NO NEED TO SAVE OUR SOULS.
HELL IS ALREADY HERE.

THE MASTER AND THE MARIONETTE

BOOK TWO

BRANDI ELISE SZEKER

99 Hudson St
5th floor New York, NY 10013

ISBN: 979-8-9855934-5-7
Cover Art: Seventh Star
Editor: My Brother's Editor
Proofreading: My Brother's Editor
Formatting: Imagine Ink Designs

The Pawn and The Puppet Series

The Pawn and The Puppet

The Master and The Marionette

Content Warning

Disclaimer: This book contains explicit content and dark elements and may be considered offensive to some readers. Check trigger warnings before reading. It is not intended for anyone under 18 years of age. Please store your files wisely, where they cannot be accessed by underage readers.

This is a dark dystopian society that is intended to be problematic. Please note that this is a fictional world and in no way reflects on the author's personal beliefs. We will see the society grow and correct its moral compass over the series.

This book contains: gratuitous violence, depression, mention of suicide, gratuitous torture, eating disorder, hallucinations, misogyny, mention of pedophilia, romanticized mental illness, gore, mention of child abuse, decapitation, female oppression, hostage situation, Stockholm syndrome, degradation, starvation, brainwashing, body shaming, sexually explicit scenes, religious trauma, horror.

Do not continue if you're unsure of the contents of this book.

For Anna,

You are no stranger to the darkness.
This book is not only for you, but for those you've lost.
Johnny & Rita, we'll never forget you.

DEMENTIA

Stormsage Keep
Hangman's Valley
North Saphrine Forest
Evergreen Dark Wood
Demechnef Headquarters
Emerald River
Nightamous Horde Cave
Dellilian Castle
Emerald Lake
Shaman's Land
Red Oaks
Emerald Lake Asylum
Chandelier City
Endograves Jungle
Midnight Se

Author's Note

I encourage all to read this before proceeding to the book. This is a work of fiction, yes. However, the mental illnesses that certain characters have are based on real disorders. The one I'd like to note is Dissociative Identity Disorder (DID). Some know it as a "split personality" or a "multiple personality disorder." That is not the correct terminology. Please let this work of fiction open the eyes to those who look at DID in fear or with a lack of respect.

The representation of DID in this novel is a morally gray, dangerous character. This is NOT an accurate representation of DID. It is a symbolic representation of how DID appears to modern society—feared, misunderstood, and a mystery of the mind to gawk at. Please know that the rest of the series will be a journey for this fictional society and the characters to understand and accurately represent. But allow me to set the record straight for this nonfictional world. This community of people is NOT the monsters. They are NOT the villains. They are kind, intelligent, wonderful human beings that were the victims of horrendous injustice and abuse.

Let this message encourage you to ask the right questions and seek to better understand. For more information about DID, please visit: http://traumadissociation.com/index

P.S. If you disagree with representations to different forms of trauma in this series, please be considerate of those who cope differently and felt accurately represented as a survivor of their experience. Everyone has their own encounters and ways of healing. If certain descriptions, situations, or explanations aren't for you, they may help or empower someone else.

Playlist

FOR EVERY BADASS SCENE

I Bet My Life by Imagine Dragons

Stick Up by Grandson

40 Cal by Heritage & Rico Act

Fed Up by Ghostemane

Bad Guy x Still Don't Know My Name by Safenokk

Bow by Reyn Hartley

FOR EVERY SCENE OF DARKNESS, HEARTACHE, AND SOUL-SHATTERING LOVE

To Build a Home by The Cinematic Orchestra

Back to You by Twin Forks

Dream by Bishop Briggs

Into Your Arms x Dandelions (mashup) by Plodentata

Heal by Tom Odell

When the party's over by Lewis Capaldi

You can find more playlists for The Master and The Marionette by searching for "Brandi Szeker" on Apple Music or Spotify!

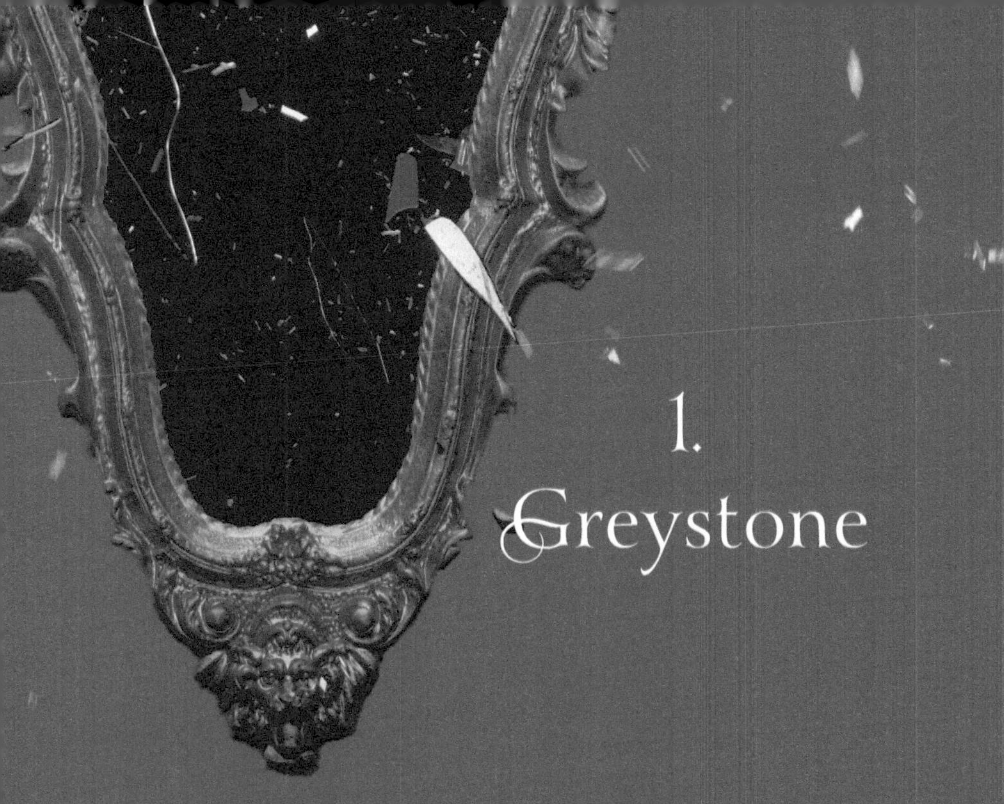

1. Greystone

Kane has left me. Gone. Vanished. A memory acting as my only comfort in the presence of this—*stranger*.

I have met a third alter.

Greystone.

But Dessin always made me believe there were only two. Is it even possible to have multiple personalities living in one mind? I have more questions than ever.

Greystone cocks his head, waiting for me to respond to the bomb he's just dropped.

"Dessin didn't tell me there were more," I say out of breath, taking a step back until I hit the wooden panel of the tree house doorway.

He licks his lips, smiling down at me as though I'm a meal he's been waiting to eat.

"No, I don't suppose that feigner is much for sharing secrets, is he?" His accent is refined, like a stroke of cursive on fresh parchment.

I shake my head.

A breeze carrying the scent of pine and lavender wafts between us. I fail at stifling a shiver.

"Are you afraid of me?" he asks.

I study his expression, his posture, the language of his body. Greystone's face holds a look of pleasure and mischief. He cocks an eyebrow, lowers his dark lashes, and wears a sensual smirk. Based on these details alone, he absolutely is nothing like Kane or Dessin. His posture is languid and cocky. And he seems to like waving two fingers around while he speaks.

I swallow. "Well, I don't know you. Should I be afraid?"

Greystone takes a step back. "If you weren't frightened by the manipulative murderer with a bad attitude, then I think you'll feel safe with me." He laughs with a closed mouth, and even the sound differs from Dessin's laugh.

I nod to myself. He has a point.

"We do not have any alters that would ever harm you." A flash of seriousness crosses his features. Relief washes over me. "As for annoying you, that's a different topic altogether."

My cheeks loosen into a smile. Wow, the asylum would have a field day if they knew how many people lived inside his head.

"How old are you, Greystone?" I decide I should start asking questions about the alters I meet. They might see themselves as older, younger, or perhaps look completely different.

"Thirty-one," he drawls, voice like luxury bedsheets and warm honey. "Quite the age gap between you and me, hmm?"

I ignore that innuendo.

"How many alters are there?"

He rolls his eyes. "I don't keep track of those details."

"What do you keep track of?" I ask.

Greystone's shadowed eyes focus on me, locking on my stare like a mousetrap. A slow, chilling smile spreads over his mouth.

"Are you sure you want the answer to that?" he teases, watching my lips with ravenous intent.

I pause midnod. *Do I?* Yes, the more I know about him, the better.

"The sexual urges of this body. And who causes them." His words drape over me like a colony of crawling insects.

"Oh," I say. "Why?"

He's silent for a moment as if questioning whether I know the answer to that or not.

"The mind splits for specific reasons of trauma. I'm sure you've figured that out by now."

I have. Hearing why Dessin ended up splitting when they were a child told me enough. But I was under the impression it could only happen once. Does this mean that every time he experienced trauma, a new alter was split off?

"You were split because of a different form of trauma," I utter. *Sexual urges*. Oh, God. Does that mean—

"Sexual abuse," he answers the question I had before finishing the thought. But he isn't fazed. The two words seep from his lips as if they carry no weight. "I believe I was split when the body was around the age of six or seven. Demechnef training was easy for Dessin to overcome. But the thirty-year-old female orderly checking in on him at night wasn't exactly what he was built for."

My heart sinks to my toes, twisting itself into a painful knot of despair. He was molested.

A thought redirects my moment of shock. "And you're thirty-one. Were you always this age?"

"Very good." He nods once. "I have always been thirty-one. A grown man that would thoroughly enjoy that kind of attention."

I might be sick. Bile coats my throat and sloshes over my tongue. How much has this man suffered? The sting of tears alerts me that I might lose my composure over this bit of news.

"It would help if you don't show me sympathy." He takes a step toward my wilting stance. "Each alter has a negative trigger that causes us to relive trauma. Mine is when I start to hate myself for sexual arousal."

I swallow down my despair and clench my hands into fists. Get angry, then. Don't let him see you cry over this.

"And to be clear… consent is a priority of mine. I figured you might be frightened of me, wondering if I—because of my trauma—wouldn't understand the importance of it. But I do. It's imperative to the other alters that I do."

I straighten up, forcing myself to show him strength. "Do… the others know what you've experienced?" The *others,* as in whoever else is living in his mind.

Greystone shrugs, looking bored. "Some do. But others aren't allowed to know. That's the point of splitting, isn't it? To keep that trauma away from those who couldn't handle it."

I'm learning so much already.

"May I ask you another question?"

"You may ask whatever pleases you. It pleases me to hear the sound of your voice." But his eyes aren't focused on where my voice is coming from. They're roaming my body with wild intrigue.

"Have you met me before? Do you know who I am?" There are still secrets Dessin and Kane keep from me about my past. But Greystone could be the loophole I need to spill their secrets.

He shakes his head. "No, I am only triggered to surface around grown women," he says. "But I do know of you, yes."

"How old was I when you first heard of me?" I ask casually, slipping in the question that might tell me everything. Or enough to lead me to more questions.

"You were—"

He blinks slowly as if he's ready to fall asleep. And those dark eyes fall out of focus. He chuckles. "I'm sure I'll see you soon, my pretty Skylenna."

Those words fade like drops of ink in a bucket of water.

His chest rises, a slow intake of breath. His once dark eyes now seem a little lighter, with a gleam of russet brown catching in the morning light.

He's switching again. I hope it's Kane or Dessin. I don't know how much energy I have to meet someone new again.

The man lets out an aggravated groan. "I was hoping you'd never have to meet him."

I smirk. "Greystone is lovely."

"Greystone has loose lips," he says, looking down at me with warm-chocolate eyes.

I study his features. I don't think I'm speaking to Dessin. His stance is usually wider, asserting dominance and power. No, this person is calm with kind eyes.

"Kane?"

His lips spread into a surprised smile. "You don't know how happy that makes me."

"What?" I ask, smiling back.

"You recognized me."

2. "Hello, Old Heart."

With a thump into moist soil, my high heels sink. I let go of the wooden planks nailed to the tree and begin my walk through the Emerald Lake forest.

After a day and a half of rest, Kane leaves to gather food.

Naturally, he gave me a strict order to stay in the tree house. Dangers lurk in these forests that I won't believe unless I see them. Beings from old folk tales. The reasons why our citizens stay within their perimeters.

But I've already made the cots, cleaned up after us, and stared blankly at the horizon of swaying trees for over an hour. I've wondered endlessly what's next for us? Are we planning on living in the tree house forever? Are we going to find somewhere to live? Build a hut? Find a safe place in the forest? Or does Kane have a plan?

The morning air is cool and refreshing, dancing against the turquoise leaves, creating an Emerald Lake symphony. But I don't make it far.

There's movement a few trees away. A flash of moss green and radiant gold.

Great, Kane was right. I didn't make it two seconds.

I press my back into a tree, staying completely still until the figure leaves or reveals itself to me. I strain my eyes past the vines and shrubs and into the shadows of the sycamores.

I force my breathing to remain shallow and undetectable. But the forest dances on without interruption of man or beast, and there is no evidence I saw anything.

With a final minute of silence, to be sure, I lean off the tree, taking a step into the soft soil to investigate.

"Be frightened not." A masculine voice like thunder and sandpaper echoes from behind me.

I spin around, the sides of my shoes filling with dirt, and I topple over as my eyes land on him. A tall, lean man wearing moss and vines for clothing, woven intricately around his body to the way veins would crisscross under skin. The wind flutters through his long, golden hair, pushing it back behind his shoulders.

I stay completely still, gauging his next actions with caution. The man narrows his hazel eyes down at me quizzically.

"My big friend will be back soon," I say.

He looks around, intrigued. When he doesn't see the big man I'm referring to, his light eyes fall back to me. "Young."

I blink twice. *Huh?*

"What are your years?"

I cock my head. He doesn't seem dangerous, but I can't be too careful.

He steps toward me, long brown legs glistening in the sunlight.

"Stay back, Forest Boy." Surprisingly, I don't flinch. I stare back at him with calm, threatening eyes. Being away from the suffocating nature of the city seems to have made me feel stronger. When normally, I might crawl backward in fear.

His brow furrows. Gazing down at me as if I'm a pet of his. He dips his head to acknowledge my guardedness. "When you are ready."

I shimmy my way back up the tree house ladder before Kane and DaiSzek return. The last thing I need is a firm scolding and an "I told you so."

But apparently, I still don't know him as well as I think I do.

"You just couldn't resist leaving, huh?" Kane throws a sack over his shoulder before pulling himself up from the ladder.

"I didn't leave," I say quickly. Too quickly.

He smiles as he removes his shoes. "Tell that to the dirt you brought with you." He nods at my high heels coated in wet soil.

Wonderful.

"That was from when we first arrived."

His dark eyes flick to me and back down to the other shoe he's untying. Amusement softens his expression. "Is that right?"

"It is."

He nods with a smirk. "You haven't learned much about lying to Dessin, have you?" And with that, he's standing again, hovering over me. "Why are your hands dirty?"

I don't even have to look to feel the grimy flakes over my palms.

"Okay! I went down for like five seconds." I throw my arms in the air. "But I came back up right away."

The amusement drains from his face like water swirling down a sink. He lifts his chin, putting pieces together he didn't catch before.

"What happened?" he asks. "And don't bother lying again. You're terrible at it."

I roll my eyes. "It was nothing. I saw a man that looked like a forest god. Really handsome. Perfect skin, like glowing…"

"To the point, Skylenna." Kane pinches the bridge of his nose.

"He only said a few words. Asked my age, and said, *when you're ready* before he left."

"When you're ready?" Kane peers down at my hands in deep thought. "How was he dressed?"

"Like a forest god. Moss, vines, shrubs, for clothes."

His gaze snaps up to meet mine. "Impossible."

"I didn't even know people lived out here. We were always told it was so dangerous because of the creatures these forests were home to."

Kane sits down next to me, running his large hand over his neck.

"My mother used to tell me tales of the colonies of the seven forests. The Emerald Lake forest was home to the Naiadales, the descendants of the lake nymphs. They looked and dressed exactly as you described."

"There's no such thing as nymphs," I scoff.

"They aren't nymphs. Their colony is descended from them, though."

I glare at him. Waiting for him to laugh in my face for being so gullible. But his expression is stone. Unflinching.

"Is it dangerous for us to be out here, then?"

"He didn't hurt you. Maybe these people aren't as vile and dark as our own."

Kane's knee leans against my thigh, and it's the first time we've touched since I met Greystone. A jolt of fire ignites under my skin at the contact. I stare down at my leg, unsure if I should move it or lean into him.

Dessin was clearly attracted to me, and Greystone must have been attracted to me if my presence brought him to the surface. But what about Kane? He's looked at me with fondness, sure. But is it more than that?

I nudge him with my ankle. "You found food?"

He straightens and pushes off the cot. "Yes, no meat today. But I'll go hunting soon." Fruit tumbles to the wooden tree house floor from the sack he brought up.

Kane tugs a sheet to the floor, placing the fruit onto it.

I lower myself to sit across from him. "Hey!" I pick up an apple as I reminisce a moment from the asylum. "Remember when we had the picnic at the asylum?"

He doesn't answer. I glance at his blank expression. *Oh*. He wasn't the one I had the picnic with. "I'm sorry—"

Kane takes a bite out of an apple. "I remember a little."

"How does that work? Do you have all of his memories? Or were you able to pay attention while he was in control?"

"A little of both," he says quietly. "I can pull from his memories sometimes. But during your sessions with him, I made sure to stay close to the front to see how you'd interact with him."

That must mean he was there when Dessin and I were close to kissing. He was there for every raw moment. I want to ask what he thought about it. But the topic seems too awkward to bear.

"Has it sunk in yet?" he asks.

"What?"

"Being on the run? Has any of that sunk in yet?"

I bite my lip. The taste of apple is sweet on my tongue.

"I don't know. I'm still not sure what comes next," I say, examining the next space of my apple I want to bite. "I had nothing in Chandelier City. You and Dessin are the only people that make me feel safe—that make me feel like I'm home. But I do need to know where this is headed."

Kane lowers the apple from his mouth, staring intensely into my eyes. The sun sprinkles over his face like tiny flickers of candlelight. "Wherever you go, I shall follow."

His heavy words coil around my thumping heart. Déjà vu sears my insides like a crackling fire trickling up my spine.

His eyes are as warm and radiant as melting copper. They dig into me with deliberate intent, unearthing my soul, flipping through the pages of my life as if there's a chapter missing.

"Right now, I'm trying to buy us time. To rest. To enjoy a little freedom. But we're playing a long game with Demechnef. They'll never stop chasing me." His head lowers, brow pinched together. "Fortunately, they aren't thrilled about the forest. They're paranoid that Vexamen lurks out here and of all the unknown species. So, it'll take them longer to track us down. Dessin's plan, however, is a bit different. He's hoping to track down people and things that may help us negotiate with Demechnef. Create a treaty, perhaps."

"What's he trying to track down?"

"Defects who ran from the government. My mother is the one who gave me that advice. She said they could offer safe harbor and secrets about Demechnef."

I nod slowly. "So, we'll take it one day at a time then."

"Yes." He smiles. "Together."

For the next few nights, Kane wanders deep into his own thoughts. Sometimes I watch him when he's tied so tightly into the safety of his mind, the comfort of his old home. I wonder if he'd rather be in there than with me. But it gives me time to understand him without the cryptic messages of a conversation. He always makes sure I am fed and taken care of before providing for himself. I see that he goes out of his way to find the sweet plump red fruit I like so much at the top parts of the trees by the water. I see that when Kane thinks I'm asleep at night, he brushes the hair away from my face, drapes his blanket over me, and tucks it under my chin.

Tonight, I fall into a sleep that is heavy and unrecognizable. I see my father hovering over me, a wooden club in hand, a look of despair twisting over his face. I can't move my arms to protect myself. I can't roll away. I can't even blink my eyes. Terror bites into my neck and wraps itself around my chest and waist. *Please, don't hurt me again.* I try to scream, seeing the itch of a violent action worming through his limbs. *Daddy, don't do it. Don't hurt me. Please don't hurt me.* My father begins to sob. *Dessin!* He takes the wooden club and slams it down into my stomach. I'm defenseless. I'm paralyzed. The shocking jolt of pain shoots through my gut. Another slam in my shoulder. Another into my chest. *You're going to kill me!*

I find the perimeters of my own mouth and finally say, "Kane," I think it comes out in a single breath. Can he even hear me? Will he know that I'm dying? *My father is here, and he's trying to kill me!*

"Think of me." I hear a voice outside of the beating. It's Kane's voice. "Think of me, Skylenna. Picture my face. Take my hands and let me pull you back." The perfect picture of Kane flashes in my mind. I see his hands reach for me, pulling me into his arms. The safest place in the whole world. My eyes open, no more pain, no more Father. I'm in Kane's arms. I let out an agonized sound. His chin rests on my head, my face nuzzled into his muscular chest.

The smell of cedar fills my nose, and I exhale in relief. He mirrors my breath and holds me tighter. "I'm sorry." I shake my head. "I don't know what—I'm sorry," I say again.

"Sleep paralysis." I hear a familiar smile in his voice. "Sometimes you just need someone to guide you out of it." An echo of a memory tugging at my mind's eye, yet it won't reveal itself.

"It was horrible. I thought my father came back to kill me."

Kane lets out a slow breath. "I wouldn't have let him."

I push against his chest to look at him. Our faces hover closely. "Can you make me a promise?"

He waits silently, smart enough to hear what the promise is first.

"Promise you'll never take your life."

Like a blow to his lungs, air catches in his chest. His weighty gaze rolls over me, pain clinging to his expression like a parasite. "You have my word."

"Goo—"

"But I'll need you to make the same promise," he cuts me off.

"I would never—"

"Promise me, Skylenna," he orders, but it sounds close to a plea.

I rest my head against his chest once more, breathing in the sweet aroma of cedar and sandalwood. "I promise."

Kane tightens his strong arms around my body, gripping me like I'm a part of him now. I'm a piece of his soul that was severed, and he's trying to mend it together again.

"Jack loved you, Skylenna. He believed removing his life from yours was the greatest act of love he could do for you."

My eyes fall closed. "I suppose you're not going to tell me how you knew any of that. How you knew my father's name, and how you could possibly know if he loved me or not."

"I have two minds about it."

An unexpected rumble of laughter barrels out of my chest. I keep my mouth closed and let it shake my body against his. I feel the pulls of his cheeks against my head.

"You haven't been sleeping," I comment, snuggling into his arms.

"I know."

"Why not?"

"I'm having trouble adjusting." He sighs, warm breath blowing over my hair. "It's nothing to worry about."

"You're also having headaches." The moments where he rubs his temples, clenches his jaw, rolls his neck are happening more frequently.

"You're quite observant."

I nod.

"I'm okay. I promise." The finality in his tone tells me the conversation is over.

"Can I tell you something?" I ask.

"Mhm." Soft, sweet, warm molasses voice muffled against my head.

"I've never felt safer than when I'm with you or Dessin."

He stays silent.

"I care about you." And I can hear his heartbeat pick up its pace under the swollen muscles of his chest.

"And Aurick?" Not jealousy, no. More like he's fishing for something.

"No."

"No?"

Sleepiness weighs over my eyes. The sounds of midnight wind singing against the trees and the crickets lull me closer to falling back asleep. "I never did." And in his arms, I drift.

But in a place less pleasant is where I wake up.

3. The Avenging Alter

Strange inhuman sounds erupt from all around.

Not loud enough to wake me fully until I feel hot, humid breath blowing against my face. This sensation forces life back into my eyes to examine the source. We're no longer in the tree house, and my face is pressed against patches of moss and soil.

A black, wet nose nudges my cheek, and I jerk away, choking on a gasp.

The RottWeilen is back, heftier than a lion. Glossy black fur with russet-brown accents on his chest and paws. He watches me patiently, with large cinnamon eyes and an enormous jaw. I remember when he let me touch him. Caress the mane around his neck and shoulders.

"You might be the heaviest sleeper I've ever met." A familiar tone. "I could have been some psychopath carrying you into the night to dump your body off a cliff." I twist around to see him standing behind me, a devilish smirk.

"Dessin?"

His mouth stretches into a grin, revealing those straight, very white teeth. "You should have run while you had the chance," he says.

A pulse of excitement runs through me. I push my hands off the dirt to stand up, shuffling over to him. He looks down at me like I'm an animal that might attack at any moment. My hands slip under his arms, and I wrap around his torso, hugging him tightly.

Silence, like a child's comfort blanket, wraps around us. My eyes fall closed.

"Was he really that boring?" Dessin asks. I release a laugh against his chest and roll my eyes.

"Not at all." I nuzzle into his chest. "I just missed you." He exhales and holds me closer.

"And did he tell you every little secret about us that you've been dying to know?"

I huff into his shirt. "Not really. And I'm really getting tired of not knowing anything." I take a moment to finally acknowledge my surroundings as they have changed. It's still dark out, but I can tell it's early morning. We are in a different section of the forest. The trees drape over us so heavily that even if it were midday, the space around us would remain drastically shadowed and cool. The Evergreen Dark Wood has areas that can make you feel utterly blind at night, areas that are the homes of predators not yet identified. The Evergreen Dark Wood is the source of many scary bedtime stories. I dart my eyes around, remembering the RottWeilen standing behind me, and look back at Dessin.

"Why did we leave the tree house?"

"DaiSzek alerted me that we had company on their way to pay us an unfriendly visit. I packed you up and moved us to a location they wouldn't dare visit." I look back at DaiSzek, who blinks twice to confirm the story.

"You packed me up," I repeat.

"Okay, I *scooped* you up."

I rearrange myself to face DaiSzek, who sits in front of me, waiting. "Hello there," I say. I reach my hand out toward him, carefully, like I'm about to touch a hot stove. He leans into me, pressing the side of his face against my palm, closing his bright cinnamon eyes. My other hand reaches up to his chest, my fingers disappear into his sleek black fur.

"You know… RottWeilens are one of the reasons why the seven forests are so highly feared?" Dessin is leaning against a skyscraping

Hyperion tree that rules this forest like an ancient king that never dies.

I raise my eyebrows at him.

"About sixty years ago or so, this country was vacant until our people settled here. They ventured through thousands of acres of forest, primarily through the Red Oaks. The pack of RottWeilen wouldn't let them through."

I look back at DaiSzek, who seems mesmerized by his words.

Dessin's eyes flick down at the calm titan beside me. A memory of a smile decidedly hiding on his face. "Not sure why."

My eyes flick between him and the great beast. "Then how did the settlers end up here?"

"They slaughtered them with chemical warfare. Only a few survived." He thinks on it for a moment. "That species is quite superior. Their understanding and ability to cognitively think is close to that of a ten-year-old. And on top of that, they're stronger than a bear or lion and faster than a mountain cat. But above all else, their loyalty is unmatched. No living creature on this planet is as loyal to family as a RottWeilen."

Loyal to family. "But why is he so tame around you and me?"

A dark shadow casts over his eyes, and he opens his mouth, forming a word that has decomposed before it can pass over his plush lips. He furrows his brow, waiting for me. Like I would have that answer, and he wants me to beat him to it. I blink at him, tilting my head.

"Kane found him just after he was born. His small pack was one of the last hunted down over a decade ago. His mother dug a hole for him to hide in until his pack was killed off."

I gasp. "Why would they do that?"

"The men of this country feared they'd multiply and eventually invade the city. When we found DaiSzek, he got used to Kane and me, and we became the only family he knew."

"But why me? Why does he trust me?"

"I suppose he senses you're my family too."

I grin up at him, then glance back at DaiSzek. "You hear that, big boy? We're family now."

How incredible to be this close to a once feared beast.

You have a beautiful mind. I think.

Dessin maps out where we are going to go from here. He draws the terrain and obstacles ahead with his fingers. The punctual movements are exact, and he needs no form of measurement to fact-check himself.

I am flat on my belly, my head propped up by my hands resting under my jaw with my elbows digging into the dirt. I close my eyes, then shift them away from the fast movements he is making. I refocus my attention on his face. The source that makes my heart flop like a fish lurching for water.

His undeterred focus is that of a savant calculating the accuracy of their newest discovery. I have a fleeting image of myself caressing his jawline and—

"Can I help you?" he asks without taking his eyes off the dirt map.

My mouth parts, but I say nothing.

"Just admiring my good looks, or do you have something to say?"

Wow, his peripherals are uncanny. "I'm waiting for you to explain what is obvious in your head and not so obvious to others. What's the plan?"

A smirk appears on his lips, but he wipes it away like an unwanted bug landing on him.

"We have to get to the North Saphrine Forest."

I look down at what I'm wearing. A *dress*. A dress that goes down to my knees, barely passing my shoulders. "Dessin, it's snowing out there. Temperatures get below freezing at night. I would die."

"I've planned for that." He nods, examining my dress. "Everything we need will be at our next stop. There's a Demechnef defect out in a small village in those mountains. People who escaped the city and wanted to live freely. They all settled to this one spot."

I frown. "So that's your big plan for us? Wait out the rest of our days in the snow until we finally freeze to death?" For the first time, I feel doubt.

He rotates to me, stands to his feet, and raises his eyebrows. "Did it sound like I was finished?"

I shake my head.

He walks up to me, tall with confidence dripping from his presence. "I know you didn't have to run with me, and I know you probably didn't picture your life on the run with a dangerous criminally insane man. I'm fully aware of this."

But I wanted to.

He's a breath away from me, hovering like a cloud of death. Thick webs of desire form over my nerves, buzzing under my skin.

"But you are with me. You chose to run, and it wasn't out of spontaneity. You ran because you trust me." He stares down at me, and all I want to do is touch him, thank him, and hold him close to me.

Instead, I say, "I'm sorry." *I don't know why I said that; I'd run until I was old and gray if it meant it was with you.* I want to say all of this. But it won't leave my lips.

He nods. "These are the routes we will take to avoid any trackers coming for us. DaiSzek will let us know if they get close. But let's just make it to the defects first, and then we'll know more about the next steps we're going to take."

The next couple of hours, Dessin leaves me alone with DaiSzek to set us up with a place to sleep and a fire to cook what he hunts. I feel a little useless when he or Kane leaves to do all the work. But what am I supposed to do? I don't know how to hunt (nor would I want to.) I don't know how to set up a fire or a shelter for us to sleep. I'm basically deadweight. Why does he even want me around?

I decide to use this time to get more comfortable around DaiSzek. To learn just how capable he really is.

He lies in the dirt looking like a black grizzly bear. I kneel down beside him and run my fingers over the thick fur on the side of his body. His brilliant cinnamon eyes flick over to me.

"Hi," I whisper to him. He sits up to face me directly. "Can you understand me?" I ask.

Something heavy falls on my thigh, scratching my skin. I look down at DaiSzek's heavy mammoth paw resting just above my knee. His fur around his paws and ankles is the same color as the cinnamon in his eyes, like he's wearing little rain boots.

"See? What does Dessin know? You don't seem dangerous." But even I can see how wrong I am. It's the ghost of a feral demon behind his gaze and the promise of imminent death to whoever crosses him.

I fall back on my bottom to stretch my legs out in front of me. DaiSzek lowers the side of his head to my lap and proceeds to slip between my legs, rolling on his back, belly up. His big head rests on my crotch. I laugh. "Can I help you?"

He grunts and wiggles slowly. I laugh again. "Ohhh, you want me to rub your belly!" He wiggles again. It's unlikely to see such a gargantuan doglike animal cuddle up to anyone. He feels more like a puppy trying to play than a RottWeilen who can demolish a night dawper. I do as he wishes and rub his chest, belly, and neck with both hands. He lies there, completely mesmerized.

"What did you do to him?" A deep voice dipped in warm butter glides over my skin.

I turn my head in his direction. "Leave us alone," I snap.

"Look at him; he's defective!" Dessin carries a laugh in his voice that hasn't been released yet. He trudges over to us, carrying a dead animal and wood for a fire. "Hey! Flea-Head! I told you to stand guard, not crush Skylenna under your big body!"

I burst into laughter. DaiSzek seems to understand the insults and rolls off of me, galloping into Dessin's lower abdomen with impressive force. Dessin doubles over with a grunt, wrapping his arms around DaiSzek's neck. "Hello to you too, lazy boy."

"Leave him alone; he just needed a break." I push myself off the dirt and walk up to them, wrestling on the ground.

"What do you think you're doin', huh? Rubbing your scent all over my girl?!"

Wait. He said, *my girl*.

I hold my breath. I could ask him what he means. But we're friends. Just friends. That's what we have always been, except for those moments that were far too friendly.

He looks up at me after quelling DaiSzek's need to play. His dark eyes search mine curiously. I wonder if he realizes what he just said.

"Are you hungry?" He dusts himself off. The muscles in his arms harden as he swiftly gathers the wood and dead animal.

"Yes." *Stop looking at him like that.* I look away.

He moves closer to me, tilting his head downward to meet my eyes. "Good, because we're having a little story time next to the fire tonight."

I chew my food. Somehow watching Dessin put in the work to feed me makes it taste that much better. But I'm careful to not overindulge. Without catching his attention, I take small bites. It's a toxic habit now. The way my mind rejects the dopamine that fills my body from the delicious flavor.

The restraints of that city still haunt me.

"Please tell me it tastes better than Aurick's fancy dinners." He's lying on his side, propped up by one elbow as he eats by the fire. DaiSzek is passed out behind us.

Aurick. I haven't thought about him in a while. He has no idea where I am. Am I a terrible person for not thinking of him? We were friends. We lived together. I left and didn't think twice about him or how this would make him feel.

But he hit me, and for that, I don't owe him a moment of pity.

"Do you regret leaving him?" Dessin is now looking up at me, his dark-chocolate eyes glowing like hot coals in the orange fire.

I break myself away from the spiral of thought that overtook me. I can tell that he is afraid of my honest answer. "You always knew he'd hurt me. How?"

"Kane's answer to this question didn't suffice?"

"Not really. It was vague."

"He was telling the truth," he says, taking another bite.

"He was telling half a truth."

Dessin shrugs, focusing on the sparks popping from the firewood.

I yawn dramatically. "Greystone will probably tell me. He's an honest man." I look off to the darkness, waiting for Dessin to react. If Kane seemed annoyed by Greystone's existence, I could only imagine how Dessin feels about him.

Dessin's head falls as he drops his last bite of meat into the fire.

"I'd rather talk about anyone *except* the little *Greyshit*," he grunts.

A laugh tickles my lungs, but I settle for a teasing smirk. "Not a fan of him?"

He scoffs

"Why not?"

"He's useless, pompous, annoying, has loose lips, and goes out of his way to ruin plans." Dessin glowers at me as if merely speaking about Greystone has drained him of all happiness.

"He told me about the other alters," I say, sitting up. "Why didn't you tell me?"

"We were in a dangerous place, surrounded by people who would use that knowledge against us. I would *never* risk the safety of the other alters." He's sitting up now, too, a stare of loyalty burning into me.

That makes sense. I can't fault Dessin for wanting to protect them.

"Will you tell me about them?"

"I'm sure you'll meet some of them soon enough." He sighs.

"I thought you were going to tell me stories by the fire!" The wind whistles through the branches around us, forcing the fire to make a sputtering sound.

I glance around the woods that are now covered in total nightfall. Extreme blackness. No light. No flicker of stars or the glow of the moon. The Evergreen Dark Wood is a black pit of blindness.

"Mmm." He pokes the fire with a stick and begins. "When I was at Demechnef's training quarters, I wasn't the only one being trained. There were others."

"Others… like you?"

"Mm-hmm. Only two came before me, and two trained with me. The ones I never met killed themselves a couple of years into training, and the two that trained with me were about fifteen years old." Dessin hands me another slice of cooked meat. That's one benefit of leaving the city—no more starving myself.

"The girl's name was Vinaley, and the boy's name was Valentine, Val for short. Vinaley could not cope with our environment, the pain, the abuse, the physical conditioning. She went through the motions but was in a catatonic-like state. The hardest part of this to watch was Val. He was in love with her, took care of her. He even found new ways to lessen her training and take more on for himself."

I remain still, keeping my breath shallow and steady. I don't want to interrupt or say anything that could stop him from sharing with me.

"He would hold her every night as she begged him to take her home. She'd repeatedly say, *I want to go home*." Dessin sighs, running a finger over his jaw. "Val was a good man. Someone I looked up to. He not only took care of Vinaley but also looked after me because I was so young. Unfortunately, when I turned eleven, he killed Vinaley in her sleep and then hung himself above her bed. He did exactly as she begged… he took her *home*."

I stare at him in disbelief. "What?"

"It was the only way to really escape."

"But,"—I set my food down—"if they were all like you, able to think differently, then why couldn't they find another way out?"

He chuckles. Looks up to the sky. I am a child to him. A child that still believes in magic and happy endings. "They were all like me. Only slightly different. We all emerged from our trauma with adverse strengths. It happens that mine is planning, human behavior observation, deduction, and deception. Val's was empathic. He could so clearly understand how each individual was feeling. He could sense if someone was afraid of him or afraid of a spider in the corner. It was a gift and a curse. A gift because he could detect weakness in anyone. It allowed him to make nine different escape attempts."

"What about Vinaley?"

He looks down in thought. "I'm not entirely sure. She was buried in something powerful. Val didn't even know. All he knew was that training struck fear in her, yes. But whatever her strengths were, they swallowed her in devastation. It destroyed him to feel what she felt."

I inch myself closer to him. The fire warming my cold toes.

"Did you know he was going to do it? Murder her and kill himself?" My knee touches his, and he glances up at me from under his black eyelashes.

"I knew." A soft cashmere blanket coats the tone of his voice. "That morning, he told me every person's greatest fears in Demechnef. He told me what causes them anxiety and discomfort. He told me everything he learned in a matter of an hour. He didn't have to say goodbye or tell me what he planned to do. But I knew. I had known for some time that he would do it."

I rub my palm over the right side of my face. "I don't understand. How were you successful with escaping and they weren't?"

"Val and Vinaley failed to hide their weaknesses from Demechnef. Kane got lucky that he had me to protect what meant most to him. Without me and several other alters, they would know everything."

The heavyweight of sleep wraps its arms around me, caressing my eyelids to take a bow. I blink slowly and lean against the side of his body.

"You want to know something?" I ask like the words have been dipped in glue.

"Hmm?"

"You and DaiSzek are definitely my weakness."

4. Friend or Foe?

My skin has absorbed a second skin, and it's called dirt. My hands feel grimy when I rub them together like I've been rolling fresh dough. The rest of my body is stiff from sleeping in the dirt. My muscles have hardened on my left side and moving them is like taking a bite of stale bread. And I dare not look at the bottoms of my feet.

Dessin pointed out a small lagoon I could bathe in. I hear the peaceful stream of water trickling over rocks and clumps of mud. The water is a sheet of black crystal.

I'm hesitant to climb in. What if there are dangerous beasts that lurk under its surface?

But I'm with Dessin. He'd never let anything happen to me. I slip off my clothes and toss them into the water. Dessin gave me a bar of soap that smells like honeysuckle and jasmine. I step in, feeling the sliminess and wet clay cushioning my feet. The water is frigid, lacking the natural rays of the sun that would keep it warm. Fog and darkness curl around the trees, slinking over the trickling waterfall like a predator.

I move through the dark lagoon faster, hoping my skin will acclimate to the temperature so this deafening urge to get out will disappear. It's up to my neck, and my body trembles like a coward on the front lines of war. I hold my breath, buckling my legs against my chest so I will sink into the arctic ice batch. When I rise with wet golden hair sticking to my neck and back, my flesh now feels numb and at peace with the cool temperatures. With the citrus soap in my right hand, I get to work.

A ring of oil and dirt forms around my body as I scrub my face and neck, working the soap bar in my thick mess of wet hair. I bounce up and down in the water, feeling the cold atmosphere of the lagoon freeing my naked body. After cleaning down to my toes, I hold my breath to wash off the remaining bubbles. When I come back up, I see DaiSzek standing in a crouched position above me, where the top of the narrow creek turns into the waterfall that feeds the lagoon.

He's facing something ahead, to my right. Low to the ground, he takes each step like the dirt is made of glass and can break at any moment.

"What're you doing up there?" I say in a lighter voice how you would speak to a child. He doesn't look my way. His stare is focused and precise.

Fear strikes a nerve in my spine.

Hands grip the caps of my shoulders and spin me in the water. I cover my breasts and almost shriek when I see Dessin, fully clothed, in the water with me. The scent of cedar fuses with the aroma of murky water.

He gently places a hand over my mouth and shushes me. His other hand shifts over my lower back. We're treading toward a low-hanging tree, grazing the lagoon's surface adjacent to the small waterfall. He angles us under the leaves to hide from whatever DaiSzek is creeping upon.

My eyes are searching his with panic. But his are calm, like a king so wise he'd reign forever. He rests his forehead against mine and closes his eyes. "Don't move," he whispers.

Footsteps shuffle around behind our heads. Whispers and the clinking of metal. Dessin's breath brushes against my lips and cheeks. Just like that, the pull to be closer to him is palpable, burning at my fingertips.

That darkened gaze of his is an avalanche. Daunting, dangerous, and cruel. I lift the hand draped over my chest and relax it over his forearm.

His eyes open. And I can see the switch, the dissociation, the change in tension over his brow. It's like watching the clouds clear after a hurricane.

It's Kane. He shifts his hand to cradle the side of my face, and I lean into his subtle embrace. This spurs something to awaken inside of him. His body presses into mine, sandwiching me between him and the wall under the low-hanging tree.

I know they are two different people, and I shouldn't be attracted to both. But they each hold something that draws me in.

He sighs, forehead still pressed against mine, lips so close I can almost taste them. And again, my pulse races, driving my need to press my lips against his.

"Kane," I exhale, moving my lips closer to his if he would just close the distance…

Suddenly a snorting sound comes from above my head that makes me jump. DaiSzek's big black nose pushes through the underbrush of the tree we're hiding under. Kane releases a long breath and lets his head fall back. "They're gone."

I keep my gaze cemented on him. If I could have had a moment longer with him.

"How did you know it was me?" he asks, dropping his hands from my body. An empty, hollow sensation fills the spaces his hands once covered.

I wrap my arms over my breasts as I recover from the sudden distance.

"You're cold. Come on, let's get you dried and dressed." He touches my shoulder blade and guides us to the edge. "Let me get out first so I can get you something to cover yourself with."

His clothes are soaked, a downpour of cold water. He kneels down to grab a Skylenna-sized brown wool blanket from his bag; stretching it out, he turns his head and looks away.

I stand in front of him, turning my back to the blanket. The crisp wind stings my skin.

Kane's hands linger after he untucks my hair. "You said my name. How did you know it was me again?"

My teeth chatter when I answer. "I just *felt* it."

"How?" His expression is a locked chest of secrets.

I shrug. "When you open your eyes and look at me. It feels like the look of a man returning home. I don't know; I guess I can't explain it." A violent shudder takes over, and I bury my face in the warmth of the wool.

He wraps his arms around me and kisses the top of my wet head. "I'd say that's a pretty good explanation." His chest moves with a sharp inhale. "Skylenna, you are my home." He speaks, and it's like hearing a thunderstorm in the warmth of my bed. A rush of pleasure burrows into my soul.

As I finish off the deer he cooked, I lie back and look at the stars. We're close to the edge of the Evergreen Dark Wood, where the trees open up enough to see slivers of the constellations.

"Do you think about your family often?" I ask.

I hear him stop moving beside me. "My family?"

I nod. "Your mother and Arthur?"

He sounds like he's holding his breath. "I try not to."

"They're up there, you know." I point up to the stars. "They're watching over us now, guardian angels."

I look over at his face tilting up to the stars.

"Only the strongest of souls can endure what your family did. And that means they are guardian angels. I think your mother and little brother are with us everywhere we go." I smile at him. "They keep us safe."

He smiles, yet there's a sudden weight of sadness in his gaze. A beacon to darkness, the way a vulture is drawn to blood. "Are all of the thoughts in your head so sweet?"

"Just the ones about you." I shut my eyes immediately. *Nice*.

I lift my hand to smack it over my eyes, but it's intercepted. Kane's hand wraps around mine, pulling it toward him. "If that's true, why don't you voice them?" He softly kisses my knuckles. A hot, jittery feeling flushes through my gut. Scattered wisps of desire flood my thoughts, clouding my focus.

"I—well, because—" *Nothing*. I can't think. Blank. My mind is pudding.

He folds my hand into his chest with both hands to keep it warm. My exhale turns into a quiet hum. "I want to hear all of your thoughts. All the time."

"You and Dessin have that in common." I blow out a nervous laugh.

"And you don't like that?"

I shrug. "I just don't think you'd really want to hear everything I think about."

"You mean, *you* don't want to say when you think about me." I hear the smile creeping from his words. I roll to my side and place my free hand on his shoulder.

"That's right." I pause while the words work to unclog themselves from my throat. "You're my friend. My *best* friend. I don't want that to go away."

He looks at me and unveils a smile that is the heat of a blueberry pie fresh from the oven. "Until hell freezes over."

I grin back. "And even then."

I wake up to the deep grinding of my own teeth and my face swallowed by a mass of black fur. The cool morning air kisses my arms, the back of my neck, my toes sunken in the dirt. I caress DaiSzek's coat and smile. I'm about to greet him when I notice Kane on the other side of him, still sleeping.

The sun has barely begun rising, and I can't believe I'm awake before him. His right hand is tucked under DaiSzek's throat. His face is at peace like a prisoner that has just been freed from bondage. I rest my chin on the ridge of DaiSzek's back to get a better look. The stubble along his jawline, his long onyx lashes, the smooth cushion of his lips.

"You enjoying the view?" Kane mutters sleepily.

You have no idea. "How'd you know I was staring?"

He pinches the bridge of his nose. "It's a ninth sense."

"*Ninth?!*"

He laughs and props himself up. “Well, look who decided to keep us from getting frostbite last night. How’d you sleep, Dai?” He ruffles the fur on DaiSzek’s head. DaiSzek lifts his head like it weighs more than a mountain. He pushes his chin in Kane’s hands while being scratched and adored.

Kane’s face morphs into surprise like he isn’t sure if he saw a poltergeist lurking nearby. His eyes flicker to me darkly, mouth parting to say something.

“What?” I lift myself off my side and sit, trying to look at DaiSzek’s face.

He shakes his head, scans the area around us. I try to pull DaiSzek’s head toward me by his chin, but Kane pushes my hand away. Something wet is smeared on my palm.

Blood.

“Oh god.” I examine it, half alarmed and half grossed out. “You must have eaten good last night, huh?”

Kane sits up. “It’s human blood.”

I yelp, wiping my hand against the dirt frantically. “Human?! How can you even tell?”

But Kane doesn’t answer. His body is rigid and taut at my side.

“Care to show your face?” That voice. Rough, cruel, and deep as it warms my lower belly.

Dessin. He switched fast. Does that mean we’re in danger? Did he get triggered by the blood on DaiSzek?

I look around the dim forest sprinkled with wisps of morning light. But we’re the only three living beings in the area. Maybe he’s overreacting from the blood. Wouldn’t DaiSzek be the first to know if someone was nearby?

“I’m losing my patience,” Dessin warns, rough and deep, like a king standing over an execution block.

The hairs on my neck stand at attention. I should never doubt him. Not when his instincts have always been correct.

There is a deafening moment of silence, not even the wind daring to make a sound. The forest holds its breath.

“If your beast trusts me, then so shall you.” A voice like a snake, slithering between us with its scaly presence.

Dessin’s eyes shoot to the source behind a wide Hyperion tree, then back to DaiSzek, who remains calm and unthreatened.

"I think I'll be the judge of who I trust," Dessin says, his tone splashing over me like a bucket of ice water.

A cloaked figure reveals itself from the shadows. The face is hidden, but instantly we're made aware that the figure is a woman. Her cloak is open, showing her bare, pale stomach and legs. Black silk and leather cover her breasts and a small portion of her bottom half.

We gawk at her in silence.

"If I were a threat to you, I would have attacked in your sleep," she says.

But Dessin isn't convinced. His eyes are scaling the length of the woman, studying her posture, her clothing, the language of her body.

"No," Dessin utters. A rare moment to hear the surprise in his voice. "You're from one of the ancient colonies."

Like the moss-covered man in the Emerald Lake forest, I narrow my eyes at her. Kane thought he was from the Naiadales…

"And which colony would that be?" Her tone is glossy and seductive. A jealous wave rips through me as I realize she's speaking directly to Dessin and not to me. I swallow down the acidic burn crawling up my throat.

"The Nightamous Horde," Dessin says slowly, still unsure of his discovery.

The woman bows her head. "Descended from Dark Elves, original inhabitants of the Evergreen Dark Wood. You know your bedtime stories."

Okay, I'm confused.

"And I remember the horror stories that follow your people. What exactly do you want with us?" The unrelenting dominance in Dessin's voice settles my nerves. He isn't afraid or threatened.

The woman lifts the hood of her cloak. A pair of sultry black eyes focus on Dessin's face. Her features are pointed and elegant, but her skin is so white it's nearly translucent, showcasing the blueish veins under layers of flesh.

The forest seems to grow smaller.

A smile tugs at the corner of her thin peach-colored lips, feline and hungry. A dazzling imitation of friendliness. And there is no shyness in her stance. It's proud, daring, and coy. She seems, if anything, to enjoy the attention of a man. Especially a man that looks like Dessin.

Annoyance flashes through me like a hot whip of lightning. My fingernails bite into the palms of my hands.

"Your presence in our territory is rare. It makes me wonder, who would dare be so foolish from the inner city?" The woman stays unnaturally still, refusing to come any closer. I'm confident she can sense the essence of death that hangs around Dessin like a storm cloud.

"I'd be foolish to tell you who we are," Dessin replies.

She licks her lips at his response. Obviously, she wants him and wears that craving around her like a scarf. "Pity." She traces a strap of leather over her chest, considering something. "How about your age then?"

Age? Isn't that what the forest man wanted to know?

Dessin's head tilts to the side. "I am twenty-three, and she is nineteen." *Twenty-three?* He had a birthday since he first told me his age months ago and didn't tell me.

I slash my stare through him like a knife. Why is he telling her anything at all? We don't know her.

She nods as if something has clicked into place. She chuckles to herself.

"I fought alongside the RottWeilen this morning. We took out a few of Demechnef's finest." The woman wipes a bloodied blade over her cloak. "There will be more. I'd think you should like to come with me back to my village for safety until they're led astray by the shades."

Shades. Scarlett told me a scary story about them once. Reimagined life forms possessed by evil spirits. They could have once been elves, faeries, dwarves, or any other fictional being.

Does she believe they actually exist?

Dessin looks just as perplexed as I am.

"And why would we trust you?" I ask, finally gathering the courage to speak up.

The woman's large pupils slide to me, only just realizing I've been here all along. She hooks her crooked index finger under a shiny strand of sunless white hair.

"Because, Skylenna. Harming you would interfere with a prophecy I would like to see come to pass."

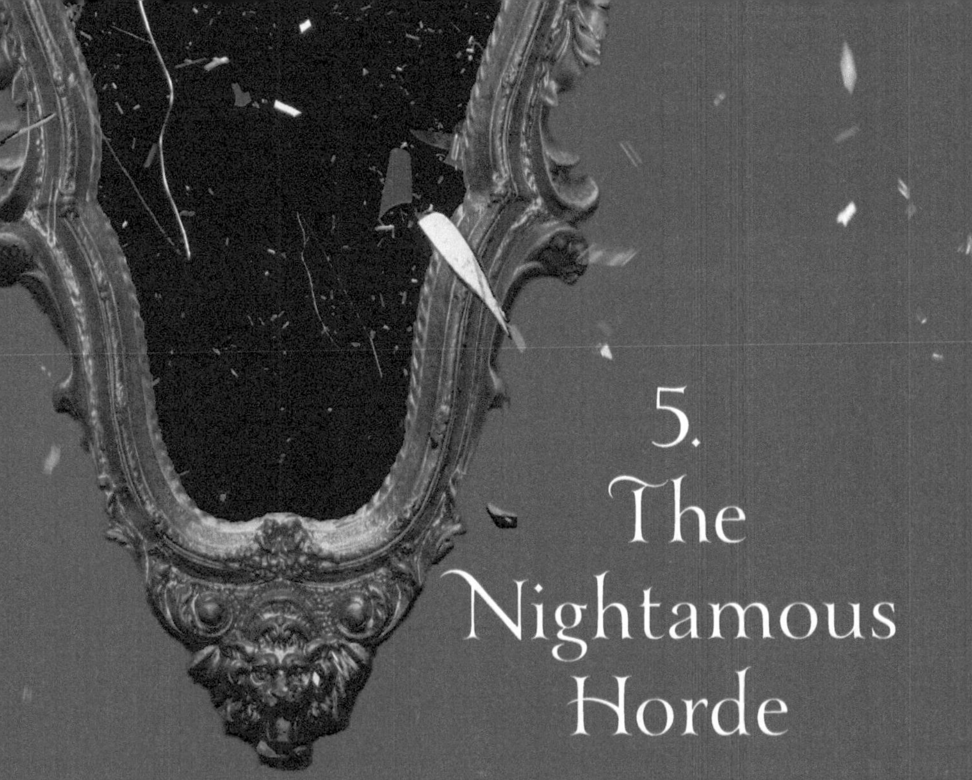

5. The Nightamous Horde

I can't help myself.

The laugh rushes out of me like a deflating balloon.

It's Dessin's face. The sudden surprise that the woman knows my name. I've been waiting for him to have a taste of his own medicine. His dark-mahogany eyes jolt back to me, offended and fighting to hide the surprise on his face.

"Is that funny to you?" he asks, tone as sharp as a new sword.

I nod.

"And what name should I call you at this moment? I know you have many." The woman takes a step forward, and Dessin is on his feet.

I stop laughing.

Knowing my name is one thing; it's another to know about his mental state. How could she possibly know of the other alters? I didn't even know that until recently.

Dessin takes a taunting step forward, looming over me like a reaper of chaos.

"That prophecy of yours knows intimate details about my life," he says calmly. Too calm. It's the peace in the eye of a storm. "Details that

I've kept hidden at great cost to me."

The woman lifts her chin, quickly becoming aware that she has treaded too far. "My name is—"

But Dessin has a sword slicing through the air until he reaches her neck. The woman is nailed to a tree, broad hands encapsulating her pallid throat.

"I've killed for less," he growls next to her ear.

I'm on my feet with DaiSzek, who is snarling at the sudden outbreak of violence. He can't kill her. We need to find out how she knows so much.

"The woman who—birthed you," she croaks. That colorless face swiftly turned a sickly shade of pink. "Sophia!" she blurts with every bit of strength she has left.

Dessin loosens his grip, awakened in a way by the name of Kane's mother.

"Speak."

"She must have shared the stories of the colonies. And when she did, she would have given you advice for when you are grown and in a time of need!" The woman's words that were once laced with sultry appeal and warm vanilla sweetness are now urgent and forced.

Dessin looks off in the distance. Listening. Waiting. Analyzing something no one else can hear.

Kane.

Sophia must have told all of this to Kane, not Dessin. He's scouring their memories or listening to Kane confirm or deny this new information.

Dessin's eyes dart back to the woman, still gasping for breath. "She said to seek out the seven forests for safe harbor. The ancient colonies know more than the city." He speculates her stance, those eyes suffused with menacing darkness. "What is your name?"

"Runa," she says, standing straighter now. "Our prophecy says you would stumble in our territory at the years of nineteen and twenty-three."

The space between them collapses as Dessin backs away, sliding his glance to me.

"You want to help us?" I ask.

"So it is written."

I find Dessin's gaze. "We should go with her," I tell him. "At least until we know more about this prophecy."

But he isn't sure. If it isn't written in his grand plan, it must not have been written at all. The confusion and doubt casting over his features are like shooting stars. Rare. Mythical, even.

I inch forward. "We owe it to Sophia to look into this."

His attention snaps back to me like a rubber band. Confusion clears from the murky water of his mind. He nods. Although, I can see it isn't easy or natural for him to be deterred from his own plans.

Dessin turns on his heels to face Runa. "If you betray us… I won't hesitate to behead you first."

Understanding washes over her cold, pointed expression. If she knows as much as she claims, then it should be apparent to her that Dessin is true to his word.

Venturing back into the Evergreen Dark Wood is a dower, silent journey. Dessin keeps me close to his side as we follow behind Runa. He's on high alert, watching her steps with precise detail, scanning the forest for threats, even with DaiSzek keeping a closer eye on the perimeter.

"Is there anything we need to know before entering a fortress that may or may not try and trap us inside?" Dessin's skepticism rolls off his tongue with lazy ease.

"Actually, yes." Runa turns her head to give us a side-glance. "We never see outsiders here. And most don't believe in prophecy anymore. It's the way of our ancestors and since nearly forgotten to our generation."

I hadn't realized I was fidgeting with my hair until Dessin's hand caressed my back, calming the nervous current running through me. My body sighs in relief, air expelling in a silent flutter from my lungs.

"I will need the two of you to blend in until I can introduce you to our elders," she adds.

Dessin rolls his eyes, knowing there was a catch.

"Blend in, how?" I ask.

"The Nightamous Horde is known for three things. First, being descendants of Dark Elves. Second, we love to drink. And last, but most importantly, we love to fuck."

I stumble over my left foot and nearly take a nosedive into the dirt. Dessin hooks an arm around my waist to steady me.

"Come again?" he says.

"It's a way of life, as natural as breathing. You must breathe to show people you're alive, right? Well, when you blend in, I'll need you two to toss your prude nature to the side and sink into the shadows of what you would consider lewd acts and improper closeness." Runa stops, facing us now with a casual smile.

"Is that all?" I scoff.

"We're not doing that," Dessin states in a clipped tone.

Runa arches a white brow. "You will if you don't want your travel companion to be swept off and ravaged by another male of thirsty intent."

Dessin makes a sound that is a feral cross between a snarl and a grunt. Before he can act on his monstrous need to silence her, I stop him with a shaky hand against his chest.

"We don't have to actually—have intercourse, do we? We just have to…."

"Blend in with those hungry enough to feast on one another? Perform like you're close to finding a vacant room to come to completion? Yes," Runa finishes my sentence with a coy grin. "If that's putting your rapport in jeopardy, I'd be happy to take your place in his arms for the night." She tilts her chin up at Dessin in a challenge.

I'm going to flick her. A quick snap of my finger to the base of her throat.

"A generous offer,"—I smile sweetly at Runa—"but his performance wouldn't be convincing with you. I'll do it."

Dessin's head has never turned so fast. He glares down at me, his brow furrowing in question and surprise. *Are you sure?* casts over his eyes like a shadow dragging its feet.

I shrug. "It's like a game, right? We're playing a part."

The emotions on his face quickly dissolve in the air, a puff of silence. The aftermath of a natural disaster before casualties are counted. "Yes," he rasps, "exactly like a game."

Aha! I knew that would do it. Dessin's magic word. *Game*.

But there's a threat wading through the treacherous waters of his mind. A warning like a powerful gust of wind. A message that looks like "*some lines cannot be uncrossed.*"

~

Runa gives Dessin and me clothes to change into. Shreds of material we would never have worn in the city. A cave Runa stays in when she hunts gives us privacy to change.

I have trouble slipping into the tight straps of black leather and the sheer tights over my legs. I am, at the very least, grateful for the black cloak that will cover half of my face. My breasts are pressed up to my collarbone, half of my stomach is bare and exposed, and the fabric covering my legs is so tight I'm afraid sitting down will cause it to split.

I can't wait to see what Dessin looks like.

Stepping out into the dim light of the forest, I see him leaning against the cave wall. He's wearing a sleeveless black tunic and matching trousers.

I grimace at his casual posture. Arms crossed over his chest, brow furrowed as he sifts through his own thoughts.

"How come *he* doesn't have to wear a death trap of wire and straps?!" I pluck a stretchy band covering my ribs and snap it, making a slapping sound against my skin.

Dessin's attention redirects to me.

"That's all I have," Ruse offers.

"She's not wearing that." Dessin sets his jaw and tightens his shoulders.

"Oh really?" I cough out a laugh. "Well, now I'm definitely wearing it!" I try to bump Dessin's arm with my shoulder as I storm past him, but he snags my wrist.

"Hell no," he growls under his breath. The sound of his hardening anger curls my toes in the boots Runa lent me.

"Fine. Would you like to take it off yourself?"

Dessin blinks, partially stunned, partially amused.

"Greystone would like it. Maybe he would be more equipped to handle this," I bite.

What has gotten into me? Jealousy? Over Runa? It's like an inconsistent flicker of fire. Some moments it burns me and spreads like a virus. Others, it's extinguished. Nothing more than a slow ribbon of smoke.

I glance up at him, my cheeks burning as if I'd fallen asleep in the sun.

Dessin narrows his eyes. "You know, I'm certain Aurick's thongs cover more flesh than this. But why not? It's only a game."

I'd laugh at his Aurick jab if it weren't for his use of the word *game*. As if it's a weapon. A tool to hurt me. A reminder that he wouldn't actually touch me if we weren't pretending.

Without further discussion, we follow Rune to the Nightamous Horde. A series of scattered caves that have been carved into taverns, miniature Gothic castles, and entryways to candlelit homes. A village of stone and fire. A kingdom of the shadows and dark elf descendants.

Runa reminds us to keep our cloaks over our heads, shielding half our faces from being recognized as outsiders. This act is common with new couples. A way to show other males and females the claim on one another has been staked.

She must request an audience with their elders, leaving us to *blend in* until she returns.

We're led into a cave that runs long and wide. Stone teeth like hanging icicles at its opening, and a mouth that glows from the fireplace and candlelit iron chandeliers. The air is clouded with a thin fog and the distinct scent of leather, liquor, and cigar smoke.

The tavern is as wild as a pack of hyenas.

Passing the threshold is emerging into a dark circus. A chilling fantasy of dark elf descendants in their habitat. Gambling, drinking, and erotic displays of affection. From a touch of violin and the low staccato of a piano, music combined with boisterous noises of clanking silverware and shrill shrieks of pleasure.

I've never seen anything like this before.

Clusters of tangled limbs, arched backs, and flesh glistening with sweat. Laughing women, intoxicated men, greedy hands, and lurkers who watch from the shadows.

My innocence is clipped like the wings of a bird as I watch the lust roll from their careless fun. Dessin stiffens at my side.

The women are dressed like Runa. Black, lacy undergarments and knee-high boots. Some are in the laps of their chosen, others are splayed on the tabletops, hair soaking in the puddles of spilled drinks. A few men pin their eager victims against the cave walls, cupping their breasts and tasting their necks, chests, and other parts with feral hunger.

What have I gotten myself into?

"Find a table. I'll get you drinks," Runa purrs to Dessin, disappearing into the dimly lit cave of moans and laughter.

We stand there in silence, in shock, in debilitating stillness.

I overshot. This is so much worse than I imagined.

"*Fuck*." Never in my life have I dared to utter a curse word. But it slips out, leaking from my lips like a string of drool. I said it under my breath, too quiet to be heard by the crowd.

But Dessin whips his head to me. And although the cloak shields his eyes with a heavy pour of shadow, I see his mouth part.

"*Excuse me*?" he says in shocked amusement. "Skylenna"—he chokes on a laugh—"did you just curse?"

I cringe. My father hated curse words. I've never even had the urge to recite one. How does this view provoke such profanity but the asylum doesn't?

His chest rumbles with unexpected laughter.

"Don't get used to it." I poke him with my elbow. "Let's sit down before I lose my nerve."

My legs move quickly through the tables, failing to avoid being bumped and caressed. I drop down to a wooden bench connected to a heavy oak table. My heart gallops in my chest, stuttering, palpitating, causing my breath to be choppy and uneven.

The voices fill the air around me. *Taste me. Open wide. You want to fuck both of us, don't you?* It's foreign and never heard of in the world I grew up in. Only words of such vulgarity are said in the beds of husband and wife.

"Bite off more than you could chew?" Dessin muses as he sits down on the bench beside me. Usually, his presence is calming. But today, in this erotic setting, it only churns my stomach into elastic putty.

I shake my head, looking down. "It's like they're purposefully trying to be the exact opposite of the Chandelier City."

"Our people have been here far longer than yours, little girl." Runa sets down two worn-down, gray chalices.

I clench my cloak in my sweaty hands, lowering my bulging eyes.

Breathe.

The overwhelming urge to draw the puppet, the strings, the sad, upturned brow, triggers a nervous twitch in my fingers.

"We can leave if you're afraid," Dessin says into his chalice.

I shake my head. Nope, no backing down. *You're the one who had to open your big mouth.* I can do this. It's just a game. Pretending.

Runa disappears from the tavern to request an audience with their elders. I make a mistake looking for her, scanning the writhing bodies of powdery-white skin and black, lustful eyes. They're worshipping each other. Teasing. Fondling.

It's too much.

I remember that Greystone is triggered to the front when the body is sexually aroused. "Will Greystone surface"—I wave a hand around the tavern—"from all of this?"

He shakes his head. "He won't come near the front when we could be in danger. Even if he's intrigued by the surroundings." A quick eye roll.

I gulp. Well, at least the thought distracted me for a moment.

Dessin's firm hand grips my knee, pushing my leg down to stop it from bouncing. But his touch, although simple and innocent, triggers forbidden anticipation for his closeness. A sharp spike of excitement and pleasure twists through me.

"Your nerves are setting my teeth on edge," he says, low and strained.

I relax my leg under the weight of his hand, softening my tightly coiled muscles. At this, his grip loosens, but he doesn't move away. His thumb traces my inner thigh in lazy circles.

I'm a vessel of electric nerve endings.

A soft moan, like a sigh blended with a hum, escapes me. I reach for my chalice, bringing it to my lips to drown out the noises I want to keep making at Dessin's touch. A silky bittersweetness fills my mouth, and I swallow it down. Wine. Chilled and passing down my throat with ease.

Without glancing down, I can feel his hand shift higher. The comforting caress is a fog that envelops me. Heat simmers between my legs.

I make the mistake of glancing up at him. Those dark-mahogany eyes are hooded and watching me closely. He's a caged animal, walking the perimeter of our boundaries. But that glazed look in his stare is dangerous. It's pure heat, an agonizing craving.

And there's a yearning in my chest. A string pulling my heart from my chest to be closer to him. I gulp and turn away.

My eyes meet a dangerously tall man walking past our table. Long white hair, down to his midstomach. Shirtless. He slows his stride to inspect me curiously.

Dessin's fingers dig into my thigh, probably aware before I am of the man's attention.

Terror runs its jagged talons down my back. He could figure out I'm an outsider. He could alert the rest of the room. I act swiftly, like butter coating my joints. I turn to face Dessin, running two fingers down the mountains of his arm.

"When are you going to taste me?" I ask, stealing the command I heard earlier from a woman spreading her legs on a tabletop.

The man keeps walking, but Dessin doesn't seem to notice. He becomes a living statue. His breath hitches in his lungs, jaw clenches, and that hand on my thigh is a steel clamp that might never come off.

"Is that what you want?" he asks with cruel decadence. "To feel my mouth again?"

That night in the lagoon is a faded dream. A hazed hallucination. His lips grazing my jawline. His tongue running over my ear. A hot, sensitive lash of ecstasy pours through me like lava.

I nod.

He moves fast. Hands on my waist, lifting me off the bench and setting me on his lap with graceful ease. My legs straddle his thighs. And if I'm not mistaken, he wants me to feel the growing length in his trousers, pressing against my center. Excited panic splashed over my face like unexpected summer rain.

"Dessin," I utter.

"There," he says, low and gravelly. "That's better, isn't it?" Those powerful hands slide down from my waist to my hips, then circling around to my curvy bottom. He squeezes, and I'm melting against him. An icicle becoming a puddle in a new season's warmth. He jerks me harder against him, pressing his heavy erection against me at an agonizing angle.

"Do you feel that?" His voice is vicious and taunting. The exact calculated tone that he used on others in the asylum. A mask. The alpha coming out to play.

I nod.

His eyes are glazed, nothing like the clear focus I usually see.

"That's what happens when you touch me, Skylenna." He reaches for his chalice, taking a small sip. "How agonizing that must have been for me in the asylum. My hands shackled to the wall while you kneeled at my feet. Those pretty hands grasping my arms."

My lips part. But I can't speak.

"You were clueless then, weren't you?" His hands tighten around my backside. "If I keep you in my lap long enough, will I start to feel that slickness between your legs?"

My gasp is audible. Stuttering and loud.

He pauses, staring down at my parted lips like he wants to lick them, bite them, take them into his mouth. For a moment, as brief as it might be, I think he might kiss me. Finally, instead, he lifts his chalice again.

"Roll your hips against me," he commands, blinking slowly as if to clear that lustful haze from behind his lids. "I want to feel how warm you are while I finish my drink."

I hesitate, unsure of how to do what he's asking of me. I arch my back away from him, then roll my hips forward to meet his hardness again. My core tightens, aching for something to fill it.

Dessin hisses in his cup.

Sexual energy vibrates through my bones. This motion feels natural. Primal. Like I was born to move against him like this. My stomach somersaults and my center is suddenly slick and hot, tingling from my thighs to my ribs.

I do it again and again until the motion starts an animalistic frenzy in me. A guttural moan rushes from my throat. Dessin's jaw flexes, and he sighs like he's been waiting for this for far too long.

"Tell me how good that feels," he growls.

"Feels… amazing," I pant, lowering my forehead to his as my hands clasp the back of his neck. *Oh god.* I've wanted to put my hands freely on him since I met him. The desire seemed unquenchable.

Movement distracts me. A man bends a woman over a table, tossing plates of food to the floor. I'm certain they're about to cross over from foreplay to actual intercourse.

Two firm fingers lock around my chin, turning me back to Dessin.

“I am the only man that gets your eyes tonight.” He looks up at me from under a curtain of dark lashes. A scolding that tastes like pleasure and euphoria. “Understand?”

“Yes.”

“Yes, what?”

“Yes, sir.” The simple response of respect spills out of me before I realize all he wanted was for me to repeat his statement to confirm what I heard.

And at my words, Dessin *unfolds*.

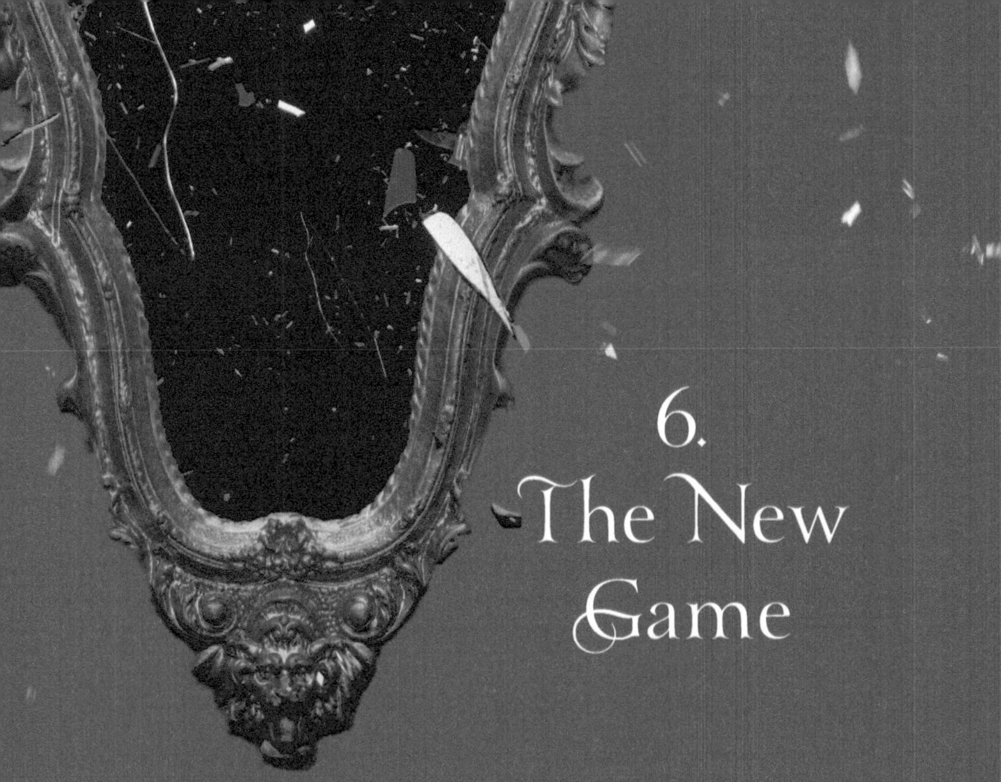

6. The New Game

There's a brief look he gives me.

A warning.

A flare of caution.

A chance for me to run, to hide, to leave without consequence. Because he's about to rip me apart.

Dessin's hands fly up to my throat, curling his fingers with a firm yet gentle touch. He brings my face closer to his, breathing heavily against my mouth.

"What the fuck are you doing to me?" he growls into my ear. His lips part, an opening for his tongue to glide against that sensitive spot. Hot. Wet. I'm writhing in his lap, losing my mind, and panting like a dog left outside in the heat.

The room fades from existence. The moans, the aroma of sweat and saliva, all gone. Now there's only the faint whiff of cedar and sandalwood. The forest during a thunderstorm.

I *want* him. And it's in his grip tightening around my throat. He wants me, too, and he would kill to have me.

"Dessin," I beg, my arms hugging his neck to me. But he doesn't stop. He's licking my neck, flicking his hot tongue against the lobe of my ear. "I want to kiss you. I want to kiss you!"

He pauses, moving his face away from my neck. "Is that right?"

I nod.

"I know you remember when I told you that I can't have your lips yet," he says.

The lagoon. *I can't have your mouth yet, but you can have mine.*

"You want to taste me, Skylenna? Is that what you need?"

"Please." My voice is the wisp of a whimper. A shred of dignity.

He smiles like a madman. Possessed. Starved. Dessin brings two fingers to his mouth, watching for my reaction as he dips them past his lips. When they exit, his index and middle finger are shiny.

"Open," he commands.

His fingertips hover over my lips. "Taste me, Skylenna." And he's in my mouth. Two large fingers spread my lips until I taste him, salty and sweet. I stare in a haze of ecstasy, stunned by a storm of fire between my legs. He's studying me. Examining my reaction.

So, I begin to suck. Drawing Dessin's fingers deeper into my mouth to savor every moment. To enjoy the little bit of him that I can have.

My eyes flick back to him, locking with his wicked gaze. He laughs darkly until I move my mouth up and down the length to meet his knuckles.

He looks angry. As if the amusement he once felt has slipped away, down to the base of his spine to relax. Now, he's roaring with another sensation. Violence. The locking of his jaw. The furrowed brow. The rigid arms flexed around me.

"You keep doing that, and I'll make you regret it." A voice of fire and brimstone. "I'll rip this pathetic excuse for clothing from your body and fuck you until your eyes water."

"*Oooh*, can I join?"

Runa.

I freeze in his lap. Dessin doesn't seem fazed. He couldn't care less who is watching.

"Need something?" he asks her without taking his eyes off me.

"A great many things," she answers. "But they'll have to wait. The elders would like to meet you."

Another cave opens into a cathedral of stone and darkness.

Dessin and I are stewing in a web of uncomfortable silence as we follow Runa. Was it all for show? Was he touching and moving to put on a performance? Or was the evidence in his pants all the proof I need?

I glance at his tan, stoic features as we descend into the shadows and dim lighting. Unreadable. Not a hint of insecurity or questioning what we did back there.

Fine.

I mimic his expression of indifference. Another game? Let's do it. He won't see how that affected me. I'll share his mask and let him wonder if his actions touched my heart at all.

I examine the musty scented cave of iron light fixtures, jagged stone pillars, and rows of seating like a church. As we continue following Runa down a never-ending aisle, I see the shape of a long table on a pedestal sitting horizontal to us. Two old men and one old woman are watching us approach. Tall black candles are perched in front of them, casting a honey-and-metallic-gold glow over their withered faces.

It's a struggle fighting the urge to look at Dessin for reassurance that we aren't in danger. He's a blanket of security. A shelter that I run to when I'm afraid.

We stop walking in front of their heightened table. The elders are at least two feet above us.

The old woman sits in the middle, no cloak, only a black lace turtleneck. Her wizened hair matches her colorless skin, and her eyes aren't beady and black; they're the color of smoke that has polluted the air, bleeding into the whites of her eyes.

The two old men look like brothers. The same sleepy expression, hooked noses, and bald heads. The right one drums his fingers on the table to hurry this along before it's even begun.

"Here they are," Runa announces nervously out of respect for her superiors. "I found them in—"

The old woman holds up her crepe hand. "I'd like to hear their ages again." Her voice is hardly that of an elderly woman. It's melted chocolate. It's low and shiny with newness.

"Twenty-three and nineteen," Dessin answers.

The woman eyes him suspiciously. "You came from the inner city."

Not a question, a fact.

Dessin nods.

"From the asylum." The old man to the right stops drumming his fingers.

Dessin's cruel eyes shoot to him like a poisonous arrow. "I hardly think that's any of your business," he grits.

The elders chuckle softly as if they expected that response.

"And are you in love?" the old woman asks.

Dessin and I stiffen.

"No," I answer quickly. Dessin doesn't move.

"Is that right?"

"Yes, that's right." I regret how unsure I sound when I answer. My voice trembles like a brittle leaf in the wind.

Why would she ask that? We aren't holding hands. We aren't gazing lovingly into the other's eyes.

The woman rests her chin on her fist, concentrating on the two of us. Committing our faces to memory. "I have one question. Your answer will determine if you are who we think you might be. It will confirm that our prophecy from ages ago is that of truth."

We wait, tension thickening the air like being underwater.

"Aside from the death of Scarlett, what are the memories that pain you the most?" Her question is a volcano erupting within me. An earth-shattering statement. Chills ripple over my arms like a colony of fire ants.

Dessin's head whips to look down at me, frozen in shock.

"I—" My breath hitches in my throat. I want to ask how they know about Scarlett. But the old woman isn't blinking. She needs my answer, and she needs it now.

My hands clench and unclench repeatedly.

I know the answer without giving any additional thought.

"The memories that I have forgotten are the ones that hurt the most," I say with pain like barbed wire tightening around my words.

The three elders straighten in their seats, glancing between each other in surprise and understanding. The old woman rises from her seat, looking down on us as if seeing us for the first time.

It's only after I slide my confused gaze to Dessin that I notice he's watching me too. Eyes shadowed with agony as he releases a slow breath.

"I know you will not trust us for some time. But our people have waited for the two of you for several generations. It's been so long, in fact, that most of our youth believe you to be fictional characters in a bedtime story."

What? This doesn't make any sense. I'm a nobody born in the Bear Traps. I weaseled my way into the city, slithered into the asylum, and now I'm here. Am I just involved in these stories because of my association with Dessin?

"This is a lovely fantasy," Dessin mocks. "But Skylenna and I aren't exactly big believers of magic. But you are correct about one thing. I do not trust easily, if ever."

The woman nods. "We know. But there are things we'd like to give you for your journey. Things we've saved in our artifacts for a very long time, locked away until the day you would arrive."

"Stay the night or as long as you require. We'll visit you in the morning with what you'll need for your travels." The old man to the left sounds like he hasn't spoken in years. His voice is hoarse, like a buggy sputtering as it has run out of fuel.

Runa shows us out, nodding her head at the cave opening to guide us to our rooms.

Not rooms.

Room.

One bed. No changing curtains. No spare cot.

"I should remind you that you are to keep up the ruse you displayed in the tavern when you leave this room. The elders believe the prophecy, but my generation won't be convinced. They'll see the two of you as outsiders. Dangerous." Runa lights a few gaslit globes, revealing the sooty cave walls, a small fireplace with wolf statues, and scattered framed paintings of dark warrior elves.

Dessin and I pretend not to notice the small bed as we take in the details of the room.

"Want me to stay for a nightcap? A lickety-split roll in the hay?" Runa asks, voice feminine and seductive.

I glare at her until she breaks into a mischievous smile and closes the door as she leaves.

"I'd like to nominate Runa for your hit list," I blurt out.

Dessin's head lowers as he chuckles. He's turned his back to me, so I watch his shoulders shake with reluctant laughter.

"Jealous, are we?"

"No," I scoff. "I just don't like how crude she is."

He glances back at me with a raised brow. "You don't like how crude she is toward *me*."

True, but don't call me on it!

"I don't care at all." I shrug, running my fingers along the cave wall. "If you're into her, help yourself."

He's chuckling again. Delight flutters in my chest. I wish that sound didn't cause such an unwanted response from my body.

"Oh, well, if you don't care…" Dessin takes three slow steps toward the door.

"Take another step, and you're sleeping on the cold, hard floor tonight," I snap.

His head tips back as he barks out another laugh. I turn my head so he doesn't see my smile. God, what I'd do to hear his laughter more often. Dessin faces me, smirking, devilish and handsome. I can't blame Runa for looking at him and wanting what she wants.

He's a masterpiece.

But his stare, although appearing innocent, lingers on me a moment too long. My heart slips from its shelf, falling the way it would when your foot misses a step.

"I should get dressed for bed," I tell him.

He turns away from me, facing the wall. I throw off my cloak, unlace my boots, and shimmy my way out of the straps and wires I'm dressed in. Runa left a black nightgown that is thinner than tissue paper and shorter than anything I've worn.

But it's all I have.

Before I can slip under the blankets on the small bed, Dessin twists to look at me, his eyes of dynamite and steel tracing over every inch of my skin. His jaw clenches.

"I won't make you sleep on the floor." I smile.

After removing his boots, he's climbing into bed with me. The goose-feather mattress creaks as his weight settles in, leg touching my leg, arm pressed against my arm. Nothing to see except the soft glow of the lamps, flickering across the ceiling.

Will he touch me again now that we're away from the wandering eyes of the tavern?

Dessin shifts to get comfortable and brushes my leg with his own. He stills.

"Not a lot of room," he justifies. I can hear his breath, his heartbeat, his mind racing. The hairs on his leg tickle my knee as I shift it to rest over his thigh.

He doesn't move an inch.

"It's more room than your creaky bed at the asylum."

"You've been thinking about lying in my bed?" There's that unmistakable mischief in his tone. I'm glad he can't see my smile in the dark.

"I haven't even thought of it until this moment."

A closed-mouth laugh rumbles under his chest. "Liar."

It's chilly in this cave room, but luckily the feathered blanket is trapping Dessin's radiant body heat around us like a cocoon. Yet I still want him to hold me. I want his arms to pull me against his chest.

"That was quite the convincing performance you put on today," I muse.

"Oh?" His voice is low and gravelly.

"I thought you were only pretending until I felt *it*."

"Felt what?"

I huff. "You know… your excitement."

"I'm not sure what you mean," he says, a smile creeping in like a slow leak from a faucet.

"Really? It wasn't exactly subtle."

Dessin's quiet for a moment.

"I'm afraid you're going to have to show me with your hands."

I bark out a laugh. "Well played."

We lie there for several minutes. And it's long enough that I think he's sleeping with long peaceful breaths and complete stillness. I close my eyes; briefly, that is until his hand caresses over mine. The tips of his fingers graze my knuckles. And he's gentle. I ache inside, a slow throb in my heart and between my legs. *Please just hold me.*

He doesn't hear my silent plea because he lifts his hand away, slow and hesitant. But I'm not done yet. That can't be all after everything that's happened today. I snatch it back, slipping my hand around his, folding my fingers around his palm. I wonder if he can feel my heartbeat through this touch.

Adrenaline runs hot through my veins.

It still isn't enough. The need to feel his lips on my neck again fills me with wanton urgency. It's a feral itch in my lower belly. A beastly need to be touched. And I don't know where it's coming from. My back arches. My breath quickens.

"If you move your body that way again, we're going to have a problem," Dessin growls, sounding strained and almost fearful.

It's right here in this moment I know how I affect him. Every muscle in his body is stiff and rigid, while mine is floppy and languid. My movements control him, and it's wildly addicting. To the man who controls all, knows all—I am his downfall.

"What happens if I don't?"

"Skylenna," he warns. If it weren't for the known fact that he won't hurt me, I might actually take his warning to heart.

"Show me what happens." It's indecent and wrong. He's my friend. He was my patient first. But that time has come and gone, and I desperately need to know what he feels like. The tavern was a taste. It was exhilarating and nothing like our lives back in the city.

His body softens like a sigh of breath. And he doesn't move.

I turn my head to see his eyes are open, but something isn't right. They're glassy and unfocused. Like a daydream. Like death, but with breath in his lungs.

"Dessin?"

He blinks once, twice, eyes giving me a sidelong glance. A look that is cold and makes me shudder. His lips curl into a smirk as he rolls onto his side.

I know it immediately. Dessin is no longer beside me. He's gone.

I can only pray I have already met this alter.

"He's certainly no fun in these situations, is he?" That accent is delicious and silky.

Greystone.

I stop moving. Stare at him.

"Is he not giving you what you want?" He uses his arm to prop up his head, gazing down at me like I'm to be pitied for wanting what I want.

"You shouldn't be here," I tell him. "It's not safe."

Greystone looks around, examining the cave room with fake curiosity. "I don't see any danger. And the vindictive brute has certainly relaxed enough to let me through."

I huff out a loud sigh.

"Oh, don't sound so disappointed," he purrs.

"I'm not. You just surprised me."

He tilts his chin closer to my face, hovering as if to taunt me with what he might do. "Are you well? You look flustered."

I swallow, remembering what he told me when we first met. He keeps track of the arousal of this body and who causes it.

Me.

He surfaced for me. Because Dessin was aroused.

"Grey—"

"May I touch you?" he asks.

"I—well, I don't know." I want him to. My insides are coiling up, and heat flares in my gut. "I'm not sure how this works."

"You're afraid of hurting the avenging alter."

I nod.

"You won't. It isn't just him that you can have. It's the entire system. The other alters are all fond of you in their own way."

I blink. A spike of pleasure twisting through me at the notion that each alter is fond of me. Do they watch us? Do they each want to meet me? I exhale, slowly, nodding my head. "Okay. You may touch me."

He waits a few seconds, and I can almost hear him grin on the inside.

"Is this what you wanted from him?" He drags a finger across my collarbone, drawing a shiver from me. He smiles confidently. "It is, isn't it?"

His fingers pass over the skin just above my breasts. My nipples harden into aching points that Greystone can see through my nightgown.

"You wanted him to touch you. You wanted to satisfy that agonizing need to pleasure yourself." His voice is still masculine and deep; only now it has a seductive tone with soft, soothing edges.

His other hand slides over my thigh, holding the soft inner side closest to my panties. A white-hot blaze of electricity burns across my stomach, sending goose bumps to rise over my arms. I whimper, trying to clasp my mouth shut in hopes he doesn't hear it.

"Is that where it aches, pretty one?" He squeezes my inner thigh. "Use your words."

I'm delirious. Drunk, even. I nod because words are too much.

One daring finger skims over my panties. I let out a gasp that fades into a moan. "There's a good girl. Would you like me to teach you how to get what you want?" My insides purr at his approval.

I'm panting. Unsure how to do this without overthinking everything.

"Your words, please."

"Yes." My lungs deflate. "But why do you want to?"

He pauses. "I like the control of it. Teaching you how to erupt from our touch excites me."

He watches me with cunning calculation as if waiting for me to take my words back. But it is written across the desire coating his eyes. He can read me without half a thought. He can recognize every tremble, every sigh, every expression and know how to touch me. It's the way this alter is designed to understand the arts of pleasure.

"Do exactly as I say," he coaxes, dragging my hands down to my panties. "We'll go slow."

I'm no longer spineless and melting. Now, I'm as rigid as Dessin once was. His hand is resting over mine, which is resting between my legs.

"Move your fingers with mine," he says. He begins to curl them, stretch them, move them until I'm hooking my opening through the fabric of my panties. It hits a bundle of nerves that ignites my senses. I groan at his guidance. The base of my stomach twisting in a tight knot, burning with pleasure.

"Do you feel that?"

I pause.

"You're soaking," he hums, pleased with this outcome. "You have no idea how bad that makes me want to taste you."

"*Oh,*" I sigh, my center contracting around our fingers, kneading and working on me.

Greystone leans down into my ear, breathing against me.

"When my breath grazes your ear, your skin, it'll make it so much easier to chase that fire in your tight, pretty cunt." His words douse me in a ferocious need to move my fingers faster, arch my back into his dirty mouth. What is happening to me? It's a fever of sorts. A virus that turns a woman into a dainty monster.

The pressure in my clit swells, throbbing against our fingers, and the tingling sensation builds throughout my entire body.

"Faster, pretty one."

I breathe in and out like I'm about to faint. Our fingers are digging into me, massaging my hot, wet center.

"You're so beautiful with that mouth wide open for me."

I freeze before I burst. An explosion of euphoric magic that coats every cell, every vein, every organ. I'm gasping like a dying fish under Greystone's grip, howling until I fall limp to the bed, pouring over the sheets like warm, drizzling honey.

Oh my god. What was that?!

I'm a mess of trembling goo. Greystone kisses me on the cheek, smiling as he pulls away.

"Sleep," he urges. "I have more to teach you soon."

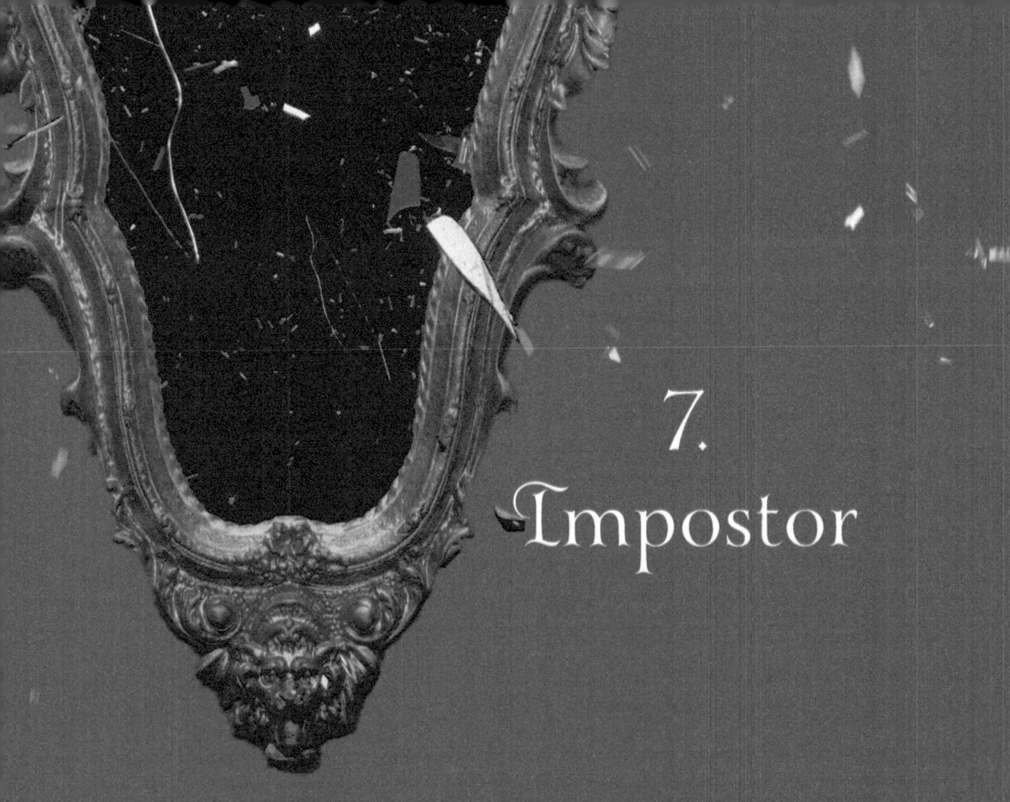

7. Impostor

I wake to the sound of a chair creaking.

My hand moves to wander aimlessly over the space Greystone was sleeping next to me. But it's empty yet still warm to the touch.

I open my eyes, blinking several times before the cave ceiling comes into focus. I shift to where the sound came from, a chair in the corner of the room. Dessin is lacing his boots up, glaring at me.

"What?" I ask, but I know. I wish I didn't. I screwed up big time.

"I've been filled in."

I use my elbows to prop myself up. My lips bunch together to keep from blurting out apologies.

"You know, I really miss the asylum. That chickenshit was too scared to ever come to the front then." He's annoyed. Not angry. My shoulders slump a little.

"You don't like him either, huh?" I ask.

"What's there to like?"

"Well—"

"Don't answer that," he orders.

I laugh. "Are you angry with me?"

Dessin lifts his chin to look down at me from under his lashes. Considering.

"No," he says.

"No?"

He finishes the last loop of his black laces.

"You're the one that had to sleep next to him," he says, cringing. "You should be the one that's upset."

"Do you think Kane will be mad?"

"No, he'll probably laugh. For the same reason I'm annoyed."

I sit up, clutching the blankets close to my chest. Is what I did not wrong? Shouldn't they be jealous or furious or hurt? I stew in my thoughts, trying to understand the meaning of all this.

Dessin kneels down on my side of the bed, looking up at me the way you would a child.

"I can see your wheels turning," he comments. "You don't understand how this works."

I really don't.

"The way I'd react to you being touched by other men versus another alter will be night and day. It's not the same. I'd cut down a man for even glancing your way. But—we all use the same body. It's different."

I sigh, a cloud of confusion thickening over my thoughts.

"Okay," I respond.

Dessin continues to watch me, eyes trailing curiously over my face.

"Get dressed." He stands, holding his hand out for me. "It's time to continue our ruse."

"Sleep well?" Runa asks, wearing a see-through dress that barely covers her bottom and thigh-high boots. We can see every detail of her backside as she walks.

Dessin has an arm around me, holding me tight to his side. I have to pretend it's normal. I have to act like being this close to him is an everyday occurrence for us. But I'm elated on the inside. My heart taking a lap around my chest like a wild stallion. I breathe through my nose to capture the scent of cedar and wood dust. Commit it to memory.

"We'll eat, then we'll be on our way," Dessin says, stroking the side of my arm with a calloused thumb.

I look up at him questioningly. I thought we would hear about the prophecy. About why the elders want to help us?

Dessin catches the question flinging from my gaze.

"I don't like staying in one place for too long. It makes us sitting ducks."

"Fine," Runa calls over her shoulder as we enter the cave tavern. "But they'll want to see you before you leave."

As we walk past the tables of clanking chalices, moaning women, and men devouring their breakfast—we're hit with the scent of cigar smoke, freshly baked bread, and leather.

Our hoods are up to disguise us, and I'm under Dessin's arm. He makes no effort to hide his aura of dominance. The shadows of death and destruction follow him everywhere. A king sauntering among peasants.

And I'm wrapped in his possession.

We take a seat at the table closest to the bar. Dessin sitting across from Runa, he glances over at me. "Up, in my lap," he commands.

It frightens me that I hardly give a thought to obeying. I'm up. I'm sliding into his lap with ease. His arms circle my waist like that's their resting position. That's where they belong.

Runa's eyes bounce between the two of us. She blinks those feline black eyes as if she's staring at a couple of ghosts.

"Out with it," Dessin grumbles from behind me.

"It's odd,"—Runa shakes her head—"seeing you two after hearing all of the stories."

"Is anyone going to tell us these stories?" I ask.

"I—" She pauses, shrugging her shoulders. "We're not allowed to. Telling you what is destined to happen could ruin everything."

Dessin is still beneath me. Deciding whether or not she's full of it.

"The elders will only tell you what the prophecy asks of our people. Instructions."

"Instructions?" Dessin asks.

She nods, smiling up at the man who sets breakfast plates down in front of us.

"From what I've heard, yes. Although no one knows what is to be given to you. It's been tasked with each generation of elders since—a long time." Runa digs into her grits and porridge.

I politely push around my food, taking tiny bites before I realize Dessin can't reach his with me in his lap. I look back at him, my eyes signaling to his food to ask, *Want me to move?*

Dessin shakes his head. "Eat."

But every couple of bites I take, I pass him a piece of fruit, forming a system. I try and shift my weight forward so I'm not suffocating him while he tries to enjoy his food. Still, he refuses my distance by tugging my hips backward, pinning me against his chest.

I fight to not let the satisfaction show on my face in front of Runa.

"What didn't you two like about the city that you'd venture all the way out here?" she asks between bites of food.

"Was it the starvation or the misogyny? Or was it the stupid bubble bath shit?" she asks again.

I scoff with a mouthful of food. "Yes." *It was all bad.* I'm still fighting the gnawing pains of the starvation. For some reason, I can't shake the need to continue my routine of eating only when I feel I might faint. It's sick. It's an illness, perhaps? And I'm careful, secretive, even, to hide these unhealthy compulsions from Dessin and Kane.

Runa nods. "You know the seven colonies don't control women the way your people do. Gender is of no importance to the way our society is run. Only heart and will. That's all that matters."

"Must be nice," I say tightly. And I mean that. I would love to live in a world that doesn't let a label limit your worth. If we cared less about a woman's appearance and more about what she could be capable of… wouldn't that be a society worth fighting for?

"How do you know so much about the city? They don't even know you exist. There are myths and rumors. But Demechnef isn't aware of your actual existence." Dessin isn't eating anymore. He's interrogating her. Uncertain of her motives.

"We have ways of watching." A knowing smile. "But there's only one colony that gets involved. Only one that watches and moves among the rest of you without ever being spotted."

"Who?"

"Crimson Kres. From the Red Oaks. They went missing after the slaughter of the RottWeilen."

My jaw drops. I turn back to Dessin. He blinks at me with the same question in his eyes.

"What do the RottWeilen have to do with them?" he asks.

"The RottWeilen were guardians to that colony. When they were slaughtered by your people, the Crimson Kres disappeared. But we think they are spies among your people. A rumor that they're pulling the puppet strings without being detected."

"What—" I set my fork down, swallowing my shock. "What do you think they're doing? And why?"

Runa leans in to whisper. "No one knows. But we can guess it has something to do with the prophecy. All seven of us have our own pieces to this puzzle."

For once, Dessin is wholly withdrawn. Unsure. Even a little confused.

I keep my eyes on him, a tickled smile blooming over my cheeks.

"What." Not a question. A demand. He doesn't even look at me to know I'm amused at his expense. My chest pressurizes with laughter.

"Am I funny to you, Skylenna?" His words are laced with edgy irritability.

I laugh harder.

"Secrets aren't so fun when you're on the outside, are they?" I'm grinning now.

He rolls his neck, his stare of steel and ice flicks to me. He is not entertained by my laughter. "Yuck it up, beautiful. You're on the outside of their secrets too."

"Careful, little girl," Runa warns, cleaning her plate. "You wouldn't want to see the other people that live in that mind of his."

Her comment is casual, yet a pang of annoyance hits my gut. How is it she knows more about his mind than I do? I want to be the only one that knows his mind in and out. I want to be the only one that knows his secrets.

Dessin seems rubbed the wrong way too. His daring eyes narrow at her, belittling her entire being with one look. "How the fuck would you know anything about that?"

Her white eyebrows rise. She realizes where she went wrong.

"*Speak*," he demands with that darkened voice he uses when he's about to attack.

"We,"—she gulps down the last of her food—"know almost everything about the two of you. You're in our mythology."

"Mythology?"

But I'm not listening. That rotten jealousy that I buried early has come back full force. I'm seething beside him. My hands grip the edge of the wooden table. I'm a doll made of stone in his lap. I get it. They know things. But hearing Runa speak about Dessin to me as though she's an old friend, someone who knows him so much better.

It pisses me off.

"I really can't talk about it," Runa says stiffly.

"I don't like my identity being public knowledge." Dessin's hands tighten around my hips.

"Well, it is, and there isn't anything you can do about it," Runa says.

"No? You don't think so?"

And I can practically hear the earth rumbling with his wrath. Dessin loves proving a point, and he'll stop at nothing to find whatever holds this information about him. Even if he has to burn down everything in these caves to do it.

"You won't because we're leaving. *Now*." I push off his lap, storming out of the tavern. But I made a thoughtless mistake. My hood flies off my head, falling down my back and unveiling my face for all to see.

A man with white hair braided down to the base of his neck snatches my arm midstride.

"I knew something didn't belong," he muses, eyes a mix of charcoal and ash. He's middle-aged, lean frame, with a tunic open at the chest. "Hello, lost one."

I try to yank my arm from his grip, but he's cold metal. A grasp of pure testosterone and dark elven blood. *Great*. I had to be the one to blow our cover.

"Let me go," I say under my breath.

He laughs loudly, alerting his chatting comrades that he's got something they'll want to see. I act quickly before they can turn around. My foot jerks forward, kicking him in the shin. He hisses at the sudden pain, and his grip loosens, allowing me to yank hard enough to free myself. But I overshoot. I pull too hard, fumbling toward the ground.

But instead, I slam into something solid and unmovable. A wall of granite muscle.

That presence can be felt before it is seen. Like a fog rolling over a mountain, thickening the air in your chest.

His hands curl around my arms to keep me steady as he stands me upright. And I don't have to turn around to feel the violence dance around him. Because he stills behind me. Signs that cold rage boils under his surface.

"Who the fuck are you?" the braided-haired man spits.

Dessin's next movements are swift and clean, rotating me behind his back. Safe. Guarded. I stand on my tiptoes to peer over his shoulder at the soon-to-be-dead man.

"Sorry, I didn't quite catch that?" Dessin's voice is relaxed and almost polite with his request for the dead man to repeat himself. He sticks his neck out in emphasis.

"She's a—"

The jab to Braid Man is quick, sharp, fluid. And he's on his knees gasping, choking on his own saliva. Dessin clutches his hand just under the man's chin, yanking him upward. And it's a terrifying sight to see. With one hand, Dessin holds my assailant above his head. Feet dangling like low-hanging fruit inches above the ground.

Braid Man's throat gurgles; bubbles of saliva foaming at the corners of his mouth.

"Apologize before I cut out your tongue with a rusted knife." His threat is a mountain falling from the sky, dropping down on the man's back. It's a storm ripping through the musty cave air.

The other men rise from their seats, hopping over the tables to aid Braid Man and attack Dessin with brute force.

And truthfully, I would be confident with the outcome of Dessin winning. But we don't know the capabilities of the dark elven descendants.

They charge like a swarm of bees to defend their nest, and all I can hear is Runa's voice shouting for them to stop.

He has to drop the man. We need to leave.

"DESSIN!" I scream at the top of my lungs, tearing from the depths of my stomach and scraping my esophagus on the way out.

The shouting of men and clattering of falling silverware fade into a slowing pace of confused looks and wide eyes. They stop themselves moments before they barrel into him. And it's a moment of caution. The way you would step away from a lion when seconds before you thought you were petting a cat.

Their gazes flicker from him to me and then to each other.

"That's right, assholes." Runa shoves past me to stand between Dessin and me. "Prophecy is real. They weren't scary stories to tell at night to scare little children."

Scary? What is said about us that could be scary?

I look up at Dessin, still strangling Braid Man.

Ah, yep, that checks out.

"Put him down," Runa barks.

I can only see the back of Dessin's head, but if looks could kill…. He lowers Braid Man to the ground. Sobs and guttural choking sounds escape him as he fights to survive the attack to his windpipes.

The men and women gather around us, gawking as if they are seeing a living, fire-breathing dragon.

Accusations are thrown from all angles.

Impostors!

Not real!

Spies from the city!

And the crowd turns from stunned to skeptical to outraged. The next moment combusts into masculine chaos. The tavern seems to decide on our fraudulent status collectively, telepathically. The cave rages with violence in the blink of an eye.

They rush Dessin like a tidal wave of white hair, black leather, and snakelike movements. They are trained. And they are deadly.

But no matter how good they might be, Dessin is worse. As I whip my head back to him, he doesn't look nervous, doesn't seem overwhelmed. He's a plague of destruction.

Their attacks are clean and precise, but Dessin anticipates every fist, every kick with calculated maneuvers. He uses them against each other, ducking when someone swings, knocking out their fellow comrades. His arms are deadly whips, devastating detonators of impact. They can't react fast enough. It's as if his actions are choreographed. Preplanned. A death dance. A symphony of organized chaos.

Except this cave is a fortress to them. They must have prepared for intruders over centuries of paranoia. Generations of planning. Two contraptions of chains fall from the ceiling, a cage of metal thorns trapping him mid-fight.

"No!" I howl, but it's too late. A pair of arms wrap around my body, keeping me from running to him. "Dessin!" I scream, watching blood drip down his arms from the spikes that puncture him in place. He can't escape without tearing holes into his muscles. And I know he would do it. He sees my struggle. That stare of insidious intent and possessiveness takes over.

I'm being hauled backward. But I kick and scream, thrashing against their hold. *This is my fault!* I'm the reason we blew our cover. I'm the reason Dessin had to fight at all.

"Please," I beg, my screams hoarse and rusty.

A woman dressed in a full-body lingerie set pulls a red poker from the giant fireplace, rushing to Dessin's cage, handing it to a man that seems to be in charge.

"Who sent you?" He taunts Dessin with the blazing tool, sizzling with unbearable heat.

But Dessin is silent, in fact, he's not even paying attention. His eyes have gone vacant, distant, unable to process the new information.

Is he… Is he switching alters? NOW? Who could possibly be more capable of handling this situation than him?!

He blinks, adjusting his focus on the poker. His gaze is lighter, less violent, and unlike anything I've seen from him. He's *excited.*

"How hot is it?" this new alter asks, breaking into a poisonous smile. "Is it searing? Hot enough to burn through flesh?"

The man holding the poker pauses, resting the sharp tip on the bar of his cage.

"Go on," the alter croons. "I'm itching to feel it."

What?

That voice never loses its weight that drops down to my gut. It's deep and low, but with a wicked humor and playfulness that I haven't heard. He likes the pain.

Trauma.

This alter was split to withstand torture. An alter that would enjoy it.

A shiver melts over my skin. I break out into a sweat, trembling in the arms of my captors.

No... I can't let him go through this. I don't care if this alter enjoys it or not. It's my fault. He won't suffer because of my stupidity.

"Stop! He'll never talk but I will!" I shout to the man waving around the unconventional weapon.

The new alter turns his head to me, faster than taking a breath. "*Don't.*"

The man with charred eyes and wispy lashes barks a laugh at me, turning back to the new alter to begin the interrogation.

But I see the flaming pointed end of the tool inching to his flesh, and I can't hold myself together. Tears spring to my eyes in a flash flood. I had to sit silently while he was tortured in the asylum. I had to hold myself together. But not here. Not again.

My agony is unleashed. I lurch forward, despite the unbreakable arms around me. And I let out the most devastating sound that has ever left my lips.

A cry for help.

A howl of endless torment.

It ripples out of my lungs like a never-ending horn of battle.

And there's a moment of silence before we feel it. A moment of peace. An energy thrumming through the earth. A rumbling like from a galloping herd of buffalo. But more than that, it's the energy of a firestorm rage that crackles through the air.

And it's not coming from the man in the cage.

A monster roars in dark fury outside of the cave, scorching the tavern with vehemence, like the devil emerging straight from hell to annihilate us all.

DaiSzek gallops from the blackened shadows of the forest like a murderous devourer of worlds. And his eyes glow crimson red.

I laugh through my tears, gasping at how his entrance has paralyzed my entire body in divine awe. The beautiful, terrifying beast charges for us, feral energy pulsing through every man and woman around us. They scatter like rats in a sewer pipe.

DaiSzek leaps in front of Dessin's cage, or whoever is in there now, guarding his friend. And I run to them. The arms have dropped from my waist. I'm sprinting like a madwoman to the cage, to the unfaltering protection of DaiSzek's ferocious stance.

When he sees that I am safely behind him, his snarl pulls back, showing off the deathly fangs that could rip a tree in half. A warning that whoever crosses him will lose their flesh, their organs, their souls.

And the crowd obeys. Staring in shock, in horror, in soul-shattering disbelief at the beast. The legends of which myths were written.

Our friend. Our protector.

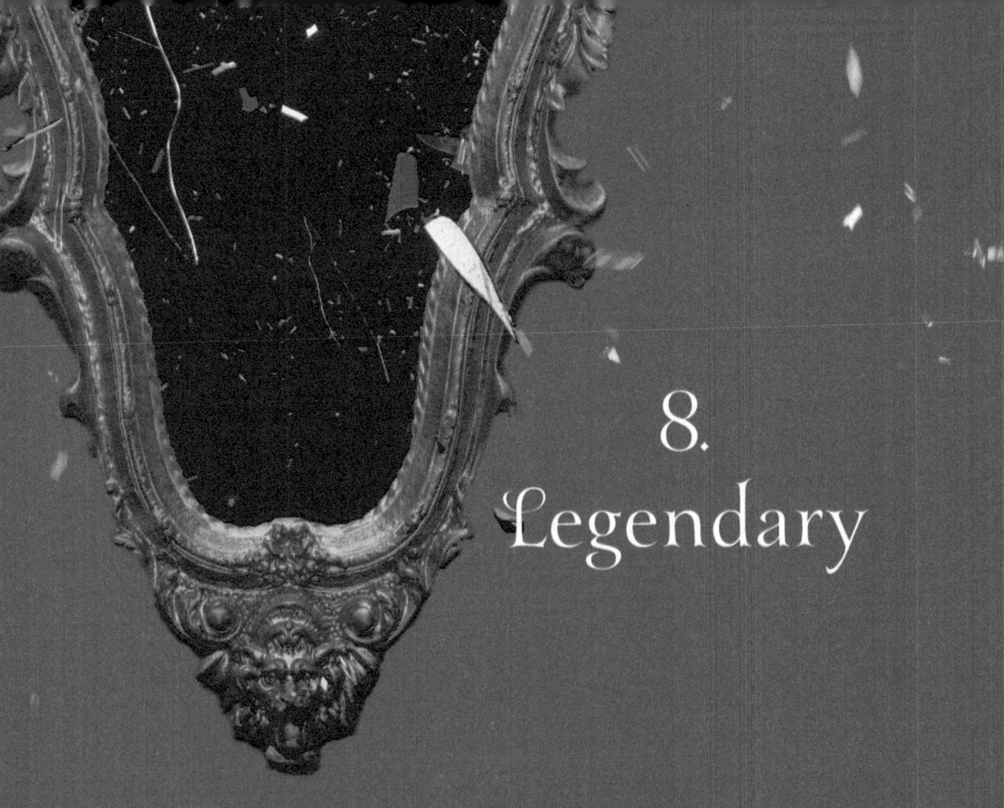

8. Legendary

The whispers are frightened and cautious.

DaiSzek does not stand down. He's waiting for an order from us. A command to eliminate the threats. His stance is wide and daring, head low, neck out, a predatory sign before an attack.

I'm shaking. I've never seen him like *this* before. It's the shock of being in the presence of something great. Something almighty. I can hardly breathe as I gaze at him in this new light. He's an unconquerable force to them. An iconic legend that is simply superior.

"Is that a…?"

"A RottWeilen," the man in the cage announces. His straight posture. Confident eyes scanning the crowd for weakness. His gaze shifts to me, asking with one look if I'm alright.

Dessin.

I nod my head, still unable to catch my breath.

The crowd breaks out in frantic whispers, flinching as DaiSzek continues to lurch forward, snarling an awful sound deep within his throat.

"They're extinct…" someone says from the back. "They're

supposed to be extinct!"

I lean into DaiSzek's side, afraid they might want to kill him. My hand reaches over his sleek black fur until my hand disappears.

At some point during the chaos, Runa was knocked over. She's up now, dusting herself off. "Do you believe me now?" She strides around DaiSzek, holding her hands up to show him she's not a threat, she wants to open his cage.

But DaiSzek isn't having it. He springs forward, teeth snapping a breath away from her face, sending her white hair to blow back over her shoulders. She falls to the ground again, gawking up at the beast that could crush her with one bite.

"Skylenna will have to free me," Dessin tells her, satisfaction seeping through his words like a towel soaking up a spill. "He'll decapitate anyone else this close." He grins down at her. I suspect he's holding back a laugh.

I walk around DaiSzek, stopping in front of his large snout to admire him for a moment. But he isn't having that either, he uses that big head to nudge me over to the cage, to hurry me along because he doesn't like me exposed to the threats.

Dessin smirks at me from behind the bars. "I had that handled, you know. I didn't need him to come save the day."

I snort. "All that blood part of the plan?" I nod my head at his arms, still being stabbed with the long metal thorns of the cage. I unlatch a few metal plates and bolts.

"Just a scratch." He tries to shrug but forgets he's nailed in place. He hisses.

I shake my head, removing the last rod that's keeping the cage from opening. I try to jerk open the cylindrical doors, but he grunts.

"*Slowly*."

I cringe. *Whoops*. The doors are attached to the spikes puncturing his arms. I have to open them inch by inch, watching the pointed tips slipping from his wounds.

"Get a healer," the man in charge barks. "And someone get this man some alcohol!"

"I'm fine," Dessin grumbles. He's going to be in a foul mood all day. *Goody for me*.

"No, you're not," he says. "And we're ashamed. We've—we've

been waiting for you for so long that we stopped believing. But seeing the RottWeilen… a beast that was supposed to be extinct. A myth that said only one would survive and that one would live with the sole purpose to protect the two of you."

I pull the cage the rest of the way, freeing Dessin from the spikes. Blood spills from the small punctures in his arms. My hands fumble to him, pressing down on the wounds to stop the blood. His dark-mahogany eyes slide from my hands up to my face. That gaze lingers. One moment, two moments… and it's intimate, it's full of feeling that's been buried, hidden, yearning for more. An ache flickers in my chest like firelight. A throbbing pain from the need to hear him say he wants me. He *wants* me.

Dessin's eyes shift back to the man in charge.

"He needs everyone to bow to him. Show him you're not a threat."

The crowd shifts uncomfortably on their feet until they're on their knees, bowing before DaiSzek.

Wow, I didn't know that's how it works. I didn't need to bow to show him I wasn't a threat when we first met. Maybe that's because I was attacked by the night dawper and it was obvious.

But right on cue, Dessin blows out a rush of pent-up air in his chest, laughing at the cave of kneeling people.

"*Dessin,*" I hiss.

The people of the tavern groan with eye rolls and embarrassed chuckles, standing back up quickly.

He shrugs, stepping out of the cage. "*That* was payment for pissing me off."

"Cute," I huff, wiping my bloody hands on my black cloak. But I want to laugh with him. To be honest, I'm glad he has a sense of humor about this instead of siccing DaiSzek on them.

"DaiSzek, wait outside for us, please." It's all that needs to be said for DaiSzek to trot out of the tavern with four long strides.

An older woman rushes in with a sack of supplies to clean Dessin's wounds, followed by a young man, not a day older than twenty, holding out a chalice of liquor for him.

Dessin glares at the boy, giving him a once-over with disgust. "I don't need it."

"You're so stubborn," I snap, taking the chalice from the boy with a smile. "Just drink it."

"I'd rather sit in the cage again."

Runa laughs.

And once again, my stomach grumbles with an ache that wants to smack her.

"Let us dress your wounds. Our elders will want to speak with you." The man in charge allows the healer to stand beside Dessin, dabbing at his arms with a wet cloth.

"We're leaving after this," Dessin says, watching the healer move her hands methodically over his punctures to clean the blood off.

"No." I clear my throat. "I want to see the elders first."

Dessin glances down at me. The tavern goes quiet.

"Why?"

"Because they said they have something for us."

He blinks twice and wrinkles his brow.

"You're right. We wouldn't want to miss them presenting us with a dungeon cell with both our names on it."

"They would never." The man in charge steps forward. "Our elders have held on to something for generations, waiting for the moment to give them to you."

I can't wrap my head around this. Elders. Colonies. Prophecy. Legends. More Secrets. I'm always left in the dark. At least these people are offering me a hint, a sliver of the truth I can hold on to. Dessin never gives me anything.

"It's settled then." I smile up at him. "When you're all patched up and good as new, we'll make them one last visit."

The elders have been waiting outside of the cave.

Someone ran and tattled on our little scandal, drawing the elders out of their dimly lit church cave to gaze upon DaiSzek.

He's currently sitting upright, facing the tavern, looking unnervingly like a gargoyle.

"Enjoying the view?" I ask as we walk up behind them.

"Incredible," the old woman says.

"How long has it been guarding you?" the old man to the left asks.

Dessin sighs, already bored. "Since he was the size of my two hands."

The old man with bushy white brows looks between Dessin and me, parting his lips as if he wants to ask something, then thinks better of it.

"As *welcoming* as the Nightamous Horde has been, we're in a hurry to leave." Dessin's voice is thick, gruff, and clearly annoyed that his arms are probably sore.

The old woman breaks away from her hypnotic trance set on DaiSzek. "My name is Qilan. My father gave me this when he passed, told me your story, told me that one day I might be one to hand you this,"—her pasty wrinkled hands hold out a rolled-up piece of parchment to me—"a map of the seven forests. And where each ancient colony is located. We've marked the ones you'll need to visit."

I unroll the aged, yellow-stained map. It's ancient, beautifully crafted, and detailed. I see the circle in the center of all seven forests, the bare land where the Chandelier City would be now. And within five of the seven forests, a pocket of land is covered in drawings of small hobbles, fortresses, and mystical architecture.

"The Red Oaks and Hangman's Valley are the only ones that aren't inhabited by a colony."

Well, we know the Red Oaks is vacant due to the vanishing colony after the RottWeilen slaughter. "Why doesn't Hangman's Valley have a colony?"

"It does. Just not one you can communicate with," Runa cuts in behind me. "It's the land of the longest living beasts. It's where the RottWeilen originated from before they manifested to the Red Oaks to bond with that colony."

"Fascinating," Dessin clips, turning to Qilan. "May we go?"

She shakes her head. "I think you'll enjoy my last gift the most." The old man with bushy white brows pulls an ash-colored stone from his pocket. It looks like a barnacle from the side of a ship. Dusty and jagged.

"You've heard of shades, yes?" Qilan asks.

Dessin and I both shrug, like *yeah, kinda, sorta.*

"They're the only bit of proof we have that these lands were once riddled with magic. Shades were once fae or elves. They turned into dark, vengeful spirits that haunt these lands." She points to the stone that the old man passes to Dessin. "*That* is a shade stone. The only object that can call to them. So, if you should ever find yourself in dire need of help. Rub the stone until flecks of ash and dust float into the wind."

Qilan's black, hazy eyes look back and forth between Dessin and me.

"And help will come."

9. Nadaskar Slayer

"All that work for a fucking rock."

It's safe to say Dessin is in a bad mood even now that we're on the move again.

"And a fucking map," I add.

His eyes pinch close as his entire upper body rumbles with laughter. He glances down at me, hugging the map to my chest, smiling smugly to myself.

He laughs again, flashing me his dimples and gorgeous teeth. I sigh at the moment, forcing it to memory, locking it away in a safe place.

"You're adapting that soldier's mouth just to throw me off."

"Or you're a bad influence."

"I am certainly that," he says, dimples prominent in the shadows of the Evergreen Dark Wood. "Do me a favor? When you see Kane again, drop one of your verbal bombs in his lap. I'd love to see how he'd react."

I scoff. "I'd never curse at him. He's nice!"

"And I'm not?" He feigns offense with a theatric hand to his chest.

"You're tolerable."

Dessin laughs again. His brow arches at a thought. "Runa was nice, hmm?"

My shoulders stiffen. *Oh, he's walking a thin line.*

"You think she was nice?" I ask without raising my eyes from the dirt trail.

"Sure, don't you?"

I grimace. "Not especially. But boy, did she like you. Laughing at your jokes, insinuating she wanted to—do *stuff* with you."

"Stuff?"

"*Yes*. Stuff. Be alone with you. Take my place on your lap." The heat of that simmering agitation comes back at the memory. She looked at him like a nice, juicy steak. I want to vomit.

"You must have been paying very close attention to her," he comments. Emotions unreadable.

I shrug, but the movement is stiff, forced, mechanical. "She might as well have been shouting it from the rooftops."

Dessin thinks for a moment. "Did you picture us together? Is that why you're this tightly wound?" A wicked smile pours into his deep voice. "Did you imagine her riding in my lap the way you were in the tavern?"

I whip around and glare at him. "You—" I huff. Grinding my teeth together. "You don't know anything!" I kick the ground, a cloud of dirt surrounds my feet at impact.

Dessin grins. "Did that make you feel better?"

"And another thing,"—I point my finger at him like a mother hen—"I don't care who you have in your lap. As long as I don't have to do it again."

"Is that right?" He smiles wider.

"Yes."

"So the thought of me with another woman doesn't get you *really* angry?" He takes a step closer to me.

I push that angry bubble away but its persistence is overpowering. It wants me to burst. My hands clench into fists. Why does this bother me so much?

"Nope. Because the time in that tavern was just a game. It didn't mean anything." Why am I saying this? I've been dying to know if he felt it too. If there were any feelings fluttering in his chest the way they were in mine.

But he's taunting me. He's dangling the idea of him with another woman in front of me and I won't entertain it. I won't be the first to tell him how I feel.

"Is that right?" He tilts his head. "No part of you liked having my fingers in your mouth?"

I visibly shiver. "Nope." *Yes. I couldn't get enough.*

Dessin chuckles as if it's obvious that I got caught in a lie. But the sound quickly sprinkles into the air and dissolves like a speck of snow hitting the earth. He stops walking, and it's several moments before he blinks repeatedly, appearing disoriented.

I breathe in and out patiently. I wonder who I'll see this time. It can't be Greystone.

The man looks up at me from a lowered head, then takes a quick scan of the forest to adjust to his new surroundings.

"Where are we?" he asks.

The jealous anger evaporates from my nervous system. For now.

"Still in the Evergreen Dark Wood. But we're leaving now, we're headed,"—I hold up the map—"to the North Saphrine Forest."

I peek up at him from over the map, hoping I can catch a single detail before he has to introduce himself. I watch him take a steadying breath, soft, warm eyes roaming past the trees. His posture is casual but confident, but his brow is knitted together; he's concerned. Perhaps about how much time he's lost?

Kane.

He's been gone since Runa found us.

"Hey," I say, taking a step closer. "What's wrong?"

Kane's eyes dart to me for a split second before he goes back to observing the forest with dread. "What happened? How long was I gone?"

"Like a day and a half. We made some new friends!" Another step. It's like cornering a frightened animal.

Kane touches his left arm, feeling the pain from where he was poked by the cage spikes. He grimaces at the tenderness and runs his fingers over the bloody bandages.

"What *happened*?" he asks again, this time with a bite of resentment.

"It's a long st—"

But he isn't listening to me. He's asking Dessin. Those soft-brown eyes look down, paying attention to an explanation that's probably faster for Dessin to give than me.

Kane nods once. Looks up at me. He releases a weighted sigh.

"You can't let him get a rise out of you when he picks on you like that." And with that, Kane begins walking.

I huff. "How can I not? He's good at finding weaknesses."

"He likes his games." He nods and glances back at me. "How're you doing with all of this? You've taken on a lot since we left the asylum."

"I'm better now than when I was working at the asylum." The answer comes out rushed. No hesitation. This life is much more suited to me.

We pass the time while hiking up the mountain with old folklore. Kane shares the many tales that the agronomists and watchdogs would entertain with over a big bonfire. He tells me about the time travelers in the woods. Some would claim that they've seen people wandering around the forests, asking the agronomist children what the date was. There were also legends that there was still one RottWeilen left alive, roaming the seven forests and sometimes would sneak into the city. They claim that this beast could carry at least a ton of weight on his back, that he kills animals higher on the food chain than himself, and eats babies.

"Babies, huh?" I laugh.

"And get shot by one hundred arrows and not die. Although, that parts probably true." We both laugh this time.

"Where is DaiSzek, anyway?"

Kane tosses a cluster of branches to the side of our walking path. "He's scanning the perimeter of several miles around us. He doesn't like to be surprised."

I bend down to tie my hiking boots. The Nightamous Horde graciously gave us packs of supplies and clothing to wear over our backs. Hiking coats, boots, hats, gloves, weapons.

"Have you ever seen him in action? Like in a real fight?" I ask.

"I have." He turns around and crosses his arms. "And you have too from what I remember."

"Yes." I stand up and look at my feet, remembering. "Aurick tried to shoot him. He thought DaiSzek attacked me. But he saved me from the night dawper."

Kane scoffs. "Aurick is very lucky that he kept his genitalia that night."

I cringe and pick up my pace. I push at his arm while I jog past him. "You're so slow, we could have been there by now if we didn't have to move like snails!"

"Oh, so it's me that has been holding us back, huh?"

I'm already out of breath from jogging ahead. "Yeah! We need to get you in shape! Have you lost all of those big muscles or something?"

He starts to jog to catch up to me. "Oh, so you think my muscles are big?"

I choke out a surprised laugh but the sound is cut off.

The ground disappears from under my feet. Without even a moment to react and process the next few seconds, I'm gliding through the air, now smelling like hot rain and moist dirt. I shriek as I hit softer ground, palms down, directly on my chest and stomach. The air deflates from my lungs like a popped balloon.

My joints explode with pain. Muscles are floppy and sore. But my ankle is on fire. Searing white agony stretches up my calf as if I've been caught in barbed wire.

"Skylenna!" His voice is finally making its way to my eardrums. A deep gravelly sound echoing in this hole. I hear my name again, this time traveling downward, closer and closer until I feel the earth hemorrhage violently under my limp body. A puff of dust spreads over me.

"Where does it hurt?" he asks, struggling to keep his tone calm. He's in the hole with me now, kneeling somewhere beside me. The left side of my face is smashed against the dirt. *Oh God, I broke my face*. The constrictions on my chest loosen and I gasp in air, coughing and choking on my own saliva and particles of dirt. His hands are on my back, examining my bones.

"Nothing's broken." I hear him mutter. He pauses. A featherlight movement on my searing ankle. "Skylenna? Can you feel your ankle?"

I finally have enough oxygen back to my brain to release a guttural groan.

"Honey, can you speak?" he asks again, more urgently.

"Yes, I can feel it. Do me a favor and cut it off," I moan and mumble into my new friend, *the dirt*.

"I see your humor didn't break your fall."

Even with the sharp shooting pains sinking teeth into my pathetic body, I smile at the kind of friendship we have. To still make each other laugh during hard times.

I try to lift myself off this *bed from hell* with my palms still embedded in the crime scene. I fall back down with a whimper. *Welp, safe travels, Kane. Send me a postcard when you reach the next colony.*

"Skylenna, please don't move," he instructs. A trickle of fear drips down my back like the first stages of a thunderstorm.

"Why do you sound cautious?" I ask three octaves higher than normal. He's hovering over my legs without touching my ankle. *Oh God, did my foot actually get cut off?*

"Your foot got trapped in a snare designed to capture larger animals. Your ankle is small, so we're lucky it didn't chop it off. It just pierced it. But it's stuck in there; I have to take it out."

"I'd rather die," I say, trying to get a good look at him. The twisty movement sends a bolt of fire through my calf. "Augh!" I lie back down and slap my hand back on the dirt.

"Don't move until I tell you to. I have to open the trap, and when I do I need you to pull your foot out as fast as you can, okay?"

I grunt in acknowledgment at his request and brace myself. I hear him bear down behind me as the trap begins to rise from being embedded into my skin. It's like pulling a thumbtack from the bottom of your foot, except a million times worse.

His movements cause the snare to dig farther into my shredded skin. I yelp and bear down at what comes next.

"NOW!"

I yank my foot out and pull my knee to my chest. Crimson blood pours down my foot and saturates the dirt. My grunt isn't ladylike. It isn't pretty. The sound is unrecognizable as it whooshes from my chest.

"I know, I know," Kane soothes. "I'm going to roll you on your back now." He grips my waist, and I howl as he twists my body until I can finally look up at him. He moves my hair out of my face with two fingers. For just this moment, I forget the painful throbbing in my ankle, my stomach flips and the depth of his stare is pouring into my soul, warming me from the inside out. And he isn't looking away. There's a silent breeze of déjà vu fluttering over my heart. A moment of recognition.

"Skylenna…" Kane's tone isn't calculated or teasing. It's heavy with memories. Caring. Kind. Brave. "Is it too soon to tell you this is what you get for telling me I'm out of shape?"

We chuckle in unison.

"You're so fun—" A low growl startles us. The sound of a bear. Like the times in the early morning, my father would watch them from a window outside of our house.

Kane turns slowly, and we come to the same conclusion together. This hole is bigger than we thought, and we're not in here alone.

Behind Kane stands a massive shadow, like a tower built behind a cottage. It has thick coffee-colored fur, the body of a grizzly bear, with the face of a—of a cat? Yes, a huge, ugly mountain cat.

"A Saphrine Mountain nadaskar." Rough. Assertive. Alpha. I know the switch was inevitable. Dessin is now standing over me, and I'm racking my brain to figure how he could possibly get us out of this one. We're at least ten feet in a massive hole, and even if we could figure out a way to climb out of here, we wouldn't be fast enough. From what I remember, the nadaskar has the strength of a bear and the agility of a mountain cat. *Not a fair fight.*

"Dessin," I whisper, failing to hide the terror choking my voice.

He stays completely still and I mimic him without question. Dessin plans a lot of things but couldn't plan for this. We're going to die here, aren't we?

"Skylenna," he murmurs while slowly reaching for something to his left. "On my word, I want you to scream at the top of your lungs. Like your life depends on it. Because it does."

I'm about to object, but I see he's reaching for a tree branch, thick in size, about the girth of his thigh. I can't question him now. This is one of those times where I need to have complete and utter faith in Dessin.

The growling increases and I can see now why it's taken time for this massive beast to attack. His foot is gone. He must have gotten it caught in the trap and ripped it out.

Suddenly, the growl turns into a cat's hiss, and I know that must mean it's about to do something. Run or fight. Please let it mean run.

"Scream, Skylenna!"

I do as I'm told. I could have shattered windows and wineglasses and destroyed eardrums with this scream. It's shrill and dry and traveling a great distance out of this hole. The nadaskar lunges at Dessin with its one leg, and Dessin swings the tree branch straight into the amputee's leg. It shrieks but this only angers it. It lunges at us again, this time I'm certain Dessin won't be able to stop it from crushing us.

Faster than I can blink, a rush of black smoke flashes across my vision and tackles the nadaskar to the ground. Another animal. A hellhound.

And they're a tangled mess of snapping teeth, blood, and vicious growls that have reached a new level of feral. But I recognize the russet spots of fur. The RottWeilen that has come for me once again. Only this time, he knew he needed to attack.

DAISZEK! IT'S DAISZEK! HE'S SAVING US!

The hole suddenly smells of death massacring a farm of cattle. Entrails spilling over the muddy floor. Bones crunching. And I look up at Dessin who is now lifting me off the ground.

"Wrap your arms around my neck and keep your body stiff," he demands. I do as he says, still unable to tear my eyes away from the mass of dark fur. I hear the nadaskar scream along with another noise of ripping flesh from bone.

Dessin hooks an arm under my knees and begins to climb us out of the hole. Thankfully, there are large curly roots striking out of the walls of the hole for him. He makes each movement seem effortless, climbing with another human in your arms is as easy as walking to the kitchen. I lean my head against the side of his temple.

As we get to the top, he lets me pull myself from his arms onto the surface. I sit up and hold my ankle. The gushing of blood has slowed down but there are shreds of my skin hanging off and I think I might throw up.

Dessin looks down at me, pulls his shirt off, and uses it to wrap around my ankle. "Just don't look at it. I'll patch it up when we get out of here." But I'm not focused on that. This is the first time I've seen him without a shirt and it is *glorious*. His pectorals are two firm hills over his chest. He has a faint yet definite lining of six muscle ridges. His eyes are on me and *oh my God, I'm gawking.*

A yelp breaks this moment from growing awkward. We both look back at the hole but there is silence. "DaiSzek!" I yell. "Oh, Dessin! Is he okay?"

Dessin leans over the hole to look down and that's when I see his back. His back without a shirt. I'm briefly mortified. Burns across his shoulder blades in the size and shape of a picket from a wooden fence.

I lean in to get a better look.

But DaiSzek leaps from the hole, graceful like a deer stepping over a puddle. Blood covers his chin and nose. I shriek.

"Is he hurt?!" I touch the side of his face. He merely pants like he's just got done chasing a squirrel.

Dessin has his hands all over him, examining his entire body, then slaps his butt.

"Who taught you how to fight like that, nadaskar slayer?" He's beaming at DaiSzek. *Okay, no injuries.* DaiSzek starts to wiggle his butt, honored by Dessin's approval. "I mean, I probably could have taken it on my own, but wow, you really did a number down there!" He glances over his shoulder again, down at what probably is a mess of blood and fur and body parts.

"So, he's not hurt?" I ask.

He shakes his head. "No, this was an easy feat for him," he states, gazing at DaiSzek now sitting down proudly.

I nod. "Good. Good." Then, tip my head over the side of the hole and vomit. *A lot.*

10. "I must keep you in the dark."

His chest smells like cedar and the forest before a storm passes through.

I breathe him in as he carries me to a place where my ankle can be assessed. There is no central point of pain anymore; the throb stems from the tips of my toes reaching up to my thigh. It clenches around my bone like an iron fist covered in thorns. My head starts to pound each time Dessin takes a step. Skinny daggers puncturing my brain at the beat of my pulse.

As we get closer to the North Saphrine Forest, the chill in the air grows. Dessin even stops to bundle me up in both my winter coat and his. I refused to take his only source of warmth, especially since he gave up his shirt to bandage my ankle, but he insisted the cold didn't bother him. He spent more time educating me about how the human brain can actually control the body in a way so that we can adjust our body temperatures to adapt to any environment. With or without a coat. It just takes more concentration and focus than the average human can handle. And he is most certainly not average.

"That hole wasn't there by accident, was it?"

"No, it wasn't. Someone is trying to slow us down, and it worked." He motions with his head at my ankle. "Stopping to clean and dress the wound is what they were hoping for."

"But I thought Demechnef wanted you alive. Why would they risk hurting us?"

He narrows his eyes in the distance. "I'm not convinced that they're the only ones after us. The hole isn't really their style. They will send soldiers, disarm us, and capture us. This is the work of an individual. Someone's tracking us. I'm just surprised DaiSzek hasn't caught them yet. That must mean they know we have him on our side and they're keeping a safe distance."

"Another enemy to add to the list. Swell."

He shrugs with a cocky expression. "I'm not concerned in the slightest."

I laugh. "Of course you're not. Because an entire government trying to capture us was child's play. Now add an assassin with a personal vendetta and expert tracking skills and we've got ourselves a semisatisfying game!"

"It's like you really get me!" He squeezes the spot under my knee, and it tickles. I squirm and squeal to get him to stop.

We walk for a time that stretches out peacefully. My muscles ache from newborn bruises, so I'm grateful to be resting in his arms.

"We're almost there," he says as we maneuver through a wall of pine trees that veers off our current path we've been on. We get poked and scratched by the green needles and the sun finally blasts its way through as we exit the shelter of the Evergreen Dark Wood.

Finally emerging from the swamp of trees grown too close together, a small house. No, not just a small house, an approximately four-hundred-square-foot cottage. It includes a river rock chimney/ foundation with half logs that serve as steps to the cedar seating platform.

It's an oasis.

"Wowwwwwww!" comes blurting out of my mouth. "It's so cute."

He walks us up closer, a soft reflection of sunlight beaming through the windows. There are hand-hewn milled sidings and a log post-and-beam porch. It's breathtaking. Aurick's giant mansion seemed less like a home and more like a museum to me.

But this—*this* is a home.

"Do you think someone still lives here?" We stop inches from the front porch. "Do you think they'll help us?"

He's silent. Staring at the cottage blankly.

"Or… maybe it's not wise to enlist help? I mean, we could get them killed," I add.

"There's no one here to help us. They're already dead." Cold, frosted glass hardens Dessin's usually warm eyes.

"How do you know that?" I gawk back at the cottage.

He breathes in and out three times. "Because this is where Kane's mother and little brother were killed."

I gasp. Loudly. Way too loudly. It's almost a shriek. I stiffen against his chest.

"*Oh my god.*" I look at him and then back at the property. "Oh my GOD!"

He moves his foot up toward the first step of the front porch. It hovers over that first step. It's stone, unwilling to bend. He drops it back down. Laughs roughly.

"What?"

A frustrated sigh. "He's not going to let me go inside." He shakes his head.

"We really shouldn't go in there," I agree.

Dessin looks around the house, clearly inconvenienced and unwilling to discuss the war waging inside of the two minds at this moment. I'm okay with that though. I'm heartbroken for Kane. I can't imagine his pain right now. I'm scared for what would come of his mental health if we stepped foot through those doors.

"There's a small shed in the back. We can go in there."

"Are you sure?! I think we just need to leave. You don't even have to carry me anymore, I can hop!"

He glances at me from the corner of his eye while he walks us around the side of the house. "He's not going to object. He knows you're hurt. The shed is a safe option."

As we move around the side of the cottage, I try to get a peek inside the windows. Something brown is splattered on the other side of the window and curtain. It's covered in frosty dust so I can't see anything else inside. The grass around the perimeter of the house is long and full of weeds. I bet it was once groomed and flourishing with garden beds. The small shed is around the back. Walnut wood, worn down by rain and time.

Dessin kicks open the door. The air is stale and musty, smelling of sawdust. Thankfully there are windows letting in light, otherwise, I don't know how well he would see to take care of my wound.

"Can you take off our coats and throw them to the floor?" he asks, still holding me in his arms. I do as he says but expect a rush of frigid air to bite and claw at my skin. But this barn is like a greenhouse. It's not exactly warm in here, but not exactly cold either.

He gently sets me down on the coats, cushioning my back and bottom. I lean my back against the wall while he walks back to the shed door to prop it open. My eyes instantly flash to the burns on his back. *How have I not ever noticed this before? When we've hugged? Where did they come from?*

"Oh, Dessin…" I whisper, my hand covering my mouth like I have to filter the next words that come out of it. "Your—Your back… what happened—"

"An unfortunate side effect of training." He's now kneeling in front of me, peeling the tunic from my ankle. It's stiff and sticky with my blood. I want to pry and ask him more, but I can see he is trying to process being within this close proximity to Kane's house, and I don't want to add more to that burden.

"Shhh!" I hiss, dropping my head back in pain and bang it against the barn wall. "Ow!" I thump my fist against the floorboards. "It stings!"

He chuckles while examining the damage. "I need alcohol, water, and clean cloth." He thinks for a moment. "Wait here."

He returns with a crate of bottles of vodka, white towels, and two jugs of water.

"Where did you get that?" I ask.

"There's a cellar under the house."

He hands me a slat of wood to bite down on.

The gesture sends me back a year, when Scarlett's wrists bled. The carpet was stained. Her dress was dark and sodden. But she missed the vein. I had her bite down on a washcloth while I cleaned it and sewed her up.

Mentally, I draw the strings, the arms, the head.

Dessin wraps a coat around my shoulders as I shiver. The cap for the first jug of water falls to the floor before he pours it over my ankle. The coolness is soothing and relieves some of the sting. Blood and water snake around each other in the streams that travel down the sides of my leg.

"Bite down now," he orders.

I groan. Place the stick between my teeth. Squeeze my eyes shut. I nod to let him know I'm ready, and for the first millisecond it feels cool like the water, then I'm resentfully biting down on the wooden slat as hard as if I were trying to break my own teeth. My skin boils under the stream of poison. A cast-iron skillet, fresh from the stove, melts around my ankle.

I whimper, gasp, and squirm under the river that seeps into my wound and straight to the bone. He switches back to pouring the water and is now dabbing my wound with a white cloth.

I spit out the wood with a gasp. "Doesn't it ever get lonely? Knowing what you know and not being able to share any of it with me?" It's a genuine question. But I'm mostly asking to distract myself from the pain.

"I share a lot with you." Another tight pinch. He's done binding my ankle.

"You tell me stories and keep me entertained, sure. But something's going on and it involves me. Neither you nor Kane will let me in on it." I try to straighten out my legs. "Must get lonely."

"Kane is *dying* to tell you. Sometimes it is all he really thinks about. But I'm afraid it's as simple as… telling you would mean the difference between life and death."

My eyes snap up to meet his. *Death?* "Whose death?"

He begins to smile again like I've just said the punch line to an inside joke.

"What? Whose death, Dessin?"

"Both of ours."

11. The Valdawell Family

When the sun is waving farewell to the earth, Dessin returns. Blankets, pillows, water, a gas lamp, and a few nonperishable canned goods. I get a peek of the sky before he closes the door. It's the color of a candle when the fire is about to burn out.

"Hi." He smiles with dimples and an endearing expression. The look of seeing an old friend after years of being apart. *Hello, Kane.*

"Welcome back!"

A few steps toward me and he stops. "Jesus, look at you. It's my fault, Skylenna." He sets down his recently retrieved supplies and takes a look at my leg. "How bad does it hurt?"

"It's not your fault. I was the one who decided to tease you while attempting to take the lead." I shift to sit up. "It doesn't hurt that bad now."

Lie. And he sees right through it, but it's too polite to call me out.

After I briefly make a spectacle about how long it's been since I put my head on a pillow, he places a fluffy white (slightly gray) pillow behind my back while I scarf down a can of green beans and then another of sliced apples coated with cinnamon glaze meant for an apple pie. I hum into the can as I clean it out and he just watches with his arms crossed, grinning.

A thought releases a momentary paralytic to my insides as I hand the empty can back to him. He watches me cautiously. "What's wrong?"

The house. *His* house. His family. I look to the back door of the beautiful cottage and purse my lips. He follows my focus of attention, then touches the back of my hand with two fingers.

"I'm okay as long as I don't go in there," he says firmly.

I take his hand and am quiet for a long moment.

"I wish I could have known them."

He looks like he's about to respond but then his eyes fall. I can feel the depression containing him in chains. *He never really escaped that house, did he?*

"Do you mind if I ask about your dad?"

"Wyatt."

We lie back on the makeshift cot he put together for us. His arm supporting the back of my head. I lean into him, breathing in the scent of sandalwood and dark musk.

"Dessin told me he got justice. Toward your father. What did he mean?"

He sighs, looking up at the brittle ceiling. "It would give you nightmares."

"He said that he sold out your family."

No answer.

"Do you miss him?" I push but immediately regret it. We're only a few yards from his childhood home. I'm sure this can't be easy for him.

"One day, you will forgive your mother and your father. It may not seem like it now, but one day… it will come easily to you. But I will never forgive Wyatt. I don't agree with Dessin about much. I almost never approve of his actions. But what he did… what he did *was* justice. It was horrible and it was gruesome. But Wyatt will suffer so much worse in hell."

I shudder at the details he leaves out.

"If you won't tell me what Dessin did to him, will you at least tell me what Wyatt did that was so unforgivable?"

He shakes his head.

"Please?" I take his hand that is resting on his stomach and bring it up to my chest. I flatten his hand out against my soft skin. "This, right here. This is a safe place."

He turns his head, and his eyes fall to my chest, then back up to me like he's thought about this—touching me—being this close, but still surprised it's happening, nonetheless.

"Wyatt was a Demechnef Bureaucrat. They had been running experiments on…" He flicks his eyes away from me. "A type of child. And when my mother was pregnant with me, Wyatt quickly realized that I would fit their requirements. Wyatt knew that the experiment called for a traumatic childhood experience done by the age of six. He knew it would affect the entire family. He sold us out anyway." A cold breeze whistles through the crack of the shed door. "He drove the buggy when they took me away. He waited outside while they hurt us. While they *murdered* us."

I hook my arm across his chest and nuzzle my face into the crook of his neck. He pulls the blanket up to my chin and encircles his arms around me. How could Wyatt do that to him? I press my hand over his heart.

Please, God, don't let this man suffer anymore. Take it all away. Give it to me. I'll take whatever pain he has left.

The gas lamp jumps side to side with the little wind that makes it into our shed. We hold each other like this for hours. Not sleeping, not speaking. But deep down, I vow to him, I vow to keep him safe. I vow that I won't ever hurt him. I vow that I will protect him from bad people. I vow that I will always fight to make him smile.

12. The Death That Follows

Days pass as we let my wound recover.

Kane makes the shed a little more livable, cleaning out some of the tools, making my cot fluffier, and clearing a spot for us to eat dinner. He cleans my ankle a couple more times and continues to keep an eye on it to make sure we avoid infection.

Today, he went back into the cellar and brought back a couple books that Wyatt kept locked away. He spent hours reading to me in a deep, soothing voice. If the story wasn't so wonderful, I would have fallen asleep. It's about nine children that get taken from their home, separated, and forced to travel to different worlds. The entire time they thought they were kidnapped out of cruelty, but the worlds were beautiful and full of magic. They later learned of their purpose to unite the nine worlds again. When we finished the book, he had been reading for nine hours, with a couple of breaks here and there.

"That's my favorite book," I yawn.

He smiles, looking up at me from the book. "Mine too."

A creak comes from the door and we both whip our heads to investigate the sound. A broadly built DaiSzek stares at us, taking up the entire doorway.

"And that's our cue to get moving again."

"How do you know?" I ask.

"He may not have found any threats within his perimeter run, but a RottWeilen knows when dangers are coming."

I sigh. "Yeah, I think I'm ready. Can you help me stand?" Kane puts an arm around my waist and lifts me to my feet. I add pressure to my foot. It still feels a little swollen, but it's bearable enough to make another journey. I may just need to take more breaks.

"I almost forgot..." Kane walks outside and brings back a long wooden stick, sturdy and solid. "To help you walk." He passes it to me. I test out the effectiveness of this concept, limping out of the shed to the grass. It's just enough support to take some weight off of my foot.

"I like it!"

Luckily for me, we were only a few miles away from the spot in the mountains where the Demechnef Defects were staying. I wanted to ask him what's the plan when we find them? How are they going to help us? What happens if Demechnef finds us there and we *out* everyone?

And why don't we just do as the Nightamous Horde told us and find the next colony?

Something has shifted with his mood. He seems overly cautious. I try to be as vigilant as he is. I scan the area and keep my feet from snapping any sticks. But he is on edge. He keeps stopping us midmovement to stare ahead. It's a mutual understanding that we don't speak the rest of the way there.

Only a few yards away, the sanctuary is hiding among large, overgrown pine trees, just like at Kane's childhood cottage farther back.

Here there are hills of snow and ice. Kane holds his hand up in front of me to stop us. This time, his face isn't cautious. It's a sudden awareness of a threat. He holds my gaze with a warning that we can't make a sound.

We close the rest of the distance and worm our way through the sharp pine trees. The clearing appears with huts, sheds, and what looks like a food market.

It's so peaceful, so quiet, so beaut—

My mouth cracks open to scream.

But one hand flies across my vision and another secures itself over my mouth to keep me quiet and blind to the frozen horror.

Bodies everywhere, hanging from the trees. By their toes. Men, women, *children*. Dogs. Cats. *Babies*. Blood gushing through the white fur they wear on their bodies. Dripping down their necks, into their eyes. Their mouths gape open, without tongues, without teeth, without any screams left.

All of them, dead.

I buckle over in agony. My own arms circle my core as a way to put a perimeter around the pain. A pair of lips brush against my ear and whispers, "We're not alone."

Dessin. I stiffen. Whoever did this is still here. The agony clings to the air, fresh, new like bacteria to an infection. I want him to remove his hand so I can look around and seek out the threat he knows is here. But I never want to see the landscape of death again. The blood staining the snow, like spilled ink on white parchment.

"Keep your eyes closed, love." The rising heat in his whisper tells me he's about to act.

Dessin steps forward in the snow, dropping both hands from my face. *Crunch*. And I know I should listen. Close my eyes. Pretend like I'm somewhere else.

But in panic and fear, they snap open. There's a movement behind a pine tree to our right. Dessin doesn't turn to look at it but I know he's aware. He reaches back and grabs my hand.

"Stay here." Dessin places an old rusted knife with a wooden hilt in my palm, closing my fingers around it. To protect myself if he can't get to me in time.

Adrenaline courses like a choppy river through my bloodstream and the drums of war come alive in the base of my chest. Dessin steps away from me, walking out into the small, dead village. An open target. A beast born and bred for destruction, for a smooth, calculated massacre.

He stops in the center of the clearing. Waiting. Breathing in the flow of his plan with ease, seeming to know where each man hides.

"I surrender," Dessin taunts. He's six feet, four inches of deception. A god standing among insects, unafraid of their mortal weapons.

Movement everywhere. Men in white and forest green, camouflaged into our surroundings. Swords. Daggers. Crossbows.

I am a newborn bird, left in the nest, sitting without fight in the rise of a battle.

They move closer, shuffling their boots in the snow, trapping him in a death circle.

The man who seems to be leading the ambush is tall, freakishly tall, like a circus act on stilts. His dark goatee flutters in the winter breeze. He wears a black top hat with a red symbol embroidered on it. A red *X* and other indistinguishable markings.

Dessin studies the men. This look of his, so certain, it makes my muscles relax. "It's been a while since I've stopped a heart. And there are thirty-seven of those here. I think I'll end with yours." He nods at the man with the top hat.

They continue their slow steps, crossbows aimed at his head, closing in on him like a wild animal that has escaped its cage.

"I'd say we can discuss this like men, but tell me, would men hang babies by their toes?"

The men charge him.

Dessin pulls a metal ring out from under his shirt, a double-edged blade, allowing it to twirl fluidly around his index finger. The first two shots from the crossbows are dodged with precise side steps. But the next two, Dessin is waiting for. He uses the circular blade to swing, twist, and maneuver, swiftly slicing through the middle of the arrows like the snapping of a twig.

And as the men close in, Dessin unfurls his wings of power, releasing the dragon waiting to scorch them with fire.

He takes off in a sprint, slashing throats with this strange circular knife. Blood sprays over his face and chest, bursting from carotid arteries. With one hand, he snatches a flying arrow through the air and punctures it through the skull of another man to his left.

The rest happens in a blur. I see entrails spilling onto the snow, I see Dessin decapitating the men holding guns with the spinning knife, and I see the martial arts breathe life into his body, revealing the deadliest dancer alive.

About fifteen men remain, all trying to charge him at once. The sight of it gives me pause. Makes my stomach twist with worry. With that many swords being swung, with that many archers firing their shots, he's bound to be cut down. It was as if the first twenty-one men he annihilated were the front lines. Only present to wear him down.

The arrows are all shot at once and he deflects, using a bloody sword to knock them from his line of sight. Except one. One sneaky arrow soars passed his defense, slicing over his arm with a wet ripping sound. It doesn't strike true. It's merely a flesh wound.

Dessin grunts at the impact. I wince as I remember his arms are already carved up from the cage he was trapped in earlier.

They take his moment of weakness and prey on it. They attack simultaneously now. Overpowering his weak arm with the crashing of swords and daggers.

It's too much, he can't—

But as fast as a meteor plummeting to the earth, a vision of black death thunders through the air, DaiSzek reigns over all. His roar shudders the trees, cracks the ice, and ends the fighting.

He towers on a hill, overlooking the violence, baring his teeth to show off his weapon of choice. I nearly fall over in my hiding spot. The mere majestic sight of him causing a rush of euphoria to pump through my veins.

His growl is the trumpet of death, a mix of a lion and a dragon. And in the same breath, he leaps from the hill, tackling six men into the snow. The sight is ferocious. His teeth sink into flesh, shredding different body parts into ribbons and fountains of blood, and doing it all with the sound of hell booming from his chest. I'm mortified at the massacre and yet I want to shriek in victory.

Dessin leaps over DaiSzek and the pile of bodies he devours, and with the speed of a horse he races to the freakishly tall man.

While he exacts his promise, my attention is snagged on a faint motion from behind a tree only a few yards away from me. A man crouched low into the snow, taking his aim with a crossbow. I know Dessin or DaiSzek do not see him because he hasn't moved an inch.

He'll hit one of them.

The shot could be fatal.

I stand to my feet, throw myself through the trees, and desperately race to the hidden soldier. He has a steady eye on one of them. His finger starts to tighten on the trigger.

No! But the cry for help doesn't rise from my panic. Words stay clogged in my throat. There's only a single action. A motion of my arm. A target I must strike.

But I stop, like my hand is attached to a puppet string, unable to protect, unable to *kill*. And before I can witness the murder of one of my friends, the sharp end of a wide sword tears through a thick layer of skin before it crashes into his spinal cord. I immediately drop the knife and fall backward onto my butt. The rich blood pours from his neck onto the snow. A ruby-red river melts the ice, steaming in the winter air.

I'm panting. Can't look away. Can't rip my gawking stare from the man choking, bleeding out, writhing in a puddle of himself.

But the arrow in his crossbow is gone. Did he shoot? Was I too late?

I jerk my head to the side, searching for Dessin and DaiSzek. There. Safe. They both are unharmed, staring not at me, but at someone next to me. Dessin has an actual heart in his right hand, thick, gooey strings of blood hanging from it.

Gurgling sounds come from the soldier, flinching with his last moments of breath. But I didn't kill him. I froze. I stopped before my knife could save Dessin and DaiSzek.

Someone beat me to it.

13. The Stormsages

A man built like a bear with a long copper ponytail and giant hazel eyes stands behind us. He's dressed in layers upon layers of animal skins, straps of weapons, and thick pelts of dark fur.

Walking up around him is a pack of white wolves. Their feet crunch through the snow quietly, carefully, as if one wrong step could start a war.

Dessin races to my side, a strong, bloody hand gripping my shoulder to let me know he's here. I'm safe from this stranger. But the wolves have us surrounded, and I can't tell whether or not they'll attack.

But something sits beside us, tall and stoic, black fur sprinkled with flakes of snow and blood.

DaiSzek.

He's not attacking. He's calm. Unthreatened.

"Wait," I urge Dessin. "Look!" I nudge him to where DaiSzek sits, gazing at the beastly man without any aggressive intent.

It's the same reaction he had to Runa. He didn't harm her.

"He's not attacking…" I mutter. "Does that mean—"

"It means he knows we're the Stormsages," the bear man answers.

A husky, masculine voice. A foreign accent that is rugged and northern.

"The colony from the North Saphrine Forest." Dessin takes a breath. "Are the wolves with you?"

Like moths to a flame, the wolves gather around DaiSzek, a safe distance, yet close enough to show him they will not harm us.

"They are a part of our colony, yes."

Dessin helps me stand, but as we get to our feet, I remember he's still covered in blood. Will they think we killed these people? That we slaughtered this village?

"We wish we could have fought alongside the three of you. It would have been a great honor for my people."

I cough out a laugh. "I did not fight. But I'm sure these two would have enjoyed your company." I jerk my head in emphasis to Dessin and DaiSzek.

The bear man lifts his chin as if he does not understand. Those giant hazel eyes trail down my body and back up to my face. "You do not fight yet," he states, working something out in his own thoughts.

That's what I said.

Bear Man nods once, looking around at the dead scattered throughout the village. Corpses hanging from trees like ornaments. "We will bury the victims and burn the demons. Will you be our guest in the Stormsages Keep this night?"

Dessin's chocolate eyes flicker to the men and women dressed in animal furs and skins, trudging through the snow and dismounting the bodies.

"My name is Garanthian. You can trust us."

Dessin considers this. "I trust no one," he says, attention still pulled between the wolves, the colony members surrounding us, and Garanthian. "But we'll accept safe harbor from you tonight."

Garanthian and his pack of wolves lead us through thick snow and plump pine trees.

DaiSzek doesn't leave my side, clearly choosing to protect the weaker link. Occasionally leaning down to my ankle to lick the bandaged wound.

"He's bigger than the legends described," Garanthian says, his voice like a shovel scraping over a sidewalk or the tire of a buggy rolling across a graveled driveway.

Dessin left us somewhere a few yards back. Kane studies Garanthian now.

"I saw a pack when I was a young boy. They weren't *that* large. Even still, no other beast compared. They were our favorite monsters to hear stories about." He continues trying to make conversation but Kane isn't humoring him with small talk.

"What's your favorite story?" I ask. It wouldn't be small talk for me. I'd love to learn more about where DaiSzek comes from.

Garanthian huffs. "I don't know how much of them are true. We'd hear lots of stories about the RottWeilen packs maintaining population sizes."

My eyebrows rise. "What does that mean?"

"For animals. Not people. About a century ago there was a mass reproduction of night dawpers in these parts. They were slaughtering women on the rag, men wounded from battle, they'd even managed to annihilate several of our hunting parties." Garanthian leans down to pet a blue-eyed wolf trotting alongside him. "They nearly made our snow elven wolves go extinct."

Each wolf continues to glance over at DaiSzek. But he's glued to my hip, not to be bothered with them.

"There was an army of them. At least a few hundred. Hungry, gnarled, ugly beasts. We eventually had to shut the gates of the keep, and they would have starved us out. If it weren't for the RottWeilen." He nods his head at DaiSzek, smiling. "It only took twelve of them. *Twelve*. And they galloped through the snow like hellhounds sent from the devil himself, wiping out *a few hundred night* dawpers. And my gods, our legends described how they fought. Strategic. Precise. It was like they planned their battlefield, decided every move, every attack together."

"He used to leave me speechless after a fight. Somehow, he'd always seem overprepared, as if he didn't need his brute strength. He needed strategy," Kane finally responds.

Sounds like someone else I know.

"Aye, they were a force. Calculated. United. They not only fought for their pack, but they fought to save our people."

I look down at DaiSzek, scratching behind his eyes with pride.

"We'd never in a million years think a species so superior would be wiped out in one fell swoop. An alchemist's warfare is for cowards," Garanthian growls under his breath.

My heart stutters to a stop. Demechnef destroyed the RottWeilen with chemical warfare. It's as if someone has slapped me across the face or stuck a knife in my back. He lost everything. His pack. His family. And now he's the only one of his kind.

Forever.

"That's devastating," I mutter.

"Aye. It is. But y'know, these creatures aren't only known for their violence. We have other myths that may ring true."

We wait patiently for him to continue.

"It's said that RottWeilens can sense the cries of their pack members from across the world. It's a telepathic connection to come when even the weakest pack member is in danger." Garanthian takes a swig from a leather canteen pouch. "Or that in the heat of battle, the strongest member can reach an octave with their roar, rendering their enemy completely deaf."

We stop trudging and gaze upon several leagues of empty space. Nothing but snow. Only trees surrounding the white opening of land.

"But my favorite is the legend of the god alpha. The strongest form of alpha that can pass through the veil of life and death in order to save their kin. We've only heard of it happening three times in their history." Garanthian shrugs. "I'm sure the Crimson Kres could give accurate stories if they were still around."

We're silent for a long moment, waiting for further direction of where to go, but also taking in the power of legends from DaiSzek's kin.

"Do you have a healer? We have wounds that need to be cleaned," Kane says. I forgot that an arrow skimmed his already battered arm. My hand instinctually flies up to his bicep, covering the open flesh.

Kane glances down at my hand, then raises those thick lashes to me. A surprised smile.

"Ay!" Garanthian shouts at DaiSzek who is kneeling down to sniff a curly red plant. "One bite of that and the saphriness oil will knock ya on your ass, beastie!"

Kane clears his throat. "A healer?"

"We do. Will you join us for a feast after you're tended to?" Garanthian asks.

But we still aren't moving. And Garanthian's tone suggests we've already arrived.

"What are we waiting for?" I turn to Garanthian, catching him watching my every move with a cautious expression.

He scratches his copper beard. "You don't see it?"

I shake my head.

"See what?" Kane asks.

Garanthian narrows his eyes at me. "We were told that you could—" But he stops himself before he can finish. "Close your eyes, both of you."

"No," Kane says.

"Then, blink."

My eyes shut without a second thought. A blink. A flutter of my lids. And it happens, a trick of the light, a split moment of insanity as I gawk up at the stone fortress now filling the empty land.

I flinch and latch on to Kane's arm.

But Kane is silent. He's gazing up at the majestic architecture the way one would stand before the golden gates of heaven.

It is not the kind of castle you'd see in a child's storybook. No, it's the kind that you'd see pikes with human heads warding off unwanted visitors. The kind that could survive a plague, a firestorm, a war. The kind that was made not for royalty but for survival. There are towers, cuts, springalds, and statues of men and women dressed like Garanthian surrounding the great walls.

It's ancient. Older than our Dellilian castle, older than the Red Oaks.

A wooden drawbridge lowers.

"I don't understand," I say to Garanthian. Kane remains completely silent.

"This keep was built on the tombs of our fallen snow elves. Their essence will forever protect us. A veil to keep your kind from stumbling upon us."

I can't seem to swallow that down. A power from dead *elves* that made me see an empty field one second, and then a stone fortress the next.

But no one speaks again as we are led into their home.

Despite the snowy weather on the outside, the inside of this keep is toasty warm.

We were escorted through the ancient, glorious castle to the main dining hall where a feast awaited us.

Kane pulls a dark-cherry wooden chair out for me to sit. The table of men, women, and children chow down on roasted pig, mounds of mashed potatoes, steamed carrots and asparagus, and heaps of freshly baked bread. There are thousands of candles lit across the hall. Candles dripping down walls from their scones. Candles hanging from the Gothic ceiling arches. Candles spread across the long table that seats at least fifty people.

Once Kane takes his place next to me, I unfold my napkin, set it on my lap, and lightly lift my fork and knife from either side of my plate.

I examine the food in front of me. Too much.

I can't eat this much.

I begin pushing the majority of the food to one side of the plate. Only keeping three shreds of meat from the pig, four steamed carrot slices, and three sticks of asparagus.

No potatoes. Potatoes are carbohydrates.

People watching.

Forks stop hitting plates. Chatter dies down. Silence.

Even Kane turns to look at what I'm doing.

"You don't have to do that here." Garanthian clears his throat. "Not while you're in our home."

I look up at him, at his vibrant hazel eyes, at the pity spreading across his face.

"I'm not doing anything," I say, cheeks flushing with rising heat.

Stop looking at me.

"Your meal, *dashna,*" the woman to his right says. Her long brunette hair hanging in braids over her shoulder. "You can eat it all here."

The room is still watching me. What are they looking at? Why do they care what I eat?

Kane uses his fork to push my food back together. He leans into my ear, close enough so no one else can hear him.

"They don't control you anymore, honey. Eat until you're full." He presses his lips to the side of my head, lingering there for a moment too long. The room jolts to life again. Silverware clanking together. Laughter. Happiness.

Kane's words make me want to cry. The urge builds in the back of my throat. Stinging behind my eyes like I'm holding back a sea of trauma.

"Thank you," I whisper before he pulls away. It's been so automatic while I lived with Aurick. While I was being watched at the asylum. To show the world how much self-control I had. To show prying eyes that I didn't need food to survive. Look how strong I am. I don't need to eat. I can survive off of scraps. I am a *woman*.

But this place is different.

The Stormsages are eating together. The women are gobbling down their food like it may run out at any moment. And the men are beaming at them. How can people be so different? How can they live on the same continent and not share the same beliefs?

Kane nudges my plate to me with a knuckle and I don't hold back my hunger. I hunch over my plate and begin scarfing it down without regret.

It's invigorating. It's stepping into the sun after being chained to the dark. It's being pulled from the bottom of the ocean only moments before you drown.

And the hot, savory flavor of the roasted pig explodes in my mouth. Juicy, maple-glazed meat. I want to sing. I want to dance.

But instead, warm tears drip onto my plate. They're pressurized behind my eyes as if someone has shaken up the carbonated bottle of my soul. The tears burst, free-falling without running a path down my cheeks. And the sound is deafening. *Drip. Drip. Drip.*

It's an echo in the grand hall. A trumpet blasting my mental instability.

I swallow the meat and shove a spoonful of mashed potatoes seasoned with rosemary into my mouth.

Stop crying.

But it's involuntary. A force far more powerful than my own restraint, like being saddled on a wild horse. I'm holding on for dear life.

A warm hand grips the back of my neck. Stroking up and down to show that he's got me. He's here. He's not going to let me go.

And this small gesture has my heart in a steel choke hold. A quiet sob breaks away from my chest, from my mouthful of food.

And I hadn't even noticed the room went quiet again until a pair of thin arms wrap around me from behind my chair. A chin resting on my shoulder. The soft motherly scent of cinnamon and roasted chestnuts.

"There you go, *dashna*. Let it go, now. Let it out, little babe." Her maternal voice is soothing, like warm milk, like sitting in front of the fireplace on a winter's night. And she holds me tightly, her soft hair against my cheek.

The gentle touch I never had from Violet. The love Scarlett never received from our mother.

The cry barrels out of me, breaking through my armor. Severing the walls I put up while maintaining a brave, unconquerable face in the asylum.

Kane's hand is now latched on to my thigh, reminding me he isn't going anywhere.

"I'm here now, *dashna*. I'm here," the woman coos in my ear.

The grand hall is filled with my howls on this night. My agony breaking out of its leash, showing the Stormsages people my raw, battered innards.

And that cage I've been locked in starts to open.

"That was so embarrassing," I confess to Kane.

We're both turned away from the other, changing out of our winter gear.

Garanthian led us to our room after supper, graciously not mentioning my breakdown. The woman that held me while I cried, introduced herself as Asena. Married to Garanthian, also known as *the white wolf queen*. She laid out extra pelts of fur for us to sleep on, a nightgown, and a hot kettle of tea next to the fireplace.

"No, it wasn't." Kane removes his boots, tossing them to the corner of the room. "I've been waiting for it to hit you."

"You have?"

"That city is poison, honey. It left its mark on you." He turns to me after I finish pulling the nightgown over my head. "Even when you're released from the cage, a part of you stays. Still trapped. Still begging for someone to let you out."

I gulp. "Is that how you feel? Like you're still in the thirteenth room?"

He thinks on this. Turns to me on his elbow as he gets comfortable under the layers of fur.

"I was never a prisoner of that room. Dessin was. A few others got to see the inside of those walls for a short time, but that was Dessin's prison. His trauma to bear."

"Then what was yours?"

"My memories," he admits. "My regrets. My guilt." His left fist clenches.

I nod, sliding into the bed next to him. My eyes are still swollen and raw from wailing like a child in the dining hall. All of those people witnessed my breakdown. Yet, they were so gracious, so understanding.

"Can I ask you something?" Kane exhales.

I mirror his position, propping myself up on one elbow to face him.

"Why did you stay with him? You stayed in that city, eating like a small rodent, obeying orders like a dog. Accepting Aurick's misogynistic behavior." He shakes his head as if to rid himself of searing anger for that last part. "You could have run."

I could have. But I made a promise.

"I couldn't tell Dessin the truth when he asked this before, because if he knew the truth, he would have been furious." The look in his eyes when he learned that Aurick hit me. "If I left, I wouldn't have been able to help him or you. If I left, I wouldn't have been able to fulfill Scarlett's dying wish. Without Aurick, I had nowhere to live. I would have accepted any form of abuse from him or anyone else just to stay close to Dessin."

Kane's shoulders deflate as if hearing that truth was harder to hear than he imagined.

"You're right." He blows out a breath. "Dessin would have raised hell."

"Now it's your turn to answer one of my questions. When Dessin fought the men from Demechnef in his room, why did he need to stab the man after he was already dead? The man with the sickle… he stabbed him three times with a rusted knife."

Kane raises his brows and looks away like that's a loaded question.

"It's a compulsion." He shrugs. "That sickle took three lives the day he came into existence. And that old knife is the last gift my father gave to me, to protect myself. It's just something he needs to do when he sees that *weapon*."

Nausea coats my stomach. And chills, like tiny spiders, crawl down my back. I nod at him, attempting to hide my horror.

"Do you like him? Dessin, I mean. I know you have to live with him, in a way, but do you actually like him?"

Kane laughs at this. "I don't always agree with his methods, but Dessin is a brother to me. He was there to fight for me on one of the worst days of my life, and he'll be there until the day I die." A cloud of sadness passes over his eyes. "He's taken beatings for me, taken demonic forms of abuse, and done so with a smile. He does it all to protect my sanity."

I smile. The warmth of their bond spreading across my chest.

"I have another question," Kane says quietly.

I arch an eyebrow at him.

"Can I hold you tonight?" he whispers. "After seeing you cry earlier… it's something I need to do. *Please*."

My chest aches. "Of course you can hold me."

I turn my back to him, wiggling backward until I'm firmly pressed against his chest. His iron arms loop around my shoulders and waist, pulling me even closer until his lips graze my hair, dropping soft kisses. And they're slow, meaningful, full of secrets, agony, and a need to be as close to me as possible. And with each kiss, my heart throbs like an unhealed wound. Tears gather in my eyes as I try to swallow them down. But these slow kisses weigh me down like anchors in a storm.

Please, don't ever leave me, Kane.

I need you.

The sun's bright morning rays bleed through the slits of my closed eyes.

I don't have to turn around to know that Kane is still holding me close, not letting go once, even after we both drifted to sleep.

Trying my best to stay quiet, I attempt to lift his heavy arm from my waist and slip off the bed to get dressed.

But that arm clamps down on me like the mouth of a Venus flytrap. It locks around the soft of my waist, drawing me closer to him.

"Hey," I object. He takes a deep breath in, nose and mouth nuzzled into my hair. "I was trying to sneak out of bed without waking you."

"Nope," he grumbles. "You're mine now."

I melt against him. At his words. At the gravelly sound his voice makes in the early morning. Why do I want him this much all the time? Whether it's Dessin, Kane, or hell, even Greystone. I can't help the force that makes me swoon over each alter.

"Besides, there's no sneaking with you." His hand moves along my arm slowly, coaxing my skin to pebble in goose bumps. "You have the stealth of a bull. There was no possible scenario of you slipping out of my arms without being caught."

"Aw, you're so sweet in the mornings."

His chest rumbles against my back with laughter.

As he shifts against me, I can feel his arousal. A firmness at my backside. Instinctually, I lean into it, arching my back against him.

Heat drips between my legs.

His laughter stops as a hiss turns into a frustrated sigh. That hand stroking my arm grips my hip, squeezing like it's his only form of self-control.

I moan at his touch, rolling my bottom against his growing erection the way I did on Dessin's lap in the tavern.

"Skylenna," he warns, breathy and strained.

"What?"

"You keep doing that, and I'm going to do things to you that would make me a very bad friend." It's a warning to himself rather than to me. A struggle to keep his head on right.

"What if I want you—as *more* than a friend?" I turn around to face him, leaning my head against his arm.

He blinks down at me, completely thrown off by my response. His index finger hooks around a loose strand of hair strewn across my face. He studies it in his hand, thoroughly, as if that golden wave of hair is a lighthouse that has guided him to shore.

"I can promise you this, honey… you need me as your friend right now. Nothing more." He wants to say more. It's edging over his lips. Straining his eyes. "It'll only make things harder."

My jaw clenches shut and suddenly his fingers in my hair, hand on my waist, the scent of cedar and sandalwood infuriates me. I huff, shifting out of his arms and off of the bed.

And this time, he lets me.

"You're right." I shrug, finding my clothes to change into. "We are *just* friends."

14. One Name to Turn The Tides

"You two look rested," Asena hums, swallowing another spoonful of porridge.

They summoned us for breakfast in the grand dining hall. But it's close to empty. Only two people sitting across from us. Garanthian and Asena.

"I thought you might be more comfortable eating in front of fewer people." She's watching me with careful intent. Asena's hair is in two long braids today. One on each shoulder. She's in her forties, light-brown skin, and wise dark eyes like the open night sky.

"Thank you," I say.

Kane is careful not to let his knee touch my own. The walk over here was cold and distant. Neither of us has spoken after he turned me down.

"We'd like ya to stay longer… but I'm afraid that isn't in the cards, is it?" Garanthian speaks up, staring directly at Kane now. Those winter hazel eyes carrying a hidden message.

Kane nods. "We have to keep moving."

"We have three gifts for you before ya go," Garanthian says, waving a hand over his shoulder to a younger man, around my age, over to us. He's tall and lean, with auburn hair and bronze skin.

The young man refills Garanthian's glass of milk.

"Not milk! Is ya little head filled with cock hairs? Get me what I asked of ya before they sat down!" His large hand lightly smacks the young man on the back of the head.

He snickers as he pulls a satchel out from behind his back. "Specify next time, old man!"

Cock hairs. Nice.

Garanthian removes a pair of leather gloves and a belt, tossing them on the table for us to examine.

"You fight yet, Skylenna?" he asks me, nudging the gloves closer to my plate.

I shake my head. "That's his job." I jerk my chin to Kane.

Garanthian exchanges a look with Asena, then back at me. "If ya ever decide to start… these are called demon's teeth."

I lift one of the brown leather gloves to get a closer look. The knuckles are lined with sharp spikes. Tiny metal thorns. I nearly prick myself as I run a thumb over its point.

"If he can teach ya to get one good strike on your opponent, these will undoubtedly ensure ya won't have to fight for long."

I gulp. Because one punch and I could rip out the skin on their cheek.

"But I'm a wom—" I stop before I can finish, because Asena raises her eyebrows. A stare of wisdom and power I've never seen before. She lifts her chin, unblinking.

"Don't ever finish that sentence out loud or in ya head again, dashna." Her voice is smooth yet dominating. "Do ya think because I am a woman, I can't *easily* overpower a man?"

I blink. Unsure how to answer.

"I'd trust her to lead in battle over my strongest men." Garanthian nods.

"Women are dragons," Asena says. "One day, ya will breathe fire too."

I release the breath I've been holding. "Thank you."

"And for you." Garanthian points to the belt. "It's an executioner's belt. Double straps go over ya chest, holding poisons, crystal explosives, and throwing daggers."

Kane studies the pockets and small blades holstered in the straps that are meant to tighten across his chest, shoulders, and back.

I wait for him to say thank you. Or nod his approval. But the silence stretches across the narrow table. My head turns to face him, expecting to make eye contact, yet his stare is empty.

Glazed.

Vacant.

He's switching again. But why? There is no danger?

He blinks several times, focusing on the leather straps, then flicks his gaze to me.

"I'd be lying if I say I'm not going to enjoy using these," the alter says.

He's sitting and not standing, so I'm finding it difficult to determine who we're in the presence of based on body language.

Garanthian shifts in his seat, lifting his chin. "And who am I speaking with now?"

He *knows*. We haven't told these people about the infamous Patient Thirteen. We haven't disclosed what goes on in Kane's mind.

"How is it you know to even ask me that question?" His voice is bordering on a threat.

Asena answers this. "Our prophecies have described your unique traits."

The alter scoffs, turning to me. "Skylenna might be able to tell you who I am. That is, if she knows me well enough." A challenge. A game.

"This is Dessin," I reply tightly. "The one who will enjoy this gift a little too much."

I realize now that the belt of weapons likely triggered him to come to the front. Just like sexual encounters will trigger Greystone to surface.

"Indeed. It, at the very least, will help me ignore how annoying it is that your prophecies know this much about my life." But there is a bright glint of pride in his gaze. I passed his little test. I knew who he was without being told.

"It is a pleasure to meet ya, Dessin." Garanthian nods, slipping his hand back in the satchel to hand a folded piece of parchment to us. "And I do apologize. I wish I could tell ya more, but there's ancient magic at play. It won't allow us to tell ya details."

Dessin takes it from him, holding it out for both of us to see.

"All we can tell ya about this gift is that time is not on ya side. Act quickly," Asena says.

The top reads: *One name to turn the tides.*

We exchange a look before unfolding it.

One word. One name. Calligraphy. Thick strokes of black ink. A cold shower of ice water floods my veins.

Judas.

15. Wolf Among Sheep

"Tell me what you're thinking."

Dessin has been silent on the hike down the mountain from the Stormsages Keep. Garanthian said he didn't know what the name meant, only that those who wrote the prophecy knew it would be of great importance to us. A name to turn the tides. I could see the wheels spinning in Dessin's mind the moment he processed what was on the note. It wasn't sitting well with him, whatever he was thinking.

"I'd rather not tell you. It's mad, even for me." Dessin's boots crunch through the snow. A wave of echoes through the quiet winter forest.

"I take it you don't know why Judas's name would be of any importance to us," I prompt.

"He's always been on my radar," Dessin says absently. "Do you remember the day you were called to the asylum because I had a *breakdown*?"

I nod.

"And when you stopped my treatment, I told you someone came to visit me, warning me of what Masten had planned for you?"

"What of it?"

"It was Judas. He's the one that warned me. Said he overheard Masten talking about it in a gentlemen's club. His plan to show you discipline under his own roof without Aurick's prying eyes." A flash of wicked fury in his expression.

What? I suppose it is possible that Judas could have learned of this information that way, but… "Why would he tell you that? Of all people? A patient locked away in an asylum?"

Dessin shakes his head, clearly asking himself the same question.

A memory tugs at me urgently.

"Remember when we escaped for the night to see the stars? Judas is the one that gave me the key! He's the one that suggested I make a grand gesture to you." He wanted me to show Dessin that he could trust me. And now that I think on it, he also asked me if I would stay with Dessin no matter the outcome of events.

He turns to me now, stopping in his tracks. "My idea is out of the question, but I'm going to share it with you anyway."

I unhook my pack from around my shoulders, flinging it to the ground.

"There's a law written in the asylum. No matter what a patient has done or is capable of, if a priest pardons them, the patient must be granted a room and treatment plan coordinated by the priest."

I narrow my eyes. "You're not thinking of going b—"

"My execution sentence would be lifted. I could find out what Judas's importance is." He crosses his arms, rolling his neck. "The only problem is, I wouldn't be able to keep you safe from in there. You are a wanted woman now."

I want to laugh. This is out of the question. There must be ways around that extreme scenario. "Why can't we just go to Judas's home… ask him our questions there?"

"Oddly enough, Judas lives in the asylum. He never leaves."

"Why can't you just break into the asylum at night, and force him to tell us whatever it is he knows?"

"I could do that. Interrogate him. Use torture methods to get him to talk." He looks down at me as if I should understand why that's a bad idea. "But what exactly am I asking him while I make him bleed? We don't know. All we have is his name, right? Not to mention, that kind of interrogation isn't effective. Manipulation is a powerful tool to get someone to talk and share even the secrets you don't know they are keeping."

I raise an eyebrow. That makes sense. We don't actually know what to ask him.

"Then how will you manipulate him into spilling his secrets?" I ask.

Dessin thinks of this for a long minute. "He tried to help us last time we were there. He wasn't willing to share why—"

"He told me once he was looking at the bigger picture. That's why he was helping me," I interrupt.

"If he thinks I was captured and brought right back to where I started… then maybe that won't fit with whatever he has planned. If he gave you that key to get me out, maybe he wanted us to leave. And if that's the case, then I can play on that weakness. Get him desperate enough to tell me whatever makes him so important."

I blow out a breath, a hot cloud of fog whooshing from my lips. *It's a good plan…*

"What if—I'm admitted with you?" I ask, knowing how he'll react. "The twelfth room is vacant."

"Not an option."

But my mind is made up. "No, it is, actually. Think about it. Judas has always been in my corner. Scarlett's too."

"No." A firm answer set in stone.

"You have your talents, but this one is mine." My stance is unmovable. "I was able to get through to every patient in the asylum for a reason. What if I convince them to let me have daily sessions with Judas?"

"Did you hit your head on some ice? I said *no*."

"It will work!"

He looks like he's about to yell or break a tree in half. "Maybe it would. But you would also have to endure treatments every day. And *that* is out of the question."

"Dessin," I utter, taking two steps closer to him.

"*Don't*. It's not happening."

But my hands find the hard muscles of his chest. "I make my own choices. I decide what I can handle."

"Apparently not good ones," he growls, but his dark-mahogany eyes are fixated on my hands stroking up to his neck.

"I can do this. Let me prove to you that I can handle whatever you can."

I won't let myself think about the simulated drowning, the chair binding, the induced seizures. Enduring Niles's treatment was enough to scar me for life.

He shakes his head.

"I. Said. No." The violent anger is now spilling from his alpha presence. He's edging over a cliff, the end of his patience, the dark tunnel of no return.

But I don't stop pushing. I won't let him win this one.

"You can't stop me. Asena said we have to act quickly."

"Skylenna! I'm the one that won't be able to handle it. I can bear my own pain and suffering every hour, every day. But it's *your* pain I won't survive. It's *your* suffering I won't be able to endure." His large hands grip the sides of my face with unfiltered vehemence. Even the act of admitting this weakness is gutting him from the inside out. "I have enough guilt to carry on my back. I refuse to add to that weight by hearing your screams echo the walls of that demonic prison."

He's searching my eyes for understanding. A rare moment to plea for my help. To beg for my obedience.

I throw my arms around his neck, slamming my body against his. The need to quell his anguish is burying me, crumbling my stubborn behavior to rumble beneath our feet.

"I know," I whisper, tucking my face into his neck. "I know. It was hell for me to watch them hurt you when I was powerless to stop it."

He smells of cedar and a crackling fireplace. Of home and warm hugs. Of everything I'll ever need.

"But I need you to believe in me the way I have always believed in you. I need you to treat me as your equal."

His jaw sets. "I won't be able to control myself if I see you in pain."

"Control is one of your strengths," I tell him. "You're going to hold it together until we get what we need. You have to let me be strong too."

The way his shoulders droop in defeat tells me I have won. That is an argument he won't combat. He lets out a sigh of pure exhaustion against my braided hair.

"If at any moment it's too much for you, I'll put them all in an unmarked grave. Do you understand me?"

I nod, but I can't let him go. Not yet. Not now. The asylum is about to unwittingly let a wolf into their pasture of sheep.

And they'll never see it coming.

16.
"I promised someone I wouldn't go in there until the time was right."

After several days of hiking and little sleep, we make it back to the Red Oaks.

We know it's not long now until we make it back to Emerald Lake. The asylum where we met, and the source of energy that pulses like a cancerous tumor between two great mountains.

The little conversation we've had has been about the basics. Food, water, shelter. And the only time he seems alert enough to give me his full attention is when I plucked a red flower. He whirled on me, yanked it out of my hand and gawked at me as though I kicked a baby.

"Phoenix stem. It's poisonous!" he grumbled, turning around to keep walking.

And that was it.

Dessin is *distracted*. He works out details to our plan in his head, sometimes mouthing words to himself, arguing silently with a voice in his mind. But a creeping suspicion claws into my chest when I look at him. I've known him long enough to spot the moments of genius. Careful calculation. Master puppeteering. Details of *his* plan. Not *our* plan.

The burning frustration harbors heat in my chest while I give myself a headache trying to figure it out. We just discussed this. We agreed that this time, I would be in on the secrets. I would be an equal.

Am I really so stupid that I wouldn't be able to keep up with a master plan? Or is this an ego thing? He's this strong and powerful man that doesn't need to waste his time explaining ideas to some *woman*.

We've made it back to the lagoon with the gigantic red oak towering over the clearing. It's warmer this way, so we remove our coats and boots to change them out into our packs.

Dessin leans over to close up his pack and I chunk a pine cone at the back of his head. It hits the target with a light *peck*! His head lifts slowly. Only just barely caught by surprise.

He turns to me. An annoyed sidelong glance. "Can I help you?"

"Yeah! As a matter of fact, you can!" I throw my pack down. "What's wrong with me?!"

With a single blink, his annoyance is replaced with confusion. He opens his mouth to answer. Then closes it just as quickly.

"Because there must be something, right? Am I mentally handicapped? Am I *slow*? There has to be a reason why you've humored me with a dummy plan and have been spending days creating a new plan that I can't be a part of!" I pause for him to answer this time.

"Skylenna—" He stops short. Sighs. "We don't have time for this."

"Can't you walk and talk at the same time?"

He grimaces. "Let's hear it, then. Anything else bothering you?" Annoyance linked with sarcasm flashes over his face.

"Fine. What about all of the secrets you and Kane keep from me? I know you have answers to all of my questions. I know there's an answer to why you both seem to know every single one of my darkest secrets!" I'm in his face now, slapping my hands on his chest to shove him backward. But his stance is unmovable.

"You think we want to keep these secrets? That I get off on knowing things you don't?"

"That's exactly what I think."

His nostrils flare. "You're starting to piss me off."

"Good. Maybe you'll start to feel half the frustration I feel."

"Jesus, Skylenna!" He invades my space with a clenched jaw and fists. "I'm doing my fucking best. The burden of what I know is on me, not you. One day, you'll thank me for that."

"The only reason you keep information to yourself is because you think I'm weak and helpless." I shove him again. "And the worst part is, I want you!" He raises his eyebrows and catches my hands before they push him again. "Yeah, I want you. I want you to touch me. I want you to tell me how you feel about me. I want to be with you for the rest of my life. Even if that means our time is spent running!"

He watches me, a roar of emotions being birthed in his dark eyes. Stunned. In momentary disbelief. And there's this pull to his body growing like the thirst for a single drop of water in a desert.

Muffled voices followed by the howl of DaiSzek echoes through the body of the red oak trees. We tense. It's not close enough that they would have a direct sight to us, but not far enough that we have time to run. Dessin guides my chin with his fingers back to him.

"We're going to hide, okay?" The footsteps are fast, running. "Hold my hand, and stay under," he instructs while turning us to face the lagoon. *Oh, of course.*

I gasp for one final breath right before we step off the cliff, launching ourselves into the body of water. And it's a single moment of silence. Of peace. A clear sky. Not a single cloud. The turquoise water sparkling underneath us, like tiny diamonds floating on the surface.

As we hit the surface, our hands are pulled apart. The temperature is shocking at first, like walking through snow without shoes. But the coolness soothes my skin pumping with hot adrenaline.

The sunlight is fracturing the water into amber diamonds and tiny emeralds and streaming gold ribbons that shine down on me. I flap my arms through the water, trying to find Dessin. A hand grips my wrist, yanking me down deeper into the lagoon. *What is he doing?* I have to muffle my instinct to kick and thrash for air. He's trying to hide us.

He takes hold of a large curly root, sponged under seaweed so we can stay under without floating back up to the top.

My lungs tighten like a fist under my chest. How long does he think I can hold my breath? But he isn't focused on me. No, that face carved as sharp as a warrior is tilted up, watching the surface the way DaiSzek looks to the trees if he senses an intruder. And that large hand is gripping my waist. A firm electric current passing from his fingertips to the pit of my belly.

He's beautiful down here. The sunlight is glistening off of his tan skin, like melted gold pouring over a bronze statue. The soft, gentle blur from the water. The silence and distorted whooshing of waves. It's as though we've fallen into another dimension. A pocket of heaven that has shut out all evil.

That bubble of peace does not last.

My body begins to violently contract, muscles clenching and unclenching. I've been under too long. I need to take a breath, open my mouth, let out the old oxygen I no longer need.

Dessin!

His trance to the surface is broken, eyes flicking down to my coiling body that needs air. Without another thought, his hands wrap around either side of my rib cage, thrusting me upward until water is silently whooshing past my face, and the top of my head breaks the surface. I suck in a long, loud breath. Coughing on drops of water that made their way down my throat.

Dessin rises next to me, holding his finger to his plush lips, then signaling for me to follow toward the only sound that drowned out my choppy gasps for breath.

The waterfall.

That source of magnificent energy beats down on the lagoon. We tread toward the cloud of white mist. *Is he taking us under the fall?* He can't be. He was so reluctant to go near there last time. Something about keeping a promise to someone.

He's about to pull me under the veil, the glass sheet of the fall, when I tug his hand.

His eyes land on my nails digging into his skin before they look to me in question.

You said we can't go in there! I mouth the words, although, I should really let it go. I'm the one that wanted to go under the fall. Shouldn't I see what the fuss was about? Shouldn't this be my chance to hear what his promise was? Why the waterfall is significant to him?

He ignores my questions, tugging me under the heavy weight, the crashing gravity of chilled water. And for a moment, I take pleasure in the sensation plummeting down my hair before we are swallowed behind its shiny curtain.

I'm greeted by the scent of moist earth after a rainstorm. Murky and sweet. It's like a wet cave, with slimy algae coating limestone, and thick briny air.

He then eases me against the stone wall, my back squishing the spongy slime. And I take another look around. Quickly, skeptically, despite his feverish eyes nailed to my body. What's the big deal? I don't see any hidden passageways. There isn't any secret code written on the slippery limestone. It's just a waterfall. A secret waterfall that seemed to snag his attention when we were last here.

My slightly unimpressed gaze slides back to him. I nearly flinch at the way he's looking at me. His dark eyes are set ablaze. An intense forest fire, with the reflection of the waterfall they are a soft shade of hickory with a warm splash of caramel. He anchors his left hand against the stone behind me, and his right hand glides around the small of my back, pulling me close to his body.

That same forest fire takes root under my skin, under the space where his fingertips rest. I swallow down the satisfied sigh that wants to slip from my lips. The automatic response to melt into his arms.

"Honey…" He utters that one word. One term of endearment. And I'm a little disappointed in myself for not guessing it was him when we ducked under the waterfall. I didn't even notice his slow dissociation from the world.

"Kane," I rasp, swallowing down the nerves his presence has caused me. "What's happening to us? Can you feel it too?"

He exhales something inexplicable. Maybe all of the thoughts he wishes he could say. But *can't*.

"Please give me something. Anything." I'm begging for mere scraps at this point. A dog whining at his feet.

Pity flashes over his shadowed gaze. "Have you ever wondered why you are the only person that can control someone as dangerous as me? As dangerous as us?"

In the half a second my lips part, Kane's left hand slips around the back of my neck, holding me steady. Holding me close.

I don't answer. Of course I've wondered. There is no keeping count of the questions that have poured over me like an endless rain. I'm drowning in his mystery.

"You ran away with me, Skylenna. Do you know why?" I hear his question. But my mind is only focused on his warm skin against mine. The hot flesh on his hand burning bliss into my neck, my veins, my spinal cord. *Please don't ever take this hand away.*

I shake my head, forgetting my words. "I—I care about you."

He nods. He knows this.

"You think there is something between us." A cool breeze sprinkles water over his back and I can't help watching the raindrops tumble over his lips.

"Don't you?"

He shakes his head. "It's more than that, but you won't let yourself understand." That firm right hand grips my waist in desperation.

"Then help me understand," I beg.

"I have *always* cared about you, honey. Even through Dessin," he explains. "And hearing you confess what you want…"

"I want it from all of you. Not just one. I know that's selfish! It is. But I want your heart. And I want Dessin's. And I'll probably want anyone else inside that beautiful mind."

"You will understand one day. But only if you promise to remember this." He surrenders his desperate gaze down to my lips, then drifts back to my eyes once more. "Promise me you'll remember… in the moment you think you might give up."

"Remember what? You'll drive me mad with these questions!"

Kane lifts his chin in understanding. "As hard as this might be for you, to be left in the dark, to have an endless stream of questions. I promise it's harder for me. It's ripping my heart out. It's,"—he takes a steadying breath—"burning me alive, honey. I want to tell you everything. But I can't. Not until this is all over."

He waits for me to argue, to chase him down with more questions. But that's the look of a broken man. The look of suffering. It renders me still. Completely silent.

My eyes fill with tears. Because the words I know I must say sift through my thoughts, the sweet woodsmoke of a beautiful memory.

"I won't let you burn alone."

Suddenly his eyes obliterate. A mushroom cloud of raging desire. An all-consuming, impatient need. His brow rises in sweet agony as though he is preparing himself for battle. His large hand tightens around my neck, luring my forehead to his, and he exhales lightly against my lips. I let a tear slip, rolling soundlessly down my cheek.

The world holds its breath.

He gazes one last time into my eyes, as if to ask for permission.

Then he kisses me. It's enough to send my soul toppling into the arms of the universe.

It's soft, painfully cautious, as if he's waiting for me to give myself to him. To remove the restraints from my heart and hand them over.

So, I do.

My hands find his soaking tunic, tugging it gently to me, and I part my lips.

Without a moment of hesitation, he's opening his mouth to slip his tongue over my own. This melts every thought, every grudge of being left in the dark. I arch my back, pressing my hips into his own, discovering his growing hardness. I groan at the pressure.

Kane releases a strained sigh into my mouth, and with one quick motion, he's propping me against the wall, hooking my legs around his hips.

And it is as if the kiss had grown wings and taken flight, morphing into a feral euphoria. A desperate search for my soul. Because he deepens this kiss, passionately, ferociously, devouring my mouth. Branding me with his need to taste me.

I whimper as his broad hands find the sides of my face, ensnaring me to his lips. The ache in my chest burns like hot coals, searing my flesh, turning my organs to ash. It's insatiable. The need to have him. All of him. Because this kiss… this *kiss*. It's what I needed. Every moment in the asylum when I visited Dessin's room and Kane stayed in the shadows. Every moment he held me in his arms while we slept in the forest. Every secret we exchanged.

He breaks apart from our kiss and looks at me. He's begging me. Searching my eyes for a sign. Reaching into me. Pulling at my heart, removing it from my body so he can hold it in his hands. *It's yours. It will always be yours.*

"Tell me I'm yours," I pant. "Tell me."

My words untie his final knot of restraint.

His soul collides with mine and he claims me with his kiss once again, his tongue grazing my own. His right hand tangled into my wet hair, keeping me close. So close. Not nearly as close as I want to be. Nothing is enough. I want more. More of his lips on mine. More of his embrace. More of his heart and his attention and his whole world.

And in all this time, I now know I have never wanted anything else but this. And I will never want anything else but this again.

17. Poison The Puppet

While Kane checks the area for lingering guests, I brush my fingers over my lips.

I close my eyes.

I watch it over and over again.

How could we have waited this long? *His lips.*

It feels as though the tension and constant yearning for more of him should have been diffused with that kiss. Dissipated. Like a raindrop on a candlewick. *Gone.*

But I caress my hand over my cheek, my neck, my waist. I burn all over. An eternal fire thrumming through my veins, splashing over the infected areas where his touch branded me. I hold that memory, bind it to my chest, swallow it like a pill that will seep into my system and never leave. I tried to hide the feelings that seemed to climb out of my heart. I tried to disguise them as a concerned friend who just wanted to help. But they got down on their knees and pleaded with me to tell the truth. I have deep and intimate feelings for Kane. For Dessin.

The wind rises in speed, carrying fallen red leaves on an invisible string, twirling around my limbs in a whimsical dance. I'm still wet but can hardly feel any discomfort. I hold a whole new jar of questions now. Will he kiss me again? Are our feelings the same? Where do we go from here? Not just with the plan but with how we act toward one another.

At least now I finally know that every time he looked at me, there was something there for him too. More than the physical heat. The sexual energy. I just want to hear him say it. I need his words right now. I need them to validate it all for me.

Just once.

Over a crooked hill of red oak trees, Kane makes his way back to me. He keeps his head down, wringing out the bottom of his wet tunic.

A herd of electric fireflies jump-starts my nerves and I'm suddenly anxious beyond reason. But it's just Kane. The man I've slept next to almost every night. The man that I trust with all of my secrets. *That* man.

"They're gone," he states, quick and curt. "Let's get changed and get moving again." Cold. No warmth. Only ice.

"Kane?" His name barely makes it out of my mouth. He doesn't look at me. "Kane—"

"We have to get moving."

I stiffen. *What is this?* A tsunami of passion just crashed into both of our bodies at once and he's detaching himself from me? *Could it be Kane?*

I step forward and lift his chin with the knuckle of my right index finger. He looks at me. A soft, sweet look. It *is* Kane.

"I just need to say something before we go." My voice is practically gone. I've never sounded so quiet in my life. "I think we need to talk about what just happened."

He straightens up uncomfortably. Hickory dark eyes look down on me.

"What happened between us was a mistake."

My breath catches in my throat. I blink once. Twice. Several times, as if it will erase the last three seconds.

"A *mistake?*"

He nods. "It was a moment of weakness. We are close friends. Sometimes mistakes like that happen."

I want to shake my head. *Please stop talking. Stop saying what you're saying.* Each syllable that escapes his plush lips chips away at my heart, cracking like frozen glass. How could it have meant nothing to him? His kiss was *everything* to me.

I try my hardest to compose my face. To hide my pain.

"So you—you didn't feel *anything* then?" I stammer.

He remains impassive. "I don't feel that way about you."

I stare at him. I want to look away but can't. Without even realizing it, I move my hands up to clutch my heart, attempting to push it back into my chest.

"Did *you* feel something?" he asks.

"No—I—of course not." My voice cracks. It so pathetically cracks. "It was impulsive. A mistake. Wrong. I don't feel—" But that's all the words I have. I. Don't. Feel.

"Well, I'm sorry for acting without thinking. I'll let you get changed and we can get moving again." He leaves me a dry set of clothes and disappears into the trees.

Grabbing a nearby tree, I hold myself up for only a few seconds before I slide down its side, begging these feelings to go away. *I did this to myself. I cracked open that thirteenth room and let these emotions seep in like a poisonous fog.*

My eyes unclog of all prideful restraint, and the tears spring freely from their nest.

I can barely breathe as his words bite into my flesh with newly sharpened teeth. The despair is all too familiar. It's the moment you see your sister crumble into suicidal depression. It's the feeling of your father's boot on your back, kicking you down a basement. It's a sea of men and women dressed like dolls, and then there's you. Standing alone. Starved. Scared. Not belonging anywhere.

It's kind of like that. Except, all at once.

18. Children in The Rain

Judas.

I only have room for one thought now. How can I get Judas to open up to me? How can I coax him into telling me everything he knows?

It's midnight and we've made it to the city. Since we left the Red Oaks, I have refused to look at him. The ache in my chest has taken on a new shape. A dagger of jagged edges with a rusted surface. My hurt finds a protective outer shell, a shield of anger, a dull throb of annoyance in my gut. He's toyed with my feelings. Feelings I've never had before. Feelings that nudged me in his direction, into the thirteenth room, into a life of running and isolation. He didn't have to put his hands on me in the lagoon the night we shared our secrets. He didn't have to kiss me, giving me false hope.

It's manipulative. And I thought Kane was different. I thought I wouldn't have to worry about those games. I have been used and abused my entire life. And now it's happening again, but in a new form. A fishing hook to my heart, tugging, yanking until I hear the ripping sounds of my arteries being torn from my chest cavity.

Kane's plan is to get caught sneaking around the city. He's

convinced the asylum will expect us to stay within its perimeters. The seven forests are too dangerous. Even though that's exactly where Demechnef will be searching for us. Once caught, Dessin will quickly take his place.

The streetlights are elegant torches of rich orange flames, reflecting off the cobblestone streets and the tall double-pane glass windows on either side of the columns from the dress shops, the barbershops, the shops for beauty, the shops for perfume and home decor. They're all lined up down Main Street, with tall mansard roofs topped, round cornices, coffee-colored bricks, and brackets beneath the eaves and bay windows.

Although the city is sleeping, we saunter down the sidewalk, completely exposed. Kane knows we have exactly twenty minutes before five city guards will do a routine perimeter check. And we'll be out in the open waiting.

A block down the road, I hear the faint sound of water bursting from a pipe, sprinkling down over asphalt. The Chandelier Fountain Water Show. On the first Wednesday before a celebration, the show automatically goes on at night to keep the water circulated. Tomorrow is the Original Architects celebration. The day the first of our people came on boats and fought to get through the thick and deadly layers of the seven forests.

The fountains shoot up to the sky and spray over the area. There's always the same record that plays during the show. A guitar, a violin and the faint beat of a drum. It's upbeat and folksy, very similar to the dancing agronomists around their campfires with hands full of bottled moonshine.

I look over at Kane who is watching the show from afar. If we're to go back to the asylum, into the mouth of hell, we need to be united. There can't be this tension. The kiss is trying to drown me, his words are pressing a pillow over my mouth and holding me down. I want this torture to end here. If anything, I need my friend back for what comes next.

A mischievous grin spreads over my entire face. He catches the change in his peripherals and raises his eyebrows at me. "I think you need a bath," I say.

He tilts his head in confusion, and then understanding tackles him to the ground. "No, absolutely not. We just got dry, Skylenna."

No more *honey*.

But I stop listening, tossing off my boots to break out into an excited sprint. He grunts behind me and heavy footsteps lunge forward to stop me.

I'm close enough now to feel the cold mist sprinkled into the air, sticking to my skin as I enter the cloud of fountain spray. The music gets louder, just as my right foot hits the cold water, the tempo thrums to life. Dancing music. Wild and careless. And just as the cannon of water shoots up to the sky, iron arms wrap around my waist, lifting me into the air. I let go of a laughing scream that feels like it's been waiting ages to be set free. How good it feels to have those arms around me again.

The water in the sky falls, plummeting back down to earth with a vengeance. We're instantly drenched, head to toe.

He lets out a laugh of relief and excitement from behind my head. I'm being twirled around in the wet chaotic air. "You are a HANDFUL!" He booms into more laughter.

I wiggle free and run across the fountain to dodge him between bursts of water, lifting my knees high enough to not get slowed down.

His face, his hair, his clothes are soaking wet and he's grinning. *I made him smile.* I spin around, following the rhythm of pulsing water shots like a ballerina. He's maneuvering around the water pumps, careful not to get blasted.

The happiness softening the tension between us is heavy in the air, stronger than the water pressure, and louder than the music. It's pounding against my chest and telling me not to stop.

He chases me relentlessly, grinning at my sad attempt to be stealthy. Finally, he catches me, takes my hands in his, and spins us around. Like children playing in the rain, a thunderstorm in the forest, a secret dance of youth and friendship. He swings me around in a swing dance, whirling me through the briny air as I cackle. There's a strong chance I've never laughed so hard in my life. *Just like children playing in the rain, a thunderstorm in the forest.*

And that elation is quickly replaced with something else entirely. A chain that wraps around my heart, tightening to the point of pain. Until I'm frozen. Until I'm paralyzed.

It's like the moment I stepped into the thirteenth room. The moment I laid eyes on Dessin. The time he showed me the wooden tokens from the satchel in the asylum basement. A familiar wave of déjà vu swirling in my stomach. Like I've been here before or somewhere like it. Like if I tried hard enough, I could fade into a lost memory.

I look at Kane from across the fountain. The water sprinkles over us, slowly, dreadfully slow like the clock of this world has begun to stop working. It falls across our vision of each other. And that's when I see it. A young boy with his eyes. Happier. Less troubled. I see him twirling a little girl around. I see the raindrops falling to the earth. I see the lightning crack across the sky and the dark-gray clouds bumping into one another. I hear the thunder that makes the girl jump. And I *feel* it. Like we've done this before. Like we've danced in the water and sang in the rain.

And this entire time, I hold my eye contact with Kane, who now looks worried. He runs to me, so slowly, as if it takes minutes to hear one foot splashing in the fountain.

"What is it?" That deep, soothing voice is muffled by the sound of the thunderstorm. The rain pattering over the leaves in the forest.

But he's holding my shoulders now, bringing me back to this world. Back to the fountain. Dragging me far away from the children playing in the rain.

I shake my head. Willing the images to let go of me. Remove me from the frozen state. Release me from imprisonment.

"Tell me," he says.

"I've been here before."

He pauses. He waits for me. I don't think he's breathing.

"Kane, have we ever danced in the rain?"

He stares at me bewildered, like watching an inactive volcano begin to quake.

"Did we play in a thunderstorm in the forest?" I ask again.

I see his Adam's apple shift. And then, a shift in his expression. A look of emptiness. Then, something dominant. Powerful. *Dessin.*

"I think you've gotten too much water in your ears." He smirks. "Let's get you out of here."

I don't object because I'm feeling silly. I should have just kept that to myself. He thinks I am insane. I'm seeing things now. *Oh man, I'm seeing things now!* And poor Kane didn't know how to handle it. He panicked and Dessin had to take over.

How the tables have turned, huh, Dessin?

We find our way out of the maze of pumps and lights. I sit down and wring out my hair.

He picks up his dry shoes. "Thankfully he was sensible enough to keep these off."

I'm embarrassed. Like the feeling when you get caught sleep talking, and it was loud enough to wake you up, but illogical enough to let whoever is around you know that you were without a doubt sleep talking. And there's no explanation or quick way to recover. You can either roll over and go back to sleep, or admit you were sleep talking. But the embarrassment is there just the same.

"Can we just forget I said that?" I'm small. *So* small.

He chuckles and sits down next to me. "Only if we can forget that Kane kissed you."

Ouch. Small doesn't even begin to describe how I'm feeling now. Why would he want me to forget? Was it really that horrible? Or taboo? Am I a bad kisser? How could that passion and unbelievable connection have only been one way?

"Already forgotten." I clip my words, short and to the point. "It wasn't great for me either. Better if we pretend it never happened." *But I want it to happen again! Can't you see that, Dessin?* The memory of it is eating me alive and he never wants to speak of it again. Well, I can be just as cold as he is. I can be bitter and nonsentimental.

I look up in time to catch the solid clenching on his jaw, the muscle flexing over and over. His eyes close slowly. Fast breaths pump his chest. What could Kane be saying right now? Or *feeling*?

19. The Welcome Committee

They find us dripping wet on the cobblestone. And they aren't gentle.

It's as if finding us is a personal victory. A personal vendetta to make us suffer.

At first, Dessin humors them. Makes a solid effort to look surprised, caught off guard, as if they managed to sneak up on him. He even fights back, putting a tenth of the effort into what he's capable of in his punches. But they "overpower him," managing to lock him in a new set of shackles. They're different, though. Heavier. Thick, weighted brass. The chains lace around his waist, down to his ankles, around his neck.

He doesn't look surprised that they upgraded. But he fakes a look of begrudging defeat.

That part is easy. The acting rolls smoothly off his broad shoulders and furrowed brow. It's all part of the plan. An effortless shift in power from Dessin to the five guards.

Until one of them yanks down my wet breeches, revealing a black lace thong from the Nightamous Horde.

"What do we have here?" The guard laughs, turning me around to show his friends—and Dessin—my bare ass. "Has he been dressing you up like his whore?"

My lungs turn to ice. I shift my head around enough to see Dessin's eyes widen, jaw flex. His eyes dart from my backside to me then back to my backside.

"Stop," I mutter, half commanding, half pleading.

"Your little boyfriend has made us look pretty bad for letting him escape." The guard still holding the back of my breeches turns his attention to me with a predatory smile. "How do you think we should punish him?"

The other guards laugh. But Dessin is a towering tree. Unmoving. Unflinching. Godlike as he decides what to do with their meaningless fate.

"Should we,"—he plucks my thong, snapping it over my skin—"play with you in front of him? Show the bastard you're not his property anymore?"

"No," I choke out. *Damnit*. He's going to have to blow his cover before we've even started. I want to swat the guard's hands away, but my wrists are shackled just like Dessin's.

The guard glances back at Dessin. "What do you think? Would it upset you to see me play with her pussy?"

I panic. "*No!*" I scream. My body thrashes against his hold hard enough to knock his hands away from me. But only for a moment. Two guards rush over, holding me steady, leaving Dessin's side, which, of course, is a mistake on their end.

I glance back at his silent fury again. Though he isn't moving, there's a current of feral alpha energy buzzing under his tan skin. A murderous frequency behind his cold stare.

Calm down! I tell myself. They're not going to do anything. They're bluffing!

But I sink into a pit of fear as a clammy hand cups my most sensitive skin. The important area that my thong covers. And he's glaring at Dessin as his hand strokes over the lace.

"Think I can make her come with my fingers, Patient Thirteen?" he taunts, pinching my clit through my thong. I wince, turning my face so Dessin can't see. "Or should I pull out my cock to finish her off?"

That's it. We're done. I wait for Dessin to detonate.

"Unhand her!" A voice of authority booms through the night, bouncing off the cobblestone street. It's familiar. Stern with an aged tone. The metal clap of a buggy door shutting forces the men to let me go after they pull my breeches back up.

As I turn around, a short figure steps under the light of the nearest streetlight post. Dark skin, short white hair, a pin-striped suit, and a thick wooden cane under his right palm.

Lyoness. The head council member that was the deciding vote for Dessin's life.

He glares at the guards, one by one, examining the situation. "What might have happened if I hadn't shown up?" he asks them, voice rough and creaky.

No one answers.

"Get them to Emerald Lake," he barks. "I'll deal with the five of you later."

I don't miss the quick latching of Dessin's shackles before we're herded into a prisoner's buggy. Despite the terror that had a hold on me moments ago, I want to laugh.

He's already found a way out of their upgraded security.

We're herded into the hall of the intricate section like cattle that strayed from the farm.

I didn't realize how it would affect me, being here again, stumbling along the checkerboard tile, hearing the moans through the thick stone walls.

My entire body trembles, because why wouldn't it? This establishment—this *prison*—was frightening enough when I conducted the treatments. Now I'll be a victim of them. I'll endure the abuse daily, keep my mouth shut until we get what we need from Judas. At least there's that. If I still have that magic touch, this shouldn't take long, right? But what if it does? What if I can only speak to Judas on a rare occasion? What if he doesn't budge?

A knot twists in my stomach, growing thorns that stab vital organs.

I don't think I will last long. Dessin clearly has alters that front when he can't take the pain. Like when the Nightamous Horde was going to burn him, torture him, a new alter took his place. An alter that seemed to enjoy the pain.

I'm not armed with that kind of defense. But I can't let him down. He has to start looking at me like an equal, even though it's clear that he holds all of the power here, and I'm merely a helpless marionette in this game.

I try to look back at Dessin, but instead I'm greeted with a boot to the back, launching me through the air until my face smacks against the checkerboard tile. A sharp sting vibrates across my cheekbone, pressurizing behind my right eyeball.

"*Ugh!*" I groan, lying flat like a pancake.

Dessin growls behind me, rattling his chains in protest. "When this is all over," he snarls. "I'll make sure I take my time with you. You'll beg for a quick death."

There's a believing silence from our audience. A sense of consideration because they know he is true to his word. They must have a suspicion that he could get out of this.

But they shake it off. "Up! Now!" the guard orders me, snatching a fistful of my honey hair, yanking me to stand upright.

If I thought my body was shaking before, it's a full-on earthquake now. My teeth are chattering. My intestines burn as we move closer to the twelfth room.

No. I don't think I can. It's like—I start panting like a dog—like being locked in a basement. A cold, dark basement. I'm wheezing, looking for an escape, for a way to stall until I'm ready.

"Wait," I blurt out. "Just wait a second!"

But they only jerk me harder to the door that will be the source of nightmares for me until the day I die.

"Dessin!" I shriek, digging in my heels to buy me some time. "Dessin, I'm scared!"

I only catch a glimpse of his face as they open my door. A look of strength. Perseverance. But also a dark glint of roaring agony.

I've got you, he mouths to me before I'm thrown into my new home, chains and all.

The room is dim with flickering sconces, and the iron-framed bed is on the right wall instead of the left. I slump a little. At least we'll share a wall when we sleep. But how many nights will that be? Only a couple of days? Weeks? Months? I guess that all depends on me. On my ability to learn what Judas knows.

I take another look around. The small bathroom. The rusted sink. The stained white sheets. The crumbling foundation, gray ceiling, unswept floor. It's exactly like a basement.

But I chose to be here. I *chose* this.

The knowledge doesn't stop the tears from spilling over my eyes, staining my cheeks and neck. I don't hold it back this time. I remove the leash from my grief and allow it to run free, just for tonight. Because I can't change out of my wet clothes and I'm cold and alone in a room that reminds me of nights locked away, curled in a tight ball at the age of six. I want to go back to the forest. I want to see Asena and Garanthian again.

It's on this night I allow myself to feel weak and afraid. Like an injured animal, I curl up on my creaky, hard bed, shivering without a warm blanket or dry clothes or the crackling of a fire to soothe me to sleep.

At least Dessin isn't here to see this. To see me splitting at the seams. To see how weak I really am in comparison to him. He would be better off without me dragging him down. Another sob rattles my body, clutching my rib cage.

I place my damp hand on the wall I share with Dessin. On the other side, I imagine him lying in the small bed parallel to mine. I imagine he's planning the demise of this hellhole. Plotting the methods of unfathomable torture he'll use on the guards.

And strangely enough, that brings me comfort.

This will end with his wrath.

"I wasn't aware you were still alive."

I flinch in my frigid wet clothes that only dried a little while I slept. But that's a gray area, isn't it? I didn't really sleep, not soundly, anyway. It was a delirious loop of drifting close to sleep, then waking in an icy panic. I was relaxed enough to close my eyes again, yet I never even heard my door open and shut.

"I thought he would have killed you. Maybe raped you first, then carved your heart out slowly. Perhaps he would have found a way to keep it attached to all major arteries, scooping it an inch above your breastbone, just to show you it to you before he ate it." Meridei sits in the conformists chair in the middle of the room. Her raven hair still short, styled in a neat bowl cut around her head. That godforsaken navy-blue uniform dress. Her black, soulless eyes.

My dry eyes widen as I process what she's saying. What she's crudely implying. She figured Dessin would have done away with me when we ran away.

"Otherwise, I would have volunteered to help lead the hunting party that went looking for the two of you," she purrs, pleased with the malice of her words, like a cat who's just had its milk.

I try to sit up but forget my wrists are bound in brass shackles. I forget about the throbbing pain under my right eye, splintering across my cheekbone.

"You two have really been living off the land, haven't you?" she asks, eyes snaking down my outdoor attire. "You'll need to be hosed down."

Fantastic.

"It's a shame I don't get more time to play with you. Three days until you're executed next to your psychotic rebel. That isn't nearly long enough for me to play with you."

Three days. Not likely. Unfortunately for me, Dessin will be asking for a priest right about now. His right under oath of the asylum.

A shiver vibrates up my spine at the thought of being Meridei's pet for any length of time.

Two orderlies collect me from the sodden clump I'm in on the bed, hooking their hands under my arms and dragging me to the hydrotherapy room. I nearly sigh in relief. Even though being blasted with cold water isn't fun, at least it isn't Chekiss's treatment. Simulated drowning.

I can do this. I already know what it's like after the first time I subjected myself to it as a way to get Niles to trust me.

I miss them, terribly. But at least they're no longer suffering within these vicious walls. By the hands of these insidious men and women.

Two doors away from our destination, my elbow is yanked out of the way to let an orderly pushing a wheelchair past. But it's who's in the wheelchair that has my jaw hanging open.

Sun Ravendi. The patient with the obsessive disorder. The woman with no hair, raw lips, and sunken eyes. A mother without a child. Her mouth is blue, veins bulging from her neck. And she doesn't even see me. She's dead behind the eyes. Another chair binding treatment.

Another inch closer to death.

My eyes fall closed. I couldn't help her. My efforts to make a better place here were lost when I left with Dessin.

And now I'm going to pay for it.

We keep moving, and I'm in a daze. A protective instinct to distance myself from these next experiences.

"Strip her," Meridei commands the orderlies as she unwinds the hose.

The room is colder than I remember. An ice chest. My boots are ripped away from my feet and I glance down at my naked toes wiggling in a puddle on the chilly tile floor.

My oversized white tunic is thrown to the corner of the room with a wet plop, then my pants. I'm left standing like a trembling baby tree in the dead of winter. Left in nothing but my black lace brassiere and thong, courtesy of Runa.

You know, compared to Meridei, I suppose I kind of like her. I suppose I'd rather be in her presence, flirting with Dessin right about now. I'd take the burn of jealousy any day.

With a rough tug down my legs, the lace drags over my skin, soundlessly dropping to the floor. Because my hands are bound, they don't try and lift my brassiere over my head. It's ripped off from behind.

And… I'm naked, chained, and shivering in front of this small audience.

I'm shoved in front of the drain, my backside lightly touching the wall. Maybe Judas will hear my screams, like last time? Maybe I'll only have to be in here for a single day. One conversation alone will tell me all I need.

"It's strange being back in the spot, isn't it?" Meridei muses, aiming the head of the hose at my face. "I couldn't let you really have it back then, though. I had to let you make your point to that patient. But now,"—she cracks her neck—"*now* I stop this hose when I feel like stopping."

It's the only warning I get. The only moment to close my mouth and shut my eyes. The lever is pulled, and it only takes half a second to whack me in the face, bloodying my nose and sending my head flying back to knock against the wall.

The instinct to cover my face is quick but useless. The water juts past my wrists, shredding my cheeks, my throat, my lungs. So I turn around, face the wall, allow my back to take the hydro-beating. And Jesus, it's so cold. Tiny needles stabbing my flesh with a vengeance. But the worst part isn't the ice, the shock, or the devastating pressure. Nope, it's the panic of not being able to breathe. I had almost forgotten that part. With water shooting at my face in ten different directions, it's nearly impossible to suck in a wholesome breath.

A true fight for survival. Basic. Primitive. Terrifying.

I start to choke. If she would just lower the hose to my legs or my lower back…

But it's useless. She knows what she's doing. I smack my hands against the wall as a plea to stop. My throat burns with the need to cough up the inhaled droplets, but I can't. I try. My rib cage coils together, attempting to suck in enough air to cough, and I do, a little, but it's not enough. My lungs will fill up. I'll drown. I'll die.

And as a natural human response, my eyes fill with tears. And animallike gagging noises combating the jet of water smacking against skin and tile.

I'm dying.

Stop, Goddammit!

My naked body splats down on the floor after slipping on the puddle of water and losing my balance. The water stops but the sensation of being beaten by a spiky club remains, prickling all over my body, flooding my ears and nose.

I don't even have the strength to look up. But I can hear Meridei snickering. My eyes follow a stream of dirty water, circling around a drain by my face.

This is a great first day.

"Get up," she orders. "Or I'll start again."

Suddenly my strength is revived. I peel my wet, heavy body from the floor, using the wall as leverage to hoist myself up.

But as I turn around to face her, my stomach collapses on itself.

The door is open and Dessin (along with five other orderlies) is watching the hydro-show. His chin is lowered, but he's staring up at me from under his thick lashes. The only movement is his chest rising and falling heavily.

There are nine people now staring at my naked body. But only one set of eyes has me scrambling to cover my front with my shackled wrists, narrowing my arms to lay over my breasts.

"Don't worry,"—Meridei nods at Dessin—"this won't be the only treatment of hers you get to watch."

His knuckles turn white, tightening around his chains.

"I can handle it." I'm looking at Meridei but pointing my message at Dessin. He needs to know. It will take one wrong phrase, just one, and he'll lose his grip on control. A volcanic eruption. An asylum apocalypse.

Meridei laughs. "We'll see."

My only saving grace now is that I am back in my room with fresh clothes.

A white patient's gown that smells of bleach and elderly body odor.

And best of all, Meridei is forced to leave my room to attend an emergency meeting with a priest and the council. Dessin did it. He bought us time. I should be thankful, but truthfully, nothing makes me want to vomit more.

Time in this place is exactly what I don't want.

I sleep most of the day and the rest of the night. No one comes to bring me food. But I don't mind. The thought of eating anything makes me nauseated. At least I have a sink to drink from until they decide to start giving me basic human rights again.

The next morning I'm woken by the chanting of an elderly man. Through the fuzzy slits of my sleepy eyes, I see a black robe with a white collar.

Rosary.

The priest.

He's waving the cross over my body, reciting verses from the Bible. Welp, that does it then. Dessin did his part. Now, I have to do mine.

"Amen," the old man says, bowing his head. "You may inject her now."

As he steps away from my bed, I notice the wide hands holding down my shoulders, then another set of hands on my ankles. Meridei kneels at my bedside with a wicked, alarming smirk on her face. A twitch of her thin lips that says, *I'm going to enjoy this*.

She waves a syringe in front of my face, ensuring I see what's about to happen.

What is that?

You may inject her now.

"What—" But the needle is already halfway in my neck. I wince at the sharp sting that lingers under my skin, even after she pulls it out.

"We'll get those demons out of you, child," the priest says loudly.

Shit. Dessin had to plead reason of insanity was *demons*. What was the injection for? Is there actually a vaccine for demonic possession?

"Dear Meridei injected you with a couple of viruses, child. When your body fights it off, I pray that it will also fight the evil. The fever will burn it out. We can only hope it doesn't kill you in the process."

Nice. So I'm going to die from a disease. I'm more than tempted to ask what the success rate of this is, but I'm sure it will only result in more treatments throughout the day.

"Thank you, Father," I mumble.

They leave me alone for a few hours and I start to wonder if they injected me with a sedative, because my world grows fuzzy and unclear. I sleep as though my eyelids weigh a ton, and my dreams are wild, foggy, and all over the place.

A cold splash of water over my face and chest jolts me awake. Sort of. I'm groggy and disoriented. But I recognize the priest again, hovering over me, with a dubious look on his face.

With a flick of his bony wrist, another splash of water sprinkles over my face.

I gasp at the temperature, so cold. Like being pelted with hail.

Meridei rests a hand over my forehead. "She's burning up, Father."

Am I? My legs rub together to make friction under my white sheets. I would give anything for a big fluffy blanket from Aurick's mansion. No… I'd give anything to be wrapped up in Kane's arms. He's always so warm. A traveling furnace at my side.

I must have a fever, because the inside of my mouth is bitter and hot, along with my throbbing eyeballs. The rest of me, however, is freezing. Trembling from the inside out. My organs are thick and achy. My limbs, muscles, and joints must have all taken a beating. A gruesome, quiet mauling.

Another sprinkle of water.

I groan. But the Father continues. "He who dwells in the shelter of the Most High will abide in the shadow of the Almighty…"

The voices around me are under a tank of water, sloshing against my ears, increasing the pounding drums of searing pain under the shell of my skull.

"My refuge and my fortress, my God, in whom I trust."

I slip under the current, plummet away from the priest and his cold water, away from the people watching me, away from the smell of bleach and basement walls.

It's like floating on a leaf that has detached from a tree, whirling along the stream of wind, and I let it take me. Up, up, up… far away from this death ditch. I won't die here. No, not in captivity. I'd rather go somewhere under the trees. Yes, that's what I think I'll do. Float away.

And I am. Flying, that is. Soaring over a meadow, surrounded by long, flowing wisteria trees. I'm tempted to land. To sprawl out in the grass, maybe call for DaiSzek to join me…

"Eyes open, child!" A bark of an order. Old and gruff and shaky. "Don't let the devil lure you away."

At this point, I could either laugh or cry. If the devil were luring me somewhere, it would be right here in this bed. Not to a pretty meadow.

"I wanna see him." My words come out in a floppy slur. At least, I think I'm the one who spoke. It sounded like my voice.

Meridei laughs. "I'm sure he'd ask to see you too if he weren't currently being drowned over and over again."

A moment of lucidity. Dessin. The simulated drowning.

"You're lucky. Another priest is trying to flood his demons out of him."

God. What is wrong with these people? My stomach lurches at the thought of him gasping for air. On his knees. Thrashing against the tub.

My head flops to the side of the bed and I vomit. A loud splash of bile and water spilling across the floor. The priest leaps out of the way, gasping at my sudden bodily explosion.

"It's working," he declares with a sense of victory.

But I have to get this out. "No. I need to talk to…" I drift off for a moment, a splash of water and louder chanting snapping me back into reality. "Judas."

Meridei scoffs, a wet choking sound. "And what makes you think he wants to speak with you? A traitor? A whore? A demonically possessed woman?"

"Do not taunt *it*," the priest snaps.

It. *I'm an* it *now, huh?*

"Judas," I say again, louder this time.

"Just because you asked so nicely…" Her tone is too soft. Too sweet. "I'll make sure he never steps foot in this room. Because it looks like I'm getting my wish after all. Since a priest is now overseeing your treatments, no more death sentence."

I tremble violently under my sheets, clanking my chains together over my lap.

"Which means… more playtime for me."

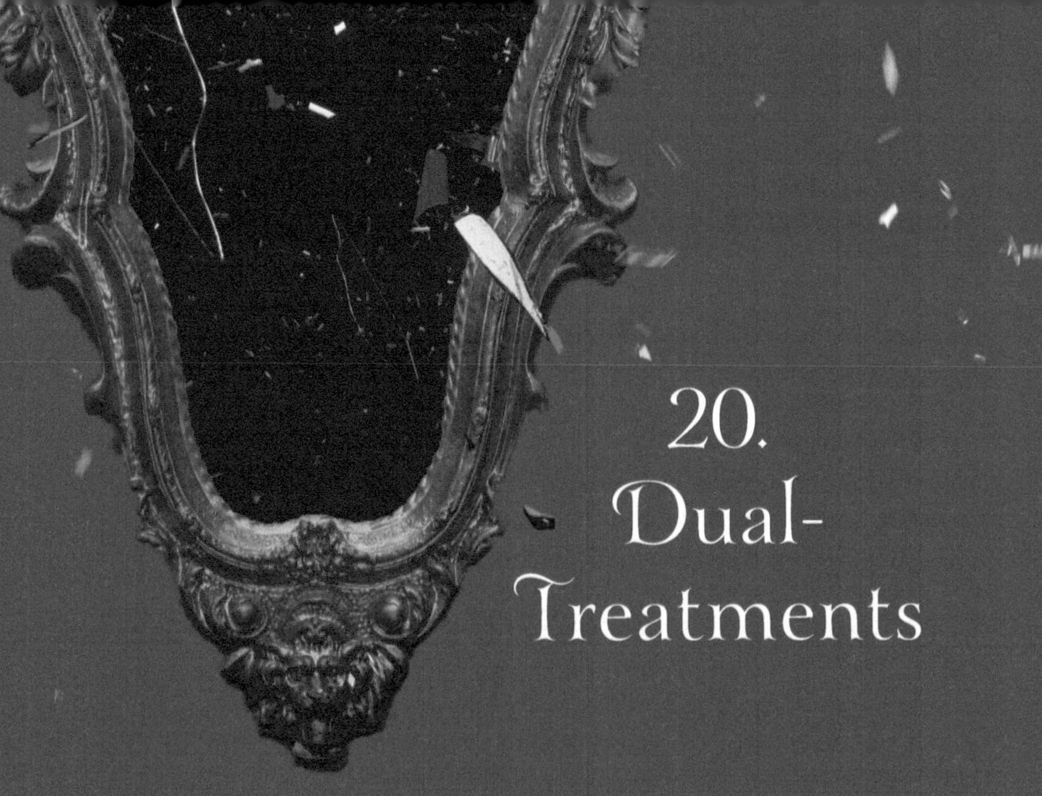

20. Dual-Treatments

I am not given days to recover.

Despite the fever, chills, vomiting, diarrhea, and achy limbs… I am treated as though my body is indestructible. In a hazy state of weakness, I'm dragged from my bed, knees scraping over the checkerboard tile as two orderlies haul me to another treatment.

If there was anything left in my system, I'd vomit again. But there isn't. I'm an empty vessel. And this is only day two.

My elbows are locked in two choke holds, tugging me along like an old, worthless doll. A puppet who has lost her strings. A run-down, vintage marionette.

My stomach is in knots and I'm shivering at the crisp draft in the air. Nothing in the world would make me happier than being back in bed. I don't even care if they didn't feed me. But it's so cold out here—

A treatment door swings open, and I strain to lift my head, afraid to see what I'm in for.

No.

A pair of shadowed eyes lands on me. And in this gaslit lighting, they're a smoky shade of hickory. Dessin is strapped down to an inclined table, raised enough for him to look back at me without lifting his head.

"Dess—" But there's something about the cold, unfazed gleam in his stare. Detached. Eager. Vigorously amused. He nods at me with a smirk or anticipated entertainment. But that can't be right. Dessin would be, at the very least, frustrated that I'm in a treatment room with him.

"Until your fever drops, you're exempt from treatments," Meridei announces, cutting off my line of sight to Dessin. "But that doesn't mean you can't watch Patient Thirteen suffer."

I didn't even have to watch that when I was his conformist.

My stomach takes a tumble. I'm going to be sick.

My heavy eyes trail over the wires on each side of him, the small machine on a table to his left, and a rag to bite down on. The orderlies on either side of me let go of their grips on my elbows, shutting the door behind me. And I want to stand. I want to rush to his side. But this fever, these viruses in my bloodstream make it hard to keep my eyes open, much less walk.

"Do you remember this treatment, Skylenna?" Meridei skips over to Belinda's side, who is turning on the machine, swiping at switches and pressing buttons.

Electroshock therapy.

Meridei turns to Dessin. "Aren't you going to grovel? Beg me to make her leave the room?"

Dessin raises an eyebrow. "Why would I do that?" His eyes slide back to mine, slowly, like slicing a dagger through skin. "I like the idea of her eyes on me."

Meridei and Belinda exchange a look, attempting to hide their disappointment.

But I can't stop staring at his expression. His slightly different mannerisms. All of it combined with his words… it can't be Dessin anymore. It must be the alter that was locked in the cage surrounded by the Nightamous Horde.

What is his name?

The different alter winks at me as if to confirm the question buzzing around my thoughts. He's here to take the pain.

Belinda places a headset with two bulbs that rest on his temples. Meridei shoves a white rag between his teeth.

And here I am, slumped on the cold floor, hands pressed into the tile, knees going numb, and completely powerless to prevent his pain.

"Should we let Skylenna decide the voltage?" Belinda glances my way.

Meridei's mouth curls upward. "Do you like a slow burn?" she asks me. "We could start it out mild and build that tension by only increasing it a notch at a time."

"That'll take forever." Belinda huffs out a laugh. "His brain will be fried by the time we finish."

Terror gushes over my nervous system.

I don't dare respond to their antagonistic taunts. Anything I do will result in this alter getting it far worse than he normally would if I weren't here. My only subtle cue that I'm writhing on the inside is my nails scraping into the unfaltering tile.

But the alter's weighty gaze is planted on me, completely unbothered by their threats.

There is no warning before they twist the knob on the machine. The table vibrates as it comes to life, rattling other tools on its surface.

The alter's body goes taut, back arching as much as the straps and restraints allow. Every muscle turning to a block of stone. Every vessel about to burst. And he's holding his breath with a red face, bulging veins in his neck, and that powerful jaw clamped down on the rag.

Bile sears my esophagus as I watch in horror, feeling the sharp pang of energy coursing through his body just by looking at him. Even through the fever, the dull pounding ache, I can't tear my eyes away from him. I forget my own exhaustion, my own suffering, my own need for a warm bed.

The machine dies, powering down, and the alter's flexed limbs come down with it. His back relaxes, fists unclench, bare toes uncurl. And he hums, closing his eyes slowly, pleased with the result. And his lids move back and forth. Could he be replaying the pain in his head?

He chuffs out a muffled laugh.

Meridei's spine straightens. This wasn't at all the response she was hoping for.

"Keep it up," she seethes. "You won't be able to fake satisfaction when we've hit the last notch."

But that's just it. I don't believe he's faking anything. The alter's eyes practically roll back in his head at the pleasure of it all.

The machine roars back on, triggering the rigid response from the alter once more. These next few rounds, his chest growls at the impact, a low groan in the base of his throat—like someone unable to hold their breath underwater any longer.

And his responses don't change. Every time the machine silences, the alter melts back onto the table moaning in pleasure.

Meridei slams her fist down next to him, shrieking like a child throwing a tantrum.

"I wonder how fun this will be for you if I leave it on! Would you like that? To die of a heart attack? To finally keel over to a brain aneurysm?" Her breathing is ragged now, unraveling to her own sadistic frustration. "Won't that be humiliating for you? The great and terrible Patient Thirteen extinguished by a little machine."

It's hard to tell, but he's definitely smiling with his eyes closed, as if that threat excites him even more.

The box screeches as it floods a new and extreme current of electricity through the alter's brain. And this is the top notch. It doesn't just cause the table holding it up to tremble, no, the walls quake, the floor rumbles. And the alter is nearly levitating from the torture table.

Wait...

I gasp, looking back and forth between the women and the body of the man I care deeply for. Every drop of moisture is drained from my mouth as I gape at the scene. I can't even swallow, but I manage to scream.

"Please," I beg, crawling toward the vibrating table. "*Please!*"

And the two women are grinning at my pathetic attempt to stop them. Because it is pathetic. The tears are rolling down my face as I suck in oxygen like a dying pig. Everything hurts but watching him slowly burn from the inside out hurts more.

"Meridei," I rasp, reaching for the tip of her black heel. "I'll do anything."

I'm sobbing at her ankles now, feverish, delirious, and unhinged.

"Anything?" she purrs.

"God, yes! Just turn it off! Please, turn it off!"

She squats down in front of me. "Will you be my obedient little pet?"

Jesus. "Okay!"

"And do everything I tell you like a good slave girl?"

"Fine!"

She pauses for a moment, watching me like a fun experiment.

"Kiss my shoes, slave girl."

His treatment table is still buzzing with agony. He could already be dead. He should be by now.

I do as she commands, leaning down to kiss the toes of her high heels. Embarrassment and disgust swirl in my stomach, triggering a wave of bile to slosh up my esophagus.

The buzzing from the machine ceases, only to be replaced with the laughter of Belinda. "He's not going to like that. Everyone knows she's practically his slave since they ran off."

Before I can hear Meridei's response, the side of my head cracks against the tile, slipping back into my fevered dreams and hallucinations now that the adrenaline pumping through my veins has simmered back where it came from.

The darkness sweeps me away, carrying me back to my room. And when I open my gooey, tearful eyes… Scarlett is kneeling beside me, smelling of blueberry pie and rose petals. She looks *healthy*, glowing, even. And with a smile like a sunset draping over the ocean. She's happy.

"Hi," I say, my mouth made of sludge.

"You're so warm." Her willowy fingers graze my forehead. "They're doing their worst, huh?"

I sigh. "Lucky me."

"It won't be for long."

I strain to look at her golden complexion through tears forming in my eyes. Those rosy cheeks, shimmering spring-green eyes, and pouting bottom lip.

"I miss you." My voice breaks.

She smiles, leaning down to kiss the top of my scalding head. "I'm still here."

Meridei forces me to crawl behind her like a dog following its master.

The fever passed, the aches of the virus have fled, and now I'm fit to take on whatever treatments the priest decided for me.

After finally being fed eggs and porridge, I'm stronger, more alert, and giving myself pep talks every few seconds. But at the moment, this degrading parade is what's tearing me down. I can only hope that someone will tell Judas, or maybe he'll see me in my chains and white gown being humiliated in the hallways.

A fool's hope.

We turn the corner to a hall of vacated rooms. They were too old and condemned to ever make use of. But an orderly opens a door, sending a gust of asylum stench my way. Stale urine. Mildew rags. Rust.

Putrid.

Heavy.

As I pass the threshold on my hands and knees, I freeze without taking another step.

Chains hanging from the ceiling, the walls. Racks of weapons. Metal clubs, pliers, pokers, knives, saws, hammers, and tweezers.

I thought this kind of room was outlawed in the early days of settlement. Dessin's the one that told me that. They used to hang patients by their toes. They'd torture them in reckless practices that served no purpose (not that they do now).

"I—Meridei—" I glance to my left and have to do a double take. Make sure my eyes aren't betraying me.

Dessin is chained to the wall by his wrists. And he—he looks surprised to see me, like he accepted his fate to be tortured in this room alone. A flash of shock and disgust passes over his face. Eyes covered in storm clouds. Jaw locking down in outrage.

"The only thing you should be saying to me is *thank you,*" Meridei says, glaring down at me. "You didn't want to watch him get fried in electroshock, then you'll be happy to know that this time,"—she leans down to speak to me like a child that hasn't learned to walk yet—"he gets to watch you."

Ohhh, Dessin is going to end her.

I can't look back to see his reaction. Meridei has my chin pinched between her thumb and index finger, digging her nails into me to the point of pain.

Just get it over with then.

She must have heard my thoughts, because her chin flicks to the orderlies behind me and I'm towed upward, aligned in the center of the room. It happens before I can object. My brass shackles unlocked and falling to the floor in a clanking heap, only to be replaced by another set of old, rusted shackles that are instantly snapped tight to my bone.

And I'm truly a puppet now. The chains are attached to the high ceiling, looped through a hook that allows the orderlies to pull my chains until my toes are dangling an inch above the floor.

I groan at the ripping pain in my wrists as they bear all my weight. And without meaning to, I look up at Dessin, chained to the wall in front of me. They gave him a front-row seat. And even though his expression is blank, unreadable. His knuckles are stark white. The rage of an alpha spills over his large, brooding frame. Beastly fury pumps silently through the veins bulging from his tan arms. And they're ripped, like trunks of a tree emerging from the earth.

But he has to contain it. We've come too far in the past couple of days to ruin it all now. All I need is to get someone to reach out to Judas. Someone to—

Ruth! She must know I'm here. Maybe if I can catch a quick glimpse of her in the hallways, I can get her a message.

"Cut it off. We'll replace it when she's done," Meridei barks at the orderly, nodding at my patient gown. The man with a groomed black beard takes two steps toward me, tearing through my white fabric with a blade I didn't see in his hand.

I yelp as he tosses the shredded white material to the floor, leaving me hanging in only a medical white bra and underwear. It certainly isn't as flattering as the lace Runa lent me.

I wonder if I hear Dessin growl under his breath.

"You think a good flogging or whipping will get those pesky demons out of you, Sky?"

I hate her. I *really* hate her.

"What about you, Thirteen?" Meridei glances over her shoulder, dark intent playing over those coy thin lips. "Break her body with a club? Or slice that pretty skin open with a whip?"

To my surprise, Dessin cracks a smirk. "You think it's wise to provoke me?"

A warning. A strike of lightning shooting across the sky. A plague in the making.

Meridei is smart enough to take pause, considering his words with pursed lips and steadying breaths. She turns to me, holding her hand out to the orderly. "A whip it is, then."

My eyes fall closed. *Don't cry. Don't beg. At least it's me and not him.*

Before I can take a deep breath in, prepare for the impact of leather to skin—I'm struck. A strip of fire is ignited across my stomach. It's a failed attempt on my part to stay quiet because the yelp bursts from my throat like vomit.

The next lash is across my chest. And the pain sweeps over my entire nervous system, forcing out a whimper. My face crumples in a tight point of agony, and I have to will myself to keep my eyes open. I release a determined breath.

I can do this.

But as the third strike wraps around my back, I'm screaming. Fire eating away my flesh, burning through my nerve endings like an infectious disease.

I really fucking hate her!

Dessin has broken his streak of stoic silence. He's grunting now, yanking at the chains bolted to the wall like a wild animal that hasn't been fed in days. He's baring his teeth, snarling at every lash, at every sound of anguish that rips from my lips. I'm sure this is it. He's going to free himself, wrap his broad, deadly hands around her neck and with one swift movement. Snap! The last unholy noise will be of her body hitting the floor.

And although I don't agree with him killing… I wouldn't blink. Wouldn't lose a second of sleep over it.

The hurdle of her arm meets my neck, punching the air from my lungs. My head falls forward in an effort to suck in oxygen. And that's not the worst of it. The stinging pain is radiating over every inch of flesh now. Even if that area hadn't been lashed yet, it still burns like a white-hot branding iron the same.

"Meridei!" Dessin is a disaster waiting to wipe out the room. "Another move and I will rip that arm off with my teeth."

I'm howling now at the swelling blisters covering my waist, my arms, my back, my neck.

Before Meridei can decide if she believes his threat or not, the door opens. Belinda sticks her head in. "Suseas wants to see you."

Meridei massages her wrist as she considers the summons. "My arms are getting tired, anyway." The black leather whip hits the floor as she descends for the door.

An orderly walks over to reel me down.

"No!" she barks, one shoulder holding open the door. "Leave them. Forcing him to stare at her blistering body will teach him not to make empty threats again."

Empty. I might laugh if I wasn't in splintering pain head to toe.

The orderlies file out of the room behind Meridei, turning the gas off to the main iron light fixture in the middle of the ceiling. The old flickering scones are about as helpful as four small candles.

As the door clicks shut, I lose the little control I have left of my vocals. The sound of a dying puppy whistles out of me.

"Skylenna." More sounds of clanking metal. But I don't open my eyes to look. That was bad. Really bad. And neither of us anticipated that they would bring back the old ways. It was a grave error that has cost me, but mostly him. He was tied up when Kane's mother was killed. This was probably a huge trigger. It must have taken every ounce of self-control he has to watch me take a beating. All for this plan. All to speak with Judas. All for one damn clue from the Stormsages.

A pair of warm, giant hands cup either side of my face, fingers weaving into my damp hair. And then a forehead touches mine. "I fucking hate this." His voice is gravel and darkness and pure, unfiltered hate.

"Dessin," I whimper. "It hurts."

"Where, baby? Tell me where it hurts."

I sigh. "Everywhere."

His hands leave my face, skimming down my arms. And his touch, his warm skin, his hot breath blowing over my face—it makes the tears stop running.

"Here?" His thumb grazes the cap of my shoulder.

I nod, and he leans forward, pressing a light kiss to the spot.

"And here?" A finger traces down my sternum lazily. "Tell me where."

"Yes," I whisper. "There too."

He bows his head between my breasts, and at first, it's only his lips, then a flick of his tongue. I melt, arching my back and forgetting about the sting there too.

"Am I making it go away?"

"Yes."

He smiles and looks up at me with pupils growing larger, swallowing his brown irises. His fingers trace over my hardening nipples under my white bra and my cheeks stain with wild heat. "Here, baby?"

I moan in response. His mouth closes over the peaks through the white fabric. Hot moisture seeps through the barrier back to my puckering flesh. And he's sucking, wet sounds muffled by the thin material covering my breasts. Another sound peals from my lips, Was it a grunt? A whimper? I'm not sure. But I need more. I have to have more. It's distracting me from the pain.

His mouth unlatches from my left nipple, only to close over the right one. He pinches it with his teeth, making me yelp at the sting. But his tongue immediately laps me over to soothe it.

I take in a shaky breath. Uneven. Shuddering.

Dessin raises his head, stealing another glance at me as he lowers himself to his knees. Two fingers stroke the covered slit, like a knife cutting through butter. He sighs, closing his eyes as my head falls back from the rush of euphoria.

"Christ." His voice is broken and hoarse. His fingers glisten in the candlelight, soaking and he is only feeling me from the outside of my panties. I can't help but want to apologize. For what? I don't know. But my body is reacting in strange ways. Scarlett warned me this would happen. We leak between the legs.

"I'd beg for a taste," he growls. "To have my head between your soft thighs."

"Yes," I answer his question before he can ask it. "Please."

His two fingers press against my clit, sparking me with feral desire. I hiss, arching into his hand.

"Fuck. I shouldn't be doing this."

But he does anyway.

He's gentle in the way his finger pulls them down, careful not to touch the welts across my skin. And his breath is skimming my exposed, private area. The place I'm throbbing the most. The pooling of anticipation. The ache so internal, I'm squeezing my thighs together to keep it all in. Dessin notices.

"Open for me," he says, low and ragged with need.

I exhale slowly, letting my thighs drift apart, far enough to let him decide what he wants to do next. He watches me like a man starved, a hungry beast waiting to devour.

"Do your wrists hurt?"

I look up at my arms over my head. I hadn't noticed. Yes. No. Yes. Kind of, not really at the moment.

He nods as if understanding my confusion about what I'm feeling.

"Hook your legs over my shoulders. I'll hold you up." Dessin guides my legs on either side of his neck, then slides his hands over the roundness of my butt. Groaning as he squeezes. And he does it, stands up straight to his full six feet and four inches. My wrists are no longer straining against the metal shackles. He's tall enough that my arms hang loosely only an inch or two above my head.

"Thank you." I breathe out, relieved.

But the moment to relax is gone. He couldn't wait any longer, dipping his face directly between my legs to consume my heat, my desire, my wetness as if his life depended on it. And those plush lips kiss my clit, once, twice, and then his tongue, testing the waters, taking a long taste of my center.

We both moan at the same time. I don't know what this is. I've heard Scarlett talk about doing it to other women, but the thought of having it done to me has never crossed my mind.

"Wider, baby," he orders. My legs slide farther away from his neck and he's done holding himself back, done making slow strokes with his tongue.

He collides with my pussy, teeth grazing my clit, and then with one unexpected motion, that tongue sinks inside of me. Blazing fire ripples deep in my stomach, curling my toes over his back.

"Fuck!" I grit out.

His growl of approval vibrates between my legs and I throw my head back again, letting out strange, needy noises for more.

"I need you." I'm practically sobbing at his savage mouth feasting on me, melting inside of me, turning my bones into pudding.

He lifts his head to look at me, eyes foggy and unfocused, as if he's under a spell, bound by a coma slipping over his consciousness. "Say that again."

I blink down at him. "I *need* you, Dessin."

"Again." He removes a hand from my backside, angling a hooked finger to slide inside of me, slowly, agonizingly slow, until he stops pushing at the knuckle. That fingertip presses against a spot in a pulsating rhythm. He's scratching an itch or soothing a burn. I can't tell. I can't think.

"Say it," he barks, but his tone is weak and strained.

"God. I need you. I'll always need you." I'm bucking against him hysterically. Ravenously chasing that energy building around his finger. I would be embarrassed if I wasn't so high on unquenchable lust.

"There," he says. "You're going to come on my tongue. And when you do, I want you to scream my fucking name."

I'm hyperventilating. His dark voice is torturous and only adding to my building tension.

"Do you understand? I don't give a damn who hears you."

I nod quickly. And he's lowered to my clit again, sucking and lapping me up. That finger drums against that spot, and it's over.

As if I'm spilling my soul to the floor, tumbling down a cliff, every cell, every muscle goes up in rapturous flames. "Dessin!" I howl, my thighs clenching around his head as the world goes black and cloudy. I'm floating above him, no longer trapped, no longer a patient. It's just me and him and his mouth eating me up.

A moment passes, and I go limp and floppy over his shoulders. He laughs, lowering my legs to dangle above the ground again. Rushing to the lever attached to my chains, twisting as fast as he can until I'm a pile of sludge on the cold ground.

Dessin catches my head before I let it flop to the tile. And he's staring down at me, wiping sweat from my forehead, tucking loose strands of wavy locks behind my ears.

"I don't care that she was coincidentally interrupted by the blonde bitch. I'll sever that bony arm from her body the moment we get to leave." His attention is sucked in by the welts burning over my skin. His brow furrows in a vengeful need to carry out his threat now.

I smile up at him, despite the fact that my skin feels like it's been shredded, now that the endorphins and bursts of dopamine have passed.

"I can handle it," I whisper. "Only if you believe in me."

Dessin scoops me up in his arms, cradling me as he leans his back against the wall.

"Until hell freezes over."

"And even then."

21. Blasphemous Manipulation

"Good morning." A deep, scratchy voice rumbles in my ear. I stir against a warm body, arms acting as my blanket. I breathe in the scent of cedar, soap, and Dessin's skin. A hum buzzes in my throat, pleased that I've slept in his arms again.

"Looks like they left us in here all night," Dessin muses, running a hand through my hair.

"This place is actually the worst," I grumble against his arm. They left us to hang like meat in a butcher's shop.

He snorts. "That it is." His lips brush against my cheek, tickling like the wings of a butterfly. My eyes flutter open, searching for his face.

"I'm sorry you had to watch that." I swallow down the lump in my throat. The memory of him yanking at the chains connecting him to the wall like a wild animal.

His jaw twitched. "They injected you with viruses for the priest?"

"Mmm."

He thinks on this. "After the first lashing, I was sure I wouldn't be able to hold back. I was going to ruin it all. But I knew you'd already paid the price for being here from the priest. Whether it was some type of exorcism or fever injection. Either way, your suffering would all be for nothing…"

"Meridei's not letting me see Judas. I need to find a way to get his attention."

"Have you seen Ruth?"

"No." I drop my head against his shoulder. "Maybe they're not letting her see me. Maybe they've made my room restricted like yours."

"That's likely."

"Then how do I get a hold of him? I want to get this over with."

"Hm." He plays with my hair absentmindedly. "You could play on the priest's beliefs the next time you see him."

Play on his beliefs? How would that help? But it hits me, knocking into my chest like a swinging door. "Tell him God told me to find Judas."

"Mm-hmm."

"That's—so *manipulative*." I smile up at him. "Have I told you lately how brilliant you are?"

"I don't think you've ever said as much."

"Not true."

"If you have, it was said as an insult." His mouth tugs upward, revealing a dimple in his cheek.

"Yeah, that checks out." We both chuckle, his chest rumbling against my back. "Dessin… who's the other alter? The one that fronts when you're about to be tortured."

He stills, hand pausing in my hair. "Foxem," he responds. "He split when I started treatments in the asylum. He's a little younger than me. Twenty, I think. A true masochist. Finds pleasure in his own pain and torture."

I bite my lip. I gathered as much.

"That's why it's harder for me to watch you go through all of this. My mind can split and defend itself for any reason, any new trauma. Yours can't."

"Are there any other alters I should know about?"

He sighs. "There's—a lot of them."

"How many's a lot?"

"I'm not entirely sure. I haven't met all of them. There are eight of us that have had to front regularly over the years. Kane, myself, Foxem,

Syfer, Kalidus, Dai, Aquarus." He pauses, looking down at me in annoyance. "And you've met *Greystone*."

"Why did each split? Other than you, Kane, Foxem, and my buddy Greystone." I smile.

"Syfer is a mute alter. He split when Demechnef trained me to be able to withstand torture without spilling secrets to an enemy interrogator." Dessin readjusts his grip around my arms. "Kalidus is a fictional alter, the idea of him taken from a story Kane read as a child. A god of storms. A powerful character that was raised among humans, degraded and belittled until he was discovered to be a god. He was split when we were trained to withstand emotional abuse and belittlement. An alter that wouldn't be affected by their humiliating words. Because he knows he's a god, cocky and powerful."

I suck in a sharp breath. To think, his poor mind had to bend over backward to adjust to the vile life he was raised in.

"Aquarus is also a fictional alter. A god of the sea. He was split during the simulated drowning treatment. A god that couldn't drown. Could breathe underwater."

Dessin clenches his fists and looks away from me like his next words are difficult to even think about.

"Dai… is an animal alter. Short for DaiSzek. He was split when Demechnef would make me do unspeakable things. Rip a human to shreds. Tear them apart with my bare teeth. He split to be able to attack without a rational thought. A mind that only knows violence and chaos and animalistic fury. To be able to obey their requests so I wouldn't be disgusted with myself." He takes a deep breath. "The rest of us stay far away from the front when he's had to surface."

"Oh, Dessin…" I choke out. "I'm so sorry."

He lifts his hand to stop me from speaking, looks to the door.

"Let's get you back to your post." And he's scooping me in his arms, rising and walking me back to the chains hanging from the ceiling. I groan.

"Why?"

"They're to think we've been here all night."

He kisses the inside of my wrists before latching the shackles back on and reeling the lever on the wall to tow me off the floor, dangling like a sad puppet.

And before I know it, he's back to his wall, maneuvering his hands in a way to click his brass restraints shut, only a half a second before the door opens.

Damn, he's good.

I let my head hang, chin to chest, as if I've been sleeping uncomfortably like this all night. And the air shifts, the energy of sadistic delight.

"Sleep well, sunshine?" Meridei. Her stupid, snaky voice.

I lift my head, blinking slowly as if she has just woken me from a dead sleep.

"Are you ready to crawl back to your nice, cushiony bed now, little pet?"

I imagine Dessin using an axe to chop away at her arm. But it isn't a clean break. He'll have to wail at it, a jagged, butchered job. My eyes flick over to where he's hanging. White knuckles. Staring at Meridei like he's thinking the same thing.

I nod.

"Good." An orderly lowers me to the ground, not gently. My knees hit the ground first with a loud thud. My welted skin drags against the tile as I crawl, following her to the exit. I'm wincing at the friction, rubbing against my blisters.

And I can't look at Dessin as I leave. I refuse. This is awful enough without seeing him look at me like Meridei's bitch.

The old, wrinkly priest visits me while I eat my lunch.

A cold chicken leg, three pieces of broccoli, and murky tap water. It's hard not to miss the Stormsage Keep. Their hot feast, nonjudgmental eyes, and the woman that helped me while I cried over mashed potatoes. Asena.

I'd love to live the way they do. Not caring what I ate in public. Not letting anyone tell me what my waist size should be. It must be heaven for women.

"How is being back in God's light treating you, child?" The priest takes a seat in the conformist's chair, clutching his Bible to his chest.

I smile at him weakly, then let my eyes fall away.

"Something on your mind?"

I shake my head. "No, Father." But I make a show of pursing my lips and keeping my eyes closed as I take in a deep breath.

"God tells me you have something to share with me," he insists. *Oh, does he now?*

But I sigh anyway. "It's probably nothing."

"Nonsense."

Showtime. Make it convincing. Be the meek, shy, fragile little girl this priest clearly expects all women to be.

"I had a dream last night. A dream of a burning bush and a booming voice that surrounded me. But I—I don't know what to make of it." I twist my hands in my lap, avoiding his eyes as if what I'm confessing is slightly embarrassing.

"A burning bush, you say?" He leans forward in his seat, adjusting his bifocals to get a better look at me. "Well, what did the booming voice tell you, child?"

"It said to find a man in the asylum… that he has chosen this man to rid the evil lurking in my mind. He can rid the evil lurking in all of the patients' minds." I huff out a short laugh. "I know, it's so silly, isn't it?"

But the priest is nearly speechless.

"What was the name?"

"Pardon, Father?"

"The name, child! What name did He give you?!" The priest is on his feet now, clutching my arms like he might lose his footing if he lets go.

On the inside, I smile, wide with my teeth.

"Judas," I say. "I'm supposed to find Judas."

The priest processes the information, blinking rapidly as if trying to figure out where he's heard the name. I give him a moment to put it together. Three, two, one…

"Judas! He is on the council!" He claps his hands together. There it is. "You must never ignore a message from God, child. He knew I would visit you today. He knew I would be able to find this man for you!"

I'd feel terrible for puppeteering a priest if it weren't for my skin burning like I've been dipped in a cauldron full of hot oil. I was raised believing in God. It was something my father and I shared before he changed. So, this isn't exactly making me feel like a saint. But it's necessary. I know that. Not to mention, there are people in this world that use God's word to attack, to judge, to hurt people.

"Oh!" He claps again, throwing his hands above his head. "Our Lord works in mysterious ways. I'll find him at once!"

I can practically hear Dessin starting a slow, dramatic clap in the next room.

As the priest leaves, I take a bite of my cold, chewy chicken and take a bow.

Dessin and I learn to communicate through knocks on the wall.

It starts while I wait for Judas to finally come and see me. I'm bored, and in searing pain from the whipping. My head falls back against the wall with a deep thump, and sure, it hurts. But wouldn't it be lovely if I knocked myself out on accident? Fell to my pillow and slept until my welts healed?

But I flinch as the wall booms back at me, like a dog barking on the other side of the fence. I stiffen, eyes widening at the coincidental replication of vibration and sound.

No, it can't be...

I ball my hand into a fist, hovering over the wall, considering how dumb this will make me look if I'm wrong. But I do it anyway. My knuckles bang against the stone twice, quick and hard.

And I wait. Anticipation eating away at my insides, crawling up my spine, and moistening my palms. This is so silly, and not worth the excitement, but look where I am. I'm sitting on a series of welts, locked away like an animal, waiting for a man that may or may not be able to help us based on prophecy.

Two knocks, thick and distinct.

I squeal, turning around to face the wall like a child opening a new present.

Dessin! I drum on the wall with both of my hands, so he knows how happy this just made me. He's here, we're sharing a wall, we're a breath away from each other.

I am not alone.

And my door opens.

I fall back down on my bed like I've been caught stealing. My eyes land on the tall, skinny man with pointed shoulders, charcoal black hair and white streaks on the sides. The face of a studious librarian.

And he stands there, staring at me. A subtle look of caution flashing across his gaze. His Adam's apple bobs as he closes the door, but not before Suseas slips in behind him.

My lips part. *No*. Why is she here? I didn't ask for her. I need to speak with Judas alone! How is he supposed to confess anything to me when she's breathing down his neck?

Suseas plants herself in the conformist's chair, scowling at me as if I kicked her cat.

"Miss Ambrose, do you even comprehend how foolish you've made me look?" She whips her curly hair over one shoulder, pinching her smoker's lips in a seething grimace.

Judas clears his throat. "Suseas—"

"I couldn't even bring myself to come see you when you first arrived. That's how sick to my stomach your betrayal has made me. Why must you be so selfish?"

I really did not miss this woman.

"May I speak with her alone?" Judas cuts in.

"After the investigation? Impossible."

"Investigation?" I ask.

Judas leans against the door, looking exceptionally older and exhausted. "My skeleton key was missing when the two of you escaped."

I hide my surprise. Judas slipped me a key to sneak Dessin out of the asylum that one night when we went to see the stars. They caught him.

"Of course, I couldn't have known that you or Patient Thirteen would steal it from my possession. But they had to do an investigation nevertheless." His voice is wise, yet quiet. He slicks back his hair with one hand.

So that's why he hasn't come to visit me yet. He's being watched.

"I'm so sorry, Judas. I should never have done that." I cover for him without a second thought.

He nods, finally meeting my eyes with a silent thank you.

"Am I not to receive an apology? I gave you this opportunity. I took you under my wing as if you were my own daughter," Suseas blusters, making a fool of herself with this performance.

"You're right, Suseas. I am so ashamed and remorseful for everything I've put you through."

"The punishment does fit the crime, I suppose." She looks down at her wristwatch. "Now, in fact. I do believe Belinda has you and Patient Thirteen scheduled for another dual treatment."

She's walking toward the door, and they're going to leave me. But he can't! I have to—

"In six months, you may finally understand the gravity of your actions. Maybe then you'll follow the drums of life and unsheathe your pride," Judas says without looking away, then he nods once and shuts the door behind him.

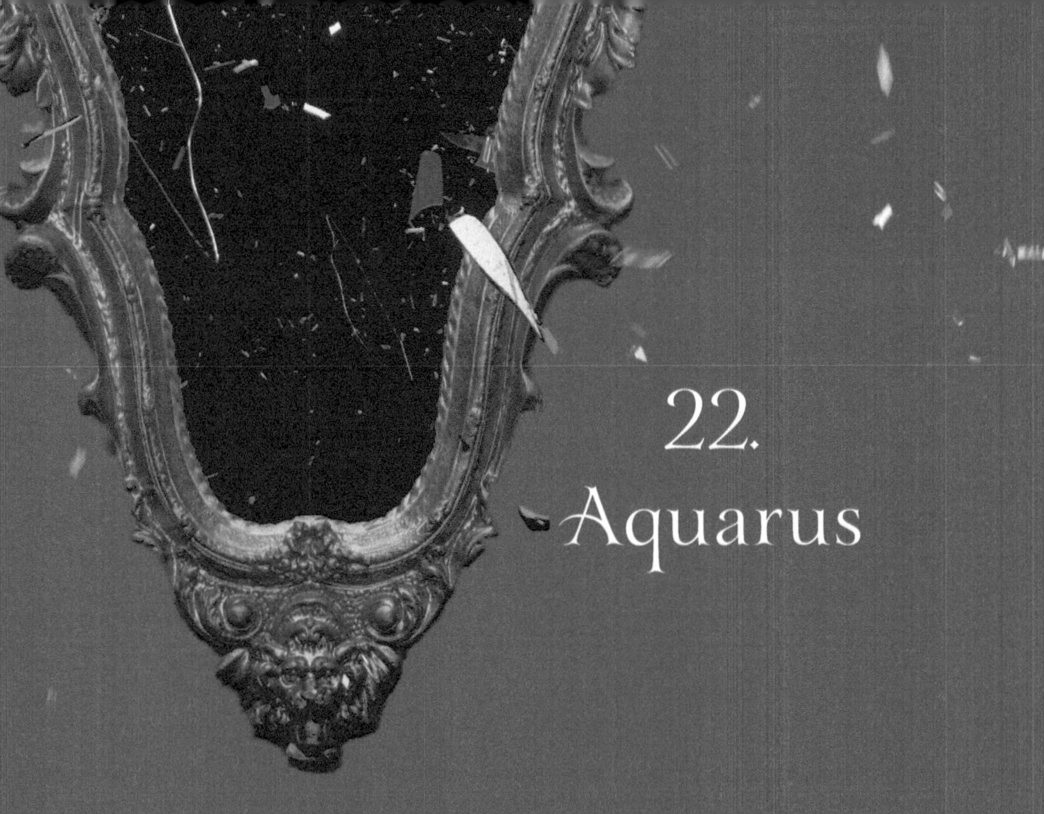

22. Aquarus

My greatest fear is coming to pass.

They finally sniffed it out. The one room I have dreaded going into above all others. The first treatment I witnessed when I was interviewed at the Emerald Lake Asylum.

"Lock them in," Belinda calls to the orderlies, ushering me to the large tub filled with cold water. "Our dearest Father is going to lead this one."

The simulated drowning. It now has two contraptions on either side of the tub. Dessin is already barred down by one of them. Metal clamps are molded around his head and neck, along with his upper body that is positioned over the cold water.

They're going to make us fight for oxygen at the same time.

I lock eyes with Dessin. And it's in one look that tells me he knows how terrified I am. We've had many conversations about this while traveling together. About how watching Chekiss drown and gag and convulse in the water was traumatic for me, and worse for him. About how more patients have died this way than any other treatment in the asylum.

I gulp as they lower me to the other side of him. My legs turning to jelly as my knees hit the floor. An icy finger with a long snaggy nail grates down my spine, filling my stomach with alarm and heaps of bile.

I spoke to him, my lips forming the words to Dessin. He nods once.

But what I don't get to say is that it was useless. He's being monitored like a hawk. I'll never get anything out of him while we're here. I need Dessin's counsel, his brains, his abilities to find the loophole.

Instead, my forehead and neck are attached to a large metal shackle of sorts, like an iron noose, a steel hand forcing me to face the small pool of water, clenching my waist to keep me still while my body goes into a rage of panic of epic contractions and spasms.

All for oxygen.

How terribly cruel.

"I'm told that the two of you have a certain fondness for one another. This concerned me. But it also opened my eyes to your ailments. The devil is using sexual attraction as a way to lure you both into his grasp." The priest walks around the tub so he can look between the two of us simultaneously. "But I won't let that happen. I will be your sword to combat him. God is stronger, God is more powerful. And so, I know exactly how to rid him from latching on to your souls."

Dessin sighs next to me, which is code for *I'd rather be drowned than have to listen to him.*

My lips twitch, but I wouldn't dare crack a smile and make this worse for us.

The priest kneels at the head of the tub. "I have blessed this water. And this baptism will not only cleanse the devil but abolish your feelings toward one another."

Dessin nods in front of me. "Effective."

Smart-ass.

"Now, I want you to think of the moment you first met. The moment you shook hands, or at least acknowledged each other's existence."

I'm flooded with the memory of walking down the hall to the thirteenth room, standing behind Dessin while Suseas told me not to say a word. Shaking his hand. The way he looked at me like he'd been expecting me.

You certainly took your time getting here, hmm?

It's like being shoved off a cliff. Like staying aboard a sinking ship. The metal contraptions begin lowering us to the water, making a creaky whining sound because it's rusted and overused. I can't help but let the panic set in, let it grip me by the throat. It digs its ugly claws into my chest, chokes the bravery from my lungs.

I'm not going to make it. I'll drown.

"Stay calm," Dessin whispers before our heads, necks, and shoulders are dunked into the frigid water.

He's right, of course. I've seen this done so many times. Chekiss always remained calm, saved his energy. If I try to fight it, I'll only increase my need for more oxygen.

But god, it's so cold. The icy tub sweeps my hair away from my face in a soft, golden web across the water. Dessin might even be able to feel it tickle his cheeks.

Stay calm.

I do as he says. I close my eyes, keep my breath locked tightly in my chest, and pretend to sleep. Pretend I'm taking a dip in the lagoon. Pretend I'm alone in my bathtub. And it's quiet. Peaceful, even. The sound of death waiting in the shadows to snatch my life from my grasp.

And suddenly, it's not so silent anymore.

Through the walls of my new cage, there's the stomping of feet throughout the asylum, vibrating the floor supporting my knees. There's the chanting of the priest, humming the Lord's Prayer over us. And finally, there's the sound of my upper body rattling the iron claw holding me underwater. My heart thrashes around against my ribs, throwing its fists against my lungs as if it wants out, it needs to escape my body draining of oxygen.

And just as I think I'm about to cross the line from silent suffering to full-on hysteria, the contraptions lift us from the water. Water streams down my face in a downpour from my hair. I gasp, controlled and deep. I know I can't start panting uncontrollably this early on. I have to replace the old air with new oxygen effectively.

But just as I peer under my wet lashes over to Dessin, I know immediately it's no longer him. But a new alter designed to take this on.

Calm, wise eyes like an ocean's horizon. He doesn't even open his mouth to breathe. He takes slow, shallow breaths in through his nose.

Aquarus. The god of sea. An alter that split to withstand the simulated drowning.

While the priest chants, I smile up at him. "I'm Skylenna," I whisper.

I know, he mouths, "Aquarus."

"Look at him, child!" the priest shouts at me in a fit of passion. "Think about your attraction to this man. Visualize it. *Feel* it."

And we're being lowered again. This is some kind of trained response conditioning. Every time I think about Dessin or another alter, he wants me to associate that feeling with drowning. I wince underwater.

Someone needs to inform this priest that he isn't saving our souls before we get sentenced to hell.

We're already in it.

We go through another five rounds of this until I'm heaving, seizing, and blubbering like a dying woman. Because *I am*. My lungs are going up in toxic flames, my chest is taking a brass-knuckle beating, and my eyes are practically bulging from their sockets.

I'm hanging over the tub with strings of saliva hanging from my mouth. And yet, Aquarus is mildly panting. I'm sad and also jealous that he's been through enough in his life to be able to have this many defense mechanisms in his arsenal.

I'm seeing spots in my vision, and the room sways like a boat in a storm. *Oh god, please don't let me be sick in this tub. Please, please don't let me vomit in the water we both have to get dunked into.*

Surprisingly, despite the internal flogging I'm suffering through, I haven't cried. I've been too busy struggling for oxygen, thrashing, screaming, begging.

The creaking noise of the contraptions flip on again and I let out a guttural moan, watching the water come closer and closer.

"No," Aquarus utters across from me. "Stop."

His contraption isn't lowering anymore. They're going to make him watch me drown alone now. These evil, vile, insidious human beings.

"I feel nothing for her! Your treatment has worked, Father!" Aquarus's voice is booming, tumbling across the echoey walls of this treatment room, complete with a hint of a northerner accent.

"Is that so?"

The tip of my nose touches the water first.

"Yes! But I don't want to watch you kill someone," Aquarus argues.

"She isn't going to die."

My face is submerged next.

"Oh no? Her lips have turned blue and her eyes have sunken in. Signs that her brain is not getting enough oxygen. You drown her for another round and you'll be carrying her out in a body bag."

The sounds are muffled and distorted as I'm lowered the rest of the way into the tub. This time, I don't have enough air to stay calm. I wasn't able to take enough breaths this time around. I sobbed, panted, and choked but I couldn't take any deep breaths. And now I'm certain this time will drown me.

Scarlett, I miss you every day.

I imagine her kneeling next to me, rubbing my back as she watches me die.

I'm sorry I couldn't save you. I'm sorry you had to relive your trauma by working in this hellhole. I'm sorry I wasn't there for you during your last moments on this earth.

My lungs are outraged. My throat is shredded to blood and acid. And my body goes ballistic, flopping, bucking, kicking, lurching like a bull being hunted.

I release the only air left in my chest to scream underwater. I have nothing left to spare.

Yet my body is reeling upward, like a fish caught on a hook. And I'm crying now. Hissing, shrieking, and wailing like a newborn baby.

I don't even hear what they're saying around me. I can't make out sounds or letters or emotion behind their statements. All there is, is the strangulated sounds of my agony. The raw, battered burning of my throat. And the bruising of my knees and legs from kicking and knocking against the tub.

It's all so terrible, so frightening. And Chekiss had to do this every goddamned day.

Suddenly, I'm being released from the clamps around my shoulders, unhooked from the deadly contraption, and dropped onto the cold tile floor to sob in a wet, pathetic bundle of my own exhausted despair.

And I wasn't aware before, but the smells of my own saliva, sweat, and now—vomit—are assaulting my nostrils. Because, yes, I'm doubling over, lurching up the rest of my lunch. But thank God for not letting me hurl in the water Aquarus and I both had to swim in.

A pair of hands, warm and calloused, are grasping my shoulders, helping me off the tiled floor, pulling me away from the mess I've made.

And when I look up, make out the furious glint in his dark-mahogany eyes through my tears, I know it's no longer Aquarus. It's Dessin. And he's unfurling those wings of murderous rage, plotting the deaths of everyone's soul in this room apart from mine.

"Hands off of her!" An orderly charges Dessin.

But Dessin puts up a single finger, pointing at the young orderly as if it were a poisonous weapon. As if no one would ever cross that finger.

"Another step and I'll carve your liver out and feed it to the priest." There is no questioning this threat. No second-guessing his meaning. The room falls silent, obedient, morbidly watchful.

"I'm carrying Skylenna to her room. If you want to follow me to ensure I don't make a break for it, by all means. But if she's touched, harmed, or interrupted while she's recovering—I'll know."

A thousand chills coat my pruney body. This entire experience must have been devastating to watch for him. And I know he must have been watching, if not from behind Aquarus's eyes.

I'm lifted off the ground, still dripping cold water between the two of us. My head falls to Dessin's wet chest. And I begin to weep again. Mostly out of relief, gratitude, and fondness for the man that would burn down the world for me.

Before he lays me down in bed, he looks away as his hands peel off my wet patient's gown, flinging it to the bathtub in my small washroom. As I stand shivering, he wraps me up in a bedsheet, patting me down like a child who's just taken a bath.

He looks over his shoulder to an orderly. "Bring her a thick blanket. Not one of these pitiful little sheets, but something warm. She'll get hypothermia if not taken care of properly."

The orderly stands in the doorway, stunned that Dessin even had the nerve to order him around. But Dessin senses his hesitation, growling under his breath before he whirls on the man.

"Do you want to risk pissing me off at a time like this? You think I can't get out of here? You think your wife Beverley won't be the first one I hunt down when I do?" He's in the man's face, itching to hurt someone. A human ticking time bomb before he loses it completely.

The orderly doesn't take another moment to consider Dessin's warning. He's running down the hallway, his chubby frame jiggling as he searches for what Dessin is requesting.

He turns back to me, cradling my face before he presses his lips to my forehead.

More tears slip from my eyes, but I hold in the audible sob that wants to escape.

"Lie down," he commands. "I'll be back tonight."

"But—what about the guards outside your door?"

"Fuck the guards."

I shake my head, feeling sleep fight to yank my eyes closed.

"You can't ruin the plan," I utter.

But it's no use. He's gone, already back in his room.

"You look like a wet cat, baby."

His voice sinks to the bottom of my stomach like an anchor, guiding me back to reality. I'm not sure how long I've been sleeping, but I don't know if I've ever been more comfortable in my whole life. I'm cocooned in several layers of thick blankets, warm, cozy.

But I'm still in the asylum.

I was nearly drowned. *Multiple* times.

My eyes snap open, then blink as if my eyeballs have dried up, sticky and thick against my lids. And Dessin is on his knees at my side, stroking my hair, lost in thought.

"A wet cat?" I grumble, rolling to face him. "You have such a way with women."

He smirks. "How're you feeling?"

"Like a wet cat."

A laugh, rough and deep in his chest. But he pinches his brows together, narrowing his eyes on my face. "I told you I didn't want to do this."

"But I'm doing it. I survived."

His jaw clenches and he's beautiful like this. The left side of his face glimmering in the dim light of the candle sconce. His large hand combing through my hair.

"The trick with the priest worked. He brought Judas to me," I say quietly.

"What happened?"

"Suseas accompanied him, so he couldn't speak forthrightly. It was a waste of time. And he's being watched because they suspect he had involvement with our escape when they found his key was missing." I rub my eyes and grunt. "I don't know that I'll ever be able to get an honest word out of him."

We would have to stay there for months.... And I'm not prepared to do that. Not after today.

"Did he say anything?"

"Well, yes, but—"

Dessin stops stroking his fingers through my hair. "Tell me exactly what he said. As accurately as you can recall."

I take a moment. Sigh. Stretch my legs under the blankets.

"Umm, he spoke about his skeleton key going missing. About the investigation because we decided to steal it to make our escape." I shrug. "That's pretty much it."

But Dessin isn't convinced. "How did he leave? I need you to try harder. Recite his words back to me."

"There isn't anything signifi—" But there is, kind of, isn't there? I watch how he turned to leave and close my eyes. But before he vanished, he said, "*In six months, you may finally understand the gravity of your actions. Maybe then you'll follow the drums of life and unsheathe your pride.*"

Dessin looks away, thinking, breathing, reciting the words in his mind over and over again until—he's on his feet, staring down at me like I should understand his sudden excitement. I'm groaning, propping myself up on my elbows to match his energy.

"What?"

"Follow the drums of life and unsheathe your pride." Dessin recites the words. Begins pacing the length of my room. "That's not right. It's supposed to be—follow the drums of *death* and unsheathe your *honor*."

"I don't understand!" He needs to do a better job of voicing his train of thought and explanations out loud.

"It's a quote from a war back in Alkadon, approximately four hundred years ago. One of the greatest devastations in history. They fought their sister country and won. But they lost a third of their population and suffered famine, plagues, and a corrupt economy soon after."

I stare blankly at him, still not getting it.

"Judas quoted it back to you knowing I would catch the incorrect words. But why?"

I shrug again. "You're on your own. I'm lost."

"Wait…" He stops pacing. "He said six months? You're sure?"

I nod.

His chin lifts in understanding, eyes wide in daunting black saucers. "It's a warning. In six months, there will be another great war. Possibly just as devastating."

"But how could he know that?"

Dessin is silent for a long moment. "We need more information. Do you think you can get him back to your room?"

I roll my neck, whimpering at the thought of keeping this act up. Performing for sadists like a little wooden puppet on a stage in a carnival for the criminally insane.

"Yes."

"I won't force you. We can leave on your word." He pauses, pursing his lips, a wave of murderous irritation taking hold of him. "Or mine if I have to watch you go through that again."

"I can do it." I smile weakly, reaching my hand out to run my fingers across his jawline. He looks like he's about to keep talking, going on about Judas and maybe another plan, until his eyes fall to my hand. A momentary distraction like my touch scrambled his brain, made him lose his train of thought entirely.

He snatches my hand in the air, examines it like a foreign entity he has just discovered.

"You're so cold, Skylenna." And he kisses my fingers, one by one, then my knuckles, my palm, my wrist. As I hum my approval, he seems to snap out of the tender trance he was in, locking eyes with me. But I don't get any warning at all.

None.

He's quicker than a strike of lightning as he swoops down, claiming my mouth with his own, stunning me with his hot, wet tongue sliding past my lips until I can taste him, I can feel his breath skimming the roof of my mouth. And I'm in his cloud of cedar and sandalwood aroma, a sharp breath to take in as much of that sweet, rugged scent as possible.

Urgent heat swarms between my legs. That tongue, wicked and invasive, makes my body tremble in hunger. It remembers his mouth licking my center. It remembers the way he threw my legs over his shoulders. It craves him like a new drug I've only gotten a small taste of.

"Skylenna." He breaks our kiss, gasping. "I shouldn't be doing this."

I make something of a needy moaning sound.

"You've been through hell today. I can't—"

"Can you take me to your room? I don't want to be here. Not in this room. In this bed."

I want to be in his bed.

I want to be in the thirteenth room.

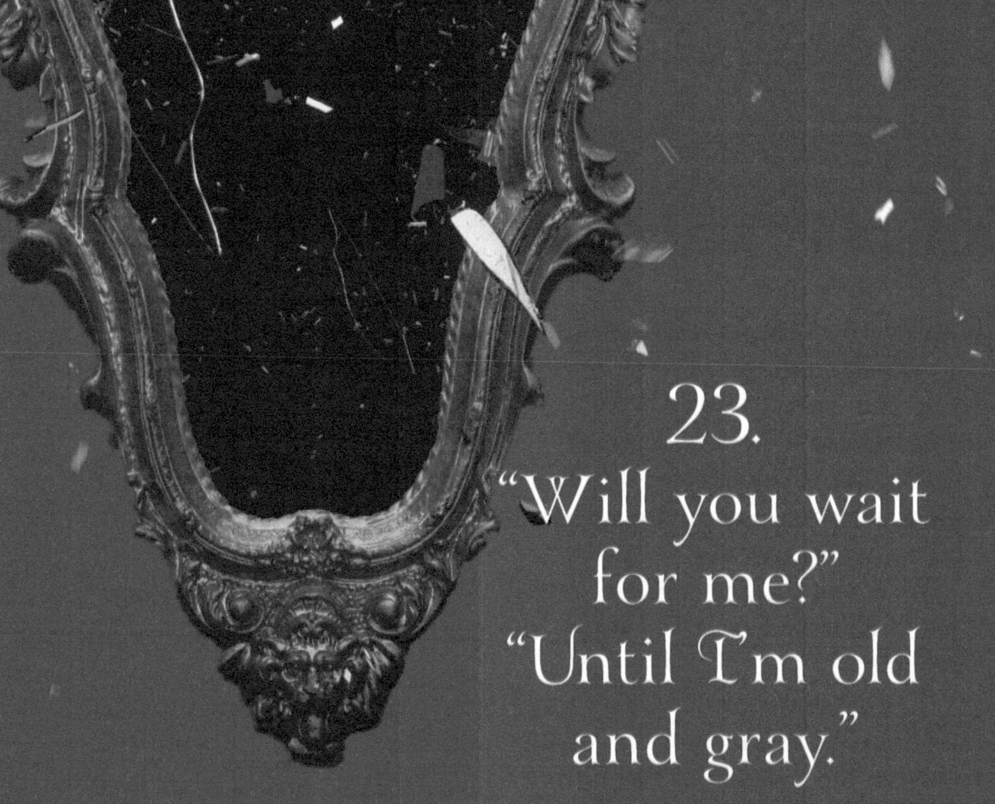

23. "Will you wait for me?" "Until I'm old and gray."

He loses his words, nodding before he scoops me in his arms, keeping me wrapped in two blankets. I'm weightless to him. A small bag of feathers. Because he uses one hand to hold me and the other to open the door. As we step out into the hallway, I tighten my hold around his neck, breath hitching in my throat as I look down at the guard.

He's—*asleep*. Head back against the wall, mouth gaping open.

Or is he?

"I drugged his flask," Dessin mutters.

I snicker. "Effective."

He closes the thirteenth door behind us, slowly, careful not to leave an echo that bounces off the walls. And I'm being draped over his bed, so carefully I stare up at him in shock. Like he's afraid to break me. He's far gentler with me than I've ever seen him with anyone.

It turns my heart to putty.

Dessin steps in front of the side of my face that's resting on his pillow. "Lift your head."

I blink twice. "Okay." I strain my neck, lifting as he tosses the pillow to the floor, sitting so that his lap is now my pillow. He coaxes me back down, combing my long hair to drape over his legs.

I stifle a shiver. His hands are the source of chills that want to run blindly down my nervous system. Bliss. Paradise.

"You're going to bruise here from the tub restraints," Dessin says, using one finger to lightly touch the side of my neck, the area I was being forcefully held underwater.

But then his hands are slipping under my shoulders, massaging the tight muscles across my upper back, then coasting up to my sore neck. I let out a husky moan.

"I never wanted you to go through that," he murmurs, more to himself than to me. "Not much throws me off, but that gutted me, Skylenna."

I nod against his hands. "I saw." He was trying to keep it together, but I know he would have carved that orderly's liver out. He would have fed it to the priest. In fact, I'm certain he was hoping they would challenge him.

His fingers dig into a knot, pressing on it gently. I arch my back, letting out another pained and satisfied moan.

But I did something wrong. Those strong fingers still, pausing midstroke. And he lets out a frustrated sigh. "That's exactly how you sounded when I had my face between your thighs."

That's all it takes. A surge of unleashed desire shoots through my core, causing my breath to hitch, my thighs to flex. His hands leave my shoulders, skating across my collarbone, and ending over the sheet that covers my bare breasts.

My entire body tenses. Because his palms are centered over my hardening nipples, poking his hands in a desperate attempt to get him to stimulate them. He groans quietly as he squeezes, letting his head fall in defeat at the feel of me.

"Fuck," he grits behind clenched teeth.

"More," I plead.

The movement of his hands is automatic, as if I've said the magic word. But his fingers surprise me. They pinch my nipples, twisting, plucking, making me squirm under the blankets. All of my thoughts and fears scattered like tiny rodents. The ache in my lower belly manifests into something wild, something hungry, something untamable.

Dessin's pants grow under my head, a steel mountain pulsing.

And he's up, slipping out from under me, darting to the wall farthest from the bed. He's mumbling to himself. "*I'll make things worse.*"

I sit up on the bed, careful to hold the sheet around my shoulders, my hips.

"I'm already yours," I tell him, swallowing down that agitated fear of rejection. "I'm yours to touch, taste, and love however you want me."

And with a calculated sense of purpose, I let the sheet drop to the bed.

And Dessin, with widening eyes and parted lips, gazes at my naked body.

It's like watching an ocean rev up into a wall, into a tidal wave. Like he's holding his breath. Like his eyes have returned home from a long journey. And he's swallowing me whole, taking in my bare legs, stomach, and breasts as if he wants to remember them. As if this may be the one and only time he gets to look at me. In this weak, golden light and cold, empty shadows.

He moves like he's falling, three hard strides to the bed, arms looping under my knees until his hands reach my hips, and he's spinning me until my head is lying where the pillow once was.

Here we are again, my legs hanging over his shoulders. But half of my back is on the bed, my lower half is hoisted up at an incline, and his hands are holding me by my ass. My gleaming pink flesh is open for him, just under his chin. Like he's carrying a meal, waiting to lick his plate clean.

"Dessin," I whine. Because I don't care for him to taste me again. I want that growing bulge in his pants. I want to feel him stretch me. Feel him pump inside of me.

He shakes his head. "I need to make you ready for my size, baby."

I'm not sure what that's supposed to mean, but he begins lapping me up anyway. Painfully slow licks up and down my center. And it's cruel. Like a punishment. The wicked wet heat slipping inside of me, bringing my body to tremble like an earthquake.

"Oh," I gasp.

"That's it," he murmurs against my throbbing clit. "Open up for me."

I lose all sense of decency. My hips buck against his face, legs clenching down on his shoulders. He moves his hands to bite down on my hips again, angling my pussy to his mouth exactly where he wants me. He's sitting upright on his knees, dipping his tongue in and out of me, until I can't take it any longer.

"I'm ready." My legs begin to drop from his shoulders. But this man, this alpha, yanks my hips hard back to his mouth. It's primal. Like an animal being interrupted while it feeds. He's blacking out at the taste of me, eyes gone dark and foggy and blind with insatiable need. I have never seen anything so sexy.

Like a rubber band, my tension burns between my legs, at the base of my gut, coils tighter, twisting until I'm sure something is going to combust.

I'm grinding against his mouth now, those plush full lips, and Dessin lets out a low sound in the back of his throat, guttural and agonized. It pulls the last ribbon of my hindrance undone. I'm screaming as thundering pleasure washes over me, legs spasming over his back.

One large, powerful hand flattens over my stomach, lowering my bottom half back down to the bed. I've transformed from a solid to a liquid, melting across the sheets.

"I want you—I want you to make love to me," I utter breathlessly.

A hand clenches around my chin, tilting my face up to look him in the eye.

"Are you certain that's what you want? You can handle me inside of you?"

"Yes."

Dessin towers over me, tossing his shirt to the floor, unzipping his white pants.

"I've waited so fucking long." He takes another look at my spread legs with feverish longing. "To have you tighten around my cock. To fuck you until you remember me."

I almost ask what he means—but his cock has sprung free, hard and enormous. I gulp or choke on my own saliva. I'm not sure which. My mouth waters at the sight. My blood, muscle, and bone crying out for it to fill me.

I nod my head, even though he hasn't asked me anything.

"I'll go slow," he says, using his strong arms to lower himself, wedging his hips between my legs.

I'm panting, watching the tip nestle on top of my center. "Eyes on me, baby. I'll let you watch me pull it in and out another time," he commands, devastatingly deep.

"Okay."

Slowly, Dessin nudges the head against my opening, working himself in as carefully as he can. And I'm needy, so unbelievably desperate to connect with him wholly. I'm undulating my hips against him, trying to speed him up.

"Skylenna," he barks. "I'm working my way in so it won't hurt as much."

"I don't care if it hurts."

He blows out a pent-up breath. "You will." And he's in a solid inch, stretching me, not painful, but it is overwhelming.

Another inch. I hold my breath and he watches my reactions closely.

Halfway in and I shriek. A ripping of flesh. A sharp stab of pain. "*Easy*."

He nods, stopping, letting me adjust. "God, look at you. So fucking beautiful. You're trying so hard to take it all."

I blink up at him, shifting my hips to let him know I'm ready for more. But now he's retreating, my slickness making it easy for his cock to glide out. Yet not all the way. Another small thrust and he's in. Retreats. Pushes back in a little farther. And he's making a mess of me, or it's the other way around. Because I'm dripping, soaking, lathering him in my aching need.

He's almost all the way in, but he keeps going back, hesitant to fill me completely.

"Dess—" A wet, slick sound comes from him, pulling his cock out another inch, and his eyes lock with mine darkly.

"Fuck, Skylenna." And I'm free-falling into his glazed eyes, his sudden feral need to take me in one bite. He isn't thinking clearly, isn't in control anymore as he pushes himself to the hilt hard enough that his hand finds my mouth, stifling the scream that tears out of me.

But it doesn't hurt. It's delirious ecstasy.

He withdraws again, only to slam back to the deepest spot of my insides. I cry out against his hand, still locked in the impenetrable gaze of his eyes.

I don't know if it's from the earlier stings of his entrance, or the fulfillment and captivating adoration of this man that we are closer than we have ever been—but I'm blinking away evidence of internal sobs.

His hand shifts away from my mouth, wiping away tears that run down the side of my face.

I want to tell him right now. How I really feel about him. I want him to tell me back. But as he pumps himself inside of me, over and over again at a slow and steady pace, I can see that look in his eyes. That yearning, that soul-shattering love. That man who will die for me. Who will tear down any man that wishes me harm.

His cock hits that spot that his fingers drummed against last time. I'm hissing as the coils inside me wind up, tighter and tighter, until I'm chasing that high, climbing that hill of pure bliss.

"I've never wanted anything more," he growls, crashing into me until I'm teetering on the edge, begging for more. I'm clenching my inner muscles around his shaft, and all I can make out from him is a rough, throaty rumbling. "Jesus. You're going to make me—"

But I'm already there, choking on my gasps as I whirl into climactic oblivion.

Dessin pauses to watch me before he unfolds. Before he attacks me in a vicious erotic frenzy, fucking me like a possessed man. Like an uncivilized barbarian.

It's too much, pounding into my sensitive area until I'm blind with the need to release again. A muffled roaring sound fills my ears, and I'm falling again. But this time, he falls with me. Roaring into my neck as his arms and hands clamp around me as he erupts, going up in smoke and flames. And even as the climax passes over him, softening his muscles, loosening his grip. He still doesn't let me go.

I hope he never will.

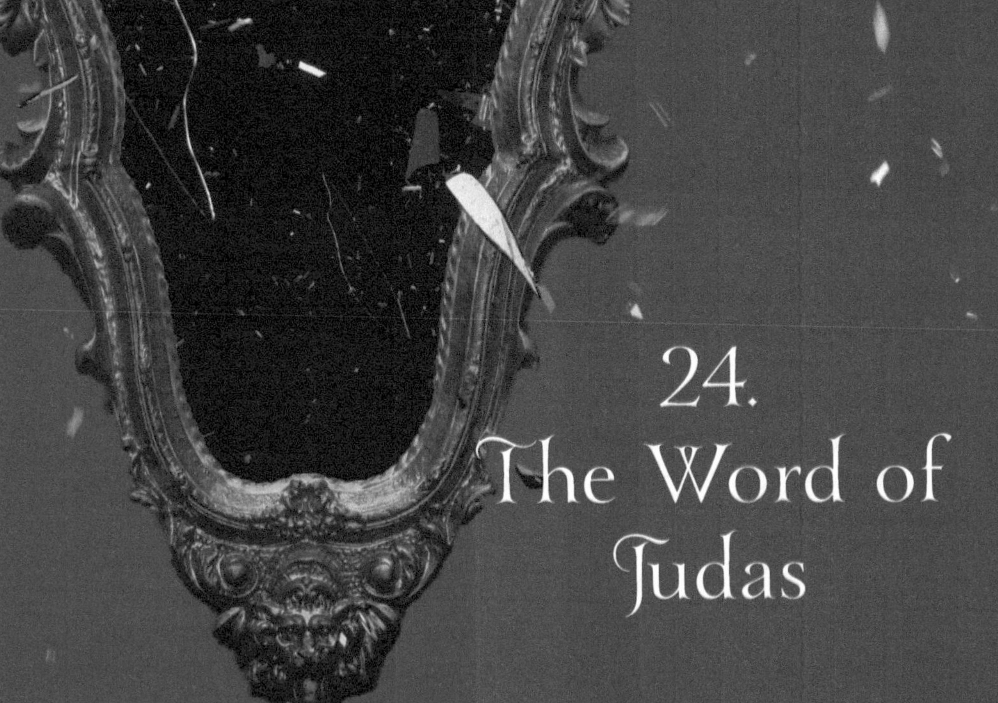

24. The Word of Judas

"Do you want to know the only terrible thing about what we just did?"

Dessin's question wakes me from nearly drifting to sleep. I blink up at him, raising my eyebrows and scowling. "Um. Not really, no."

"The little Grey bastard got too close to the front. I didn't notice until it was over though."

I laugh. "Oh. I guess that would be a trigger for him."

He rolls his eyes.

It wasn't twenty minutes after, as we lay next to each other, panting, recovering from the rigorous entanglement of limbs, that Dessin was in urgent need of being inside me again. I was still dripping, ready for him to work himself in again. And it was lazier, like he was in no rush, had all the time in the world. Taking his time, teasing me with slow strokes.

I don't know how we'll go another night without doing this. How we'll be able to look at each other and not collide like passing waves on a shoreline.

But when I turned over to get some sleep, Dessin folded himself behind me, curling around my body with his giant arms to keep me safe and secure while I tried to sleep.

Only, he hasn't been able to close his eyes. I can practically hear his thoughts bouncing off the walls of his brain.

"Have you always been like this?" I ask.

"Like what?"

"An insomniac."

He sighs against my hair. "Not always."

"I've seen you sleep very little since we ran away. And I've noticed the headaches."

"It's nothing."

Liar.

"Symptoms of when there's tension—among the other alters, I think." His tone is hard and clipped, like he'd rather talk about anything else.

"Anything I can help with?"

He chuckles. "You already have."

This deflates me more than he'll know. Is that what all of this was for? To release pent-up tension for him? To relieve him of stress?

The notion gnaws at me while we remain cuddled on his small bed.

"Is it safe for me to go back to my room?" I ask.

He hesitates before responding. "You're not going back. Not yet." Those arms tighten around me. It's misleading. It's dangling a carrot over my head. I have to remember what Kane said to me after our kiss. He doesn't see me that way.

"I am." I make an awkward attempt to wiggle out of his arms. "The priest will visit me again this morning. I'll get him to bring Judas to me again." I shake my head, looking over my shoulder at a shirtless Dessin. So handsome with his jawline of stubble, huge swollen chest, glistening, tan skin. "I'm ready to leave. This place is a cancer."

Dessin nods as I sneak back to my room.

Moments before the guard wakes back up, moments before someone comes back in my room.

The priest, dripping in sweat.

"Child!" he exclaims, rushing to my side. "Judas, the chosen! They won't let him speak with you alone as God has intended, but he gave me a message to give to you."

I straighten in bed. *Thank God.*

He slips out a rolled parchment from his white collar, passing it over to me. I do my best not to look too eager, faking slight interest, placing my fingers delicately around the roll.

Skylenna,

They say when the Lord has given you a dream, it should not be ignored. Have you read the script from the Bible—what book was it? Ruth. You should read the passage "Your people shall be my people, and your God, my God." Must I be the only man that God has chosen in this asylum to do his work? Leave it to me. I accept this responsibility. Will you let me know if He passes on other dreams? Find me if He does. You need only speak through one of God's children, the priest. Soon, please.

Judas

(And there's a symbol of a burning tree).

There has to be a message buried in this. I read it over and over again, trying to find a hidden phrase that maybe I would know.

I nearly forget the priest is still in the room, hovering over my bed. He raises his eyebrows expectantly.

"He's going to do everything in his power to follow the Lord's request of him." I smile, nodding. "Thank you, Father, for having the courage to do God's bidding."

After the asylum falls asleep on this night, the howls and moaning of its patients dimming as the moon reaches the top of the sky, I knock on our wall three times to signal to Dessin that I need him to come over.

It takes him three minutes.

He closes the door quietly behind him. And that tall, broad frame, devilishly handsome eyes, and powerful presence brings a violent rush of heat between my thighs. I have to pinch my knees together, take a deep breath, and avert my eyes just to focus on why I asked him to come. But before my gaze bounces away, I swear I see his hands clench into fists.

"Judas sent me a message. But I can't figure out what it means." Truthfully, I've gone over it a hundred times, although I won't admit that.

Dessin holds his hands out to take the letter from me, but as I place it in his palm, our fingers glide over each other, causing a wave of friction, a small jolt of adrenaline.

He sighs, reading it quickly. Blinking. Looking away. Then reads it again.

"An anagram," he says.

I wait for him to continue.

"The first word of each sentence is a message…" But his pause, his slow hesitation, twists my gut. His eyes snap up to mine, mouth parting as if I'm supposed to know why he's suddenly taken aback.

"Skylenna…"

"What? What did he say?!"

His throat bobs as he looks down at the letter again. But it's too late, I'm on my feet, snatching it from him. Pointing at the first letter of each sentence, reading it out loud.

They say when the Lord has given you a dream, it should not be ignored. Have you read the script from the Bible—what book was it? Ruth.

"*They—Have—Ruth*," I say slowly, then stop. Read it again. "Ruth!"

Dessin paces.

"Who is he talking about? Who has Ruth? Is the asylum holding her as a patient now too?"

But Dessin wouldn't be worried about the asylum. He could break anyone out of here in his sleep. No, something is poking at him. Something has him flustered.

I begin reading the rest. *You should read the passage "Your people shall be my people, and your God, my God." Must I be the only man that God has chosen in this asylum to do his work? Leave it to me. I accept this responsibility. Will you let me know if He passes on other dreams? Find me if He does. You need only speak through one of God's children, the priest. Soon, please.*

"*You—Must—Leave—I—Will—Find—You—Soon.*"

Dessin stops pacing to examine me. "Demechnef. They've taken Ruth as a way to lure you out. And if they lure you, they know I'll follow."

I'm on my feet, letting the letter slip from my fingers. "Dessin." My voice is a husk of sound, a broken echo through the wind. What have I done? I thought I was without loose ends when I ran with him. I've been alone, without family. I never thought my actions would hurt my friend.

Ruth. Sweet, kind, doe-eyed Ruth.

"We're leaving now." He aims for the door.

"Will they—do you think they'll hurt her?"

Dessin stops, hand hovering over the handle. "I've seen them do worse for less."

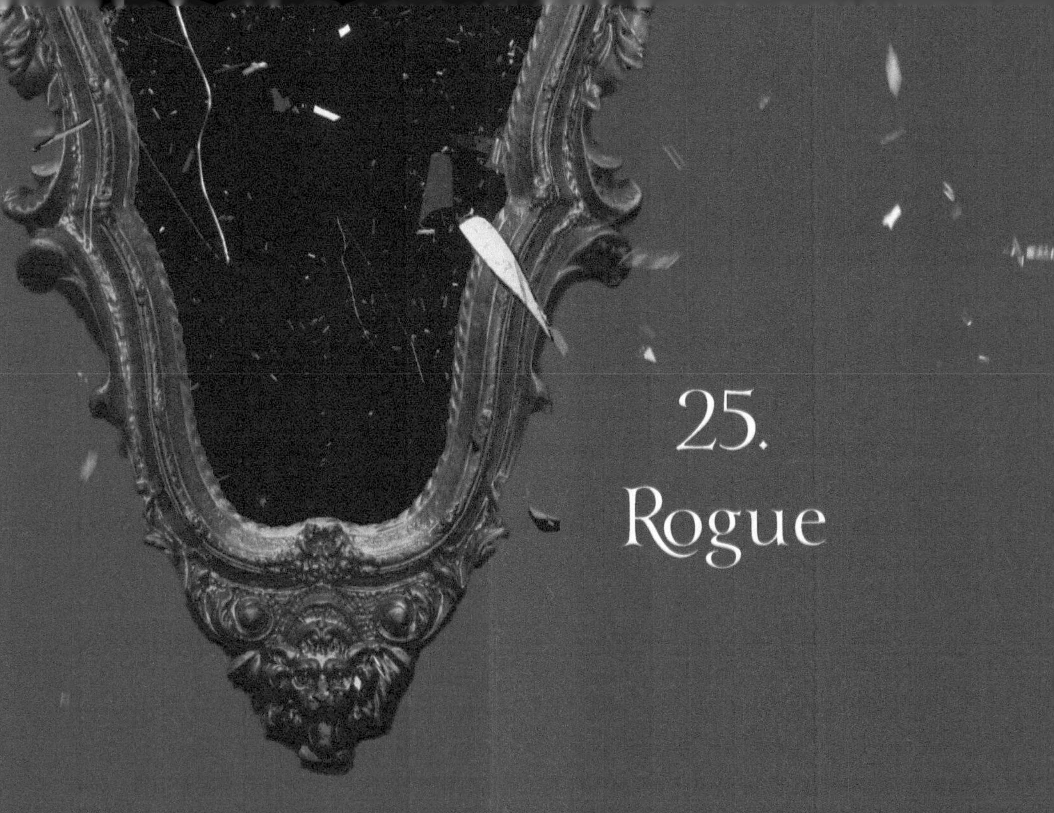

25. Rogue

As we duck our heads through the hidden door in the asylum basement, a crisp morning breeze greets us, along with an early morning sunset. We rush to uncover the motorcycle from its shelter of branches, weeds, and vines.

"We need to get out of these clothes when we find somewhere safe to stop," I tell him. My white patient's gown is thin and nearly see-through.

"Our packs are—"

The engine starts. But that isn't what stops him from speaking.

Another engine starts. *Behind us.*

We turn around to see another motorcycle. A man rolling up slowly behind us. Black leather pants and jacket. Black helmet. No face.

"Hold on," Dessin orders.

I hook my arms around his waist and cling tightly. We're moving. He must be pressing down on the gas enough to dig a hole beneath us, because we're now flying as fast as DaiSzek runs through the trees. The faceless man is following behind us. I should be more worried than I am. But it's *Dessin*. The same man who could unarm, and cripple all of the guards that tried to restrain him on more than one occasion at the asylum. The same man that wiped out soldiers in the North Saphrine Forest. This *one* man on a motorcycle isn't a match. I know it. Dessin knows it. But does Faceless know it?

Dessin takes sharp cuts around trees and over large roots to throw off our tail. It doesn't work. But I can practically feel the engines working harder and faster in his brain. He's got something. I sense the smile peeling over his mouth.

"Skylenna?" he calls out. I tap the muscles over his stomach to let him know I hear him.

"Yes?"

"Whatever you do… don't let go!" he roars and a grin is sharpening his voice like a new blade. I nod against his back. *Oh, god.*

Dessin jerks the bike to the left in one forceful movement. I clamp down on my teeth to brace myself. The tail end of our bike grinds against the dirt, spinning around, mud and leaves and pine cones fly up around us in a wave. We take off in the faceless man's direction.

Twenty miles per hour. Forty. Seventy.

We are moments away from meeting with the other bike in a nasty collision of metal and blood. But Dessin veers slightly to the right, swinging his right leg over the bike to meet his left leg. His hands remain on the handles, but his legs fly out to the left and kick the faceless man off of his motorcycle.

The force is a tremor in the earth. A blast from a bomb.

Faceless is ejected like bread from a toaster. He hits a tree, back first, no grunt or cry. He only lies there.

Dessin maneuvers back onto the bike and speeds off.

I can't see his face, but oh, how that smile suits him.

26. Missing Memories

I recognize the direction we are heading in. It feels like I'm retracing my steps in a dream.

Holding on to Dessin, I wonder how this will end. Surely he knows we can't run forever. What if… death is the only way out? We're fugitives. We don't get the chance at a peaceful life. And what if we are caught? What would happen to me? They want *him*. Not me. I'm deadweight. A liability. Would I be killed for my association with him? No, Dessin would never let that happen.

I rest my cheek against the center of his back. The wind beats against us, the sound of it rushing past my skin. I've forgotten how sweet the air smells in the city, like baby powder, vanilla, and roses. Being among trees and dirt and endless diverse plants, that artificial sweet scent was cleansed from my nostrils.

My thoughts skip back to last night. The way our bodies moved together in a frenzy, the way his arms bore down on either side of me. The cedar scent of his skin. The fullness I felt as he stretched his way in. I can't stop my stomach from flipping around like a happy child. Or the way my heart gyrates in my chest at the memory.

But the cold look in his eyes, the way his lips shaped those awful words.

I don't feel that way about you.

Maybe it's because he has too many opinions in his head. Maybe one of them is attracted to me while the others look at me like a friend or a sister. My fists clench against his hard, ripped stomach. It doesn't matter. They shouldn't toy with my body or my feelings.

"We're here," he says.

I sway off of his back, adjusting my eyes to the sunlight. The motorcycle trembles as he turns it off. He's standing in front of me with a look that tells me he knows he's in trouble but I should listen to what he has to say before I freak out. My direction of focus falls on the house behind him.

My house.

My *father's* house.

The house he nearly beat me to death in.

"Let me explain." Not Dessin anymore. Kane. Soft sweet eyes, begging for mercy.

"What the hell did you do?!" My tone comes off angrier, and far more violent than I have ever spoken to him before.

"Skylenna—"

"No!" I grab his forearm and yank it toward the bike. "Get me out of here. Now!"

"Please, just let me—"

"You know what he did! You were *there*." My voice breaks off at the end, to something broken and weak. "You saw what he did to me."

His strong, rough hands are covering my ears, fingers combed through my hair.

"I *was* there," he says sternly. "I saw you. I saw your helpless body covered in blood. I thought you were dead!" Agony. Raw agony like someone has just jammed their hand into his chest and pulled out his heart, still beating, still connected to his other organs. "It wasn't until you saw me through your tears and blood that you smiled. You *smiled* at me. Even through your pain, you had hope that I had come for you."

I drop my head. Grab the back of his wrists for support. "Why are we here?" I whisper.

"Jack left something behind for you."

My head springs back up. The question of *what* is written all over me.

"He left it for you as a last resort. In case you ever came into any trouble."

"How do you even know that?"

He blinks slowly, working his jaw. "He told me before he died."

Oh.

"Can I wait outside?"

A sad smile of reassurance. "Of course."

He tells me he'll be right back. I can imagine him walking through the front door. Through the door cut from an oak tree. Squeaking when it opens. Air decompressing when it closes. I remember the scent of the living room. The scent of old books, the scent of the living dead. A lifeless home.

I remember when he would come down from his fits and find enough room in his heart for remorse. Sometimes he would cry. His pale-green eyes would bleed tears that would last forever. His cheeks would glisten and his forehead would perspire out the remaining alcohol in his system. I'd watch him as he'd kneel down in front of me, holding my small hands, explaining through heavy sobs how he tries to resist the madness, how his love for me can't defy science. A grown man whimpering like a child. It was so easy to forgive him when he'd hug me so tightly and say over and over again, No matter what I do or say, *don't ever forget how much your daddy loves you.* He'd put ice on my bruises, he'd feed me after leaving me in that basement for ages.

I believe *that* man left me something for Kane to go find. The man that felt remorse. I wonder if Violet ever felt remorse for selling her daughter's body? Maybe Scarlett was right, maybe I did get it better than she did. Being locked in a basement is better than being locked in a closet. Being neglected by my father is better than being molested by strangers.

Looking at this house, two stories, with three windows on each floor, the charcoal paint has chipped so much the house almost looks brown. The room is three-fourths covered in black shingles. A painting of a haunted house.

Kane reemerges in the front doorway of the house. He looks at me apologetically. Holds up a wooden box. I straighten my back. A million guesses of what it could be flopping around my head.

"There's something else too." He holds up an envelope. "This is what I really came for."

I reach out for it. He jerks his hand back. "Give it!" I order, lunging toward him. "My father left all of this for *me*."

"Not all of it." He sighs, turning the envelope around. One. Name.

Kane.

Shut up. "No…" Eyes drop to the name. Jump back up to him. I gasp. "Explain."

He wears a reserved expression. Pained. Tired. "That day I saved you from him. That was not our first encounter. He left something for me that will get us out of this mess. Or at least give us leverage."

I step away from him. "If that wasn't your first encounter with *him*… then it wasn't your first encounter with me either."

He nods. *How many secrets are you keeping from me?*

My frustration pressurizes in my gut, morphing into something ugly, something angry with clenched fists and burning flesh. I scream. This is my limit. I spin around and scream again. His hand touches my shoulder. I swat it away.

"How can I trust you?" I shout at him, throwing my hands in the air. "All I've ever wanted is to know you! But you keep everything from me. I swear on my life if you don't tell me why right now, I'll—I'll just—"

"When you first met Dessin, what did you feel?" he asks, voice rough and demanding.

I blink. The thirteenth room. His white shirt, white pants. He knew my name. He knew everything. He smiled. His smile was kind. His eyes were warm. He wouldn't hurt me. I *trusted* him.

I look down. "You know how I felt," I say through my teeth.

"You felt safe with us. You trusted us despite everything you were told about him. Despite how he treated everyone else around him."

"So? What does it all mean?"

His eyes are pleading. He reaches out and takes my hands before I can pull away. He kisses my knuckles softly. I close my eyes. A shiver of memorable pleasure pulses through my soul. And it shows up again, that sense of trust and safety.

"Because you have trusted me long before that moment in the

asylum. You just don't remember it." He's holding my hands against the sides of his jaw.

What? "Oh, god." I gasp. I've known him long before. *How?* The holes in my memory. The beating from my father. "I don't understand."

"Skylenna, I shouldn't have even told you that. But I can't live with myself if you don't trust me. You have to know. There's a plan. There's a reason I can't share with you how I know you. How I knew Jack. I made a promise. There's a plan in place. This envelope—" He waves it in the air again. "It's part of the plan. I swear to you, you'll know everything soon. *Everything*. But we have to get your friend back. Okay?"

I'm numb. I can barely nod. Ruth is the only thing more important than me being enlightened by the missing memories of my past.

27. The Ambrose Trust

Kane and I take a moment alone against an ancient angel oak tree, sitting on separate sides of its thick trunk. I stretch out my legs, holding the wooden box on my lap, running my thumbs along its rough edges.

The box is heavy, like its purpose is to be a glorified paperweight. I tap at the gold lock attached to its opening. "It's locked," I holler over my shoulder.

I hear him dig into his pocket. He passes me the small golden key, reaching his arm around the tree to hand it to me. *What if I get a letter too? What if he explains his illness to me?*

I unlock the box, set the lock down on top of my left thigh, and lift the lid to unveil a heap of shiny objects. I lean down and narrow my eyes to get a better look. So many colors, red, green, gold, silver. Glittering under the sun. They sparkle and wave hello to their new owner. I recognize some of the gems. Rubies and emeralds. *Diamonds*. Gold and silver. He left me valuables. But for what? What am I supposed to do with them? Find a jeweler and get them attached to earrings and bracelets so I can finally look like a respectable woman in our society. Kane and I don't need diamonds where we're going.

I sigh, using my index finger to push a few diamonds aside, mixing them with the green tint of the emeralds. I hook my finger around a chain. A golden chain. Attached to something heavier and bigger than the gems piled up among each other. A circular gold piece. Two rings hanging on either side of the thick locket. *Oh, it's a necklace.*

I hold the locket in my hands. The ring hanging on the right has a marquise cut diamond on it. *Are these wedding rings?* I see the line opening on the side of the locket. My fingernails dig in to open it. *Clink.* Open. An oval photograph. My father's face. *Violet's* face. Babies. Two of them. It's our family photograph. I feel my lips part ways, sucking gusts of air through my open mouth.

The photo is black and white. But I know that cheekbone. That dark hair. He's kissing Violet on the cheek. Her mouth is open like she's laughing. She's wearing a white gown in a bed. Was this just after she gave birth to us? They each hold an infant. The two happiest people on earth. *What the hell happened to them?* I've only ever known them as the two coldest people on this earth. How can one photo hidden in a locket tell me otherwise? I caress the back of the locket as I try and imagine how different their lives were before we were born. How long were they together? Did we ruin their marriage? Their minds? I feel a rough texture on the back of the locket so I flip it over. Words are engraved on the back. Words I never expected to read.

You will
always have
our love and
our hearts

I stare at their message in shock. Love? *Love?* The man locked me in a basement for days at a time. He nearly beat me to death. Violet sold her daughter's body for money. Had strange men come into their home and molest her. How dare they say we have their love and their hearts? They had enough to put into this locket but not enough to give us a decent childhood?

I throw the box and locket out in front of me and cross my arms.

Kane is kneeling at my side. The envelope is sticking out of his pocket. I reach forward, pull the locket out from the mess the open box made and stick it in Kane's palm.

"*Here,*" I say. "Behold, the loving parents that raised Scarlett and me."

He examines the locket, opening it to see the photo, flipping it over to see the loving words they left for us. Holding the rings between his thumb and the tips of his fingers.

His gaze moves at a glacially slow pace to meet mine. He wants to say something. *Please just say it, Kane.* He purses his lips. He holds it back. His eyes bounce back and forth between both of mine.

"You should keep this." He holds out the locket.

I shake my head.

"I think it's important that you do."

I gasp. "You remember how my sister died, right? Violet, the woman in that photo, did that to her. She *killed* my sister." I push his hand away. "I'll never put that around my neck."

He looks at me, holding back, edging on advice he wants to give. His hand reaches for the jewels now covered in dirt and grass.

"It looks like Jack left you a trust fund." He changes the subject.

"I don't want it."

"I think this was his way of making sure you would be taken care of." He pauses. Watches me with uncertainty. "He left it in the basement for you to find."

At this I can't help but laugh. "In the basement, huh? He gets one last laugh from the grave." This is both ironic and simply ugly. The one place I would never step foot into again is the one place he leaves me valuables to start a new life. If Kane never went down there, I would have gone the rest of my life without it. Surely he knew that, surely he could have guessed that the basement was not kind to me as a child. *He* was not kind to me as a child.

"I'm going to put it back where I found it," he says quietly. "Until you're ready to open it again."

28. "Please comeback for me."

Thirty years ago, Vexamen soldiers launched a missile from inside the Dark Wood, it blew up parts of the old Demechnef headquarters, forcing the government to evacuate, to find new protection and go into hiding.

Since then, no one has figured out where they reside now. It's one of the most famous secrets. But of course, Kane knows where they now hide. It's impressive, really. One of the greatest secrets of the last couple of decades and Kane knows the exact location. And not just that, he knows how to get in. He knows their weak points. He knows how to escape.

The only issue I foresee is how does he plan on getting Ruth out undetected? A valuable prisoner. The only leverage they have to lure him back.

I can see he has been working out the small details of his plan since we left my father's house. I want to ask him what the envelope was. How could my father possibly have what we need to help us?

We pull up on his motorcycle back to the Red Oaks. His back and shoulders are filled with tension, like he's hanging from a wire hanger in a coat closet.

My fingers touch the center of his back. "Kane?"

He doesn't look back at me. "You have to stay here." Something like a heavy, occupied coffin weighs down on his voice.

Stay? "No, I'm going with you."

He shakes his head. "You can't." It gets heavier. "I'm going to get her out alone."

I push him in this back. "I can help!"

"Skylenna… if you come with me, you'll be my priority. You'll be the only person Dessin cares to keep safe. If he has to choose between Ruth or you… he'll choose you."

I can feel the outer edges of my eyes stretch beyond their resting point. He gets off his motorcycle and looks at me. His eyes are tired. Tired of having to update me on the knowledge that runs on an endless loop in his mind.

The sadness of having to separate for the first time casts a dark shadow over me. It rolls over my organs like cookie dough. I grab onto his hands. His warm skin soothing my trembling hands.

"Can you tell me everything's going to be okay?" My pleas are aggressive.

He leans his forehead against mine. And with the warm floating scent of forest and cedar, he whispers, "Of course it will be."

"And you promise to come back for me?"

I fight to understand the complex agony in his eyes. It's familiar and crippling for me to look at. It's the look of a warrior recalling the most brutal moments in battle.

"I will *always* come back for you. Until hell freezes over."

"And even then." He pulls me into his body, harnessing his warmth, and projecting it over me. My face finds the soft spot above his collarbone. I squeeze hard enough that he won't be able to forget the way my body fits into his.

"DaiSzek is going to stay with you. He'll watch over you until we get back."

Hot oil jolts through my nervous system. "No!" I object. "No, he's going with you! You need all the help you can get!"

He shakes his head. I can see his mind is made up.

"Kane—listen, either you leave me here alone, or I go with you.

You're not going on a suicide mission. You'll need him to have your back. Besides, I know how to hide in small spaces."

He looks behind him, in the direction of where he needs to go.

"*No*." Firm. Gruff. A growl from the bed of his throat.

"This isn't negotiable. I let you take the lead, make the decisions, figure this all out alone. Not this time. Give me *this* decision to make. He's going with *you*."

His forehead is knotted together with permanent fury. "Don't make me do this," he says slowly through his teeth. He's... angry. He's *furious* with me. I've never seen Kane angry. Not like this. It's Dessin's trait. But those eyes are still warm, kind, gentle—despite his fury.

He gets back onto the motorcycle. DaiSzek is farther along, waiting for him.

Kane finds one last second to look at me, and through that barbed wire fence of anger, he looks at me with eyes that say, *please be here when I get back.*

29. Demechnef Hide-and-Seek

It's been *far* too long.

I did just as he asked. I found myself running through the tall Red Oaks, jumping into the lagoon. Hiding under the waterfall. I watch a leaf fall from a branch, landing on the surface of the water, and although it reminds me of a sweeter time, with summer warming my skin, picnics, and chirping birds—I can't shake the painful kneading in my gut. My fingers turn into flesh-colored raisins, and *it's been far too long.*

I fight the *what-if* thoughts that pollute my train of thought over and over again, because what if they were caught? What if I have just lost everything? What if I'm alone? Completely *alone?* What would I do?

Maybe there's something I can do to help them. If I draw them out, Dessin and DaiSzek might get the time they need to make it out.

I duck under the curtain of water hammering down on my back. I could lead them to the Evergreen Dark Wood, and if I scream loud enough, maybe the Nightamous Horde will find me, hide me, take me in. But I'll need to do something that they can't ignore. I know I promised him I'd wait and hide, but they won't kill Dessin. They need him. DaiSzek, on the other hand, is a thorn in their side that they would gladly kill. *I'm doing this for him.* I'm doing this to make sure they all get out safely.

I jog through the shallow side of the lagoon. My knees practically touch my chest as I raise my legs to get out of the water and to the trees faster. I cling to a baby red oak tree as I fish my hiking boots out of my pack, my hands snatching and throwing them on my feet faster than a spring on a mousetrap. I have to find something that would be suitable for a distraction.

The contents of my pack are dumped and scattered in the grass. A few knives I'm careful not to cut my hands on, a thin roll of rope, a blanket, extra clothes, fire starters, and—

Fire starters.

These little packages, wrapped in yellow plastic with a red flame symbol, are something Dessin packed for me. He said *if we ever get separated and you're in trouble, crack these, then put some distance between you and it.*

Well, I'm hoping Dessin isn't the only person's attention I will get from setting them off. I cram everything back into my bag and haul it back over my shoulders. There are seven fire starters. *Seven.* I scan the area, mapping out my line of destruction.

I wince at an image of DaiSzek being hunted down and killed by men with machetes, cutting him open, mounting his head on their walls like a prize. Without another thought, my hands are unwrapping and pulling out the brick of chemically soaked wood. There's a dotted line I trace a finger over, then break it down the middle, like cracking an egg. Smoke seeps out the middle, carrying a scent of gasoline and ammonia. I set it on the crook of a tree trunk and its branch. *Run. Run. Run.*

It sparks and crackles as I tear off to the second tree, ripping off the next wrapper and splitting it to ignite. The loud sound of a cannon erupts from twenty yards behind me. The sudden impact sends an invisible shock wave, shaking the air around my ears. Even my skin vibrates. But I keep going, tossing the fire packs over my shoulder.

Soon enough, it sounds like a war of good and evil is erupting behind me. Like fireworks and grenades collaborated at the same party. And when I turn around, I am standing upon several Red Oaks engulfed in flames, a page directly from Revelations torn straight from the Bible to play out before me. With the vibrant blood leaves dancing in the chaos, and dark mushroom clouds growing wider and higher to pollute all of the innocent white clouds in the sky.

They're going to see it. They're going to *hear* it. They're probably already coming after me. I break my trance from admiring my work. But I'm all turned around, in the high of the panic, I can't remember which way I am to run to seek refuge with the Nightamous Horde.

I suppose my only option is to just *run*. Get as far as I can, give Dessin enough time for him to escape with my friends, and come get me. I start moving my feet again. Maybe if I'm lucky, an animal like a night dawper will emerge to hunt the men that are hunting me.

I wish Dessin were at my side. He would know what to do. He'd know where to go and how to trick them. I jump over a root climbing out of the ground and duck under a low-hanging branch. I evaluate my options, just in case they do catch up with me. I could climb a tree. I could scream. Other than that, I really don't have much else.

Normally, I wouldn't have the endurance to run this long. Before I left on this journey with Kane, I was out of shape, never used this much energy for an activity. But hiking mountains and running away from Demechnef have been the workout of my life.

I think about my sister. About how she never would have lasted this long, about how she hated the outdoors. Hated the smell of rain before a storm. Hated dirt under her nails.

I think about her and pray.

Scarlett, I have a bad feeling about this. I don't think he'll be able to save both me and Ruth. Please watch over me. Please don't leave my side.

My long strides are becoming taxing and the burn in my muscles slows me down. With the stretch of my right leg moving forward, I realize I've come up on a hill going downward. A steep slope. I drop my body to the ground to roll down a bumpy slide of dirt and weeds.

As a tide of dust kicks up in a cloud, I wrap my arms around myself to protect vital organs from the rocks and sharp edges. Something unmovable stops my course, slamming into my back, knocking the air out of me.

I'm momentarily paralyzed, unable to turn my head, unwilling to open my eyes. Pain bursts through every cell, every joint, especially my lower back. What's even worse… there's a good chance no one is chasing me. How would they ever react that fast? I might be running like a madwoman through an empty forest.

I groan and prop myself up against the back of the tree, patting myself down, getting rid of the dirt and leaves, but also checking for any broken bones. All good, I think.

A gentle vibration and humming skip off the bark of the trees, along with voices. The humming roars louder. Is it—no, it couldn't be. A buggy?

I lean my head back against the tree. There's nowhere else to run. And even if there were, I can't outrun a buggy. I wonder if they have Dessin and Ruth. Maybe this is a good thing. Maybe I'll reunite with them. Let's face it, I wouldn't have survived out here alone. At least now we can plan an escape together, wherever they're taking me. I release a shaky breath.

"*Skylenna*!" My name is roared from the far distance.

I sit up straighter. No…

And again. My name. Only one voice sounds like that. My whole body recognizes it. Buzzing with heat and excitement, that tone shoots through my veins.

Men in the same uniforms they were wearing when they fought Dessin in his room. With the man that brought the sickle. Merlot-red blazers with bronze tassel linings. They swarm me, surrounding the tree I'm slumped against like approaching a wounded animal.

I wasn't going to resist. But now the fear of being taken away from Dessin has set into my bones like a cancer. As the men lift me from my seated position, I jerk my arms, trying to free them from captivity. But there are too many of them. Their hands tighten around my wrists, forearms, back of my neck. And then I hear it again.

"*Skylenna!*" So far it's practically a whisper in the wind.

"Dessin! Dessin!" I scream, stiffening in a panic. I start letting my body thrash against the brute force. "No! Please! *Dessin*!"

But his voice is worlds away, nowhere close to us. If I could just run to him.

Hands cover my mouth now but I still fight to scream against the pressure. I'm lifted into the air and thrown in the back of a buggy that isn't really a buggy at all. It's as if they transformed the back seats into a cage. It has metal bars shutting me in. Closing off the fresh air, now stale and reeking of chemicals. I throw myself against the bars, all while continuing to scream for him.

The buggy races away from the flaming trees and smoke signals filling the atmosphere. "Dessin! Dessin!" I bellow. And I don't stop screaming, not until a sting pricks into my neck.

We move faster. The trees blur as we speed away from them.

Away from Dessin.

30. ...And The Devil You Don't

I feel the separation more than I thought I would. It's almost like ripping a warm blanket off of someone while they sleep through a cold night. Almost, but worse. It's losing a limb after war. A soldier waking up after a long slumber, glancing down to find a missing leg.

No Dessin. No DaiSzek.

I woke up in a cage. A cage, like the one you lock your dog in when you're away. It's big enough for me to sit up, but not enough to stretch my legs out. The room has a ceiling with arches so high it could make a second room. The chandeliers are as dim as candles, providing very little light to the cherrywood walls and matching hardwood floors. I thought I'd be brought to a dungeon, a torture chamber. But this resembles a grand study, a gentlemen's seating area.

There's a metal table in the center of the room holding tools like scalpels and needles and gauze. My pulse does an uncertain dance under my skin. *What are they going to do to me?*

I look down at my knees and see a white cotton gown. The kind like the one I wore in the asylum, but softer, finer quality.

I can't believe I just got out of the asylum to be locked up again. And I don't even know where I am. The room is silent. Still. Have my captors left me? Will they come back? The idea is too close to the basement. Cold, murky, lonely basement.

I wrap my arms over my chest and am jerked by a tug. There's a skinny clear tube connected to the inside of my elbow, connected to a needle sticking inside my skin. I try to pull it out, but a shock shudders through me, up to my arm, my shoulder, spreading out like a spider web into my neck. It makes a popping sound, like a whip making contact with skin, and I scream, falling back onto the bars of the cage. I examine my surroundings, frantically this time, straining to see movement in the shadows. *Am I alone?* There's a strong aroma of bergamot and amber with an underlining kick of cigarette smoke. The windows on either wall are frosted with bars. Thick sets of brown curtains are hung over each window. There are velvet tapestries, shelves of books, glass cabinets of glass bottles—perhaps for a chemist or a healer.

As I start to relax, but not quite, I catch a brief movement off to a dark corner of the room, a subtle shift, like the uncrossing of legs.

"How are you settling in so far?"

I jerk both backward and upward, hitting the top of my head on the cage. *Was someone watching me the whole time?* I grip the sides of the bars and gawk at the dark corner. It's as if someone sits in a chair, out of the flickering glow of the sconces and chandelier, because all I can see are the caps of their knees.

"You have curvier birthing hips in person than I would have guessed." His voice is slippery like a water moccasin with a slight lisp where his teeth touch his bottom lip. The personal remark leaves me stiff while the restraints of my cage mold into my back.

"I, myself, have always hated the starving look on our women. It's just so peculiar how folks can think that attractiveness is based on how tightly a woman's skin hugs her bones. Should we start digging up graves, plucking the dead from their tombs and showcasing them in the windows at boutiques? They're all bone, right?" Did I say his voice was slippery? I meant *slimy*. He sighs. A thin cloud of smoke rolls into the atmosphere. "No, all of that…" A long, arthritic finger wafts around like a wand directed at me. "…Extra cushion around your bosom and rear is what *should* be admirable. The plump consistency is like biting into a juicy peach, don't you think?"

From the pitch of his voice, I conclude that he is in his mid to late thirties. Maybe slightly younger. The knobby point to his knees and finger make me imagine a tall, scrawny man. With a pointed nose and bladed cheekbones. He still does not show his face.

"Are you in the habit of ignoring your superiors when asked a simple question? Or are you one of those deaf and dumb girls?" An edge to his tone. An irritable pinch.

"Deaf and dumb," I answer. My impatience and sarcasm getting the best of me.

"I see." A flippant smile paints his words. "At some point, you might find my conversation to be quite stimulating. It'll certainly be a highlight of your day."

The fear that springs to life inside me is almost visible when I look down at my sweaty palms. If his slimy voice is ever the high point of my day, I'm in for it. Sadly, I don't sense even a syllable of dishonesty in the time since he first spoke.

"What's your name?"

He crosses his legs again. Dark-scarlet-red pants and shiny black dress shoes. "Albatross Ivast. Demechnef royalty by day. Savant by night." An awkward beat of silence, like he's waiting for me to give him applause. "And you're Skylenna Ambrose. Homeless. Conformist. Fugitive."

I let my head rest against my new bed, letting my chin face upward. I'm done talking for now. I don't know what any of this is. I'm scared to ask because he might tell me. Right now, I don't want to know. I know I've been captured by Demechnef. I know wherever I am, it isn't good. I'm locked in a freaking *cage*. There's a tube that's hooked into my arm that sends sparks of pain if I try and remove it. Right now, ignorance is bliss. Right now, I want to forget I'm sitting in a cage, talking to Alba Knobby Knees and close my eyes. I want to pretend, just for tonight, that my head is on Kane's chest, with his arms and a big blanket around us, sleeping under the stars.

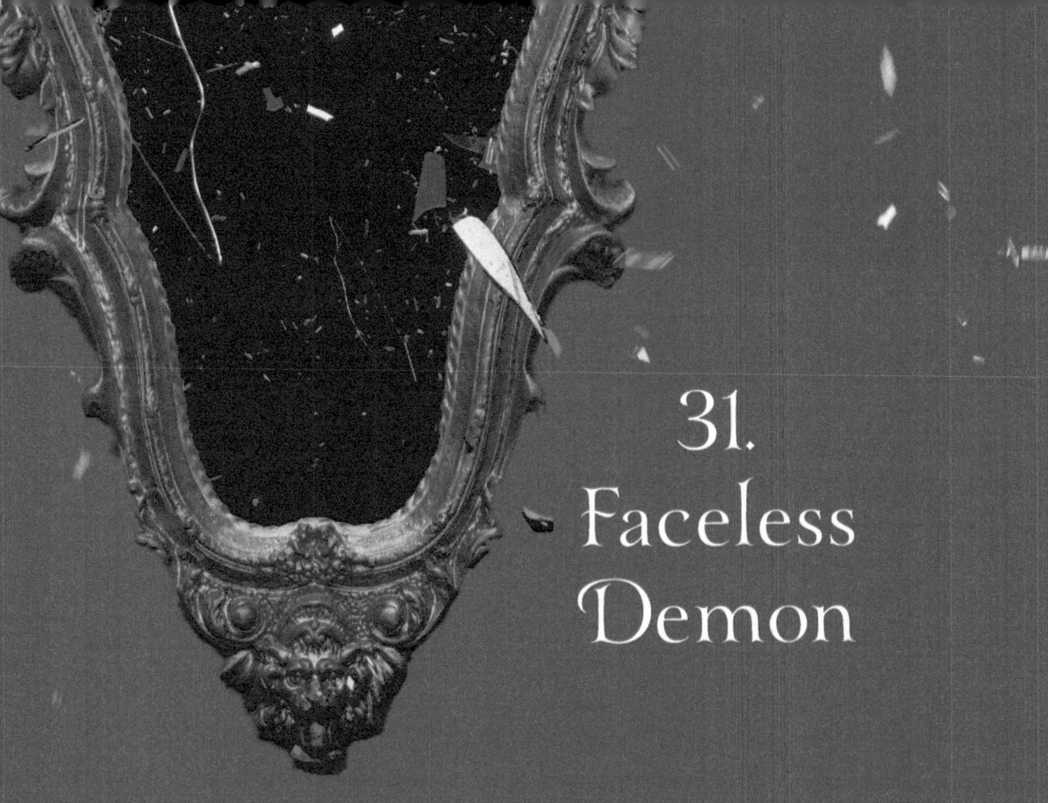

31. Faceless Demon

The smoke seeping off of this morning's roast is making my stomach growl with each breath I suck in through my nose. This is sometimes how Kane chooses to wake me up. Hot, fresh food. Right out of the fire. The smell of roasted deer, rabbit, or boar triggers my empty stomach. The aroma coaxes it out of a deep sleep and it gently shakes me awake.

"Are you hungry?"

I groan. *Not all of us can survive on four hours of sleep, Kane!*

"It's going to be fascinating seeing you get used to constant hunger. Most women in our society have to get used to it, but you clearly didn't follow protocol. How'd you get away with that anyhow?" Before I open my eyes, the chilling voice throws the memories of last night back into my mind like grenades. The disparaging shock of not waking up to a campfire with Kane and DaiSzek is like eating expired food, fully expecting a delicious treat.

"Thought we discussed your poor response time, girl!" A touch of anger. Only brief.

I part my lips to reply, but there's a snap, like stepping on a branch, and a blinding pain stabs along the left side of my body. I yelp and thrust my eyelids open to examine what force assaulted me. Nothing. Cage. Cabinets. Chandelier. It's my collarbone, it feels broken, definitely broken, like it's sticking out of my skin. I gulp down the nausea swelling up my throat, the taste of bile and dread coating my tongue. And I can't move, can't examine myself, can't dull the searing agony blistering under my skin.

A whimper slips from my gaping mouth. *Oh, god. Please help me, God.*

"Well, aren't you going to cry?" His input adds to my urge to vomit.

"Drop—dead," I say between labored breaths.

Albatross spits in disgust. "Now listen here, girl, I make the rules. If I dropped dead, you'd drop dead. I demand appreciation for my company due to that fact, *at least*."

I can't answer. Sweat is forming a glossy shine on my skin, and the pain is debilitating, it's as though someone stabbed me in the neck, and then broke the blade off inside me. It's lodged, and with each movement I make, a new rumble of pain ignites.

He sighs. Adjusts himself in his seat. "Now let's move on from this! I hate obedience conditioning, it's catty and boring." That long brittle finger emerges from the dark corner, into a warm spot that the glow of the chandelier reaches. "You keep sweating like that, I'll have to give you a bath."

As if time reverses, like rolling yarn back into a ball, the pressure, the sharp discomfort, the blazing pain in my shoulder and collarbone start to disappear. The ugly jolts of sensation from a broken bone crawl back to where they came from. I release a groan of sweet relief. My head falls back against the cage, my muscles let go of their fighting stances. I breathe again. In and out. Rotating my shoulder around. *Wait, what?*

I stare at Albatross's dark corner. "What happened?"

"Oh, now you want to talk to me, hmm?"

"Yes. I'm sorry. I thought you broke my collarbone."

"I know. Neat trick, hmm? There are so many advantages we have over Vexamen. We're quite clearly the dominant country. Far more advanced in most areas of war, technology, alchemy. It's entertaining that most civilians are consumed with their looks, their bony bodies, their floral-infused baths, and their grand balls. And then you have what's here, going on under their noses, and no one cares to try and find out. Such a superficial breeding ground."

"But what did you *do* to me?"

Hands slam down against what sounds like a leather chain. "Does everything I say just go in one ear and out the other? My god, I would have never guessed you to be so dense!"

"I'm sorry. Please continue."

"When I had you delivered, I really thought you would be this bright, astonishing young woman. I thought we'd have a lot of fun. Especially considering who your travel companion was. This has been a *monumental* letdown for me so far."

I cower back into my corner. *No more broken bones, please.* If Dessin knew how Albatross was treating me, he'd be torn to pieces. Where is he? Does he know where I am? Does he know what's happening to me?

"I can imagine where your feeble train of thought is going right about now. Usually, at this time, the thoughts that blossom from fear is reason to keep hope alive. Is someone coming for you? You won't have to suffer too long. Am I hitting the nail on the head?" Albatross is no longer a man to me, sitting in a dark corner. Albatross is a faceless demon that has no human form. It only exists to torture me with its desperate need for conversation. I wish I was like Dessin right about now. I wish I could find my way out of any situation like he can. I don't ever want to be a prisoner again. At least when I was a small child, I was locked in a basement with lots of room. This cage is going to deform my limbs. I won't be able to stand up straight. If I were like Dessin, I'd imagine all of the terrible ways I would make Albatross suffer for this. I would even taunt him the way Dessin would. I would play mind games with him and love every moment of it.

"You have permission to relieve yourself of those thoughts. After studying your travel companion for years and years of his early life, we have installed every precaution to keep him out. There will be no rescue mission."

But unfortunately, I'm not Dessin. I'm Skylenna, and I don't have a way out.

I can finally stretch my legs. It's almost euphoric to be able to let my muscles expand. Point my toes. Roll my ankles around. My spine was starting to feel cramped, a geriatric soreness and ache building in my lower back. My neck feels like a doorknob in a snowstorm. Completely coated in ice, not enough warmth to get it moving again.

"My name is strung along a family tradition. I can't remember if I told you that yet or not." Albatross's weaselly voice knocks me back into my misery. "Oh well, I'll tell you again. My great-grandfather's name was Crow Ivast, and my father's name was Cardinal Ivast. I think it's oh so fascinating that my name also can mean *psychological burden*. Which in your case, the irony is downright cruel."

I attempt to roll my shoulders and ease the new birth of tension. They won't move. There's a pressure like a seat belt or a straitjacket keeping me nailed down. My eyes peel open, sticky and hot. And there's an old woman hovering over me, eyes of a Siamese cat, the grim expression of a gravedigger. My body is strapped down by leather restraints. I wiggle abruptly, testing my bounds, unable to control the rising panic. What could they possibly plan on doing to me strapped down like this?

"If you didn't catch the tradition pattern, Crow, Cardinal, Albatross—it's that we are all named after birds. It's the family crest. Because we're a family of savants, it means the sky is the limit for us. Isn't that interesting?" Albatross asks from the same dark corner of the room. I can't lift my head to look at him, but I know he's in that same spot.

I learned my lesson last time. *Always* answer him. "Very interesting," I say, trying my hardest not to pant. The woman injects each of my limbs, a jab followed by a quick sting. I squirm to get her to stop.

A hand smacks me across the cheek, a nail scraping underneath my eye as it makes contact. I gasp at the electric pang of shock that devours my face. My eyes involuntarily begin to water, and my nostrils burn the way they would if you swam upside down underwater.

"You move again and I'll use my fist, girl." Her old shaky voice matches the crow's-feet around her eyes and lips. She walks over to adjust the IV, filling it with a cloudy, gray liquid. I can't stop my legs from trembling. The more I try to keep them still, the harder and faster they shake.

"Oh pardon me, Skylenna, I haven't introduced my grandmother. This is Absinthe Ivast. She was married to my grandfather, Crow. She assisted my grandfather way back when they lived in Alkadon. My grandfather was viewed as some sort of psychologically impaired freak there."

"Oh," I mutter, unsure of how to entertain his incessant need for conversation.

"He migrated to Vexamen but was recruited by Abraham Demechnef and Orin Blackforth. They truly saw the value of what he was capable of."

"I, uh, always forget that Demechnef is the name of a person."

This makes him chuckle. "Of course you do. It doesn't surprise me, only special bureaucrats know that it is indeed a family and not a faceless government or military agenda. The Ivasts are a prized value to our leadership."

Old Grandmother Absinthe is now measuring the lengths of my limbs. She takes the measurements of my ankles to my kneecaps and then my elbow to my shoulder cap.

"I didn't realize your family was so honored."

"My grandfather, Crow, has begun the greatest trials of experimentation the world has ever seen." His knobby knees, covered in red velvet, cross. "My father and I have each helped carry it out after his death. I'm going to win the war for our country with what we have uncovered."

"That's wonderful. So you take your orders from Abraham Demechnef and Orin Blackforth?" I ask, keeping my head still under the restraint that's making my forehead numb.

"No, not anymore. Now it's from—" He stops himself. Hesitates for several moments. "Your travel companion doesn't tell you all of Demechnef secrets?" There's caution and baffling amusement in his tone.

Why does he keep referring to him as my travel companion?

"Told me what?"

He snickers, sounding like a rat feasting in the garbage.

"Well, I certainly cannot tell you. And you know that clearly pains me to withhold information as I do love educating you." I'm beginning to understand the nature of Albatross's personality. He's narcissistic and deeply enjoys the thrill of knowing what others don't know. Privileged. Shallow. Insecure.

"Could you educate me on something else then? Like what you have planned for me?" I ask quietly. I've decided I'm rather talented at playing alone with mental anomalies like this.

He clucks his tongue. "Part of what I have planned includes you being in the dark about what I have planned. If you knew, it would all be corrupted."

The old crone examines the insides of my ears with a tool I can't see. When she opens my mouth, I realize the lining of my tongue, mouth, and the inside of my esophagus are drier than the taut skin on Absinthe's elbows. I haven't had food or water in... in.... How long have I been here? A day, I think. Perhaps two days. I've blacked out and fallen asleep a couple of times.

The ache in my stomach is growing like the constant need I have to stretch my body out. The discomfort has been so constant, it's turning into a dull and annoying pain. I want to ask for water or a couple of crackers, but I'm scared of getting the back of old Absinthe's bony knuckles. My under eyes still throbs.

"Her vitals say she's dehydrated and low on several key nutrients." Absinthe turns to the dark corner, the red-covered kneecaps.

Oh, thank God. I don't even care what they give me, I'll take anything.

Silence.

"Feed her then."

Yes! I could have gone longer, of course. I spent half my life hungry. But the thoughts would overtake me. Will they ever feed me? Do they want me to starve to death? How long will I wait until I have even a small sip of water?

Absinthe leaves my side to fetch a meal and in the time she's gone, Albatross stays quiet. Watching me. Or maybe he left too. A deep, controlled breath comes from his corner.

Definitely watching me.

I wait patiently in the awkward silence, knowing he has his eyes glued to me, knowing that he knows I'm aware that he is watching me. But I don't even mind. I'm going to eat. I'm going to have some water. I'm going to be okay, this might not be that bad. Sure, there was the illusion of my collarbone breaking. That was rough. But now I understand him better. I can keep myself out of harm's way until Dessin comes for me. Maybe I'll even ask Dessin to spare him.

Absinthe approaches my side with a rolling table. I try to suck in any whiffs of hot food but so far, I've got nothing. My eyes strain to my right to try and see what she has set out for me. Is she going to feed me herself? If so, I won't argue. I just need to keep up my health.

Another deep, controlled breath from Albatross's corner. Absinthe looks in his direction. She nods. Picks up what sounds like a cup or a plate. Touches it to my lips. *Thank you, Grandma Absinthe. Seriously, thank you.*

"Open up." Her grumpy tone demands my cooperation. *Say no more, Absinthe.*

I open my mouth, unable to prop up my head to swallow whatever she pours into my mouth. Probably water first. I'll manage. Something metal enters my parted lips and sits between my front teeth. My pulse picks up. Absinthe hovers over me with a rubber tube, aiming it for the hole of the metal mouthpiece, the contraption that is prying my mouth wide open. The tube is inserted. It moves against my tongue, slowly pushing against the back of my throat.

Wait... I make a grunting sound as it touches the part of my tongue that makes me want to gag. It's going too far. *That's enough!*

Adrenaline and terror shoot down my spine. My tongue and throat spasm in my mouth, a natural response to force an unwanted object out. The tube is pushed out, only by the tiniest centimeter.

"Just for that, I'm not going to be gentle, girl." Absinthe thrusts her body forward and jams the tube past my best muscular defenses. My throat opens up for the tube as its edges scrape past my uvula and tonsils. A throaty, gargled scream involuntarily generates from my chest. I start to gag as it moves farther down my esophagus, followed by choking and exasperated sobs. My eyes fill up with fluid, not the kind from any particular emotion, but the kind that happens when you get hit in the nose or get something like a speck of sand stuck in your eyes.

Dessin, please come now! I need you! Please, help me! Help me!

Help me!

The more I jerk around, the heavier the urge is to dry heave, so I hold still. Just like the broken collarbone, it helps not to move.

With wide, bloodshot eyes, I gawk at the raw eggs being dumped down a funnel connected to my tube. The orange globs and clear, slimy fluids swirl as they drain down my tube. I lurch at the sight of it falling into my mouth. This triggers the gagging, like a contagious attack of my body rejecting the objects prying me open. My abdominal muscles burn from the rapid contractions, loosening and tightening, making my chest, gut, and back inflamed.

By now, the eggs must have completely filled my stomach to the brim. Because the pressure in my gut is stretching my tummy outward, protruding against my ribs. *TAKE IT OUT, I'VE HAD ENOUGH!* But she picks up another pitcher, pouring clear liquid into the funnel. It's water, I think. Just water. But the pressure is building in my core, my stomach protruding and my rib cage expanding. *I'm going to explode! Is this how I'm going to die? I'd rather starve!*

Choking sounds escape my mouth, like a deer with an arrow plunged through its throat. In a guttural heave, the water sprays back up from the funnel, showering both me and Absinthe with water, runny eggs, saliva, and bile. It gets in my eyes and nose. Absinthe shrieks, shaking her head back and forth, trying to dodge the downpour.

"You awful girl!"

The tube is snaking back up my throat, slimy, gushing, stretching the walls of my throat. I blink furiously, trying to rid my eyes of the water. But Absinthe isn't being gentle. She grunts in frustration as she tugs in sloppy movements, trying to avoid the egg and saliva coating the tube. I cough and choke and gag as the feeding machine is taken away from me. The ghost of the sensation still lingers. I want to sit up, to cough out the phlegm and whatever else remains. But my body is still bound to this table and I'm not going anywhere, anytime soon.

Scarlett? Why is this happening to me? Can you ask God to protect me?

A blazing sting like the back of a frying pan makes contact with my cheekbone. I yelp as the blow glides against the bone. Absinthe made true on her promise to strike me with her fist. Both the cold, aching feelings of fear and anger form in my chest.

My first assessment was wrong. I thought if I played along, responded to Albatross like he wanted, then I could survive this without torture. *I was wrong.* They're going to keep hurting me no matter what I do.

"I would have willingly eaten whatever you wanted me to! You didn't have to force it inside me!" I release dry sobs formed from anger and hate.

Albatross chuckles. "So would most women, Skylenna. Want to know a secret?"

"Sure!" The sarcasm I intended fails to saturate my scratchy throat.

"When a woman in Dementia gets a little extra skin, perhaps she has trouble losing the baby weight after giving birth, or maybe she doesn't have self-control around sugary treats—she gets brought to the woman's ward of the asylum for reconditioning. Force-feeding."

"I know all of that," I snap.

"Fine. But what you don't know is that the women who never come back, get sent to me. For my own studies. And when I'm done with them, Demechnef uses them as fucking dolls for our soldiers." His tone is suggestive, like I should be personally offended. "Including your travel companion."

I may as well have been slapped across the face. Again. "You're lying."

"A fucking doll is a woman, near death, unable to move or speak. The soldiers bury their cocks into her so they can think clearly when their hormones start to dominate their thoughts. Barbaric, isn't it? And to think, your travel companion was by far the most gruesome—"

"I don't want to hear anymore!"

Dessin would never do that. He couldn't. But—I remember the way he thrust into me, filling me like a madman. Is that because he no longer had access to these—*fucking dolls*?

No. This man is a liar.

I wish I could glare into his eyes. See the evil that is tucked away. Know the color of his hair so I could accurately visualize myself pulling it out of his head. Or perhaps I could visualize Dessin doing that for me. Where is he? I know he must have an idea of where I am and what's going on, but then why hasn't he come for me yet?

Strings of my saliva hang from my mouth, connecting me to

Absinthe like a gooey spiderweb. She swats at them like they're lethal, like they'll cause her wilted skin to sprout boils.

I squeeze my eyes shut, smelling my own bile and the saltiness of my spit covering my mouth and chin. I hear Absinthe's footsteps as she shuffles away to clean herself off. I'm cold again, wishing I were back in the asylum after the simulated drowning treatment, when Dessin made the orderly bring me lots of blankets. I imagine waking up again to his soothing, deep voice, those rich brown eyes. But I'm here, exposed on this table, my medical gown as thin as a baby's eyelash. Trying to get warm in this position is like sleeping naked next to an open window in a blizzard. Goose bumps creep up my legs and arms, and once again, I shiver involuntarily.

"I would stop shaking if I were you," Albatross warns. And I flinch, absentmindedly I forgot he was still here.

"Why?"

"If Absinthe sees that you're cold, she'll give you a reason to be cold." A long slurp of what I would guess is from tea or hot soup. "You really wouldn't want an ice bath so soon after being force-fed."

Another shock of fear clamors inside of my nervous system. *What is their goal here? At least at the asylum, they believed they were treating insanity.*

"I'd suggest thinking of something nice and warm to get the cold sensation off your mind." Albatross confuses me with his help. First, he makes me believe my collarbone was broken, then he instructs Absinthe to force-feed me in the most violent way, and now he tries to help me from being forcibly given an ice bath.

I try to nod my head but I'm still firmly strapped to the table. I remember the first winter I was living with Scarlett. We were snowed in, the ice hardening over our windows and door. I was sitting in the family room, pressed into the corner of the couch without a blanket. My body was shaking much like it is now. I was too scared to let her know I was in need of warmth because it wasn't my house. I was just a visitor, a guest. I didn't belong. It wasn't my place to start a fire or go find a cozy blanket. I just had to sit and tremble, rubbing my hands against the back of my arms to soothe the bumps away. And I remember when Scarlett came in. She stared at me, watching me shake. She quickly ran out of the room and came back with the comforter from her bed. I could tell it was hand knitted. It made me wonder if our mother made it, because as far as I knew, Scarlett did not know how to sew. She draped it over my body and ran out once more. The second time she came back, it was with hot cabbage soup in a cup so I could hold it in one hand and drink it without a spoon. It was bland without any flavor, but the hot steam washed over my face, thawing the tip of my freezing nose, and the broth ignited a soft flame in my core as it traveled to my stomach. And if that wasn't enough, she started throwing wood into the fireplace, and before I knew it, there were the yellow flames licking the tops of brick. And my body was surrounded by both the pulsing heat of the fireplace and the kindness Scarlett shared with me that day. She snuggled under the blanket with me that night. Our hands entwined and our toes tucked under our legs.

The memory of her thin body pressed into mine stops the trembling. I open my eyes and Absinthe is back, glowering down at me like a hawk getting ready to pick apart a field mouse. Staring back up at her, I notice she doesn't have eyelashes or eyebrows. That must be why she looks wild and feral and withered down to the bone.

Thank you for saving me from the ice bath, Scarlett.

"Do you wish to sleep now, dearest?" Albatross speaks softly. Like he is a king granting a homeless man land and title. At least, that is how I feel. Because right now, there is nothing greater than sleep. Sleep to escape this madness. Sleep to shut the door on this putrid slice of hell. I make a sound to verbalize my gratitude and melt into a cloud of blackness.

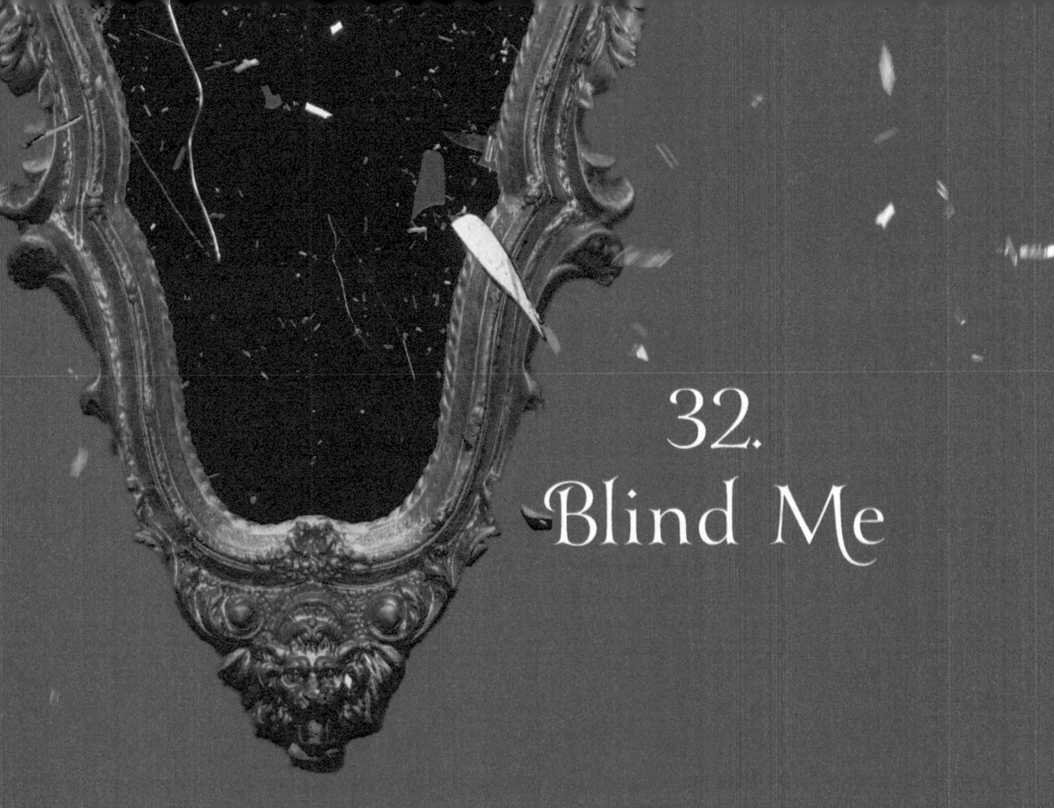

32. Blind Me

As the shelter of sleep is slowly peeling off of my body like an oversized bandage, I try and pull it back. Becoming more and more aware of my surroundings. Feeling the bars of my cage making painful indentions in my skin. I beg for that sweet relief of sleep to stay longer, stay forever. That sweet, clouded oblivion of heavy eyelids, numb body parts, and dreams that whisk me far away from here.

I want to wake up to Kane lying next to me. To DaiSzek facing the woods on guard. The mere glimpse of the future I desire most puts me in a good mood. A great mood. Despite the impending death of my sanity within the barriers of this cage.

A surge of energy makes a sudden path through my veins, tingling my skin, curling and uncurling my toes. Reluctantly, I open my eyes. Or maybe I don't. *Did I go blind?*

I can feel the perimeter of the cage holding me prisoner, but I see only darkness. I squint my eyes to focus on the tiniest bit of light. *Nothing.* I hold my hand in front of my face, wave it around. Tension creeps over me like a slow-rising tidal wave. I can't see my own hand.

Why can't I see my own hand? Perhaps with the harsh conditions I'm living in, my mind is susceptible to night terrors.

I slam my hand against the side of the cage. *Clink!*

"Hey!" I call out. My eyes darting around blindly. "Albatross! I can't see."

He must know that. Is he even in here? Maybe everyone is asleep. He has to sleep at some point. Silence. Not a whisper. Not a footstep in the hallway connected to the door.

This time I twist to my left and ram my hands against the cage. The sharp sound confirms I, at least, am not deaf.

If this is another form of Albatross's strange trials, I have to admit… it beats being force-fed. At least I'm not being strapped down. I'm sitting in a cramped cage, yes, but I'm not in pain, I'm only slightly uncomfortable.

I lie back, deciding to think only of what will distract me. And right now, it's the shift between Dessin and me. It's the night we spent in his bed in the asylum. The things he did to my body, the way he made me come apart. I wish I would have told him how I felt in the moment, but he's been so elusive, so complex with what he feels and when he feels it. I'm constantly on the defense, wondering if his emotion toward me runs as deeply as mine does toward him.

I want him as more than a friend. That much is certain. But one moment he's worshipping my body, threatening anyone that will harm me, or looking at me like I'm the something he's wanted his whole life. The next moment, Kane's telling me he doesn't feel that way about me. He's resisting my touch. He's ignoring my confessions about what I want.

And then there's Albatross's statement. Dessin took part in fucking dolls. Innocent women that couldn't lose the weight, that couldn't conform to the society designed by men for men. The terror they must have been sick with after being tortured in the asylum, only to be assaulted by lonely men in uniform.

And evidently, one of those men was Dessin.

It makes me sick, numb, beside myself thinking about him not only with another woman, but with a nonconsenting woman.

I'd like to say that he wouldn't do that. He'd never dream of it, but perhaps there is a side to him that I haven't been introduced to. Perhaps the only reason he fucked me was because he's been away from lifeless fucking dolls for so long.

I grimace at the darkness. This is exactly what Albatross was going for. To put doubt in my mind. To second-guess that man who would rain hell over the world just to save me.

I can't give him that. Can't doubt Dessin's ability to free me.

I shift to my side to relieve some pressure on my neck and head pressed up at the top of the cage. I wonder what the five of us will do when I get out of here. Yes, five. Because when I am freed, I want to find Chekiss and Niles. I want them with us for the rest of the journey. I don't trust that they're safe from Demechnef.

Will we find a place in the forests where Demechnef can't reach us? Will we travel beyond the forest? Has Kane thought this far ahead? I wouldn't mind that life. I'd like to wake up to the sound of Niles and Chekiss bickering. To Ruth, smiling and adjusting to the wilderness. I can imagine that Kane, even though he is patient on all sides and angles, will grow weary of the talking and bickering and will often want to pull me away so we can enjoy our late-night talks under the stars, or a few moments alone with DaiSzek.

"Are you thinking of your traveling companion?"

Albatross's slippery tone knocks against the corners of my cage. I flinch. Has he seriously been sitting in the dark this entire time? Does he ever move? Does he just watch me for hours on end?

"Yes," I answer plainly. There's no point in lying now.

"And you probably are wondering when he's going to save you, I presume?" Albatross asks.

I nod into the darkness, knowing he can't see my movement. Or maybe he can. A dark and forced chuckle comes from deep in his throat.

"I'm sorry, it's really not fair of me to find that amusing. You don't know how this really works, you're practically an infant in a crib, waiting for the swollen breast of your mother. Your dead mother that will never come. But of course, you're a fetus, you don't know that you'll starve waiting for milk."

I stiffen. My lungs clench together like grinding teeth, pulling my organs closer to the core of my body like they're connected to string. *Dead?*

Another chesty chuckle. "Well, your travel companion isn't dead, per se, but he'll never come for you. You'd accept that if you knew the details of his condition."

I release a toxic breath that was turning into dangerous fumes against the tender lining of my lungs. I, once again, play along. "Will you help me understand, Albatross?"

He hums. Pleased and contrite with my request to be educated once more.

"I do find it utterly cruel and unusual to let you run about without a stroke of cells in your brain that hold information so important to your survival. What kind of world do we live in these days?" Creaking of wood, like the frame of a chair, and fabric rubbing together. "But that's another conversation. The most important bit of knowledge you need to know is that *no one* is coming for you, Skylenna. You see, your travel companion has a masterfully inflated ego. He believes whatever we conditioned his brain to believe. We wanted him to believe he could conquer absolutely anything. That no amount of security could contain him. Sound familiar, right? You probably have this deeply rooted idea that this man is indestructible and his mind exceeds far past the simple identifier of genius, correct?"

I nod again. Where is he going with this?

"I said, *correct*?" His tone sharpens.

"Yes. That's correct."

"You also probably believe that Demechnef couldn't contain or control him. That they've been chasing him for years, and he's outsmarted them every time. Because with a mind that is *so* far passed any technological or scientific advancements, how could anyone possibly be able to stand in his way from what he wants? *Correct*?"

I'm gripping the bars now. Feeling anger pressurize against my rib cage.

"*Yes*."

I hear a tapping sound coming from the corner Albatross is sitting in. A stuttering beat of silence. A slurping sound from a cup.

"Now, I'm going to try my best to say this with the utmost delicacy and sensitivity I have in my heart, without laughing, I might add." An exaggerated sigh. "This is a *lie* he was fed as a small child. Everything he knows now we have made him believe. He is part of an experiment, that much is true, but the experiment is to make his young mind wholeheartedly believe he is superior to the human race. He hasn't pulled off a single action without our blessing. He hasn't fulfilled a single escape without our unlocking the doors first. He will never be able to break into this room. This building. This territory. He will try and fail and try and fail. And that will be the conclusion of the experiment. You see, your travel companion will have a plan, and not have a single doubt in his mind that he will be able to save you. But the closing remarks will be the moment he realizes his entire life was staged. He has been our puppet, and we're about to cut his strings."

I stare into the darkness; I blink furiously. I can't digest what he is saying. The words are skimming off my ears like skipping a rock over water.

"Another way to look at it is if we made a man believe he could fly. We attached a harness, made him forget he had the harness on, and for his whole life he believed he could soar through the clouds. Then, one day, we rip the harness from his body, and he falls to his death. Isn't that a carefully thought-out ending? What a theatrical conclusion it will be for him. We'll get to see what happens to the human mind when reality melts through his fingers and he's left with a disgusting mirror that shows him the sad and helplessly ordinary person he truly is."

My teeth are scraping against each other and I feel his pointy words deep in the bed of my loyalty to Dessin. For Kane. And that's just it, I feel it like it's another part of my body. My respect for him is attached to me like the way my arm hangs at my side. It's attached and to remove it would be to cut it off and bleed to death. I can't believe what he's saying. My respect won't even allow me to consider it. But the fact that Albatross thinks I would fall for that is pathetic. It's vile.

"You're a liar!" I scream. The height my voice reaches stuns me. "You think I would fall for that garbage? You may have made me believe my collarbone broke, or that I'm blind, but you'll never scratch the surface of the hope I have!" My fingers are squeezing the bars, creating small blisters as I twist them back and forth.

Albatross snickers, like two champaign glasses clinking together. "Why would I lie about that? I never lie about education. And this, my girl, is a seminar taught by *me*, just for *you*." The smug smile leaks into his voice like pollution from a sewer and the remnants of gunk from under a swamp rock.

"He'll come for me," I whisper with the hot branding iron of resentment searing through my words. It's a whisper of certainty. A whisper of confidence.

"Even if he does, my girl, these walls are impenetrable. We have security precautions in this facility that will make your old place of employment look like a child's playground." He laughs again. Adjusts in his seat.

I release my grip from the cage. "I'm done talking."

"Yes, you are."

33. Into The Darkness

He will come for me. He will come for me. H e w i l l c o m e f o r m e.

My pulse is so quick, so loud, it beats against my jugular, a drum of battle in my ears. I'm woken up by a dull throb of hunger only to feel the shock of lying still in complete darkness again. I don't know how long I've been asleep. I don't even remember falling asleep. How long have I been here? Is it weeks now? Dessin would never let me be held captive this long. Something must be wrong.

Being all alone in this long stretch of darkness makes me want to scream for help, kick the cage until my teeth rattle. I want to fight to escape. But what if Albatross breaks another bone? What if Absinthe force-feeds me again? I'm torn between doing what would make Dessin proud and cowering in fear of the unknown.

I try to stay calm. *There is no need to overreact now.* That's probably what Albatross wants. He wants me to go into hysterics. This must be a tactic of his. Use isolation to make me go insane. Let the darkness turn into hallucinations. Wait me out until I'm begging for company. A stiff chill like a set of long jagged fingernails drags down my spine.

I won't give him that satisfaction… *Yet*. I can only breathe like a jackrabbit caught between my lungs. It bounces around furiously. This reminds me of my time in the basement, the cold, hard concrete floor, the way the walls would start to breathe. My small child mind would conjure up new and unimaginable terrors that would lurk all around me. My heartbeat knocks against my skull, stomping on the arteries in my brain. My palms remain pressed firmly to the bottom of the cage and they moisten with single, microscopic drops of sweat.

I blink desperately, silently begging the lights to come on. My stomach twists, gallops, and lurches forward.

Please Dessin, don't let me go through this again. Come save me, Dessin! I don't want to be here anymore! I promise to listen to you next time! I'm sorry I didn't know what I was doing! I swear I'll do what you say!

A drop of sweat drizzles down my neck, tickling the center of my chest. And I hold my breath, biting down on my tongue to distract from the panic. My bottom lip quivers while my teeth grind together.

Somebody help me!

Terror is suffocating me with a feather pillow. It's wrapping its chains around my back and chest. It's locking me in this cage forever.

I might never see the sun again.

I curl into a small ball; my knees jammed against the bars, and my feet ice cold against the metal floor. My mind does strange flip-flops as I try and make sense of being locked in this cage like an animal, of being force-fed, of having believed my bones were breaking. If they only want Dessin to realize he isn't all-powerful, then why would they want me to suffer?

I think several days passed in the darkness. I've waited in fear, every hour, that these shadows will never end. The silence will make my ears bleed. I've waited for Albatross's voice to show up once more, giving away more useless information, and talking to me like a small child. I've waited for food, water, crumbs—anything to keep me alive. Perhaps they've forgotten about me, perhaps they've lost interest and are simply waiting for me to die.

With the black scenery becoming all that I know, I wonder if I made Albatross up? Maybe when I was captured, my mind created moments. Maybe my mind gave me a source of entertainment to distract me from all-consuming darkness.

I try to sleep mostly. Count the seconds, count the bars around me. Recall stories that Dessin or Kane would share with me to play out in my head. But the doubt starts to creep in like an infestation of cockroaches. What if Dessin isn't coming for me? What if I am trapped here forever? What if there is no Dessin and I'm insane? I want to bang the side of my head into the bars until it stops working. I want the thoughts to be silenced and to go back to sleep. I don't want to wake up until he comes for me, even though that day might never come.

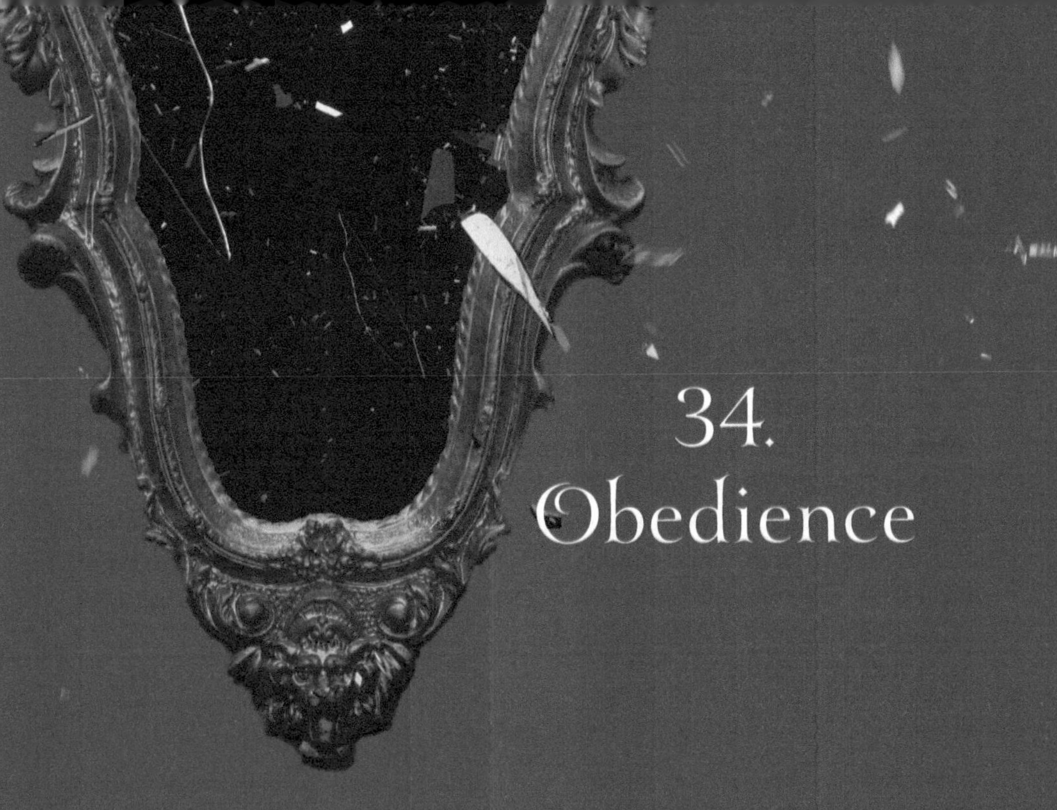

34. Obedience

I've tried to ignore it, but the smell has woken me up. No one has let me out of my cage to relieve myself. I—I'm lying in my own feces, my own pitiful excretions, my own reminder that I am, in fact, still alive. It hasn't been much because I have no food or water to release, but it's enough to burn my nostrils and cause soft sores on my backside. Every time I reawaken, I hope to God that I open my eyes and see the sun and feel the wind on my cheeks. I hope to God that Dessin has finally come.

But, shamefully, I don't want him to see me like this. My hair is a matted pigeon's nest, and my hygiene is not far off from a disease-ridden rat. Has it been weeks now? I can't recall. When you can't see the sun come up, and the moon cools the sky, you can't count the minutes that keep you captive.

Time is not my friend.

I don't even care about escaping anymore. I just want a sip of water. I just want to talk to someone. To soak in a warm bath. To brush my hair. To take a bite of a piece of bread. I want the next breath I take in to be clean and without the toxic scent of urine.

But maybe this is it. This is where I die. They've clearly abandoned me in this room. I'm never getting out now. They locked me away and are waiting for me to starve or die of a bacterial infection. Dehydration is certainly a strong possibility too. When I imagine dying, looking into a light, slowly drifting away… it's not the worst thing. In fact, give me a few more hours and I might beg for it. Isn't that weak to say? I'll beg to die. I'll beg God to bring me home so I can shed this disgusting suit, this heavy, filthy body with welts, sores, and bruises.

I won't have to wake up cold anymore. I won't have to readjust my position in hardened fecal matter. I'll spread my wings and fly away. I'll watch over Dessin and my friends, and I'll be their warrior angel that will fight for them on the other side.

It will be beautiful.

White blinding fire glows everywhere. It's shining through the slits of my eyes, leaking past my eyelashes, making my eyes water and burn.

"You're foul, girl. I'd breathe in through my mouth but then I'd taste it." Absinthe. *Absinthe! A person! Light! Oh my god! Can I see again?*

I force my eyes open, to adjust to the lights painfully. As it comes into focus, I see that the light is not white, it is a soft glowing chandelier above my head. Golden crystals sparkling, hanging off the gaslit wicks, the golden arches. I scan the area, small space, mahogany walls, designs carved into the trim. I see a sink and a small, cracked mirror. My hands grip the surface they're lying on; it's an armrest. And there are wheels. I think I'm in a wheelchair. I look to my right and see Absinthe hovering over a copper bathtub, running water from an old tarnished faucet.

"Don't even think about trying anything. I could've let you sit in your filth for several more days. But the smell was fogging up the mirrors in the hallways." She hand tests the temperature in the bathtub. Her voice is strong, yet old and unstable with weakening tones.

"I won't," I say. Scratchy. Hoarse. Raw.

"'Cause I'd beat you dead if you did," she adds. I believe her.

Absinthe steps in front of me and removes my gown. I sit in the wheelchair, completely bare, cold, shivering, waiting for the warm bathwater. For the first time in—days, maybe—dopamine seeps into my brain, tingling behind my eyes, spilling into my chest. It's nearly enough to bring a smile to my face.

A bath. It'll raise goose bumps from the back of my neck to my bare feet. I'll lie in there with my eyes closed for as long as she lets me. I'll ignore my stomach growling and my cotton tongue stuck to the top of my mouth. I will float, hum, relax, and when she's not looking… I won't miss the opportunity to drink it. I don't give a damn if it's in my own filth. I'll die without a drop of water.

With her bony arms, Absinthe lifts me out of the chair. Her frizzy, gray hair grazes underneath my chin, and I catch a whiff, a quick inhale—the scent of licorice and mildew. But who am I to judge anyone's personal stench? She grunts and hisses as her wilted skin touches the back of my disgusting legs. With a single heave and a close-mouthed groan, she chunks me into the tub. I'm silent before I scream. My body is stabbed in every direction. Tiny incisions are made, sharp sensations shake the skin off of my bones violently and I'm instantly wide awake.

"It's colddddd!" I wail, throwing my hands above my head to reach for the edges of the tub. Flailing. Flopping about like the tail of a dolphin doing tricks. *Help!*

A choked gasp. "You splashed me! You awful girl! You stupid, ugly girl!" Absinthe spits on the floor next to me. She wastes no time charging from the other side of the wheelchair. I see the point of her pinkie knuckle first as her fist swipes across my left cheekbone. A shock of pain bolts under my skin, and it throbs like a heart, pumping blood to the wounded area before I can accept that punishment for what I did. But there's no pause between assaults. No time for me to take a breath. Another punch to my jaw, slightly to the left of my chin. My head shoots against the side of the copper tub with the blast of her third swing. I am unaware of where she hits next, my whole face is screaming. Is she breaking my bones? Is she beating me dead? I can't feel the coldness of the bath anymore. My skin is completely numb. But my cheekbones are being filled with sharp stabs, as if someone was hammering an ice pick into my bone. Between her next force of impact, I'm able to let go of the breath I was harboring in my lungs and scream like it's the last time I'll ever be able to use my voice.

"Enough, old woman!"

Her fist freezes in the air, a breath away from my nose. She leaves it hanging, gritting her teeth, panting with me. I lick my lips and taste the rusty metal that is my blood. My eyes fall to the cold water, and like drops of fresh ink, the crimson-red blood spirals around my body, like a murderous cloud. Like the washing of paint brushes.

Albatross yells again. "Did you hear me? I said that's enough!"

Absinthe grunts and rolls her decaying blue eyes. "I heard ya," she mumbles, leaning into me, nose to nose. "You make another fuss in here and I won't stop again. Not even if he tries to break down the door."

I move my head down, unable to lift it up again. Runny, warm blood trickles down my chin and neck. *Tluck. Tlock. Tluck.*

Absinthe grabs a bar of soap and a yellow sponge. She dips both in the water and rubs them together, sudsing the sponge with bubbles. There is no gentleness to her touch, although that doesn't surprise me. Those gnarled, hard hands work like she's scrubbing a pan of dried food and grease.

I don't suck in a sharp breath at her lack of a sensitive touch, I don't squirm as she washes my breasts violently. I hang my head in agony, watching the drops of blood saturate my bathwater, staining the shiny soap bubbles. My breaths are quiet, shallow, afraid to upset Absinthe by existing.

"Had any visitors in your cage as of late?" Absinthe's tone is bathed in eager cruelty.

I raise my eyes to look at her. She gives me a sidelong glance and smirks with an ugly show of a sharp snaggletooth.

"Our minds invent monsters when there's no light." A garbled, throaty laugh. "Better get used to it, girl." She flips me on my right side and scrubs the sores on my backside. I wince, leaning my head against the tub.

"Just don't scream and wake us up when your mind attacks itself. Darkness drives us all into agonizing madness."

I try not to tremble at her warning. This keeps getting worse and worse. How am I going to survive this? I'll go insane before I see my friends again. If I ever do see them again, that is.

I make the mistake of wincing as Absinthe uses the sponge to scrub my private parts raw. She backhands my bloody face and the red residue splatters to the floor.

"Damn you, girl. I'm the one that has to clean up this mess." She takes my face by the chin and uses that same sponge to wash the blood off of my face. I hold my breath and shut my eyes, trying my hardest to keep from whimpering under her feral touch. She's about as gentle as an angry hive of bees.

She dumps a cup of ice water over me to rinse off the soap, then reaches for a stack of white towels. Absinthe studies my naked body with a raised eyebrow and scornful eyes.

"Can you stand?"

I release a shaky breath. "I think so." *God, I hope so. If I fall, you'll only beat me again.*

She nods and holds her hand out, those arthritic knuckles, the gray tone to her flesh, and dark-blue veins pulsing under the crepe skin. I extend my arm from the tub and let her support my weight as I push as hard as I can to raise myself from the water. The task would have been hard enough without the weight of the water holding me down like a human-sized paperweight. My legs are wobbly, and my spine might have been replaced by a spaghetti noodle. It burns every joint, every ligament, every muscle to try and steady myself successfully. But I know that the price of giving in to this weakness and collapsing back into the tub will only encourage her to fulfill her promise to me. She'll beat me dead. She will.

When I'm fully upright, water cascades down my nakedness in a downpour, like dragging a wrecked ship out of the ocean. Absinthe scrapes the towels across my wet body and watches me for a pained reaction. I keep my face still, refusing to give her even a twitch of my eye as she rakes over my sores, my breasts, my battered face.

After I'm patted down and semidry, she puts my white gown on. I stretch my arms out and let her pull it over my head. Small drops of blood saturate the pure-white cloth around my neckline.

"Sit," she orders. I drop my butt into the wheelchair, noticing that my arm is still connected to the IV.

Absinthe stops pushing the wheelchair and pauses. "Has a man ever touched you, girl?"

I would say yes, but what if she calls me a whore? What if she beats me again for letting a man touch me out of wedlock? "No, ma'am," I mutter. Safe answer.

She doesn't say anything. The wheelchair moves again and I let my head hang once more, letting the blood drip down my throat, hang from my nose, seep past my lips. I hope I fall asleep once more, close my eyes and sink back into my mind. She opens the wooden door and rolls me back into prison. And there's the cage, the metal table, and the kneecaps in the corner. *Hello, Albatross.*

As instructed, I crawl back into my cage and get into position to lie down. Absinthe parks the wheelchair in the back of the room, then shifts something across a surface quietly. Opens and closes a door.

"Here." She reaches her hand into the right side of my cage, above my head. A slab of raw meat, the size of a stapler in her palm. Red, plump, and even a little bloody. "Eat it before I get hungry myself."

I take it from her hand hesitantly. Normally, I would never eat this. Kane always cooked my food before I ate it. I wouldn't even watch as he carved the meat from the bone. But with my shriveling stomach, trembling limbs, and weak pulse—I could die. And this thick chunk looks like it's packed with protein. I could really use protein right now. My eyes shift back to her, questioning, waiting to get a last sign of nonverbal permission to eat it. She raises her eyebrows and nods.

Not a second wasted. I shove it into my mouth, not minding the raw taste, not minding the blood and juices running down my chin. I work mindlessly to chew and chew and chew. *Oh, it's so good. It's so heavenly. Oh, I'm so happy. Thank you, Absinthe. You saved my life.*

A metal cup hovers through the bars of my cage. I look up at her again as I swallow the last of the meat. She nods once more.

It's only a little water. But dear God, IT'S WATER!

I want to say thank you. I want to tell her that this has made me so happy. But all my body and mind will allow me to do is guzzle that small puddle of water down my throat. It eases the roughness of my tongue and soothes the insides of my cheeks… but I want *more*.

I won't ask though. No, absolutely not. That might prevent her from ever bringing me anything again. It may even encourage her to continue the force-feedings.

"And how do you show your thanks, girl?"

I grip the bars frantically and hum my praise. "Thank you, Absinthe! Thank you so much! Thank you!"

A smug tight-lipped smile smoothes the crow's-feet across her mouth.

"That's right, girl. Very good."

35. The Ambrose Oasis

I miss you, Kane. I have a reoccurring thought of you coming for me, finding me, and holding your arms out so I can jump into them. The thought makes my heart yearn for you. I think about you so much it burns my insides like letting a blender tear me apart. Can you hear me when I think this right now? As I lie in this sardonic darkness? I want to cry out your name in hopes you'll hear me from wherever you are. But I know that will only bring on another beating. So, this is my attempt. I will think these thoughts as loudly as you need me to.

I open my eyes and a river of fear breaks through a dam that enters my nervous system. I am blind once more. But what did I really expect? Last time it lasted for days, I think. I don't want to go through it again. I'd rather have the ice bath. My face still throbs and aches from the mark of her fists.

This time, I can't control the firestorm of panic that cripples my limbs.

The blood in my veins runs rampant, yelling and screaming at all internal operations to go into crisis mode. My nerves tingle and my stomach sours, bile splashing along the walls of my esophagus. I'm a short circuit. Loose wires buzzing and fusing. Pops and explosions of misguided electricity.

And I am a coward. Because those instincts that possess someone to fight or flee the scene aren't here at all. My only instinct is to freeze. To not move a muscle.

This is the moment I would scream for my daddy to let me out of the basement. I'd howl until my throat felt like it had been whipped. I remember the moment I went under the asylum with Dessin for the first time. The way he kept me calm during my attack of fear and flashback.

If there was ever a moment that Dessin would swoop in, make a scene, rage with an unholy fire of vengeance—this is that moment. I'd beg on my hands and knees to be that lucky.

My heart stops and stutters, and I stay still. I am unmoving, cold, hard porcelain. A doll that isn't alive. A doll that doesn't have a heartbeat. I am not real.

I begin to picture dangers that wait in the corners of the room. Beasts that hunger to rip my flesh from my bone. Monsters that my mind is conjuring up just like Absinthe said. The taunting warning stirs my anger.

He's going to come for me! He's going to kill you! I scream in my thoughts. Further in my mind, I hunch over and yell at the top of my lungs! *COME BACK FOR ME, DESSIN! THEY'RE GOING TO HURT ME!*

…I'm so scared.

I can hear the phantom growls lurking behind me. My teeth bite down on my tongue until a bitter stream of blood coats my mouth.

This is it. I'll lose my mind. I'll lose it and I won't find it again. It will disappear into this blind landscape and it won't wait for me to escape this hell.

Scarlett, I'm scared!

In my mind's eyes, the darkness shifts, transforms like a puff of smoke. There's a figure. An animal. A dark shadow that looms over me, waiting while I imagine the monsters are closing in on my cage. And it's patient, unthreatening. I focus, trying to see the details. A beast, massive in size, far too big for this cage.

DaiSzek? It sniffs me, nudges at my hand to rise. *It's time,* he tells me this with his set of cinnamon eyes.

I realize what he's trying to get me to do. My body isn't mine while they have me in this cage, but my mind will keep me safe. But here, behind the lids of my eyes, is DaiSzek, offering to take me someplace safe. Someplace where I can wish my body well while it withstands this isolation.

I rise as DaiSzek bows the front half of his body so I may climb onto his back. With my legs securely on either side, I wrap my arms around his fluffy neck and hold on tight. He roars at the darkness, at the monsters who exist outside of my mind, and begins to run with me latched on tightly. We vaporize through the cage, gliding through this prison with long, triumphant leaps to freedom. We race to a small golden glow, an orb of rich light at the ending of this black room.

His strides take us farther than the length of a horse.

Within moments, we reach the end of this dark pit of hell, and bright colors begin to smear the edges of this reality. Blues, pinks, greens, yellows, mixing with the black paint. And we soar from its shadows. My fingers grip the length of his fur, and I can't imagine a better feeling than the blustery wind giving us the steps to *fly away*.

As the darkness drains from existence, we stride into an open field, with tall avocado-green grass, lilac flowers, swaying wisteria trees, and huge evergreens. The sun is out and shining, beaming down on my once cold skin, warming my insides, coating my long hair.

His stride melts into a slower trot. I was worried I'd never see sunlight again. I was afraid I'd never breathe fresh air again. I focus closer on the ground, to see the flowers that are evenly distributed throughout the meadow. Sunflowers in full bloom, and violet candytufts. The smell of the lavender herb fills the fresh air around us.

DaiSzek lowers himself to the ground in the middle of the field. I bring my right leg over to the left side of his body and step away. His large eyes pinpoint a spot across the horizon. I follow his gaze to a slight movement in the trees, the shuffling of leaves and branches.

A boy pushes past a cluster of twigs and leaves, stepping out into the open meadow of blooming flowers. He looks back at me, smiles, and waves.

I think I know him...

From this distance, I can see he has brown hair with cowlicks, wearing a white T-shirt with black suspenders and tan trousers. He walks over to me like he's greeted people here many times before. As he closes the distance, I step back to be closer to DaiSzek. The boy wears a glowing white smile and a set of dimples. *Wait...*

I scan over his face again frantically. His smile grows wider.

"*Kane?*" I ask with a loss of breath.

He chuckles with a closed mouth. The sounder is lighter, less husky, less deep than I'm used to.

"Who else would be here?"

"You're—You're so... *young.*"

He laughs again. Shrugs.

The wind is choppy, big gusts, then calmness. The sky is cloudless, Aegean blue, so vibrant if I were upside down, it could be the ocean.

I think I'll stay here forever.

Young Kane has a softer forehead and happier eyes. There are fewer creases of stress and sadness wilting his expression. He motions to the ground.

"Let's sit?" he asks.

I follow him down to the grass and crisscross my legs. I don't know how to rationalize what's happening. It *feels* real. Have I lost my mind? First, DaiSzek whisks me out of my cage and jumps through hoops of reality to get me to this beautiful meadow where all my problems seem to swim away. Then, a younger version of Kane emerges from the forest that surrounds us. He doesn't seem surprised to find me here. Have I gone mad?

"What is this place?" I finally peel my eyes off of his soft face and take another look at the blossoming flowers, swaying like dance partners in a ballroom.

"I call it Ambrose Oasis," he says. "The safe place you can go when you're scared or in pain." His eyes almost look like honey, with a direct ray of sun setting them on fire.

I nod. But I don't understand, not in the slightest. I'm just glad I made it out of there when I did.

"Do you want to talk about it?" He plucks a stem of lavender from the ground and hands it to me. "Here, smell."

I take the herb from his fingers and hold it up to my nose. I inhale deeply, the lavender-infused aroma wafting up my nostrils and the edges of my brain like taking a warm shower. The scent is strong and clean.

"It'll help keep you at peace," he adds.

"I don't think I want to talk about it," I respond to his first question carefully. "I don't think I'll ever want to talk about it. Not for the rest of my life."

"I thought you might say that." A sad smile tightens his mouth. His tone implies he's had this conversation with me before. But why am I seeing him so young? Why not the man I know now?

"Are you sad, Skylenna?"

I shake my head. "No, I'm much happier now that I'm here." And I am. I feel an overwhelming amount of relief. Like I had a tight rope hugging my neck, and DaiSzek cut me loose. I can finally breathe. I can let the muscles in my neck relax. I can enjoy the warmth of the sun on my skin. The breeze carrying lavender running through my hair.

But that feeling of relief is suddenly replaced with a twinge of fear.

"Wait. I don't have to go back, right? I can just… stay here." My back is stiff and I'm ready to run. Sprint away from the reality that might be fast enough to catch up with me.

Kane's eyebrows knit together in empathy. "You can stay here."

My shoulders fall and I let go of the air trapped beneath my chest.

"But if you do, you'll never find your way back to *him*."

"Him *who*?"

His eyes narrow. The way Dessin's does when he wants me to figure something out for myself.

"You mean—"

"I mean, Kane and Dessin. The Kane and Dessin that are nine years older than I am now. The ones that are waiting to see you again." Even in his youth, he's always had those intense eyes that are both warm and concrete with knowledge. I miss those eyes so much it hurts.

My lips part and I feel the pain of losing them in the outskirts of my soul.

"I want to see him again. More than I've wanted *anything*. But I'm starting to lose hope. It's been months. There's been no sign of him. And that's not like him! He would never leave me in a place so horrendous this long. He would cross over every layer of hell and beyond to rescue me. There would be no force strong enough to hold him down."

My words shiver as they leave me and float to him. They are weak and heavy with a heartbreak that sits on my shoulders like a backpack full of cement blocks.

"Why do you think he hasn't come for you yet?"

I frown. "I don't know. I guess I'm afraid something terrible happened to him. I won't let myself think about the possibility that he might have been killed. If he was, then why would Albatross keep me locked away? I'm leverage. I *must* be. But if he is alive, then maybe… maybe Albatross was right about him. What if Dessin isn't as superior as he believes? What if he is a sad victim of a horrible psychological experiment? It will destroy him if he figures that out."

Kane tilts his chin downward to get a better look at me.

"Those aren't your only theories, are they?"

I look up at him from under my lashes. I shake my hand and place my face in my hands. I can't talk about the last thought that dwindles around my subconscious like a murky devil swimming through my feelings in toxic wastewater.

I exhale roughly. "I'm scared… I think there's a chance I imagined him. It's not entirely ridiculous. I was experiencing great loss at the time we first met. I lost my father and then Scarlett back to back. I witnessed both of their deaths. There's only so much pain a person can take before they crack into a million tiny pieces. What if I made him up to survive it all, Kane? What if he isn't even real? What if I lost my mind?"

He sighs. Clasps his hands over his lap. "What would you do if that were true?"

I unload a frustrated laugh. "What would I do?" An uneven sigh. I lower myself, settle on my back, facing the sky and the purple wisteria frolicking in the heavy wind. "I couldn't go on. He's the reason I'm alive. The reason I'm still going. I wouldn't have joy without him. I wouldn't have happiness."

Kane lies down next to me. "Why is he your reason for happiness?"

I laugh again. "I guess you started psychoanalyzing at a young age, huh?"

He shrugs and grins back at me. "Just talented, I guess."

"Very." I nod. My smile slips away. "I don't exactly know why I'm so happy when I'm with him. Maybe because he's the one that saw me at the asylum? Really saw me, flaws and all. He brought me out of the dark place I was chained to when Scarlett died. I guess our friendship is more of a connection than I've ever had with anyone. I've clung to him through everything."

Kane watches me carefully. His young face full of curiosity.

"I don't know why…" I add. I turn my head to face the sun again. *I do know why. I'm just scared to say it out loud.* He rejected me after we kissed. And then we slept together. After that, I've done my best to not beg for him to want me romantically. I don't want him to think I'm desperate.

"It's okay to say it here. We're in your safe place, remember?"

I blow out another breath, dig my fingers into the grass, and shut my eyes.

"I love him." The words are like double-edged swords. They shock me as I pull them from my heart. "I love him so much. I can't lose him. I have to see him again."

"I *know,*" he whispers.

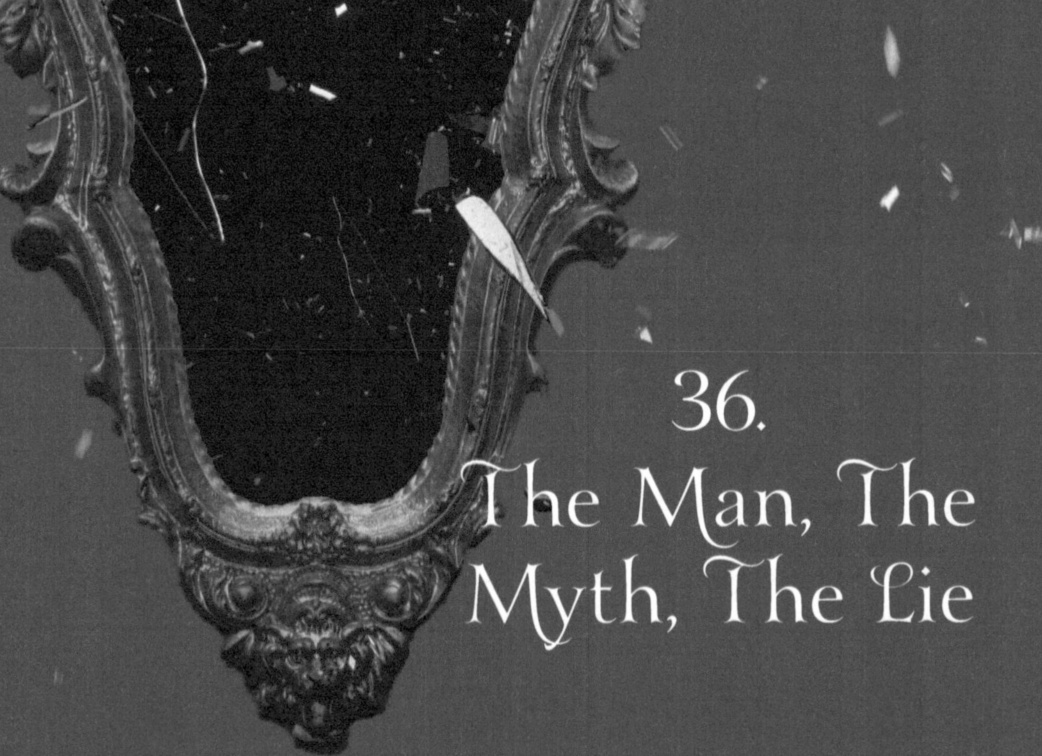

36. The Man, The Myth, The Lie

DaiSzek carried me back to the room with my cage. I didn't plan on returning. I could lie in that special place for the rest of my days. But my truth, the hidden secret weighing me down, was finally acknowledged. Finally said out loud, or at least in my head. I want to see him again. I have to.

Young Kane told me that the men were gone now. It was safe to go back.

I hugged DaiSzek around his neck and fell back into the body that lay still. Cold and defiled. Trembling and sad.

I remain as I was with my eyes still closed. I don't want to open them. I don't want to reenter this reality I just ran from. As I flex my fingers and wiggle my toes, my nostrils fill with the scent of cigarette smoke, a light waft of cleaning chemicals, and the sweat of a man.

"What did you *do*?!" Albatross raises his voice. It forces my lids to flicker open. The light is back on. The chandelier reflects off of the metal of my cage. I see the red velvet material over his kneecaps tucked away in the corner of the room.

"What do you mean?" I ask wearily.

A teacup soars through the air and shatters against my cage. Scalding hot tea splatters over my skin, fragments of porcelain puncture my arms, legs, and cheeks. I screech, fanning my burning skin while trying to pluck the shards from my new tiny wounds.

"What the hell happened? You were terrified one moment, your vitals were through the roof, and then suddenly you completely leveled out!"

I keep my face composed. "I fell asleep." *I'll never tell you where I went. Never tell you who I saw.*

An angry chuckle. "You fell asle—" His long finger reaches out past the shadows into the light. "You blacked out, didn't you? Went someplace far away in your mind?"

I shake my head. *No. Don't tell him anything.*

"DON'T YOU LIE TO ME, BITCH!" Albatross swipes at a table and knocks everything to the ground with a loud crash of glass and books. "I've done nothing but help you since you arrived!"

I grip the bars on either side of me. I know it's not wise to anger him like this. I could just make up a good lie, but they'll hurt me either way. They'll keep me locked up like an animal.

"You still think he's coming for you, is that it? You were probably there with him… in your *head*!" he bellows, that nasal voice pinging around the bars of my cage.

That's technically true…

Albatross sighs now, heavily and with a touch of theatrics. "My dear, I really didn't want to tell you this… it would only make your time here harder for you. But seeing as you aren't cooperative in your cage because of a false string of hope that your travel companion is on his way… I'll have to stop you there. You see, he arrived two weeks ago. He managed to get past the first entrance, but when he discovered everything I told you before, he malfunctioned. He completely lost his mind. He slit his own throat."

I stare at him, wide eyed, with a parted mouth that lacks the function to speak. The visual of Dessin standing in shock, finding out he wasn't as powerful as he always thought he was. Taking a knife to his throat and—

"*No,*" I growl. My teeth grinding down to the nerve.

"Excuse me?"

"No." A new kind of hatred rips through my core, quick and violent, I fear I might split right down the middle. "YOU'RE LYING!" I scream. It takes more energy than I have in me, but I'm powered by a rainstorm of toxic rage. "He is everything he believes he is and becoming more every day! That much I know is true!"

He laughs with intentional cruelty and belittlement.

"Your travel companion is nothing but a rat in our maze."

My jaw locks and my entire body begins to shake, tighten, *burn*. I slam my fists down on the floor of my cage. "SAY HIS NAME, YOU COWARD!"

Albatross clears his voice. "I will not."

"HIS NAME IS *DESSIN*! AND WHEN HE FINDS YOU, HE'LL DO UNIMAGINABLE THINGS TO MAKE YOU *BLEED*!"

Unless I'm mistaken, I hear his throat gulp. Wet, loud, and terrified.

I kick my legs out to the cage door. The peak of adrenaline is enough to give me a second and third wind. I hike my legs up to my chest, then kick the bars as hard as I can with bare feet. I can hardly feel the impact vibrate up my shins, cracking against my kneecaps.

"Let me out!" I scream again. Thrusting my legs full force against the bars of the cage. Once, twice, nine more times. "GET ME THE HELL OUT OF HERE!"

I thrash about, throwing my arms and fists against the sides of my cage. Beating the metal until my knuckles swell, blood spilling down my arms, dripping off my elbows. But I can't feel the pain or what I'm sure is a monstrous throbbing sensation under my skin. The fury fills up my bloodstream like a downpour of hot oil. It strengthens my muscles and my bones. It jolts through my veins as if my IV were connected to an electric generator. I want to tear this cage to pieces with my bare hands. I want to yank Albatross out from the shadows and clutch his throat, ripping my fingernails through his veins. I want out.

He's not dead! He's alive and he'll come for me.

"I'm warning you, girl!" Albatross finds his voice. But it isn't louder than mine.

"No, I'm warning *you*! If you keep me in here any longer, I won't hold him back! He will look to me for how much is enough. He will wait for me to tell him to stop. But I will watch as you suffer. And I will enjoy every second of it!"

Albatross slams his hands down on a leather chair.

First, my panties feel wet. Soaking. Dripping without my control. I look down and blood is gushing out of me. It happens so fast that my rage winks from existence.

Then, a flood of sharp pains jabs my uterus, like tiny knives carving me up from within. I double over, grip my lower belly, suck in a fast breath through my teeth.

Next, it's my lower back. I wouldn't be surprised if someone is massaging me with a hammer. It punctures my sides like hot pokers from a firepit, stabbing my gut, leaving me with a heavy surge of nausea. The sudden dull need to vomit slithers up my throat, coating my tongue with bitter stomach acid.

I lean my shoulder to the side of the cage, holding my belly, wincing at the shards of agony that blast through my back repeatedly. Like I'm being attacked from within. Like my body detected a foreign enemy, and it's throwing all of its best defenses against it. My eyeballs are swollen and hot. My tongue, heavy in my mouth. The natural instinct to heave is strong, drowning out every thought I have. The muscles in my abdomen contract, forcing my jaw to unhinge; I gag dryly. *What's happening to me? Is he killing me?*

My heart rate jumps as another lurch of bile pumps through my throat. I lean over and a stream of pink juice is shooting from my gaping mouth. The pain in my stomach subsides for three and a half seconds, and then returns, gripping my stomach so tightly I can't breathe.

The pain is atrocious. It's beyond comprehension. The only thing I can do is hold completely still while my stomach acid sloshes around, burning holes into the lining of my intestines. A single gasp followed by a whimper drips off of my lips with a string of my own bodily fluids. I bear down as my innards churn and twist, and more pink vomit is ejected from me, spraying through the bars, landing around my cage. The smell and taste is sour, like sweet wine and pickles. Like choosing to sit in a decomposing swamp of curdled milk and sewer water. I gag again at the scent that fills my nose, and the fluids spreading across the cage floor, drenching my nightgown.

The thought slices its way through my ongoing hell. *Why would Dessin let me suffer this long? I must be wrong about him. The man I know would never let me undergo this kind of unimaginable torture.*

He's never coming for me! He's never going to break me out. I'll be trapped like this forever!

A flood of more vomit and blood burst from my chest. This time, it saturates my gown down the front of my body. Everything hurts. From head to toe, I tremble, waiting for the next roll of vomit. I don't know what's happening to me, or how long it will last. But this can't go on. I can't go through this forever. I'll die. I'll lose my mind. More so than I already have.

The whole world is dark and I'm falling endlessly through a realm of evil humans taunting me, kicking me while I'm down. I want to leave it. I should have stayed in the safe place. *Where is DaiSzek?*

Underneath my loud groaning, Albatross clears his throat again.

"All at once, I gave you endometriosis, kidney stones, and a rather severe case of appendicitis. Your poor body is trying to fight. You have a fever of 104, and *oh,* you've also come down with the flu."

Please make this stop! I moan again in agony as the stabbing pains attack my midsection with impressive combat skills. *Please!*

I look up through glossy eyes. Albatross stays hidden in the shadows, only the caps of his knees showing in the light of the chandelier. I plead with my quivering lip, hoping he takes pity on me. I shouldn't have yelled at him. I should have stayed submissive. *What was I thinking?!*

"I could make the pain go away, dear," he announces, legs crossing.

I hold my breath as another tub of vomit is dumped across my tongue and out of my mouth. The taste is too close to rotting meat and expired dairy. *I want it to stop!*

I can't even look up again to respond to him. A migraine. Hot flesh. Violent chills. My soul is begging him for a warm bed.

"But I can't make it stop if you're still in denial." He sighs. "This all is so trivial and barbaric. I could be spending my time explaining more about my good work here. I don't like seeing you like this, dear girl. I don't like it at all."

I choke on another uprise of bile and swallow it back down. I've never felt so weak and horrendous in my life. "I'm not!" I spit the words out before my uterus is being squeezed again.

"Sorry? You're not what?" Albatross asks.

I whine as my stomach feels like it's being pinched between a piece of hardware.

"You don't want to have to keep feeling this way all for a dying cause, do you? It's just not fair! It's been over a month since you were brought here. A month! Tell me, would this strong, indestructible travel companion of yours really need months to come break you out? I mean, he's far too clever for a task this small, isn't he? But if that's the truth… then what could have stopped him?" He waits for me to answer, but I'm too busy writhing on the floor aimlessly. "It hurts me to see you giving your best self to a false perception of a person."

My thoughts, chained down by pain, are clear for a brief moment. He's right. Even thinking that makes me feel like a traitor. Like the scum of the earth.

But it hurts. *I* hurt.

Disappointment possesses me, dragging every hope I have to hell. He isn't coming for me. If my version of this man was the right one… I'd be out already. It's been too long. I've suffered *too long*. It had all been lies. My connection might have been real, but the lion, the dragon, the great beast that encompassed the all-knowing, master manipulator, the strong-willed warrior he has always been to me… has been a lie. *A LIE.*

"He's—not—coming—for—me." I make out my words evenly through the rapid inhales and exhales. "He's a *lie.*" A dry sob breaks through my pursed lips and gritted teeth.

Albatross hums in agreement. "Would you like the pain to go away now?"

"Yes, I would," I groan. *Please make it go away.* With a click coming from his side of the room. The pain sinking its teeth into my stomach, my back, my uterus, all lift like a poisonous cloud floating back up to the sky. I force out a shaky, grateful sigh, hooking my hands over the top of my head. It's all gone now.

He's all gone now.

37. Set in ~~Stone~~ Skin

With my newfound, heartbreaking resolution Albatross helped me to see clearly, I have gained some trust from him. Which is good. *Really* good. Because he's my friend, my mentor, and all he's tried to do since I've come here is help me see the truth. He didn't want me to live in a sea of lies any longer than I have my whole life.

After the mess I made all over my cage floor, he allowed me to clean it up myself. Absinthe reluctantly brought a bucket of soapy water and a stack of white rags. I was strategic with how I approached such a task. I haven't had any real purpose in months, I think. I've been detoxing in my locked space from the reality I knew. It was necessary. Albatross tells me it was like breaking a drug addict from his addiction. Sure, it's painful and atrocious to live through…. But once you're out of the worst of it, it's smooth sailing. He told me that I was in a weeded section of the woods. There were thorns and sharp branches, and lots of poisonous insects. It was a nightmare to travel through alone, which is why he wanted to sit with me the entire time. He wanted me to know I had a friend. And that was very nice of him, indeed. I am grateful for my new friend.

I took my time, scraping up the vomit and blood with my hands before I began to deep clean the area. It was thrilling for me, actually. I am finally useful. I can do more than just wait around and feel the pull of depression tugging at my gown to ruin me, waiting for a man that would *never* come. I tried not to let that concept peel layers away from my heart, but the burn was still fresh. And I am still recovering.

After I proved myself useful, Albatross now lets me crawl out of my cage and sit while he shares with me more of his work. I recognize that I'm not allowed to come near his shadowed area. His feet and knees cringe inward if I scoot too close. I've wanted to ask him why he won't show me his face, but that's not my business. That kind of curiosity would earn the strike of Absinthe's bony fist. While I sit and listen, sometimes Absinthe brings me a glass cup of fresh eggs, and sometimes another slab of beef. I always show her my appreciation. She tells me I've lost thirteen pounds. I don't know where that weight went, but I share the same smile she gives me. If she thinks it's a good thing, I think it's a good thing.

There are still days when I am blinded and surrounded by darkness. And then, I see DaiSzek hovering over me in my mind's eye. He waits for me to follow him. But I'm no longer allowed. Albatross asked me to remain present. And I'll do just as he asks me, even if I'm swallowed in terror. I wave DaiSzek away, but he begs me with his eyes. He wants so desperately for me to jump on his back and go far away from here, to meet young Kane in Ambrose Oasis once more. But I swat that dream aside like a gorgeous butterfly trying to land on my shoulder. I can't go there anymore. Adjusting to the madness that engulfs my mind when I'm swarmed with hallucinations of my father or other beasts waiting to attack in the night. It was hard at first, of course, to mold myself into this nightly routine. I would rebel against it. I would lash out at Albatross for forcing me to endure such evil. But rightfully, I was put into my place. I've felt the pain of childbirth, without the love of having a child. I've undergone the pain of a broken leg, with bones sticking out of my skin like the jagged edge of a broken porcelain plate. I've choked on fluid in my lungs for several minutes as I experience the torment of being several stages into horrendous lung cancer.

After so many correctional forces, I have understood what my role is. To listen. To abide. To never question what is asked of me.

"Might I ask you a rather serious question?" Albatross speaks to me while I sit upright inside my cage.

I nod eagerly. "Please."

"I put you through certifiably strenuous tribulations. Every day. Every night. Yet, you never cry. Not even close. When was the last time you did cry?" He wiggles his gangly fingers through the air like he's trying to rid them of spiderwebs.

"I'm not sure," I answer mechanically. But I don't give specifics. A steel-plated wall rises in my mind, a warning, an impenetrable force that won't let me give details. That I cried to Dessin, and without him here, I've held it in—trapping it in my chest, only to be released when I see him again.

He hums in curiosity. "Ahh! You must have a block then?"

"A block?"

"Yes, yes! A block. It makes perfect sense. A block is a curious thing, indeed. Very hard to locate and even harder to remove. But it allows you to shut out the side of you that falls apart. Oh, but dear girl, if I removed it… do you even realize what would happen?"

I shake my head. I wish I could see his face and understand the expressions that hold his motives in a glass jar.

"Of course you don't. I'll inform you. If the block were lifted, your emotional floodgate would burst into billions of unearthly pieces. No one would be able to contain the universal explosion that would happen to your insides. It would be magnificent. *Magnificent!*" He gasps again. "That's probably how you're able to escape in your mind when bad things happen. Did someone teach you how to do that?"

Another quick shake of my head. "No, it just happened."

He's silent for a solid minute. His breathing becomes heavy. "Are you sure about that, dear?" His hands fold over his kneecaps, fingers drumming against them. "Have any holes in your memory that you're aware of?"

Even though I know better by now than to ignore a question or refuse to interact with him, I can't answer. I bite down on my lip and attempt to find a decent response.

"When my father beat me and hit me over the head with a club… I think he might have left me with some amnesia." I sigh.

Hands clap together. “Fascinating. *Truly*. I can’t wait to learn more.”

Before I can respond, the walls shudder. The chandelier vibrates like it’s attached to a large piece of machinery. A teacup falls to the ground, crashing into pieces, sending a piece of glass gliding across the floor, hitting my cage. I reach through the bars, pick it up and look back at Albatross for answers. I hear him shift in his seat. His knees are pressed together. And there’s a moment of searing silence that passes through this room like a ghost.

Another shudder rolls through the walls and furniture, followed by a *boom*. The sound of a strike of thunder. I grip the bars of my cage. *What’s happening?*

The door flies open and Absinthe is holding a crossbow. The skin on her cheeks is flushed, the color of wine. And she’s so sweaty, her thin forehead covered in a runny sheen of oil.

“We need to take the girl to the panic room,” she pants, looking at Albatross’s corner.

I can hear him stiffen.

“*Why?*” he asks through his teeth.

“He—” Absinthe gulps, face pinching in discomfort. “He decapitated thirteen soldiers. Their heads are on spikes around the mountain.”

He? He, who?

“We’re firing the perimeter but haven’t found his body.”

My eyes dart back and forth between the two of them.

“He won’t get in,” Albatross tells her.

Absinthe laughs, a strained old woman laugh. “You still feeding the girl that story?” She cackles some more, pinching the bridge of her nose. “Guess she hasn’t seen your face yet, or she wouldn’t have believed you.” Absinthe looks back at me with a wicked smile. “You really are a *stupid* girl,” she says with spite.

“What is she talking about, sir?” I ask Albatross.

A grunt turns into a shout and he slams the palms of his hands down on the leather chair.

Absinthe leans against the cabinets, the crossbow in her left hand, and holding up her weight with her right hand. She squeezes her eyes closed, like she’s in pain, then unravels a whiny laugh that howls like an old violin from her chest. Tears bulge from the corners of her eyes as she crows harder.

"Oh, goddammit," she chokes out between fits of laughter. "Were you going to hide it from her *forever*?! Did you really think she would want to be with someone in a shadow?!" Her laugh grows scary and aggressive. Albatross remains concealed in his corner. Without so much as a flinch.

Absinthe pushes off of the cabinet and rushes over to his side. "Get up, you little coward! Your father would roll over in his grave that he raised such a recreant. A *craven*! I let you play your little game of hide-and-seek with her, now it's time to be a fucking man!" She reaches down into his chair and snatches his arm. I see his hand dangling from her grip in the light. "He's coming for us *now*! Show the girl what he did the last time you pissed him off!"

What is she talking about? I sit up straighter to get a better look as Absinthe yanks Albatross from his seat. At first, I see that he is dressed in black slacks, a white button-up, and a red velvet robe wrapped around him. She heaves her body backward again, and he is fully in the light. My jaw falls into my hands and I gasp, loud and impolite.

Albatross has shiny red hair, the shade of a carrot. He is, by all accounts, skeletal. With gaunt cheeks, pallid skin, and small, mouse-like eyes. But my eyes fall first to his mouth, then his forehead. Above and below his lips are deeply indented lines with holes at the top and bottom of each line. I blink a couple of times, realizing they are markings of someone who has had their mouth... *sewn shut.*

I suck in an unsteady breath and my eyes travel to his forehead. Something written. Pink scars across his brow line. I have to squint my eyes, crank my neck forward to make out what it is.

"D-E-S-S-I-N," Absinthe spells it out and chuckles again. "He carved his name into Albatross's forehead. He cut in so deep, that blade scraped down into his skull!" She pushes him toward my cage. "He got tired of hearing my grandson talk, so he sewed his mouth shut too! I'm the one that found him! Considered leaving him a mute too!"

Albatross's cheeks turn bright red, and he stares at the floor in humiliation. His face, defiled, punctured, carved, made *hideous*. Made a product of Dessin's infamous wrath.

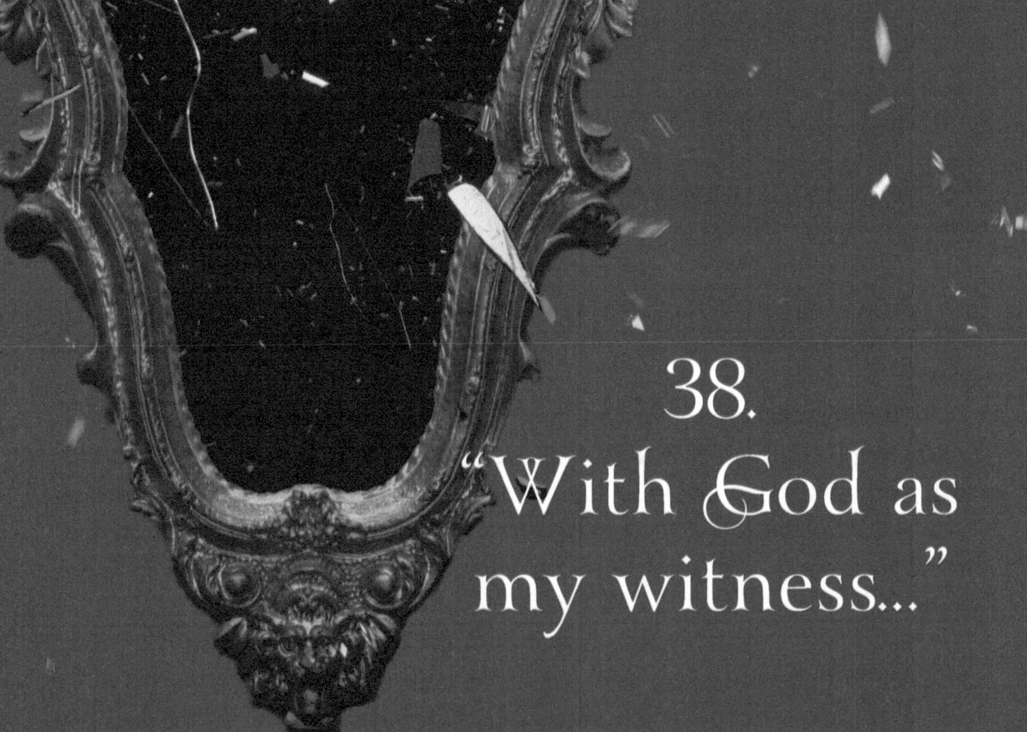

38. "With God as my witness..."

Albatross snarls, his face twisting in a revolting expression of annoyance. The thick pink scars on his forehead scrunching up together, making Dessin's name hard to read.

"He's not going to get in! This place is sealed tight! God himself couldn't break it down!"

I stare at them in disbelief. *There's no way.* My head mechanically starts to shake back and forth. *No.* Dessin? *My* Dessin? But Albatross said that he wasn't all of the wonderful and terrible things I thought he was? He said Dessin isn't powerful or destructive. They just wanted him to think he was. Would Albatross really go to these great lengths and let Dessin carve his name into his forehead and sew his lips shut? Just for this… experiment?

What—is—happening?

Absinthe shoves Albatross in the back with the head of her crossbow. He steps behind my cage and begins to push us to the door. I hold on, my fingers curled around the cold metal. *Where are we going?*

Dessin is alive. Could this be another trick? An experiment?

Absinthe guides us through the hallway. Another shudder echoes the halls, and a wave of dust floats downward from the ceiling. Albatross continues to make frustrated noises. *Is he embarrassed? Why won't he explain to me what's going on?*

"You said he was… *dead,*" I mutter, taking shallow breaths. A deliciously creamy, sugary flavor of hope coats my tongue. *Was he lying?*

Albatross scoffs. "You probably think I'm this absurd liar. But I assure you, I'm not. You have no idea how much progress I've made with you. Once we abide by this old woman's security measures, I'll take you back and we'll expedite the process. It'll be harder and far more agonizing for you, but I'm beyond certain the result will be glorious."

"Why do you have his name written on your forehead?" I ask cautiously. I need to know how much of what he said to me is true.

"Because that conceited sociopath, that behemoth of a man had no desire to learn from me! He wasn't like you! He wasn't eager like you are to be educated by what I have to teach you! That despicable human was vile and pure evil." Albatross pushes me faster down the hallway as he gets worked up by the haunting memory of Dessin and what he was capable of.

My attention is drawn to the glittering light fixtures dressed in crystals spaced apart as we move farther down this endless hallway. The walls are made of rocky stone, and the floors are dark hardwood. I suppose I would have imagined being tortured in a less elegant estate. With dudgeons and leaky ceilings. Or white walls and people with lab coats.

Absinthe uses the tip of her crossbow to tap a stone on the wall. It falls inward, and a stone door cracks open. A hidden room. Albatross wheels me through the doorway. First, I can't help but notice the many glass screens embedded into the stone wall to the right. There are at least fifteen monitors capturing the views of several angles, both outside and inside.

BOOM! Louder, closer to us, and a shock wave that passes through me.

Albatross shoves his weight into the back of my cage until we are out of the doorway and completely into this panic room. The inside looks like a different building entirely. The walls, ceiling, and floor seem to be made of steel. There are compartments along the floors parallel to the built-in screens. A bar of light stretches across the ceiling. The room is chilly, laced with the scent of mothballs and gasoline.

I watch Albatross and Absinthe gawk at the screens, scanning them for the source of the commotion. We can no longer feel the effects of an earthquake. They whisper back and forth as they point to different screens and compare notes. I shrink into the corner of my cage, rubbing my hands over the backs of my arms and my legs to keep warm.

My attention falls back to the scars on Albatross's face. Including the ones that cut into his lips. It makes me wonder what Albatross must have done to Dessin to provoke such a reaction. *And* if he was willing to mutilate him like that… what would he do to him for hurting me? But that would mean he would have to break into the facility. It's been months since I arrived. I can't cling to that ideal of him again, the pedestal I had him standing on, I can't fall for this trick. It's a sick delusion to test my loyalty.

Besides, of course it isn't real, because Dessin would have saved me in a matter of *days*. Not *months*. I would never have been belittled, isolated, or beaten. I wouldn't know what it feels like to have kidney stones, endometriosis, appendicitis, go through childbirth, endure a broken leg, and die from lung cancer. That man would have saved me from all of it.

"There! You see? He can't break in! He's embarrassing himself! He's giving up!" Albatross exclaims, throwing his twiggy hands at the monitor that he sees something on.

I crawl to the front of my cage, straining my eyes to see what he sees on that screen. On four of the screens surrounding his hands, there are mushroom clouds of dust or dirt. My eyes scroll over the destruction to peer between his hands plastered to the screen. I see a figure walking out of camera view. *Is that…? No. He isn't here. It's not him.*

Large groups of armed men close the distance from screen to screen, coming right for him. But that man walks with steps that are slow and intentional. He wants to be seen. He wants to be chased. I *know* that walk. It's drowning in confidence and the unfaltering ability to dominate all. I feel the candlelight within me flicker with excitement, with hope. I haven't tasted from that chalice of sweet victory in what feels like a lifetime.

And it feels damn good.

My two captors turn to me, smirking. Albatross's lips peel apart, separating in space, showing his teeth even though it is a close-mouthed smile.

"Looks like the legend of his royal psychopath isn't everything we thought it would be, hmm?" He taps his hand on the screen and sighs with satisfaction. "I told you I wasn't lying. He's a small man who believes he can do big things."

I keep my eyes level with him. Trying to hold back an emotion building in me.

"Tell me, Albatross… if that's true, then how did he get inside of the building?" I feel the malicious smile cutting through my lips and exposing my teeth.

He isn't dead.

Albatross and Absinthe whip their heads around to face the screens again. Their heads frantically swivel and pivot from monitor to monitor. When their eyes finally catch it, the muscles in their backs turn to stone.

Dessin stands in what looks like a sitting room, with a fancy rug, leather couches, and a low-hanging chandelier. He stands in the middle of the rug with his arms crossed over his chest. A brown leather jacket, white T-shirt, and brown pants. He's staring into the screens, smiling. It's *him*. Oh god, it's really him. It's his face. His stunning, tan, rugged face.

He came for me!

I'm filled with a blustery excitement that flutters around under my skin like a disturbed hive of bees. The rush of adrenaline has me wired and alert. I look over at the screens where Dessin once stood outside and notice the seven-foot-tall spikes, topped with human heads.

"*Shit!*" Absinthe slaps her hand across the screen.

"Listen, you little street child, he thinks finding you in here will be a breeze! Our advancements surpass everything! Every security measure is meant to kill any intruder on sight! So if I were you, I'd wipe that smirk off of your face and prepare yourself to watch this man die a sad and painful death!" Albatross's face is bright red, causing the name scar to protrude and turn a grayish red.

But I can't wipe the happiness away. I don't want to get my hopes up—because this could all be a test, a trick of the light, a confusing trial to ensure my loyalty to Albatross. This could all be in my head, the way DaiSzek rescued me from the hungry pack of men. But I haven't seen his face, his body, those glorious dark eyes in so long. I've longed for this feeling to return to my heart, like melting an ice cube over a fireplace.

Hearing Albatross laugh brings my focus back to the screens. In the far-left monitor, Dessin walks down a long hallway with an axe slung over his shoulder. His eyes are glazed with a ruthless certainty. Like a time traveler that's already witnessed the destruction of his enemies.

Albatross stomps his foot and looks back at me. "Flesh-eating acid," he says with a nod. "The sprinkler systems are about to shower him with it. In…"

"Three… two… one…" Absinthe counts down.

I press my forehead to the bars at the front of my cage. The shower of acid starts at the opposite end of the hallway, one section at a time, springing to life. I wait for Dessin to turn the other way, to find a place to hide from the storm of chemicals. Like a sheet of fog, it covers every centimeter of the vicinity. *TURN AROUND DESSIN!* He stops in his tracks like he's just now noticing the downpour coming from the ceiling ahead. Only a few yards left until it burns him into a puddle of bubbling skin and bones.

Slowly, confidently, he continues his walk into certain death. Doesn't stop to assess, doesn't wear a look of caution, doesn't seem to care at all that this is a security measure to keep him out.

But that isn't really his style, is it?

I half expect Absinthe to laugh, call him a fool for falling into the trap without a second thought. But the grandmother and mutilated man are gaping at him, silent, still, barely even breathing.

They clearly know him well. Know what he's capable of. And have the good sense to fear his confidence.

I think about the moment Demechnef came for Dessin with gas masks, throwing a canister into the room to stabilize him, knock him unconscious. But he smiled, breathing it in his nostrils, making a show of how many steps ahead he always is.

Today is no different.

As he walks directly into a veil of streaming acid, the room holds its breath. We wait for the screams, the howls, the melting flesh. But he keeps walking, unfazed, unharmed. A puppeteer holding a performance for this hidden audience.

And each step he takes is that of a hunter, a soul-sucking grim reaper coming to end them. To send them straight to hell.

"How did he—"

"He switched it out with water," Absinthe spits.

I laugh. It comes out as a loud scoff. "He's playing with you!"

At this, Absinthe takes a sharp spin on her heels, cranks my cage open, and crawls inside as I shuffle backward. Her knuckles crunch against my jaw, under my eyes, and a final swing to my bottom lip. I scream as her fist fills my eyes and nose with pressure, hot tears. Blood comes trickling down my lips. "Shut up, stupid girl! Shut up! He's not going to get in here without the fist of God to pound his way through that door!"

"Grandmother!" Albatross calls. Points to the screen. Soldiers flood the hallways, an organized formation of men trained to annihilate their target. But Dessin is already on the move, running up the side of the hallway wall, does a flip, a full rotation of his body through the air over the cluster of armed men, and it happens so easily. A clean move, a swing of his axe slicing through their necks like butter. Seven heads roll. Shreds of skin and spewing arteries soak the walls, the hardwood floors, and Dessin's clothes.

He takes no time to examine his work, study the massacre he's left behind. With a spin of his axe, he's darting down the hallway, turning the corner and—

"He's not aware of the latest addition to our security," Albatross mutters nervously.

The hallway he's in shudders, the floor throwing him off balance. He's stopped, looking from wall to wall. But he isn't responding fast enough. Metal walls rise on each end of the hallway, shutting him in. With an abrupt boom, the walls begin to move toward him, dragging against the floors, closing in, aiming to crush him.

No... do something!

The screens go black. The lights turn off. And we're submerged in total darkness.

I'm so used to this sight. No color. No movements. Just me. Alone. But the gasps and groans from Albatross and Absinthe remind me that this is really happening. I'm not trapped in my mind again.

"What did he do?! What the hell did that boy do? Is he dead? Did it crush him? We've never lost power before!" she shrieks each question like a dying black crow.

I feel a tremble from something hitting my cage. "If you so much as breathe too loudly, I'll take this crossbow and blast your blonde head off!" Absinthe is scared. I've never heard her sound remotely afraid of anything. It fills me with even more hope. *Please, let this be real.*

"He's *dead*, grandmother. He couldn't have survived it. The purpose is for the walls to move so fast that a human won't have enough time to even blink, much less think of a way out of it." I can hear him try and convince himself of this certainty. But Dessin is no average human. He plans ahead, moves strategically, and is always the smartest man in the room. I have to believe that he knew those walls were going to be there just like he knew the acid sprinklers needed to be switched with water.

Since they can no longer see me, I relax my face again into a smile, and get a rush of pride when I see him do what he does best. It's infinitely attractive.

Albatross grunts and suddenly he's at the left side of my cage. Breathing hard against my face, smelling of cigarettes, herbs, and grass.

"Now, we can still finish this! We can still see the progress I hoped for! Do you know why I put you through all of this?" His slick voice is an urgent whisper in my ear.

"No," I answer. "I have no idea why evil people do evil things."

"It wasn't evil! It was necessary! You were beaten. You were locked in a cage, a small, enclosed space. You had to sit in your own filth. You were force-fed. You were given ice baths." He's panting now. An ominous fear creeps inside of me. "This was all to trigger your childhood and your sister's."

My blood turns to acid. "*What?*" Memories of the basement, my father's episodes, and Scarlett's horrid stories pierce me. I'm stabbed from every direction. When she first told me about how she lived in a closet. She used the bathroom in the same place she slept. She was left alone for days. It was always dark. She would feel paralyzed with fear, and she would never fight back—because she was a child. Small. Helpless. I didn't know about the force-feeding though, or the ice baths.

She kept a lot to herself. Much like I've done.

"I was hoping being in her shoes would help you lower that mental block," he adds thoughtfully. I want him to step away from my cage. I want him to drop dead and decompose.

"You made me relive Scarlett's darkest years? So I would *cry*?! So I would break down for you?"

"Well, to put it in layman's terms, yes. I wanted you to self-destruct in your anguish."

I laugh. It's edgy and hoarse. A rope of blinding anger wraps around my neck. It's choking me with a desire to explode and murder. Scarlett's experiences were so much worse than what he put me through. She was only a small child. And getting a small taste of that fills me with horror.

"How. *Fucking*. Dare. You!" Smoke might as well be steaming from my scalp.

"I'm trying to help you!" he argues, his hands shaking the cage.

"NO! You're trying to get to Dessin! You're trying to turn me against him!" The more I scream, the more my brain swells against my skull and throbs from the beating.

"Look around! He's dead, dear! He couldn't have survived that moving wall!" Herbs. So many herbs blowing into my face.

I pause. "…Then why do you sound so scared?"

And like clockwork, the lights come back on, a low whining of machinery powering up. Albatross is on his feet, jumping back to the monitors to find Dessin. Alive or dead. The spot that Dessin once stood is closed off by the walls that are now smooshed together. I try and scope the area to see if there was any way he could have escaped… but my eye is bloody and swollen, clouding my vision with red tears. What if Albatross was right? What if there was no way he could have survived that? My heart contracts in a desperate need to see his face again. *Alive*.

Albatross starts to laugh and shriek in excitement. "There's blood!" He claps his hands together. "Look, there's blood on the floor where his body was crushed between the walls. I told you he was dead!"

Absinthe looks back at me with an insidious smirk. "No one is coming for you, stupid girl. *No one*."

No. He's not dead. He would have thought this through. He would have planned for this thoroughly. I can't believe that this would have stopped him. But what if it did? My heart sinks into a dreary place. Desperation. Hollowness.

"Let's get out there and see how many soldiers we have left. We need to pull his body out in the open," Absinthe instructs. "But *you-know-who* will be furious with us. We'll have a lot of explaining to do to save our own necks."

Who would she need to explain his death to?

Absinthe pushes a button next to the door and a waterfall of air decompresses, blasting Absinthe's gray, stringy hair away from her shriveled face. Albatross walks around her and touches the door, his fingers curl around the handle. With the brute strength of an explosion, the steel door is blasted off of its hinges, flying across the room as if it were cocked into a cannon and fired. It takes Albatross's frail body with it, his arms and legs flopping like earthworms being burned in the sun.

Absinthe and I both shriek in unison, looking back to the doorway.

A pair of legs hang from the ceiling just outside the door. The source of the blast that might have crushed Albatross under its weight. The body drops, his weight making the ground shake as his boots hit the floor. The dark hair, the brown leather jacket, and those fierce eyes like two nuclear weapons ready to devastate humanity.

It's him. He's alive.

Dessin.

Absinthe lifts her crossbow, points it at Dessin's chest, and as her hand trembles, attempting to aim it, Dessin's eyes slide to her. And it's over. With a quick kick upward, the crossbow is knocked out of her brittle hands and snatched up by his. He tosses it into the hallway as he has no need for that kind of weapon. He wants to feel their death, their pain with his bare hands. The next steps he takes are like a tiger, heavy, masterful, the thief of life.

"Dessin, I had nothing to do with this! *Nothing!*" she whimpers. And there it is again. The crippling terror. She's petrified. Her wilted eyes are glassy with pupils the size of cannonballs. For the first time since I met her, she looks like a sweet, gentle old woman. "Please, I've been very good too. Taken good care of the girl."

Oh, please. She says this as blood drips to my hands from my cheek.

"You've been good to her?" *Oh, god. That voice.* I've waited thousands of inhumane moments to hear the deep waters of that voice once more. "You're forgetting I was once a victim to your impatient outbursts, you vile bitch!"

I like that name for Absinthe. *Vile bitch.* He's so great with nicknames.

"But I've changed since you were a boy!" That old violin whines into this hollow room.

He takes another step. "Did you use a cane or your fists on her?"

She backs into a wall. Her drooping bottom lip quivering as he gets closer. But he stops, turning his head to face me in my cage. His gaze is a cold plague, sinking to the bottom of my stomach. He goes completely still as he examines my bruises, my swollen cheekbones, and my blood. *She used her fists*, I want to say. But I'm sure he already knows that.

I catch a movement below his hips and notice his hands shaking, clenching into a half fist. I've never seen him display his anger so uncontrollably.

"Now, listen here, boy…" Absinthe tries to reason with him, but it's too late. It's far too late. He closes the distance with a jerked step, takes her chin in his hand and forces it to face me. Absinthe's noises vary between crying and panting.

"Look at her!" he shouts into her ear like a combustion of thunder from God himself.

"Don't kill me!" she wails, globs of saliva forming in the corners of her mouth as she sobs hysterically.

Dessin laughs darkly, leaning closer to her ear. I can almost hear the hairs on her neck stand. "I have no intention of killing you. No, I have a punishment that will give me so much pleasure, my children will feel it when they're born." He smiles, wide, with eyes finding joy in pain and destruction. He's losing pieces of sanity.

"But I—"

Before her next plea, he pushes into her back, hard, the sound of lightning striking a tree, snapping a thick branch of wood. Absinthe's eyes lose focus, lose that glint of light. She falls to the ground sucking in shallow breaths. Is she in shock? Did he break her back? Paralyze her?

Dessin stares at the ground in front of me. Like he knows he has to face me again but isn't ready yet.

A weak, pathetic whimper squeaks from under the collapsed door. I glance over to see Albatross squirming like a rat caught in a trap. The door must be at least seventy-five pounds. I can't even believe Dessin kicked it hard enough for it to tear off its hinges. How strong does a person have to be for that to happen? How angry?

Dessin closes his eyes and listens to a voice inside of his head. I wonder how Kane feels about all of this. He smiles as he opens his eyes again, soaking in a single thought... probably what he's planning on doing to Albatross.

"Hello, old friend," he greets the frightened man under the door.

"DO YOUR WORST, BASTARD! You already condemned me to a life in the shadows! What could be much worse?!" He's howling under the obnoxious weight of the door. The scars on his face turning purple.

Dessin takes in a deep breath. "I branded you a slave to my reputation for causing me utter annoyance. What do you think I'll do to you for..." His next words are caught in his throat. He looks down. Swallows. Looks back up only with his eyes, from under the thick wisps of his lashes. "For hurting... *her*."

A burst of doubt erupts in my gut. What if this is another trick? What if I've lost my mind? I'm playing out a fantasy in my head. Dessin wouldn't have left me in here this long. *It's not real, is it?*

Albatross says nothing. He stays perfectly still, held captive under his steel door.

Dessin shifts his head to face me without taking his eyes off Albatross.

"What did he do to you?" Dessin asks quietly.

He's talking to *me*. I don't know how to respond. I don't even know if this is actually happening.

"I needed to trigger her childhood and some of Scarlett's! Just so she could remove the horrible burden of being mentally blocked! I was trying to help her!" Albatross is stuttering, scrambling over his excuses. Trying to push the door off. But Dessin doesn't need the door to keep him exactly where he wants him.

With an overwhelming sense of disgust with myself, I drop my face into my hands and start to shudder. My bones vibrate under my skin.

Dessin sticks his jaw out, fists squeeze together until they turn ghostly white. He cocks his head to fully face Albatross. Chest moving faster than my body can tremble. Not another second is wasted. He lifts the steel door like it is made of cardboard, lunging to the ground to take Albatross's neck into his wide, grizzly hands.

"Skylenna—close your eyes!" Dessin instructs with a voice that could split the earth in half. I do as he says, shut my eyes and drop my face back into my hands. But it doesn't block out the screams that sound like his throat is being shredded into fine wisps of tissue.

"I'll do more than condemn your life to the shadows. Let's see how brave you are without the pieces that make you a man!"

And then a boyish scream, something between a malfunctioning machine and a boiling teakettle. I hear sounds of peeling, ripping, or maybe unzipping. And then the screams are muffled and choking. Gagging, sputtering, gasping. Then, nothing. Silence.

Silence.

I keep my face cradled in my hands, rocking back and forth. I feel broken and underwhelming to a man like Dessin. If this is real, he did all of this for a sad, weak young woman who can't even defend herself from a captor. I couldn't even stand up for myself as Absinthe struck me in the bathtub. And then there's that part that secretly hopes this isn't real. That prays this is all a trick. If it is all in my head, then he can't really see how ugly I really am. He's strong, and handsome, and full of fire.

Without success, I try to minimize the compulsive shaking of my muscles. But I'm cold. I've gone so long without the warmth of a simple blanket. Or a decent meal.

Click. Chink.

Something touches my cage door. If this is real, I'm guessing his revenge was short lived, and he's ready to assess the damage. Strands of my hair are hanging down in my face. I lower my hands and peek out to see him. Or to see Albatross, waiting to tell me I imagined it all.

But it's not Albatross. It's *him*. It's Dessin kneeling down in front of me, gripping the cage door like he might kick that off of its hinges too. He opens it up, his stunning face unmasked by the bars. And all in one swoop, it's not Dessin anymore. It's Kane. *My* Kane. His lips part and he raises his chin, he blinks several times, like it's his body's way of trying to process the shock. His dark eyebrows lift upward in an empathetic expression, then turn to remorse, agony, and anguish.

He reaches out to me. That large abrasive hand moves slowly through the air, timid, adjusting to the memories Dessin is offering him. When it finally hovers over my cheek, I lean into it, closing my eyes.

If this is a trick… it's worth the beating.

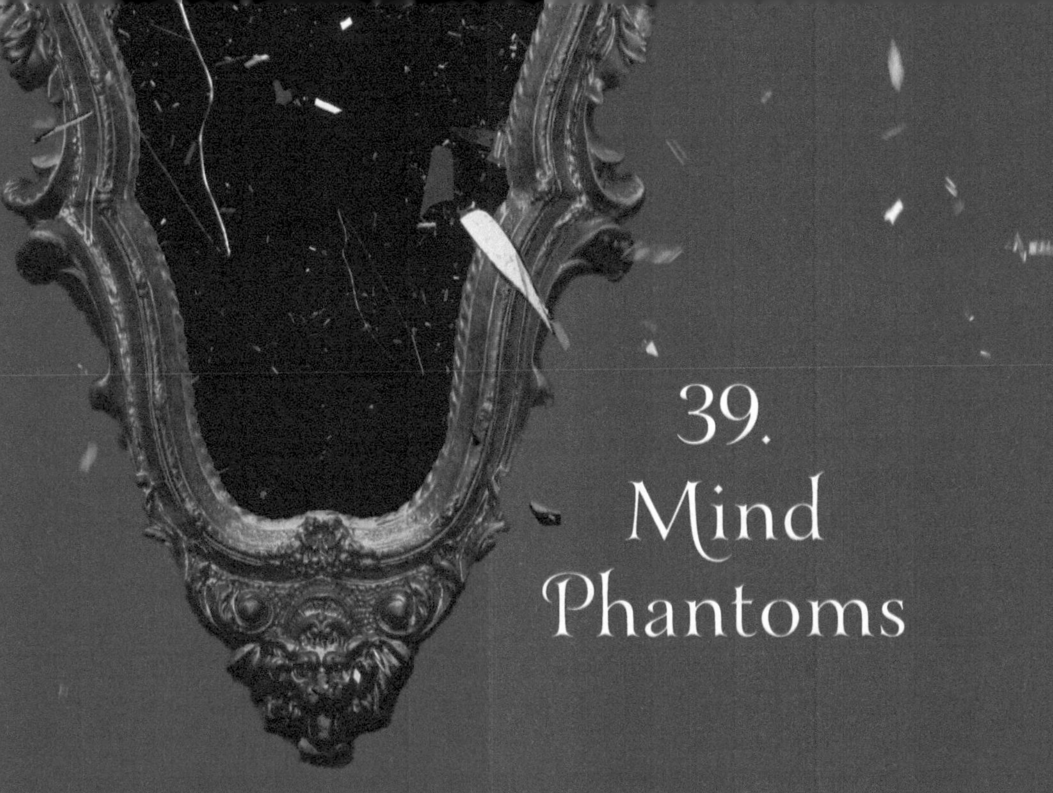

39. Mind Phantoms

For at least a whole minute, Kane holds my wounded face in his palm, blood dripping from my skin to his. When I open my eyes once more, I see that his are filled with tears. Thick, glossy tears. He says nothing, only watches me, breathing through parted lips. Stunned and unable to shift his weight.

"Is this—*real*?" I ask. The question rubs against my throat like it has teeth.

Kane sighs like he's been holding his breath, dipping his head under the cage to crawl in like a bear in a buggy. But he manages. His shoulders graze the bars as he shifts on his knees. And suddenly, with those four inches he's crossed, I don't feel alone anymore.

His red, misty eyes trail over my face, absorbing my injuries, assessing my trauma. He takes my hands in his, fingertips caressing my knuckles, and in one gentle motion, he pulls my hands up to the sides of his face, placing them on his cheeks, his stubbled jawline. He's covered in splattered blood and sweat, but nothing could ever repel me from wanting to be close to him. These are the war markings of my rescue, and I'm eternally grateful.

"Real."

He reacts to my cold touch with a small flinch, yet closes his eyes at the feel of my skin. I almost forgot how warm he is, how his touch is like a blanket to keep out the frost.

"Skylenna." His deep voice breaks, weakens, suffocates. "I'm so sorry." He's angry, hurt, and full of remorse. A guilt that may never leave him. But all I can feel is the clenching muscle in his jaw, the permeating heat from his fury. *I've waited so long to touch you again.*

"I'm sorry it took me so long…" He leans forward, kissing the top of my hand.

"But why? What were you doing for four months?" Maybe it was *three*. Or more.

He straightens up, as much as he can without hitting his head at the top of the cage. His eyes grow large and wet, like I've spoken another language. "Four *months*?"

I nod slowly. "Yes. But it's felt like a lot longer," I say with a dry mouth. "I was convinced you were dead… or that their experiment worked and you discovered you weren't superior. You weren't capable of everything Dessin can do." I don't want to tell him what I've been through. It's unmentionable. It's humiliating. I know he'll want to know, and he'll press me to tell. But I've been a prisoner for this long, my mind is still trapped here, with long periods of darkness, eating like a dog, and being beaten without reasonable cause. I've fallen apart and he wasn't here to pick up the pieces.

His head lowers, a flash of agitation and disbelief. "You thought you were in here for *four months*?" He weaves his hands into my dirty hair. "Skylenna, it took me four hours and thirteen minutes to save you. And I'm ashamed it took us that long."

What? Hours? NO. NO!

I think I'd know if I were in the belly of Satan for only a matter of hours. That's not possible, unless… "Have I lost my mind?"

I have, haven't I?

"God, no. Albatross and Absinthe were injecting you with *Mind Phantoms*. It's a chemical. The more concentrated it is, the more susceptible you are to believing the delusions you are given. They must have known I'd come for you quickly and that they would only have a short time with you. They needed to have a lasting effect." He presses his forehead to mine. "It kills me to think you thought I wasn't coming for you. It would have been a couple of hours faster if Dessin didn't have to disable all of their security traps."

I shake my head in shock. "It was all so real… I thought about you every day. It was the only thing that helped me endure the suffering." I breathe in his alluring cedar scent. I want him to hold me, to press my face into his neck. "I'm so scared I'm going to blink and this will all have been inside my head."

With very little room, Kane leans forward to fold me in his arms, tucking me away into the safety of his warmth and embrace. A thick emotion clogs my throat, burns my eyes, and causes my chin to tremble.

And like many times before, he's the key to unlock my pain, unveil my truth.

"You can let go, honey. I've got you."

My sobs break free of their chains in a single breath. It whooshes from his chest, spilling out over his shoulder with shivers so violent I think I might break in half. But Kane's grip is stronger, holding me together, keeping my severed pieces from scattering across my cage.

"I will show you every day that it's real. You're going to fall asleep in my arms tonight. And DaiSzek will sleep on your other side to keep you warm. And when you wake up with your head on my chest, I'm going to tell you how grateful I am to have you." Kane leans away and glances down at my lips and back up to meet my eyes. "Skylenna, I—"

Movements across the screens, men filling the halls, dozens of them. I tense up and look back at him. My eyes darting chaotically from his eyes to the screen. Back and forth. As if seeing the reflection, he backs out of the cage. His hands wait patiently in the air for me to take them. Without protest, I hook my fingers around his wrists and let him guide me out of the tunnel that only leads to my demise.

He glances at the screen, examining the movements and the direction of the soldiers. His expression now calm, calculated, and simmering with violence. *Hello, Dessin.*

"The trap that they thought crushed me is where the soldiers will stop to investigate first. They'll need to pry it open to search for my *supposed* body. That's on the south wing. We can make our way out to the north, but we only have one minute and forty-eight seconds." He studies the hallways for another moment like it's a chessboard and he's finding the ten moves to put him ahead.

"I'm ready," I tell him, holding his hand between us. Even if this is in my head, it will always be better than the alternative.

He looks down at me from his peak of six feet, four inches and smiles, dazzling me with his white teeth. "I'll lead."

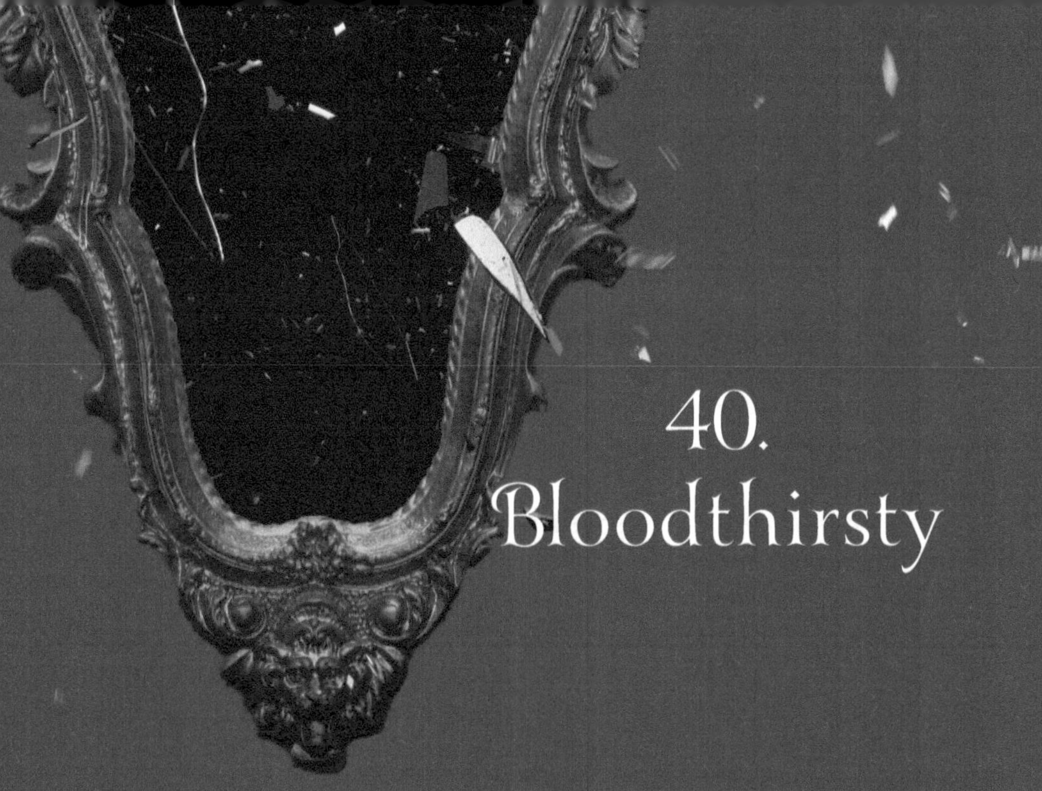

40. Bloodthirsty

The two Emerald Lake mountains near the asylum are where Demechnef relocated. We escape from a tunnel that leads into the forest.

Albatross was right, it certainly is a fortress.

He hops onto his motorcycle and signals for me to mimic his action. I nervously tug at the white medical gown I'm still wearing, smudged with blood around my neckline. I look back up as Dessin removes his brown leather jacket and passes it to me.

"We'll get you changed when we're safe in the Dark Wood." He nods again for me to get on the bike. Sliding my right hand into the sleeve, I smell him everywhere. His sweet natural scent that is both soothing and intoxicating.

Hiking my leg over the bike and latching on to Dessin's waist, I see a group of twenty soldiers come tumbling out of the tunnel. Conveniently, also with motorbikes. We are equally matched with speed as Dessin starts the engine and fishtails us out of the perimeter of the mountain/Demechnef fortress. But I can't imagine that Dessin would come this far without a plan, without an effective escape route.

decisions, weaving through trees, staying ahead of the mob only by a few yards.

"We can't lead them back to where we're going…" I shout into his ear, fighting the force of the wind. "So, what's the plan?"

He glances over his shoulder, lips curling upward, not enough to make a smile, but enough to answer my question. "Are you still doubting me?"

Dessin accelerates the speed by thirty miles per hour and we're flying through the forest like a wildfire devouring dead leaves and plants in a drought. The branches are cracking under the wheels, the healthy trees whizzing past us, while my hair dances behind me in the rush of strong winds… I lift my face from Dessin's back. The rays of the sun leak through the speckled peepholes of the canopy of trees. They shower me in their warmth, welcoming me back to my home, to the blessings of Mother Nature, to the humming sounds of honeybees, and to the early morning taste of earthy air.

Something clinks against the back of the bike. I look back to find a crossbow pointed at us, with a fluffy red feather attached to the back of the arrow.

"It's a tranquilizer. They don't want to kill us. Just knock us out!" Dessin lifts the handles of the bike upward to jump us over an overgrown tree root. We hiccup in the air and come slamming back down to the ground without skipping a beat. One or two bikes don't make the same move and are ejected from their seats, breaking bones as they are flung into the trees.

The next red-feathered arrow is shot through the air with perfect aim, blundering toward Dessin's head, he seizes it by the stem with two fingers as if it were unmoving, sitting on a shelf like a book waiting to be snatched. He uses the same hand to launch it back to its home, soaring into the neck of the man to our left.

We can't take them all out like this.

Is he going to steer us off a cliff into a body of water? Are we leading them into a trap? Is he going to pull over and fight them off one at a time? I wish I could take a dive into his mind and comb through his plans.

The ride starts to get bumpy as we drive over a passage of rocks, some small like pebbles, others jagged and the size of my head. This slows us down and allows the fifteen or so other riders to catch up. We're bouncing up and down, jerking over the uneven obstacles. The ending of the rocky terrain is in sight, a flat dirt path ahead. I strap myself against his back, hugging my face to the muscles flexing over his shoulder blades, desperate not to be taken away from him again.

The other bikes succeed at closing in on us. A half circle of roaring engines moments away from causing us to wreck. Arrows are being shot from different directions, but Dessin is crafty with his shift of weight from one side to the other, driving in zigzags. I release a breath as we tumble over the last of the rocks, but the riders are still so close, and Dessin isn't speeding up.

"Dessin!" I shriek. Why is he slowing down? "*Go*!"

He turns to give me a side view of his face, a flash of dominance, a flash of the alpha in his dark-mahogany eyes. They say, *fear not, we've already won.*

And just like that, a black shadow dives through the air from behind a sheath of trees. A pouncing beast with an unhinged jaw, showing off its white, sharp teeth. And those cinnamon eyes are in hunting mode, locking in on his prey, blazing with certain victory.

Something between a laugh and a scream comes out of my mouth.

DaiSzek makes a clean leap over our bike, wiping out three soldiers, knocking them off their motorcycles. Gasps and grunts of impact come from behind us. I regret turning around, regret the gory image of DaiSzek sinking his teeth in a soldier's head, popping it like a balloon.

He's merciless, fast, and unreasonably *feral*.

Dismemberment. Skinning. Scalping. An overwhelming amount of flesh and blood. It seems DaiSzek shares Dessin's vengeful temper.

We accelerate again, aiming for a broken tree, slanted like a ramp.

"Hold on!" He grips the handles, leaning forward with focused precision.

A violent wave of panic crashes into me as we speed up the inclined trunk and eject into the forest, airborne, soaring over a small cliff. The humid air of wet tree bark and wildflowers blasts me in every direction. At least ten more soldiers are following us, coming up from our right and left sides. My teeth and bones clank together as we land, and I flinch at the sound of grown men screaming all at once, and then… *silence*.

We slow down to a stop, and Dessin reaches back to grip my hand.

"What happened? Did we lose them?" I try to look behind us but he stops me.

"Don't look," Dessin instructs.

"*Why?*"

He parks the bike against the tree and steps off of it to face me. I can still catch a hint of that murderous temper, quelled only slightly, but still remaining unsatisfied.

"I set a trap," he says like I'm supposed to know what the result of that trap was.

I blink and nod for him to continue.

"It was a very thin string blade. It's why we had to be launched over it. Because we needed to fly over it—not *through* it."

I remember the sound of the snapping. The splash of liquid. My mouth parts as it all comes together.

"You sliced them *in half?*"

His focus is redirected to something behind me. I whip my head around, my entire body jerking as if I'm preparing to be hit, smacked, beaten. But his large hands hold me steady, covering my shoulders with slow, reassuring strokes.

"It's DaiSzek," he says calmly.

Dessin pulls a rag out of his pocket and wipes DaiSzek's mouth and neck. The blood of my captors soaking through every fiber.

"You did so well, Dai."

My heart swells with gratitude. I forget everything that had me questioning my morals just a moment ago. The dead soldiers. The way they were killed.

As of an hour ago, DaiSzek has only been a figment of my imagination. This herculean, wondrous animal has saved me multiple times. And every time, it's always a great risk. He's always outnumbered or facing beasts larger than him. He never hesitates or leaves me to fend for myself. Somehow, I have gained his loyalty and his love. I don't know what I've done to deserve him, but witnessing him soar over us to tackle our attackers. The looks of shock, disbelief, and childlike terror. DaiSzek is the monster that is supposed to be extinct, risen from the grave, delivering them to hell. I've only been starstruck with one other being, and that's Dessin.

I kneel as DaiSzek walks up to me, slowly, like he's very much aware I've been living in a hostile state. His gigantic head presses up against my chest so gently it breaks my heart. I swoon and sigh in relief, hooking my arms around his neck. A familiar warmth, like sinking into a hot bath. I know this feeling, I haven't touched it in so long. Months. But that's a lie. It's only been hours.

I tangle my fingers in his black fur, and remember how he saved me in that cage, he brought me to young Kane. And it's like DaiSzek can sense my need to hold him close, because he stays tucked in my embrace.

"Thank you," I whisper. "You didn't just save me out here. You saved me when I was trapped in that cage. You took me to a safer place."

DaiSzek snuggles his head into me. I can sense Dessin's eyes watching us both.

"I love you, DaiSzek." My lips are lost in the fur around his ear. "I'll love you until the day I die."

And I will. *I'll always love my boys.*

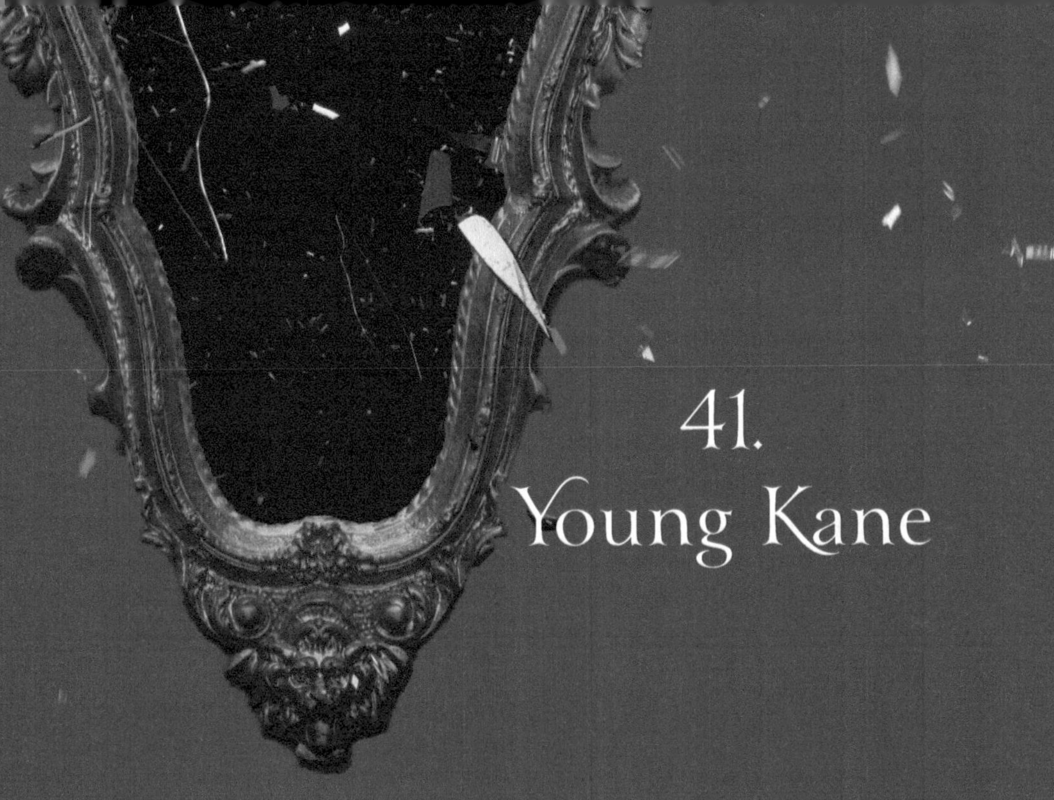

41. Young Kane

After getting far enough away from Demechnef mountains, we stop so I can quench my thirst.

I drop to my knees at a skinny creek trickling over shiny pebbles and rocks. Maybe it's all in my mind, the dehydration, the sandpaper mouth. Maybe it's a side effect of the chemicals. But I'm not ladylike as I scoop the water into my hands and lap it up like a dog on all fours.

Those brown eyes burn into my back, watching me slake my thirst. It's in his silence that tells me he knows this feeling all too well. He's been starved. Beaten. Convinced of his imminent death. He can relate as I slurp from the source, dipping my mouth into the stream.

Once I'm finished, I look over my shoulder with cold water spilling down my chin. Dessin's shoulders stiffen.

"Why did you do it?"

"Do what?" I ask, drying my hands on my gown.

"Why did you lead them to you? I asked you to hide…" This might be the first time I've heard him struggle to get a sentence out. Normally, he's confident and collected. But now, he looks at me like I've plunged a stake through his heart.

"You took too long. I wanted to make sure you'd get out safely."

He leans down in front of me, uses his thumb to wipe the water from my chin, letting it linger below my bottom lip.

"I had it under control. I had everything under control." His jaw tightens, hand falling away. "You had no right to go rogue like that. If you would have just stayed hidden and waited patiently for me… *none* of this would have happened!" His words are soaked in oil and fire.

"I just wanted to help—"

"Do you have any idea what it did to me? What it did to Kane? To hear your screams as you were hauled away from us?! To know what was going to happen to you when Albatross got a hold of you?" He steps away from me in a fluster. Veins bulge from his arms. Brow tight and clenched together.

"I—I'm trying really hard to understand how you could be the one upset right now." I lock my jaw and hold my breath. Trying to contain the river of frustration.

Dessin paces in front of me, shaking his head. The sunset hovers over the horizon behind him, a deep golden orange, like the start of a forest fire.

"After everything we've been through, you didn't believe I'd make it back? Jesus, it nearly destroyed us to see you like this!" he shouts, pointing to my bloody, bruised face.

I flinch. Every muscle, cell, atom, and fiber—*flinches.*

His face falls, all anger and resentment sliding from his cheeks to his chest, tucking itself back into the toxic space of his heart. He blinks slowly, relaxing all features, including those hickory-smoked eyes, smothered in warm butter.

It's the slack look, the emptiness that tells me he's dissociating again.

And as the darkness clears, he walks to me, a heaviness in his steps, a defeat and a longing that bows down to me. With the weight of his shoulders, he lunges into me, lifting me off of the ground, arms tied around my waist, his face tucked into the side of my neck. And his lips caressing my cold skin.

"Kane?" I choke out, my chin resting on his shoulder and my chilled hands grasping his neck. "You should let me know when you show back up."

"Why would I do that?" he hums into me. "You recognize me before I get the chance to tell you."

I relax my face, closing my eyes, inhaling his woodsy scent. "It was bad," I confess.

"I know," he says, understanding that even though for him it was four hours, for me it was four months. "I'm hurting with you, honey."

"It was horrible. It was so horrible." My voice cracks, ripping down the middle. The pieces fall to him in heartache.

"You're safe now."

"I just wanted to come home."

His hand finds my hair, comforting me with its gentle caressing. Before he says what's building in his mind, stirring in his thoughts, Kane pulls a rag from his pocket, swiping it through the stream.

"Chin up," he whispers, hovering the dripping cloth over my right eye, asking for permission. I nod, swallowing down the stumble my heart makes.

With soft dabs, Kane cleans the blood from my cheek, under my nose, the clotted cut over my left eyebrow. I wince yet melt into his gentle touch. There are so many things I want to say. Why don't you feel the same way I do? Why did you kiss me? Why did Dessin make love to me? What does it all mean? And how—*how* can you look at me like this? Like I'm your most valued piece of treasure. Like I'm the beating of your heart. I'm the flowing of your veins.

"Can you tell me something?" Kane asks. "Dessin says you thanked DaiSzek for saving you in your cage. You said he took you to a safe place. What did you mean?"

I'm reminded of the great shadow of DaiSzek, hovering over my defiled body in the cage. In the bizarre darkness, climbing onto his back and him carrying me away to the meadow. Where young Kane sat with me until it was all over.

"When I was blinded and left to go mad in the darkness, I was in a paralyzing panic, I think I was in shock. I think I became delusional. I saw DaiSzek in the cage. He took me somewhere far away into the forest. It was a beautiful meadow with purple flowers. And… *you* showed up," I tell him, refusing to let go of his embrace.

"*Me?*"

"Yes, but it wasn't who you are now. It was you when you were thirteen years old." I sigh into his shoulder. "You were smarter than me even at that age."

Kane leans back, holding me an arm's length away by the caps of my shoulders.

"Did you learn a name for that place?" He searches my eyes for the answer he's looking for. *Wait*… does he know what it's called?

"How did you know it has a name?" I ask cautiously. I thought I made it up in my mind. I thought it was as fictional as a dream? A hallucination?

He smiles like the answer is obvious. "Ambrose Oasis."

"*What?*" I gasp, stepping away. "How did you know that?"

"Because I'm the one who named it."

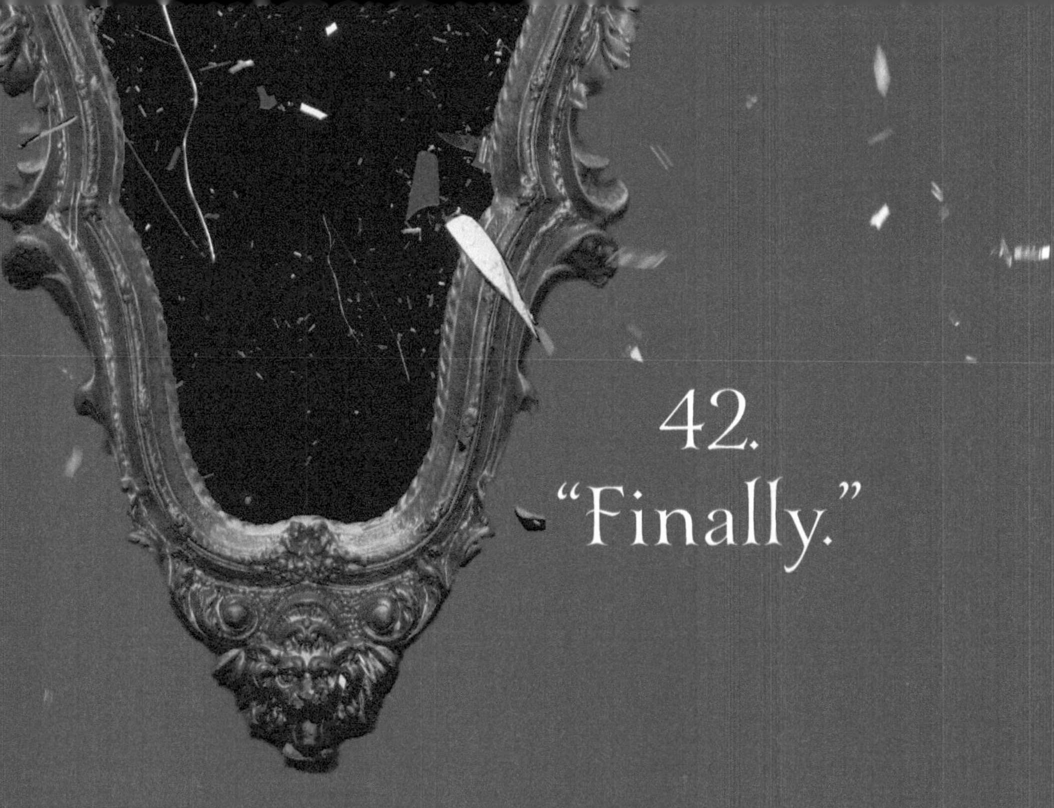

42. "Finally."

Dessin told me that the day I learned everything… it would be the worst day of my life. But it's not enough to keep me from prying.

"I might be as bad as Greystone with letting secrets slip," he says.

I hiss and beg and tug on his coat as we get back on the bike to get back to the Evergreen Dark Wood. It's dark, and after a while, I give up. My head falls against his back, and I watch the moon touch the top of the sky, shimmering down on the bushy evergreen trees.

Kane slows down for a few yards before we come to a complete stop. I blink sleepily as Kane helps me off of the bike. Immediately, I can't wait to change into my clothes, remove this thin white gown and toss it into the wilderness. I can't wait to eat, to sit in front of the fire and fall asleep in his arms.

I turn away from Kane, searching for his pack. Instead, I'm greeted with three sets of eyes. Under the glow of the moon, there are two men and a short woman. One of them has tears streaming down their soft cheeks, and the other two look like they're fighting to keep it together.

My heart gallops in my body, springing to life like a young stallion.

He didn't just rescue Ruth. He went back for Chekiss and Niles, too. He brought my friends back to me. I whip my head to stare at Kane. He nods in heartwarming confirmation.

"Sky?" Ruth mutters, followed by an exasperated sob. I hold my arms open as she runs to me, and as we collide, her body shakes from a heavy cry.

"I thought I'd never see you again! I can't believe you sacrificed yourself to make sure we got out safely! I was so scared—"

"It's okay, Ruthie." But my words are thick and heavy like molasses in my throat. "We're all together now," I reassure her as my hands rub up and down her back.

"You promise?"

I nod against her embrace. But I'm not sure. I don't know the outcome of anything. That cage left me numb, the torture left my heart bruised and barely beating. When my eyes open, I see my boys waiting patiently for their turn.

Ruth and I separate. She wipes her nose on her sleeve and steps aside, smiling.

Niles charges me first, lifting me into his arms and spinning me in circles. He's beaming with excitement, laughing as he squeezes my ribs to the point of pain. He sets me down and grabs the sides of my head to demand my full attention.

"You made a promise to me. You said you'd get us out of there, and that we would have a home with you," he reminds me with glistening eyes. His cheeks are a shade of watermelon pink, and his golden hair is just as groomed and thick with styled curls as I remember. "Thank you for keeping that promise."

"It was all Kane. But you're welcome. We would have never left you in there."

He caresses my cheeks with his thumbs, noticing the swelling, the cuts, the result of my time away. His throat bobs as he nods.

But as I step up to Chekiss, my chest coils inward and my bottom lip quivers. I experience the rush of what it was like when my father would come home, in the early days when we would share an ice cream cone and long hugs. That same feeling of longing and emotional attachment.

He wears his frown as if it's a zipper, holding in a long-overdue tsunami of tears. Our foreheads touch gently, hesitantly. And just like that, we release the air we were both holding in our lungs. A sob shudders from my chest, and he lets me weep, patting my back, cooing in my ear that I've done so well. That I have such a big heart. I've gone most of my life without affection, love from a father, hugs from a mother. Scarlett was the closest I ever got, and even she had those days of madness, of violent coping, or morbid darkness. But today is different. Today I'm surrounded by people that care about me.

"Finally," Chekiss says, pulling away to wipe my tears.

I smile. "*Finally.*"

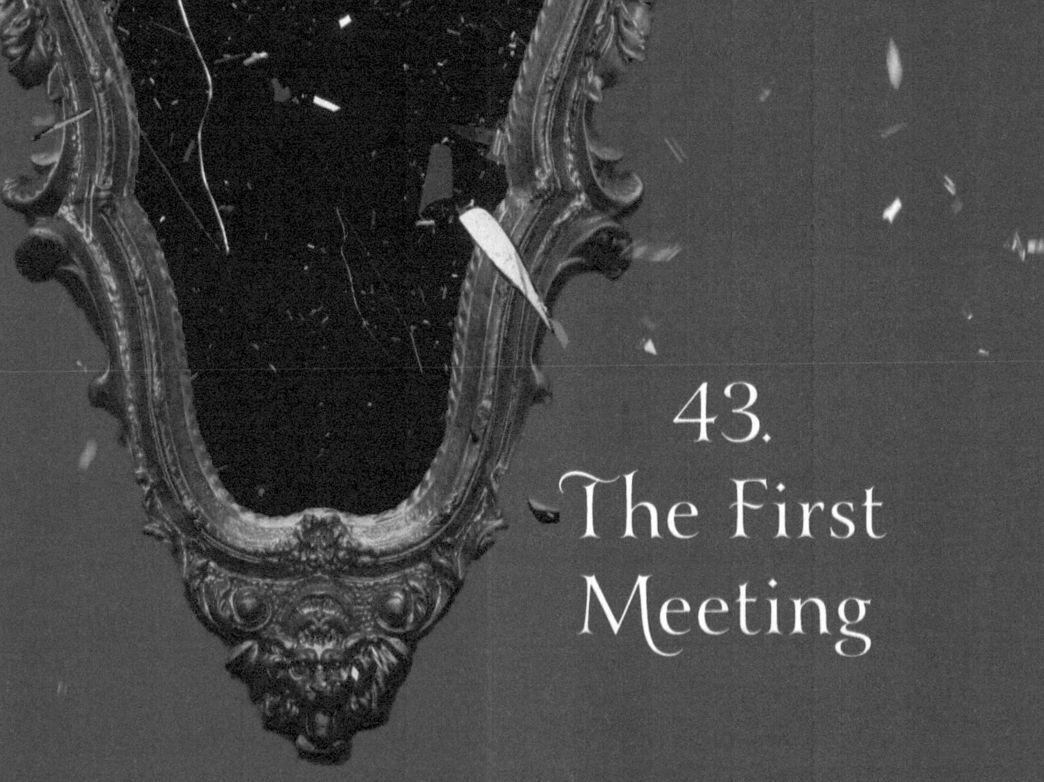

43. The First Meeting

Standing in the center of the symphony of crickets and the howling winds, my friends are smiling, wiping their tears. It all feels like a dream.

"I want you all to officially meet Kane." My eyes burn with exhaustion, but I nod him over. He's been leaning against a tree, watching us with a look of peace and relief.

"We already met," Kane assures me.

Niles laughs. "If you call that a meeting." He struts over to me to stand between us.

"*Hey ugly, you're coming with me,*" Niles mocks. "Then skip ahead to us watching him slaughter soldiers next to the black beast who likes to chew on human brains like they're a toy you can buy at the market!" He looks at the group then huffs. "It truly was a pleasure."

Ruth chokes out a laugh that comes from deep in her chest. Chekiss rolls his eyes.

"I did not call him *ugly,*" Kane corrects.

I can't help but laugh at that.

"*You* didn't. But your evil twin did." Niles crosses his arms.

"*Niles...*" Chekiss warns, using the authoritative voice of a father. "Remember who you're talking to."

Kane pushes off the tree and takes three confident strides up to Niles who is still pouting in front of the group. "The man you met was Dessin. He doesn't have the best bedside manner."

Niles cocks his head back awkwardly, like he's preparing to be hit in the face.

"No murderous rages?" Niles asks cautiously.

"No."

"Affinity for gutting the male anatomy?"

"Nope."

"Maniacal needs for vengeance for those who've wronged Skylenna?"

Kane sighs. "No."

"Not even when I do this?" Niles holds unblinking eye contact with Kane as he reaches to his left, flicking me in the arm.

"*Hey!*" I hiss, rubbing the stinging area with my other hand.

"You're pushing it," Kane says, unamused.

"Niles!" Chekiss barks from behind him. A thick hand smacks Niles in the back of the head, hard enough to hear his teeth clack together.

"Alright! God, I was merely testing his patience with me."

"You're lucky he has a lot of that," I tell him.

Niles nods slowly, narrowing his eyes into small childlike slits. "And how often are we going to have the pleasure of enjoying Dessin's lack of manners?"

"He only surfaces when there's danger. And when those times come, you'll be glad for it. He might be a dick, but he's a dick that'll keep you alive."

"Mmm, yeah that part was kind of nice." Niles shrugs.

Ruth greets Kane with a rosy-cheeked smile. "You're very tall," she blurts out. "I met Dessin the first night I met Skylenna."

Smooth, Ruth.

"And you're very short." Kane smiles back.

Chekiss then approaches Kane with his hand extended. "Thank you for saving us. And thank you for taking care of her."

"And thank *you* for getting her to leave that prick, Aurick!" The inappropriate remark comes from Niles… *again*.

Before I can flick Niles for not keeping his mouth shut, Kane laughs. Unlike any other noise, it fills me with blind rhapsody. He's chuckling at Niles, squeezing his eyes shut like he was taken off guard by that comment. I look around and Ruth is giggling with her fingers covering her mouth.

"I'm thankful for that as well." Kane winks at me. A surge of galvanic energy takes me by surprise, galloping through my bones. "I think we should have a group hug!" Ruth suggests.

"I don't think so." Chekiss swats Niles away from trying to pull him in.

"Me too," I agree, reaching for Chekiss to join. He sighs dramatically and closes half a circle with Niles on his other side.

I look back at Kane, showing him the empty space between me and Ruth.

Kane raises his eyebrows. "I don't really do *hugs*."

Pfft. That's a lie. We hug all the time.

"Ohhh, just get in here! You deserve some love after all you've done today," Ruth coos at Kane, then snickers at Niles who is tickling her side as he tugs her closer to him.

Kane glances back at me as I mouth the word, *please.* He looks away and laughs.

"Okay, but this is the first and last group hug we do, agreed?" Kane looks around at the group, everyone nods in agreement. He closes the gap between me and Ruth, placing his large arm over her tiny shoulders.

My breath hitches. A familiar chill of terror crawling up my back. I'm reminded of the cage, the blinding darkness. And this close contact triggers me. My pulse races under my skin, pounding like a waterfall in my ears. I fight like hell to keep my breathing less than noticeable. *This is a trauma response*. Hide it. Put it on a leash and lock it away.

I don't want to worry them. They've been through hell too.

"Aw, we just started a tradition, you guys!" Niles grins.

Chekiss grunts. "No, we did not."

"We agreed this was the first and last time," Kane reminds him.

An unwanted thought surfaces, sticking thorns in my side, nudging me to the side of doubt. What if I didn't escape? What if I went mad? It's entirely possible. I hallucinated DaiSzek. I went off to a meadow.

My mind could have collapsed on itself, could have shut down and stopped living.

Either way, I needed this. I don't care if it's real or not. I don't care if I've crossed over into insanity.

Kane is gazing down at me with a look of bittersweet relief. Like he knows what's going on in my head right now. Like he knows this is exactly what I needed after breaking out of hell. I needed a family to come home to. He drops a kiss on the top of my head.

"So, did you two have sex yet?" Niles blurts out like the little monster he is.

Our heads snap up to the pest. "Niles!" I scold. "There was the line back there. Did you see it when you crossed it?" I unhook my right arm from around Chekiss and reach across the circle to shove him, hard.

Now Chekiss is laughing. "You know what that means, Niles? Means you're sleeping with the black beast tonight. And every other night until you learn to keep those uneducated thoughts to yourself."

Our circle separates, and I catch Kane giving me a curious look. It's fleeting but interested. Does he know that Dessin and I were intimate? Of course he does. But is that upsetting to him? But before I can look any deeper, he takes a step away, breaking the trance.

"There's a spring nearby." Kane nods his head behind me. "Let's get you cleaned up."

"I can help her." Ruth touches my shoulder. I resist the urge to jerk away, hating myself for reacting this way after only being captive for four hours. "If you want me to."

I smile weakly. "Thank you."

Kane hands us towels and a soap bar, pointing us in the right direction, just down the hill, in the middle of scattered boulders.

The soothing white glow of the moon softens Ruth's pale skin, smoothing out creases around her eyes, highlighting her freckles. She looks simply… angelic.

We remove our clothes, backs facing each other. I pull my gown off over my head, throwing it to the dirt with a huff.

Ruth holds the soap close to her bare stomach as we gawk at the black water, only a brief flicker of moonlight drifting over the ripples.

"If we go in quick, we'll hardly feel the shock," Ruth says.

And we go in, wading through the ice water, squishing the mushy bottom with our toes. We hiss as the chilled spring covers our stomachs and then our breasts. It's like being in Absinthe's ice bath, except—not horrible. I'm choosing to be here. I'm glad to be out in the open, kissed by the cool night's breeze.

"They hurt you?" she asks, lathering soap and water in her small hands.

I throw her a quick glance with my swollen eyes and bruised cheeks.

"What about you?"

She shrugs. "No, actually. I wasn't the one they wanted."

At that I'm surprised. I try to hide the shock from my face but fail. I wasn't the one they wanted either. They wanted Dessin. They tortured me to get to him, yes, but why wouldn't they do that to Ruth? I'm relieved, of course. But their tactics just don't make any sense.

Ruth touches my head with fingers ready to clean, but I wince, unable to protect her from seeing my reaction. She lowers her gaze and takes a deep breath. "May I?" she asks.

I nod. It seems to be when I'm caught off guard that the contact shocks me. She begins making big shiny bubbles in my hair, gently cleansing my scalp. I massage the soap down my chest and arms.

"I was mad at you, y'know," she says.

"Me? Why?"

"You left me. You didn't say a word. You didn't try and get a message to me. You just left the asylum in shambles. It was bizarre. I figured… I must have not really been your friend if that was the case."

I sigh, hanging my head. "Ruth, you have to know I'd never—"

"I know now." She sighs, leaning my head back to rinse my hair. "I didn't realize what was really going on. That you two were fugitives, running for your lives. The asylum concocted all sorts of lies about you. That you ran off with your patient because you two were madly in love. That you were just as sick as he was."

Oh, goodness. They really didn't like me there.

"I mean, unless the in-love part is also true, then this would make a little bit more sense." A subtle smile creeps into her voice.

I groan. "No, it all happened so fast. I wanted to save his life. He was going to be executed." Demechnef came for him. There was no warning when they swarmed his room. "We had to act fast."

"*So*, there's nothing romantic going on at all?"

I wince as a pathetic, dopey smile tugs at my throbbing cheeks.

Ruth's doe eyes widen, matching my sloppy expression of tickled-pink giddiness.

"Oh my god, is there?"

"No. *Yes*. I don't know. It's strange. Things have happened, but Kane told me he didn't feel that way about me." *Ugh, the kiss.* I hate thinking about what came after it.

"He's *definitely* lying." Her face twists with suspicion.

What? "How do you know?!"

She looks behind her to make sure no one is listening, then proceeds to scrub me down gently, cleaning the grime and blood from my pruning body.

"Skylenna, that man doesn't look at you like a friend…" She leans in closer, cupping her hands around my ear. "To me, it looks like you're the world, and he's the moon that revolves around you. When we were all laughing at Niles, Kane was smiling because *you* looked happy. It's like that's his only goal."

I nudge her. "I think you've been spending too much time with Niles." But a swarm of fluttering birds takes flight in my soul.

She chuckles. "That may be true, but a woman knows that look. *Trust me.*"

If she's right, then why would he lie to me? My feelings for him have grown stronger every day since I met him. It's like our bodies can't hide the chemistry. But he is trying to with his words.

Ruth wishes me a good night's sleep and finds a spot around the fire that Kane started for us. The night grows quiet with a special hum, an ambience only the trees and wind can make. I change into the clothes Kane laid out for me. Pants, one of his white shirts, and a wool coat. It's not that cold out currently, but I appreciate finally having something to keep me warm when I sleep. It's sad how much I took for granted. Even something as simple as a blanket to sleep with.

Kane's legs are stretched out comfortably. He's using a tree as a headboard to sit up and read. As I get closer to him, I recognize the label on his book. *Holy Bible.* I've never really seen him read it before. He looks as concentrated as a healer performing surgery. His left hand is holding the wooden cross that hangs around his neck, fidgeting with it, outlining its shape with his index finger. His eyes bounce up to the campfire, keeping an eye on a meat cooking over the top of the flames.

I lower myself down quietly next to him. The trunk of the tree is illuminated by the orange glimmer of our campfire and large enough to provide back support to the both of us. Reaching down to our feet, I pull up our usual sleeping blanket, but pause midstretch realizing we're the only ones with a blanket.

"I gave them their own backpacks with blankets, clothes and necessities for the trip." He answers the question that is taking a train route of panic around my head.

"*Really?*"

He nods, bookmarking his place, and setting the Bible to the side.

"Wow. That's… kind of amazing." I search for our friends across the fire, only now noticing them tucked peacefully under their own blankets.

He completes my paused action and pulls up the rest of the blankets, covering my arms and shoulders.

I smirk up at him. "Cuddling up with Niles all night under one blanket wasn't appealing to you?"

He raises his eyebrows and hums a closed-mouth laugh. "That was the driving motivation behind that act of kindness, yes. And not to mention, Dessin would have a temper tantrum."

I nod in agreement. My attention flickers over to his Bible that he set down. I reach across his body, my chest hovering over his lap, as I pick it up. Kane lowers his eyes and fixates them on my body grazing his. He doesn't seem to care what I'm reaching for. The attraction radiating from his body is as tangible as steam from a boiling teakettle. I drop my gaze back down to the book as I get comfortable in my spot.

"May I?"

"Sure."

I open the Bible back to his bookmark. He points to the spot on the page he left off at.

"Jeremiah 29:11-14," he reads. "For I know the plans I have for you, declares the Lord, plans for welfare and not for evil, to give you a future and a hope. Then you will call upon me and come and pray to me, and I will hear you. You will seek me and find me when you seek me with all your heart. I will be found by you, declares the Lord, and I will restore your fortunes and gather you from all the nations and all the places where I have driven you, declares the Lord, and I will bring you back to the place from which I sent you into exile."

I'm moved by the sentiment in his voice.

"Why is this passage important to you?" I ask, setting the Bible down.

He levels his gaze to look at me from under his top lashes. "Because I have to believe we're going to find a way out of all of this." He rubs his hand across his jaw in thought. "This chaos… it's all I've known my whole life. I need to believe that we're going to find peace one day. That God will bring us back to a good place."

"Your whole life… that's a long time to keep fighting."

"Yes, it is." Kane shifts his weight to face me with his entire body. "In all truth, this fight won't be over for a long time. This won't be the last of the terrors we face together."

Together. That word creates floating feathers in my stomach.

"And how long do you expect us to stay together?" My tone suddenly turns cold. "Because let's just say we do make it through all of these terrors in one piece. Let's just say ten years from now, we're free to live in peace. What then?"

He keeps his eyes on me, steady, unwilling to break the connection that's holding our gaze. "I expect when that day comes, we'll build a house in the Red Oaks where we'll live out the rest of our days in peace. No more fighting. No more running."

I clasp my hands together and press them to my mouth in frustration.

"As *friends*, right?"

His lips part slightly. He takes several seconds to answer. "That's right."

"Really… well, what if I want to marry someone one day? And have babies?" *Please don't break my heart again, Kane. Please don't hurt me.*

"Skylenna…"

"No." I shake my head. "Don't you say it again." I slide my hands up his chest to grasp his neck. He takes a shaky breath as our skin touches, sharing warmth, sharing a pulse. "Don't hurt me again, Kane."

His eyes are swelling with a suffocating emotion. He looks like he wants to pull away and pull me closer all at the same time.

"I know what I'm feeling isn't something as tame as friendship. And I know we both feel it. I can see it in your eyes when I touch you. I can feel it in my stomach when you look at me."

He inhales a sharp, unsteady breath, still unable to speak.

"You can try and convince me that you don't feel that way about me. But you're lying. And if you're unable for some reason to tell me the truth, then fine, I get it. But don't lie to me again. If you can't tell me the truth, then don't say anything. I can accept that. I can live with that. But I can't live with you saying those words to me again." Hope and desperation flood my veins. The pain in my jaw, my busted lip, my eye gnaws at my skull, begging for me to sleep.

Kane curls his fingers around my wrists and holds them tightly.

"When I was rotting in that cage… I replayed your words in my head over and over again. I felt the heartbreak over and over again. It hurt me more than living through broken bones and abuse. But I also relived our kiss. I held on to it and it was the only light I saw when they blinded me." My chest clenches and my throat fights to swallow down a heavy lump. "That kiss meant *everything* to me. And you stole that when you crippled me with your rejection." My hands are shaking. I can't believe my own boldness as I confess my feelings so bluntly. And by the look of his stunned expression, he can't believe it either.

Kane's breath hitches before he lifts me off the ground, pulling me onto his lap. His strong arms circle my waist, and his head burrows into my neck. Instinctively, I fasten his neck and shoulders securely against me, feeling his heavy breath against my skin, and his nuclear passion unfolding from his body into mine. My heart floats around us in a mist of stars and solar flares. His hands travel sensually under my shirt, his fingers running softly along my spine, summoning goose bumps and small shivers within his embrace.

I want him to confess his feelings to me. I want him to tell me that he is falling in love with me. I want some kind of verbal affirmation.

He reaches up to my face and lowers my head to his lips, placing a soft kiss on my forehead, and then meeting my ear with his mouth.

"You're *everything* to me. I'll never lose sight of you again," he whispers into my ear. I lean the side of my head against his, impairing my ability to keep myself upright. I'm bulldozed with paralyzing relief.

I know that's all he can say and I won't ask for more.

After we spend long stretched-out moments holding each other, like we're about to be ripped away by a violent tide, kicking and screaming, reaching out endlessly to be held again, he offers me dinner and then does as promised. Kane lies back, holding me against his chest, his fingers tangled in my hair. He whispers to me how grateful he is to have me in his life. The magnetic energy flows through my veins every time he places a kiss on my head. And after a while, DaiSzek shows up, planting himself on my other side to comfort me further and keep me warm.

Tonight, this was enough. This was so much more than enough.

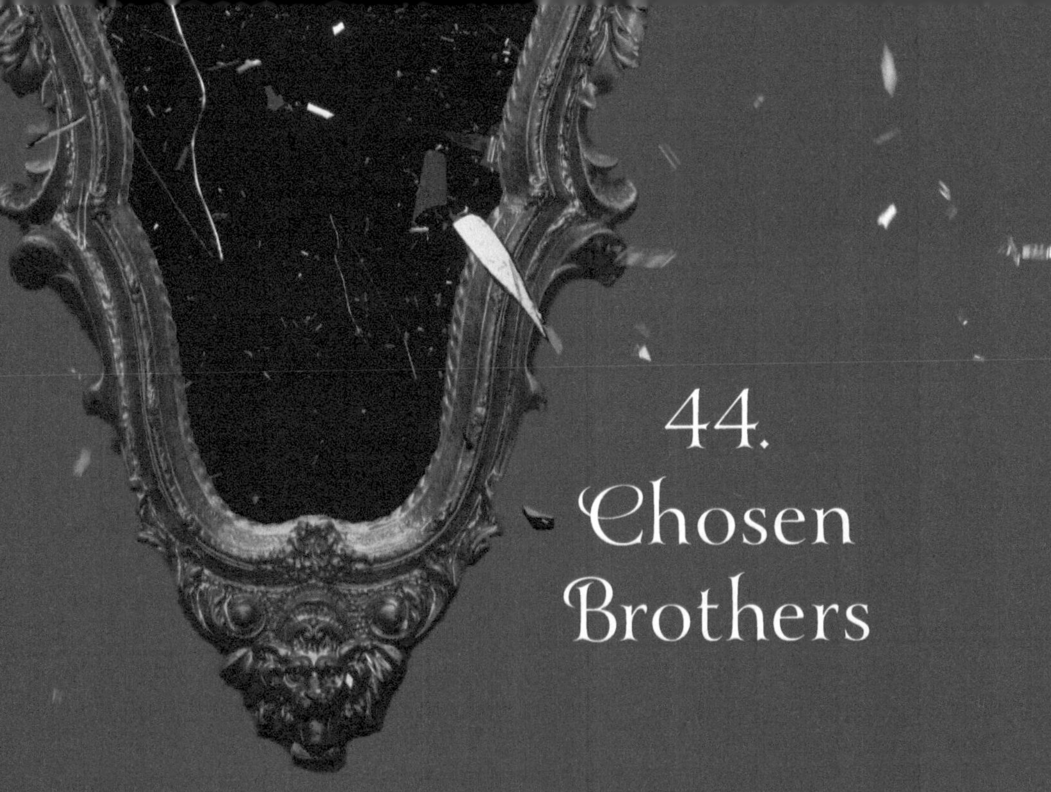

44. Chosen Brothers

"I'd like to vote Chekiss off the island!" Niles announces while we all pack up to keep moving.

Kane glances over to me, raising his eyebrows with a *do-I-really-have-to-entertain-this* look. I shake my head. Chekiss just rolls his eyes and continues packing. I hear Ruth try and scold him for his obnoxious remark.

"He snores, *Ruth*." Adding extra emphasis to her name as if she should know how silly she is for not noticing.

I turn around so Kane can put my winter coat on, applying a scarf and fluffy beanie.

"Your winter gear should be in your packs. It's going to get a lot colder where we're headed," Kane announces to the group.

I notice Niles staring at DaiSzek who seems to be guarding our area, sitting at his post to look out for intruders. Niles takes a few excited steps toward him.

"I wouldn't," Kane calls out while shuffling through his bag, his back facing Niles.

Niles doesn't realize he's the target of Kane's warning and keeps shuffling closer to DaiSzek.

"He's talking to you, Niles," I warn him with a higher tone of caution.

Niles stops and glares over at Kane. "Will he bite me?"

"Most likely."

"Well how *likely* are we talking here?"

Kane turns around and crosses his arms over his chest. "If you directly approach him, he'll assume you're a threat and attack."

"Whoa! You said *bite,* not *attack*!" Niles takes slow steps backward.

"I thought bite sounded less scary." Kane smirks, fully amused and Niles is holding his hands up like he's about to be shot down.

Niles scoffs. "Well, how scared do you think I would have been if I were expecting a little harmless nip and instead was greeted with my face being torn off?"

"Niles!" Chekiss reproaches. "You're being a nuisance. Just leave him alone."

"*I'm* a nuisance?! Who's the one that was gargling saliva in their sleep? I was so disturbed I almost cuddled up to man eater over there for some sweet relief!" Niles saunters off to pick up his argument with Chekiss.

"Hey, maybe we should tell Niles what Dessin did to Albatross for being annoying, huh?" I nudge Kane in the side with my arm.

He glances up at me after he finishes fitting everything in my bag. A considering smile rises, then falls. "That's not funny," he decides.

I start laughing. "Yes. It really is."

After a while, we pick up our feet and begin our slow journey north. Kane tells the group that our continuous movement is merely to buy us time. Time to plan. Time to have together. But he leans in close, telling me he's still looking for one Demechnef defect. A man he didn't see among the bodies we found.

Kane and I lead in the front, taking on the brunt of the crisp blizzard winds, cutting through trees and running past our cheeks like razor blades. It only happens a few times. But I'm sickened by flashbacks. My entire body aching at the memories. The false time lapse. The beatings from Absinthe. The cramped cage digging into my shoulders and neck.

I just want to forget. But it's still fresh.

I spend the rest of the hike drawing the puppet in my mind.

Ruth requests for a few more stops than Kane and I would have taken if we were on our own. Her legs are shorter and unconditioned, but the altitude and frigid winds weigh heavily on us all. I run back to her many times to remove my gloves and place my warm palms on her rosy cheeks. Chekiss has never looked so pleased. He gazes at the highest branches of the trees overhead, watching them as they overlap and clap together. At cracks of lighting and the drumming of thunder, his mouth gapes open in an astounded smile. And for the first time, Niles says nothing. He looks up from his boots sinking into the snow and catches Chekiss admiring the beauty of the wilderness, and he makes no comment to ruin it for him. He smiles to himself and continues to trek on.

Kane points out a cave up ahead, a small dark hole barely visible through the mass of falling snow. He tells us that the storm is strong enough to keep any unwanted visitors away, at least for a little while. But something catches his attention through the heavy fog of falling snow. His feet stop crunching through the ice, his body an impassive stone.

The group follows his iron stance, straining our eyes to see what he sees, blinking away the flurries and melting ice.

DaiSzek snarls at my side, lowering his posture, hovering one paw in the air like he's a moment away from breaking out into a sprint.

I open my mouth to ask Kane what's going on but stop myself as he slides his glance to me. A look of darkness, gore, and violence. Not Kane. A quick, effortless switch. His look tells me to stay behind him no matter the cost. I can only nod. Because this isn't the look of a man who is about to face another small army of men. This is a look of a man who knows he's outnumbered.

The sound of feet stepping through cracking ice breaks my attention from Dessin, and through that blinding sheet of a blizzard, dark crunching steps get closer. Hunched. Crawling. And it isn't the sound of their feet…

It's the sound of paws.

Oh no. Beasts? They may be crouched low like DaiSzek, but their massive forms cannot be overlooked. A few are the size of an elephant, others are leaner, like a panther or jaguar. And as they inch closer, it becomes perfectly clear that we're surrounded, at least ten of them closing in on our unprotected sides.

But DaiSzek notices this weakness before Dessin, falling back to cover Ruth at the back of the group. A monstrous roar bellows from DaiSzek's chest, breaking frozen branches off of trees, vibrating the earth under our feet, stretching through heaven and hell.

But they keep advancing, fearless in their attempt to challenge a RottWeilen.

What do we do? They're going to have a hard time protecting all of us.

Dessin fastens something across his chest, unsheathing a long dagger that could almost pass as a sword. "Here," he says under his breath. "Take this." He unhooks a small knife from his chest belt, the gift of weapons Garanthian gave him.

I take the knife and clutch the hilt in my fist. I don't know how to use it. But at least I have something in case they overwhelm either one of my protectors.

"Everyone stay in this circle and don't you dare move."

Chekiss, Niles, Ruth, and I huddle closer together, holding our breath, reaching for the other's arms, shoulders, or quivering hands as we watch them crouch low. Then, like a firework of fur and fangs, they attack.

DaiSzek is a dragon from hell, leaping high into the air, assaulting in a downward spiral from the sky, crashing down on top of two blond mountain cats. They don't even have a moment to react before his teeth carve so deeply into their flesh, he's ripping out full gushing arteries, flinging them to the snow.

Dessin moves nearly as fast as the animals. One the size of God's fist charges him like a bull, but before it makes contact, Dessin is spinning, dagger lashing out, sinking into the neck of the gray beast. He's a silent assassin, moving so quietly, so calculated, it seems choreographed. Each lashing of his legs, his dagger, his flips through the blizzard winds are those of an angel of death—a warrior god.

And for a moment, a brief blink of an eye, I'm certain they are more than capable of defending us from the pack. Two against ten. But Dessin's specialty is with human combat. And I'm reminded that he is still a man, they might not be able to predict each move of an animal when a sharp set of jaws clamps down on Dessin's arm.

He grunts, sinking his dagger into the neck of the large mountain cat. After it falls into the puddle of its own blood in the snow, Dessin continues to fight as if he hadn't been maimed at all. Yet, blood rains from his forearm, sprinkling over the white ground with each movement, each gutting. It doesn't slow him down until another mountain cat jumps on his back, biting into his shoulder.

I nearly fall to my knees as he roars in agony.

And this awful sound is enough to distract DaiSzek, getting him to look over for one fleeting moment, opening up a new weakness for three snapping animals to bombard him, toppling DaiSzek to the ground with the unexpected force.

No! It's too much. Dessin is bleeding. DaiSzek is outnumbered and distracted by the scent of his family's blood spraying through the arctic air.

And one tall gray bear gets past Dessin's line, approaching us in a dead run, a loud, earth-quaking gallop that tells me we are no longer safe in the circle. I hold out my knife, hoping the bear will run right into it, stab himself trying to maul us.

My name is screamed from Dessin's vocal cords as he's held down, bombarded in the snow and puddles of his blood.

I am our only hope.

The bear opens its mouth, taking one last deadly lunge to devour us. I scream and close my eyes, holding up the pointy end of the knife.

There's a wet, snapping sound followed by a feral gurgling, then a thud, like dropping a sack of potatoes. I open my eyes, feel the hands of my friends gripping my waist, my back, my arms as they stay tucked behind me.

I killed it! I—

But my knife isn't bloody. It hasn't been used. The body of the bear has collapsed at my feet, and his head lies next to it.

I look up, expecting to see Dessin or DaiSzek standing in front of us, the cause of the decapitation. But no, they're still overwhelmed, bodies slammed into the earth. And more animals have arrived, twenty, if not thirty.

Instead, I see a stranger wearing a black mask that covers his entire face, dark hair that hangs nearly to his shoulders, sleek feathers of a raven that coats his body, and a whip that might be made of chains or tiny blades. A weapon that decapitates with one swing.

I stare at him in horror and gratitude, sucking in fast breaths.

But the man doesn't stay put, he winds up his arm, throwing the metal whip out toward Dessin, snaking the tail end around the necks of three mountain cats, swiping their heads clean off their shoulders with a slurping *crack*.

The whipping man doesn't wait for Dessin to get up, he rushes to DaiSzek's side, whirling through the air to reach a large group of the beasts that keep piling up, cutting through their necks like butter. A gory show of flying heads and spraying veins. It's a clotted mist, a crimson thunderstorm over their falling bodies. And the man keeps going, waving that whip around like his arm will never get tired, like his body was made for the combat of beasts.

The killing slows to a painful stop as DaiSzek shakes the last bear like a rag doll, rattling the loose bones in its body.

My friends and I shiver, holding each other as we blink in shock, waiting for Dessin to confront the strange man. The soldier that turned the tide of this battle. He could be from the Stormsages. Maybe someone of this territory that was looking out for us.

The silence is smothered by the sharp winds, the gurgling necks, and our frantic breaths. Dessin and the masked man watch each other from over the carnage, waiting for the other to say something.

"What the fuck is wrong with you?" Dessin says with clenched teeth. "I thought you were dead."

With that notion, the man removes the charcoal mask, tossing it into the snow. Deep-blue eyes. Sleeping, dreaming blue eyes. Stubble along his chin and jaw, and olive skin. And that look I've seen a thousand times. The eyes of a murderer. The excitement of war, violence, and chaos.

He grins at Dessin. "You think that little of me? I just saved your ass."

"We had it handled." Despite the hard expression, Dessin's mouth curls into a faint smile. They shake hands first, then pull into a manly, back-slapping hug.

"You smell like a horse's ass." Dessin cringes as he pulls away from their embrace.

The masked man barks out a laugh. "Couldn't handle a few little kitties, huh? I guess that asylum softened you up."

Dessin snorts. "I guess so." His dark eyes flick to me, then back to the masked man. "This is Skylenna"—he points to me—"Chekiss, Niles, and Ruth."

The man turns to us, studying our colorless expressions, our mouths still gaping open to pant from terror. He nods his head at me. "Skylenna," he purrs with a look of secret amusement. "You are as beautiful as he's always described you to be."

I look to Dessin for confirmation, but he only stares back at me blankly. Unashamed.

"This is Warrose. We've trained together since we were boys." Dessin nods his head back to the blue-eyed man that is currently watching me without blinking.

"You were taken too?" I ask, holding in my aggressive need to shiver.

"I was." He exchanges a look with Dessin. "He broke me out when he was eighteen. I fled to this mountain,"—he motions his hands to the North Saphrine Forest—"where I stayed with the rejects of the Chandelier City."

"Which is why I thought you were dead."

"If I had been there a day sooner, you'd have found an entirely different set of corpses." There's a wicked flash of violence dancing in his eyes. "But you beat me to them. Were you there to look for me?"

They're talking about the slaughter of babies, women, and children from that small village. The one where Garanthian found us. I wonder why he never mentioned this man before.

"Obviously," Dessin says.

"Well, I followed you—" Warrose's attention shifts to a focal point over my shoulder. Ruth sighs shakily, trembling against my back at the sting of the winter winds. I look back at her, wrapping one arm around her shoulder. Warrose continues to stare. "Let's get them in the cave. Before the small one loses her toes."

Dessin nods, signaling for us to step over the piles of bodies to the cave up ahead.

"We're going to stay here for the next couple of days," Dessin informs us as we step through the threshold of the darkness made of stone and hard shells of ice.

"What happens after a couple of days?" Ruth asks.

"After a couple of days, we come to a final decision on what we'll do from here. We'll have a plan on how we're going to handle what comes next." He sets down his bags and clears his throat. "I need to catch Warrose up. Get warm and we'll go collect what's salvageable to cook."

After they leave the cave, the four of us sit on the cold stone floor with our hands outstretched to the wild lickings of the fire. There are long sweeps of silence while we all enjoy the warmth spreading to our toes and fingers. The rush of tingling goodness caressing our insides and melting away layers of ice clinging to our skin.

"I've been thinking…" I say to the others. "There's a way we can get the three of you out of all of this."

Ruth picks her head up.

"My childhood home and Kane's are off the grid and unoccupied. They're completely empty. Maybe we could show you the way, Kane could teach you how to hunt, and you could live there freely. Then you all don't have to be dragged down with whatever Kane and I have to do. You won't be hunted anymore or at risk of being thrown back into the asylum."

My friends sit quietly, staring in different directions. The marmalade-orange light paints new shadows around the peaks of their faces. The cave's opening whistles and hums with the warrior winds that sprint to battle. Our fire pops and the cozy aroma of burning wood mixes with frozen pine trees.

Chekiss speaks first.

"We're not going anywhere without you, dear." His statement is final. Unwilling to negotiate or fold in any which direction.

I feel the movement in the air to my left as Ruth nods.

"We're a family now. Family sticks together," Niles adds.

Ruth's arm stretches around my shoulder and her head leans gently in the crook of my neck. I breathe in her sweet scent of strawberries and rainwater.

"I know we are. But I couldn't sleep at night if anything happened to any of you," I say.

"And we couldn't sleep if anything happened to you." Chekiss rubs a hand over the side of his head, his light-brown skin changing shades in the shadows. "We're going to keep each other sane by staying together. One wolf can't survive alone without its pack. It would die of starvation or be hunted down by a predator. We're stronger as one."

Except Dessin. He's stronger and faster when he only has to worry about himself.

"It's just... Demechnef has more weaknesses to hold against Dessin now. Before it was just me, now he has four of us to watch over. I can't imagine how much of a burden that is for him." I think about the guilt that bound Kane in his own personal hell when he found out what Albatross had done to me. He blamed himself and as much as I'd try to convince him otherwise, I believe that remorse will stay with him for the rest of his life.

Ruth's small hand slides up my wrist to hold mine. It's warm and soft, like it has just been freshly lathered in lotion.

"Then how should we settle this? Because if it were up to us, we'd stay with you. But we don't want to make this any harder on either of you than it is already. Truthfully, we don't even know why you two are running and what Demechnef wants with you," Ruth says.

I think about this carefully, like her question is made of glass, wobbling on the surface. I want them to stay and to keep us company during this journey. I want to watch Chekiss's face as we travel through the shade of the trees. I want to hear Niles complaining about something trivial. I want to hear them argue. I want to keep talking to Ruth about Kane and hear her opinion on what I should do about my feelings for him. I *really* want them to stay.

"I think it's only fair that Kane decides. He's the one we'll all have to rely on for safety. He should be the one to decide if we stay together or not," I answer with confidence.

We tense as Warrose steps through the veil of cold dust, carrying a mountain cat over his shoulder with a pinched brow that indicates he's cold and maybe a little grumpy. I stand, racing to the mouth of the cave in search of Dessin. The shrill wind slaps against my skin like a wet towel. The white blinding flurries and harsh gray lighting of the sky make my eyes water, but I see him approaching, DaiSzek trotting alongside him.

He meets my eyes as he slips out of the storm, tossing the dead animal in front of the fire.

"Hi," I utter.

"Hi." He smiles, warm and deep, hitting the pit of my stomach.

Kane.

I look back at Warrose who is watching me from over the flames, skinning his mountain cats as if he could do it with his eyes closed. "Hard to keep up, isn't it?"

I smile at him. "No, not for me."

"I met Dessin when I was ten, then Foxem when I was eleven. And Syfer when I turned fourteen." He nods at the memories attached to each alter. "I thought he was a faker. A theatrical son of a bitch."

Kane listens while he prepares the dead animals. I sit down between the two men, waiting for Warrose to tell me more, fill in the missing pieces that still make up the mystery of who he is.

"It wasn't until I met Dai that I fully believed in what he is. The many faces of who he is." Warrose smiles at me sadly, knitting his brow together as he considers whether he should tell the rest of the story or not. He's handsome. An inch shorter than Kane, thick lashes, a dimpled chin, and a voice of sand and gravel.

"You met DaiSzek?" I ask.

He glances at the massive beast guarding the entrance, diligently watching for movements. Pellets of snow melting on strands of his fur. "No. I met the animal that *he* turns into when it is forced out of him." Warrose stares at Kane, asking silently if he can tell his story.

"I'd rather you didn't." Kane doesn't bother looking up.

"And how mad would you be if I told her anyway?"

"It's not just her you're telling." Kane looks up from the meat, making eye contact with Ruth, Chekiss, and Niles who are all gathered around, listening eagerly. Completely mesmerized by Warrose.

"We can keep a secret," Ruth offers quietly.

Kane sighs. "Please leave out the graphic details."

Warrose smirks, raising his eyebrows at me with an *I will tell you later* look.

"There's a point in training where Demechnef wants you to be able to destroy an identity after you kill. Meaning, make the person unrecognizable. Meaning, rip them apart so no one will know who they were."

"That's graphic detail," Kane scolds.

"I was given the task of doing that to an elderly man." Warrose sighs, shaking his head. "And for the first time in my training, I couldn't do it. I refused. There had to be boundaries at some point. Well, that was it. But because I refused... they brought Dessin in before he was ready, before he hit the right age. He was only twelve."

I can't help but watch Kane rotating the meat on a stick, focusing his attention on feeding us. My heart throbs, clenches, and sinks into my stomach.

"I watched it happen. The split. The animal he became. It—" He blows out a breath. "It wasn't human. I felt like an ass for thinking the worst of him for years."

This man knows Dessin, Kane, and the others so well. They're practically brothers. And here I am, lucky to know anything at all.

"What were they training you for?" I ask, feeling that edge of irritation grip me by the lungs, burning a hole in my stomach. The story reminds me of the bit Albatross mentioned. The fucking dolls. How Dessin would take part in their assault. "Why the two of you? And what do I have to do with any of it? Has he told you how he knows so much about me?"

My timing is terrible. Pathetic. Inappropriate. But this desperation to learn everything he knows is eating away at my insides. It's searing my patience.

Warrose parts his lips and scratches the side of his jaw. "War with Vexamen. Some children were experimented on to make the best quality of soldier." He blinks a few times because that's all he can really say.

"Okay. So I get tortured for what feels like several months, nearly brainwashed, starved, beaten, isolated and no one can tell me what my part is to play in all of this? Doesn't that seem a little unfair?"

Those dreamy blue eyes fall to his blood-stained hands.

"No? Okay, another question. Who wants to explain to me the fucking dolls that Demechnef used to offer the soldiers?" The aggressive intent comes pouring out of me like a volcanic eruption. I don't know what brought this anger on.

"How did you—"

"How could a stupid girl like me know about the fun activities you boys took part in?"

"Skylenna," Kane warns, voice alarming yet low with caution.

"Tell me! Was it a manly thing to do? Rape a woman when she's unable to fight back?" It's acidic fire shooting from my chest. I can't stop it. I can't slow it down.

Draw the strings. The legs. The arms. The eyes.

The sketch in my mind fades. It doesn't calm me down.

"You don't know what the fuck you're talking about!" Warrose is on his feet, towering over me like a great oak tree.

"Is it true? Am I at the very least entitled to know if I'm sleeping in a cave next to men that assault catatonic women?"

"Jesus! We never took part in that!"

"No? So Dessin wasn't the worst offender in Demechnef? Because that's what I heard."

"He was. Want to know why? Because any chance he got, he'd sneak into their rooms and slit their throats so they didn't have to endure that abuse any longer! And for every woman he freed, he suffered weeks of blinding torment in the arena!" Warrose is clenching his fists, glaring at me with resentment for making him explain that out loud.

"That's enough," Kane barks.

The cave is speechless. No one has an answer for me. No one can give me peace for what I just went through. My jaw still feels like it's been wired shut. My head is throbbing, my cheeks splintering with pain, and I'm so weak I could pass out and sleep for ninety years.

I push myself off the ground, brushing past Kane to put some distance between me and the others. But DaiSzek is a safe location, I plop myself down alongside him, hearing the echoes of Ruth whispering to Niles, the contrast of a whistling wind in front of us and the hissing fire from behind us.

DaiSzek smells woodsy, of wet bark from a tree and frozen rain. He glances down at me with his ember eyes, following my hand as it combs through the fur on his back. His deep, rumbling breaths level me back down to earth, extinguishing that burn in my stomach.

I don't know what came over me.

"Will he attack me if I sit next to you?" Niles approaches from behind us.

I watch DaiSzek's eyes flicker back and forth between the threat beyond the snow and the threat trying to sit down.

"Not sure. Maybe just sit an arm's length away," I advise. Niles obeys, lowering himself to the ground slowly, like a bomb will go off if there are any sudden movements.

Success. Until they make eye contact. Niles gawks into DaiSzek's eyes eagerly. A long guttural growl slides between sharp teeth and a curled upper lip.

"And maybe never make eye contact again," I say.

As soon as Niles darts his eyes away, DaiSzek's growl decreases in volume and aggression until it fizzles out to an agitated sigh.

"Eventually I'm going to get on his good side." Niles pouts.

Maybe one day.

"I wanted to ask you…" he prompts.

"I don't want to talk about me and Kane."

"But—"

"Ruth beat you to it."

He straightens up, twists his head to look back at her. "She did?"

I nod.

"Not sure I like that."

I shake my head and sigh. "I know why you want to talk about that though."

He cocks his head.

"You're afraid to ask me about the trauma I experienced when I was taken. But you also want to know if I'm okay," I say. The smell of cooking meat fills the cave. "I'm okay. You don't have to ask and I don't want to talk about it."

His hand clenches my shoulder. Squeezing, *hard.* I look up at him to find tears welling up in his sharp sea-foam-green eyes. I lean in, as if he'll tell me his pain in whispers.

"You didn't sound okay back there. Far from it." His words are unsteady from the dam of a cry that could break any second. "When Dessin realized what happened, that you sacrificed your own safety for ours, he went ballistic. He began talking to himself. He went into an awful rage, bouncing back and forth between two personalities. It was devastating for us to watch. We, of course, felt our own fear, loss, and regret over you being taken. But his pain was so far on another level. I'll never be able to fully explain it to you."

I'm tingling with goose bumps from head to toe. I can understand his reaction as if it were my own. Because that's how I would feel if Kane were taken from me. But still, I'm in amazement. That much feeling must be linked to something.

"It really scared me seeing a man that powerful, that strong, that fearless… be that afraid. I thought we were going to lose you again. And the first person that's ever fought for me, and listened to my problems, and shown me that I'm not crazy, just lost and misunderstood… that person would be gone forever." Niles leans over and uses the sleeves of his coat to wipe his eyes.

I prop myself up on one knee and pull his wide shoulders in for a hug. He sniffles against my chest and I rest my cheek on top of his head layered with golden curls. I can't believe I started my life living with toxic, violent acts of love. I lived with a man who locked me in a basement for days on end. I lived with a resentful twin who would beat me up when she had a meltdown. To this. This group of friends who cares deeply for me. Even through the stress of running from an enemy, being left in the dark, I can be grateful for this. For Niles.

"I love you, Niles. You're my chosen brother in this life."

45. The House of Ash

I find a place to sleep away from the others, deeper into the cave. After my outburst, it doesn't feel natural to chat like everything is normal. Like I didn't just air out Kane's dirty laundry. Like I didn't just assume the worst of Warrose.

As I tuck myself in, Kane slides under our fur-lined blanket, cupping my body with his own. His chest is against my back, moving slowly with the speed of his breaths. I'm instantly less sleepy by the buzzing in my head, like hearing music for the first time. A warm layer of familiar comfort, longing to be held by him again.

He swivels his hips to match up with my lower back. His arms close around me, locking me inside the safety of his embrace. Fire and bursts of chemical reactions implode in my skin. How quickly my brain responds when our skin touches, when our bodies cling together like arteries to a heart. Kane's lips make a trail of light kisses against the back of my head, dropping like bread crumbs down my neck as if he is leaving himself a map. As if he is afraid he might get lost. Firecrackers pop and crackle in my lower belly. Galactic energy hums through my fingers and toes, forcing me to arch into him.

"I'm hurting you." His voice is soft, like rippling water. I sigh at the sound.

"Hmm?"

"With the secrets," he clarifies, a rush of hot breath tickling my neck. "I'm hurting you by keeping you in the dark."

"Yes, but that doesn't excuse how I acted." I frown. "I'm sorry. I don't know what came over me."

"Mind Phantoms. Your body's metabolism is burning the last of it off. But the side effects are mood swings, fits of anger, hormonal imbalances. Temporary, though."

"Oh." *Thank God.*

"About Warrose," he prompts, shifting closer against my back. "It's hard for me to talk about my time being trained. It was hard for Dessin because Warrose was his best friend, and he had to say goodbye when he admitted us to the asylum."

"You don't have to explain."

"And the—women that were brought for soldiers. Dessin went into a rage when he learned what they were for. He put them out of their misery and was beaten mercilessly for it."

"Kane—"

"Please don't ever do that to me again," he whispers, the smell of his breath is dynamite to my attraction. It's sweet and I want to taste it.

"Do *what?*"

"Run away. Go rogue. Give up your safety for my own." He's breathing so close to my ear that my eyes slightly roll back into my head. *The euphoria.*

"I'd do it again."

He readjusts to roll me on my back, his left hand cupping the back of my head, a pillow against the cold stone. I roll farther than he intended, purposefully letting my body snuggle into his.

"No you won't," he says.

"So you can make sacrifices for me but I can't make any for you?"

His dark eyes burn in the firelight, growing in sentiment, like he's preparing to read my eulogy. "You've already sacrificed so much. But for now, I just need you to be safe. We won't survive on our own. Our only chance out of this is to stay *together*."

I touch my hand to his chest in response. *Yes, I want to stay together.*

"Promise me you'll stick with me. No matter what happens. You'll never stop believing in us. In our freedom together. *Promise me.*" He's breathing heavy, gripping my waist like I might slip away.

"I promise."

Kane lowers his head to mine, breathing deeply as if he's about to go underwater. I lift my chin, offering my lips up to him, giving the permission he needs.

And it's soft, yet strong enough to braid my heart in a knot. His warm lips brush against mine, thumb grazing over my fast pulse. And then he kisses me. Slow and sweet, allowing me to explore him, slipping my tongue past his lips, and that throbbing ache between my thighs springs to life.

My body remembers the night Dessin and I had each other. It remembers the feel of his shredded muscles, the growing hardness in his pants.

But this is someone else. This is Kane, who cradles my face, kissing me like he's died for me a thousand times. Like he's known me a thousand lives.

He pulls back, parting our lips, holding his forehead against mine.

"I think it's time I give you answers." He exhales.

This is the *only* acceptable reason I will allow the kissing to stop.

"You've been so patient with me. But you have to know, there's a plan. A plan that wasn't just created by Dessin. There's so much at stake. So much involved." He leans us up against the cave wall behind us, holding my hand while he gathers his thoughts.

I stay quiet, careful not to scare him away, or make him rethink telling me anything.

"I told you that we've known each other before the day I saved you from Jack and carried you to the hospital. It goes back much further than that." He squeezes my hand a little tighter. "Skylenna, I've known you since you were two years old."

My last gasp of air comes to a halting stop in my throat. *What?*

"My mother was friends with Jack and Violet. They introduced us when I was five."

"Your mom knew my parents?" I can't show enough surprise on my face at a time like this. It's physically impossible. I've surpassed the quota.

He nods with a solemn frown. "I first saw you when you were sleeping in your father's arms. You had a head full of honey curls and these squishy cheeks. Your arm was hanging over the side of his arm. I remember walking up to you, and I held your little hand while my mother spoke with your father. After a few minutes, you woke up briefly. Your green eyes opened and you stared at me. You weren't even the least bit curious as to who I was. You just smiled at me like you'd been waiting for me to hold your hand, and then you fell back asleep. I don't know how, but I knew you'd be in my life for as long as I live."

"I can't believe this…" I say with my other hand pressed up against my forehead.

"That's as much as I can say right now—except…" He trails off, looking away in a muted argument. Kane lets go of my hands, an impossible load of anguish in his warm eyes. He levels himself on his knees and turns his back to me, removing his shirt. Burn marks cover his back in the pattern of tic-tac-toe. Vertical and horizontal, narrow, rectangular slats.

He turns his head to the side to give me a sidelong glance.

"The day Scarlett died, Dessin knew something was coming. Call it a sixth sense, call it intuition, call it a careful calculation of her behavior. But he knew. And we were too late."

Wait. Is he saying… was he there? My hand acts on its own accord and finds the damaged skin on his back. I caress the scars starting from his shoulder blades down to his lower back. Was he burned in the fire I started?

"When I finally got to you… Scarlett's childhood home was set ablaze. I fought my way through the flames and found you passed out, holding her hand. I saw the noose around her neck and—it all hit me. I'm the only other person alive that knows the truth. I know you didn't kill her, despite the senseless rumors. She ended her own life and it… it broke your heart." His voice grows weak and raspy. "I carried your body out of the fire and left you on the sidewalk. When I went back for Scarlett, the house was caving in on itself… but I just knew you'd want to bury her, so I went in anyway. I made it halfway to her room when half of the ceiling came crashing down on my back. By the time I pulled myself out of the fire, her body was a pile of ashes."

"*Oh.*" Pieces of my heart come sprinkling down to my gut in thin flakes, and I'm failing at holding in my sobs. I don't realize my cheeks are wet, drenched with ongoing tears.

"It's something I'll never forgive myself for. It's part of the reason why I couldn't resurface when we met again at the asylum. Dessin knew he had to take over. I couldn't face you after failing you the way I did."

I lunge into him, pulling his body to my chest with impressive force. My arms curl around his neck, and my face snuggles into his shoulder. "You didn't fail me. You saved my life. Kane, I knew… I *knew* you meant more to me for a reason." I pant into his neck.

"I wish I could tell you everything, honey."

This touches my heart like dipping into a hot bath. I have more respect and feelings for him than I did before.

"But why didn't Dessin tell me? When he met me again in the asylum, he acted like it was the first time. Why was it a big secret?"

Kane pauses. "You won't believe me until I show you."

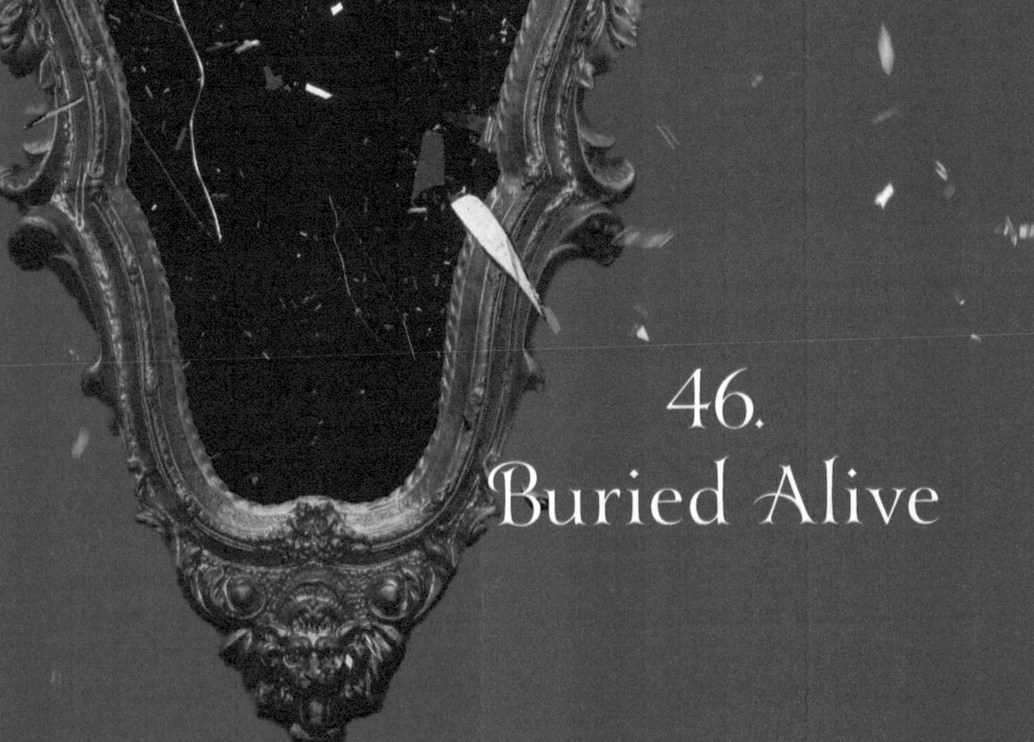

46. Buried Alive

Unhinged screams from a banshee echo through the walls of our cave. Screams of a man. Screams of a woman. Fear and impending doom fall over the group as the bloodcurdling sound wakes us up early, just as the sun kisses the horizon. The winds are calmer than they were last night, but the snow still falls. Kane is the first one to jump to his feet. DaiSzek is already gone, most likely following the devastating sound.

Warrose sprints out into the cold morning, not bothering to wait for anyone.

Kane turns to me and shoots me a look of cold caution. "No one leaves this cave." His voice is a devil's grenade to our sleepy ears. *Good morning, Dessin.*

He takes off running into the falling snow. The screams are now from one person, a man bellowing at the top of his lungs. Niles whips his head around to gawk at me. "We're not going to listen to him, right?"

And before I can react, Ruth and Chekiss are on their feet, waiting for me to make the first move of disobedience from Dessin's direct order.

I rub my face to wipe the tiredness away. "*Okay*. But we stand back to see if he needs us." As we exit the cave, the screaming is coming from the tall pine trees to our far left. I expect to see groups of armed men and Dessin fighting them all with DaiSzek by his side. But it's just Dessin staring at a tree. A tree on fire. He nods once as if taking directions from someone and takes a few steps to the right, digging in the snow with his bare hands.

I nod to Niles, Chekiss, and Ruth. We sprint through the snow, lifting our knees to our chest with each stride like we're jogging through water. Attached to the burning tree is a man.

"Get him loose!" Dessin barks at Warrose. The man is screaming as the flames lick his boots and pants. Warrose yanks a dagger from his belt, sawing through the ropes that bind the poor man. I look up and the victim has curly black hair and arctic-blue eyes that are filled with welling tears.

"What are you doing?!" I shout over my shoulder to Dessin.

"His friend was buried alive!" he shouts back.

Flames are getting too close to Warrose's hands, so I sneak a knife from his belt, circling to the back of the tree to help him cut off the restraints. I hear Dessin panting as he digs deeper into the ground. He stops, grunting as if he's pulling someone from a grave. A woman begins to whimper.

"Are you hurt?" I hear Dessin ask, followed by the woman breaking out in hysterical sobbing.

We cut the man free and he falls to the ground with a sigh of relief. His eyes look up immediately. I follow his stare and see the woman's arms around Dessin's neck as she continues to cry. Her friend doesn't move. Doesn't stand to check on her. Just stares with tears streaming from his pink cheeks.

Dessin's arms stay suspended in the air around her quivering body. Unsure how he should react to her outburst. I have the urge to smile, but I don't. It would be inappropriate, we don't even know what just happened. It's just… I remember the first time I hugged Dessin. He was in shock. His persona doesn't do well with emotions or human interaction. I can only imagine how uncomfortable he is.

I greet the crying woman with my hand on her back to help Dessin out. She looks up at me from the center of his chest, gazing at me through hot tears still hanging loosely from her long lashes, making clean streaks through the mud all over her fair face. The woman's golden-copper hair is covered in dirt, standing in wild waves all over her head. Her eyebrows knit together and she jumps from Dessin to me. Thin, frail arms choking my neck. Dessin raises his eyebrows at me with a *thank you for the assist* look.

"What happened?" I ask her.

The man steps forward, touching her arm in reassurance. "I don't know if you remember us… but the two of you found us in the woods a few months ago…"

"I remember," Dessin says through his teeth. "And you only have a minute to explain before I tie you back to that tree."

The man opens his mouth to speak.

"—And before you think about lying, I'll know. I don't like liars. I *burn* liars."

The man blinks several times with eyelids stretched to his eyebrows.

"What's your name?" I ask, still holding the frantic woman.

The man looks at me nervously. It's now I realize he holds more boyish features than manly ones. He might be a couple of years younger than me.

"Niklaus," he answers hesitantly.

"How old are you, Niklaus?" I ask again, the girl finally gaining enough strength to part from my arms.

"Twenty-one."

Dessin takes a step forward, probably to do something rash. I hold my hand up to him, signaling him to let me keep talking. He stops midstep.

"Niklaus, my friend here has many gifts, but patience isn't one of them. I need you to tell me why this is our second run-in with you two, and I need you to be honest."

The wind carries the scent of smoke from the burning pine tree. I notice Ruth, Chekiss, and Niles still standing back. Waiting to see if we'll need them.

Niklaus takes a breath, careful not to look at Dessin. "We're being chased by people who think we are in cahoots with the two of you. We just broke out of where they were keeping us. They followed us here and you saw what the end result was."

"Why would they think we're affiliated?" Dessin steps forward.

"They said they saw us with you that night. I guess they had eyes on the two of you."

Dessin begins to pace. "No, that's not right. Demechnef wouldn't have taken people we only had a random interaction with once." He narrows his eyes back to Niklaus. Suspicion forming new theories in his mind.

"Because it isn't Demechnef that has been chasing us," Niklaus responds with a higher level of confidence. "They're called the Vexamen Breed."

Dessin's brows rise slightly. "I see." His dark eyes search the snow as if there were more answers buried there.

"Who are the Vexamen Breed?" I cut in.

Dessin's eyes flicker over to me like he forgot I was here.

"They're children, well, teenagers that the leaders of Vexamen trained to be vicious soldiers from birth. The same men that slaughter that village." He looks away, unraveling more questions. "But wait, that doesn't explain why they tied you up and buried her alive."

"Maybe they were trying to draw us out?" I say.

Dessin's eyes fill with panic, an alarm going off in warning red lights and loud claps of thunder. "Where's DaiSzek?!"

We all look around the area. He was out before us. He took off toward the screams.

"What, the animal? The black wolf?" Niklaus asks. "It took off after the Breed left us here."

Dessin moves like his body is going up in flames. He yells back at me to stay put. I don't dare to go against his wishes this time. He has to put all of his focus and energy into making sure DaiSzek is going to be okay.

I usher the group into the cave. The only thing I can do now is restart the fire. The thought crosses my mind that this is a trap for me, that these two strangers are here to kill us. But Dessin wouldn't have left me with them if he didn't think they were telling the truth. I feed the couple leftovers from last night and let them get some sleep. Meanwhile, I wait at the edge of the cave with Dessin's machete and Warrose standing guard.

After what feels like a couple of hours, I watch Dessin trudge through the snow. Fury painted over his face like a warrior coming home from a battle lost. I stand, unable to breathe, unable to feel anything but hopelessness.

"They have him," Dessin says, completing his last steps to me. "It was a trap to capture him all along. They must have injected him with the saphriness oil."

"Wait, the country we're at war with has DaiSzek? Why do they want him?"

Dessin stares down at me with anger boiling under his surface, then shares a quick glance with Warrose.

"Demechnef isn't the only one after me, Skylenna. It's been a race for who can get me first."

Oh my god.

He takes a deep breath, blows it out through his mouth. His eyes might as well be glowing red, cold isolation and a thirst for enemy mutilation.

"It's time to turn ourselves in. We're going to need Demechnef's help."

"No." The firm response comes out with a cold bite to it. "There's no way I'll go back there. We can get him back ourselves. We can ask the Stormsages for help. Or the Nightamous Horde, right? They all seem built for battle."

Dessin watches me with a patient, remorseful expression. "If there were any other way, I'd take it. But Demechnef is the most suited for a fight with the Vexamen Breed. Their soldiers have been trained from birth, and I, alone, won't be able to infiltrate. But Demechnef has the resources, the spies, the manpower, and years of learning the war strategies of their enemy."

"Dessin… I won't go back to that cage." My hands shake with determination. A white-hot flash of uneasiness drapes over me. "And I can't believe you'd try and make me."

His furrowed brow softens, and he's reaching for my hands, stopping them from balling into fists. "You will never go back to that cage. *Ever*," he promises. "I have a plan. Something to trade for our immunity. A treaty that will keep us safe while we work with them."

My stomach rolls. "What if you're wrong?"

"I swear to God, Skylenna. I won't ever let them put you in that goddamned cage again."

I drop my head, still feeling the darkness around my cage. Still stewing in the hopelessness of never getting rescued. Of believing I am all alone.

"I've got to save him, baby. Please trust me."

DaiSzek. My boy. What is he going through? Would they have him in a cage now? I take a deep breath, nodding. I won't let my fears of stepping foot in that place again stop me from freeing the beautiful animal that has never failed to save me. To protect me.

"I'm in."

47. The Family Pact

We travel halfway to Demechnef headquarters, a.k.a. one of the two Emerald Lake mountains behind the asylum. Dessin stops us. He's having a heavy argument within his own head. He closes his eyes and turns his neck, like he's enduring a high-pitched sound that's painful to his ears.

"What's the holdup?" Niles sets his pack down to sit on.

Dessin snaps his fingers at Niles like a parent would to scold a child without causing a scene. "Another word out of the contentious little prince and I'll sew his mouth shut."

Niles raises his eyebrows. I mouth the words, *he's done it before!*

I wait patiently at his side, sensing the retaliatory anger coming off in clouds of steam from his skin. I can only imagine the amounts of pressure he's under. Pressure to appease Kane, protect Kane, make sure nothing bad ever happens to Kane, protect me, protect my friends, save DaiSzek, follow his carefully curated plan he's constructed for years. I can see it swelling inside of him like a cancerous tumor, eating away at the good cells he needs to remain healthy.

I let my hand follow its desires and reach out to him. I move slowly, like the first time I touched DaiSzek, careful not to scare him away. My index fingertip touches his palm, a knock on the door of his humanity. He doesn't move, doesn't make an effort to meet me halfway. So, I slide my hand within the strong, larger-than-average hand attached to Dessin. My fingers interlace with his fingers, clutching him with any comfort I can send his way.

He looks down at our hands, takes deep and controlled breaths. His close-set, dark-mahogany eyes flicker up to mine with a disarming sigh.

"I had every intention of dropping you all off at a safe location," he says to Ruth, Chekiss, and Niles. "But Kane is insisting on bringing you lot along for the ride."

Ruth tightens her lips together in an excited smile.

"But I have a few rules that need to be followed. What I say is the law. No questioning my judgment, making your own decisions on how situations need to be handled, and no trying to be the hero. Skylenna does that enough for everyone."

He's still bitter. Good to know.

"I'm going to make a deal with Demechnef's leader that will keep all of us safe and exempt you all from their cruel methods. With that being said, if you all insist on standing at Skylenna's side… I want you three to train for war. Demechnef wants me for a reason. Everything in Kane's life they put him through is to create a human nuclear bomb. They want me to end the war they have with Vexamen. And now that the Vexamen Breed has discovered and captured one of my weaknesses, I have no choice but to help Demechnef put them down."

A pit of silence hangs between the five of us. No one knows how to respond to him. Niles normally would, but he fears Dessin will make good on his word and sew his mouth shut.

"I'm going to give you three one last chance to walk away. If you decide to stay, above all else, I need your loyalty."

My three friends exchange glances, coming to a wordless agreement.

"You wouldn't last a day without me." Warrose grins, walking past Dessin.

"I'm in," Chekiss says, then nods to me. "We're family."

Niles smiles. "I'm clearly a tumor you can't get rid of. Count me in."

Ruth glances between Dessin and me, swallowing down her fear. "Family."

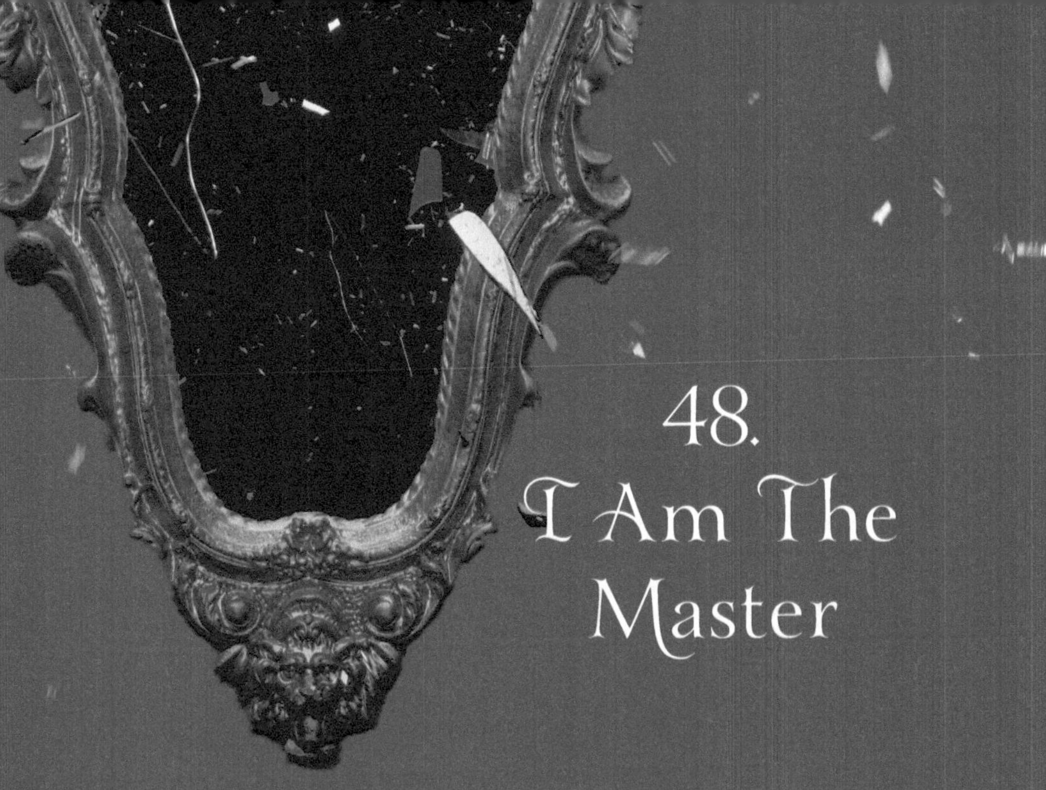

48. I Am The Master

I have an infection that needs tending to. Like I fell off my bike and scraped up my knee, then let the dirt and gravel snuggle into its new home. I want to clean it out, I want to bandage it up and start the road to recovery. But there's no time. No time at all. And I don't want to tell someone that there's a deeply rooted infection taking hold of my ability to gather strength and stay focused. It's not something you talk about out loud. You keep it to yourself. You bury it in a cell like a criminal that's done unspeakable things to innocent people. Because talking about it would make other people uncomfortable, and if you're making them uncomfortable, then that makes the infection much worse. It makes it harder to pretend that it's not there.

My infection is a devastating rope of fear looped around my neck. I don't want to go back to the people that made me believe I had broken bones, endometriosis, or kidney stones. These people violated me. These people made me believe I was a prisoner for four months. I never want to experience anything like that again. I'd rather die. If it were to happen again, I'd go with DaiSzek to Ambrose Oasis and I wouldn't come back.

But it's too late to speak up, not that I would. I want DaiSzek back just as much as Dessin and Kane. I feel a constant stinging in my chest at the thought of never seeing him again. But more than that, if they do anything to hurt that glorious friend of mine, I will kill them all myself. The rage boiling inside me is enough to wipe out a continent.

We stand before the great Emerald Lake Mountain, about to enter the underground entrance. Dessin is in a foul mood, and I don't dare try to calm him down. I can't imagine how he's processing this. He just got me back, only to lose his beloved friend too.

We live in a malicious world.

Walking toward the iron gates of the mountain tunnel, I stop to look back at Dessin who is staring at something in the trees.

"What's wrong?" I ask. But I see it, standing behind a veil of ivy. The tall, lean man that I met near the tree house. Forest boy. Brown glistening skin, long golden hair, with moss and leaves covering his private area.

"Which man are you?" The voice of thunder and sandpaper stops the group from moving.

"Dessin."

The man's bare chest is slick with sweat. He nods his head once. "Come."

No one moves. Even Warrose looks back and forth between us like we're missing something.

"I have what you need for what you plan."

Warrose leans into Dessin. "He's one of the Naiadales. The Emerald Lake people."

But Dessin already knows this. He starts to approach the man, so I follow. One hand stops me. "Stay here. I'll hear what he has to say alone."

I want to argue, but the man said *for what you plan*. Meaning I'm not supposed to know. I give a reluctant nod as he joins Forest Boy behind a cluster of trees and vines. It's only a few minutes before he's walking back to me, tucking something into his pack.

"We meet again when you are ready," the Naiadales man says to me before disappearing into the forest.

I open my mouth to speak to Dessin.

"Don't ask because you know I can't tell you."

Warrose nudges me with his bulky shoulder. "He's so sweet in the mornings, isn't he?"

Dessin and I lead the group through the gates that lead to a hallway underground, with antique chandelier light fixtures lit by candles, rosewood walls, and rib vault ceilings. The vintage northwest rug runner cushions our steps from echoing. With the waft the air vents bring, I catch hints of pink pepper, ginger, and sandalwood, much like the aroma of a wealthy man. Spicy and loaded with wealth.

"We're going to be fine," Dessin assures me. I'm sure he can practically smell my fear, like an extra sense he might not quite understand. "I have something to trade. Something that will ensure everyone's safety." His confidence gives me more comfort than I thought it would. I trust in his judgment more than that spike of fear prickling under my skin. He touches the small of my back with his finger, and I can't hold the shiver from breaking out across my body.

"You leave the talking to me. We'll get him back. *I promise you.* We'll get him back."

I nod, unable to respond with my voice. It's tucked away for the moment. Scared to come out and mess up any part of his plans. I don't know who we're meeting or if we'll even be able to see the leader of Demechnef. Someone Albatross and Absinthe feared. He probably smells like this hallway, like old money and expensive booze.

I glance behind me and notice my friends walking awkwardly close together, shoulder to shoulder, hip to hip, like knives might shoot out from the walls and impale them at any given moment. And no one wants to be left at the back of the line. Except Warrose, who is keeping his pace slow and predatory, daring a threat to attack the group. Ready for a fight. Itching for the violence.

Like a magnetic pull, my hand wants to reach for Dessin. The fear that holds me down is becoming lighter and less prominent as I watch him walk like an undefeated warrior. Owning everything. Time stopping at his convenience. The cloak of confidence drags behind him. I can't help but succumb to my mesmerization by this man that stands tall and walks proudly into a chamber of powerful people and dangerous weapons. A territory of conspiracy and pain.

A few minutes later and we're walking through a common area of soldiers, businessmen, savants. All men. No women. No surprise. They look at me like I'm breathing underwater or flying without wings.

The hallway grows wider, opening up into a common area, with the same rib vaults, cherrywood floors and no runner rug. At first I think the eyes are on me, gawking like they'd been shot by a poisonous arrow. Alarmed and unsure if they should run, fight, or hide. I follow their petrified stares, pointed at Dessin. They look at him like… the king has returned home. I didn't notice it at first, but once you see it, you can't unsee it. He's either an idol or a raging mad tyrant that no one dares to stand up to. Some men step out of the way as we pass, some fall against the glossy walls like they never expected in their lifetime that they'd ever live to see the day he'd come back.

He's a walking plague, and every inch of this vicinity holds its breath.

An important member of this organization leads us into a private room. Oily face, cleanly shaved, sleepy eyes, and thickly built. He doesn't seem as afraid of Dessin as the rest of them, but he certainly isn't wanting to stick around us much longer.

We wait inside a private room, a single walnut ball and claw desk. It has a dark-brown leather top, and gold antique-colored tooling. There's an antique oil lamp on the left corner, a scotch-filled crystal decanter with three matching glasses. The rest of the room is gently lit by oil lamps mounted on the surrounding walls. The soft light reflects through Dessin's eyes like two tiny glowing orbs floating in his pupils. No windows because we're buried inside a mountain. I take in a controlled breath and am stunned by the smell of coffee, scotch, and cigarettes. All very potent, mixed together in the air to concoct something stale and old.

"I can't believe how much I did *not* miss this place." Warrose leans against the back wall, toying with a knife.

"There's something we haven't told you yet," Dessin says delicately, placing the sentence an inch under his breath.

"What is it?"

Dessin closes his eyes slowly. "Because we wanted you to see it for yourself…"

The second door to the left of the desk cracks open, only showing a sliver of darkness and a hand resting on its handle. My peripherals catch Dessin raising his chin in reaction to the hand, challenging the dominant shift. And there's a sinking feeling in the bed of my stomach, a nausea wave that inches up my throat. It's that feeling that you're about to catch someone in a lie, about to swing open a door to expose a personal betrayal.

Dessin's body is tense as if he's preparing himself for an explosion or spontaneous combustion. As tangible as a cloud of thick smoke, I can practically breathe in his anticipation. My heart begins to rattle, clench, bang under the bone wall in my chest.

The door suddenly opens the rest of the way, and a tall man emerges from the slither of darkness, followed by three other men. But I don't waste another moment looking at them. Dessin turns his head completely to face me, watching for my reaction with discomfort. My eyes flicker in panic from Dessin to the first man. And like a bolt of lightning shooting down from a massive thunderstorm directly into my chest, I fall to my knees with a *bunk*. My lips are separated and drying up as I suck in oxygen like the air is running thin. I choke on my own harsh gasp.

No fucking way.

"You're back. I was worried I might have scared you away." That voice. That familiar, *horrible* voice. And those pale-blue eyes topped with black, perfectly arched eyebrows. The angelic porcelain face. The face that was once my friend. My only resource to starting my life over.

"What are—you doing—here?!" I stutter, clutching my hands to the cold hardwood floor.

"Skylenna..." Dessin's voice comes from above me. His hand squeezing the cap of my shoulder. "This is the leader of our country."

Silence. Cold claws cut into my spine and drag down my back. *This isn't real.*

Dessin clears his throat with disgust.

"This is Aurick *Demechnef.*"

To be continued in the third book of this series:
The Puppeteer and The Poisoned Pawn

Acknowledgments

I quit my nine-to-five job to become a full-time author. A dream I've had since I was a little girl. I originally was not prepared financially when I quit. I spent my savings on making sure I did everything right for my debut novel. But I was miserable in my position. I was belittled. I was made to feel less than for being a woman in a male-dominated industry.

And the only reason I was able to quit, was because my mom believed in me. She knew it was a huge risk, a jump of blind faith, and she supported me anyway. From making me food while I forgot to feed myself from long hours of writing to making sure my bills got paid until I was officially paid for *The Pawn and The Puppet*. Momma, everything I do, everything I write, is to make sure you never have to work another day for the rest of your life. Thank you for being my guardian angel. My best friend. My biggest supporter. And when the internet hit me hard, and took me under—you kept swimming for the both of us.
Because of you, I can *keep going*.

Thank you to my soul sister, Anna, for being the first person to read this draft when it was garbage. You must really love me! To my cover designer, Stefanie Saw, I freaking love you. You are an artistic genius. To my format designer, Amy Kessler, chef's kiss. Thank you for hustling for me! And to my editors, Ellie and Rosa, you're doing the Lord's work. Because I seem to really like my typos.

To my incredible beta readers: Sarah Leach, Danielle Caballero, Kayla Watson (who also did my book trailer), Jessica Latta, Heather Heath, Taylor Symon, Megan Oswalt and my superb sensitivity readers Hannah Rutgers, and Allison Sharrer! Thank you all for dealing with my crazy deadlines and committing to making this book the best it could be.

To my readers, thank you for supporting me at my lowest. Thank you for believing in me when I no longer believed in myself. And a special thank you to the people who sent me loving messages on Instagram when I thought I lost everything. Your words pulled me out of a dark, terrifying place. I owe you so much.

As many know, I worked with a system that has DID. Loki, PJ, Percy, and a few other alters helped me understand the delicate details that surround this disorder. I have learned the terror, the struggles, and the different forms of trauma a child can face that result in the mind splitting. I will never be able to thank them enough for giving me their time and sharing their heartache. They have contributed to so many people around the world learning about Dissociative Identity Disorder in a new way that they won't soon forget.

Kék pillangó, fehér nyúl.

About The Author

Brandi Elise Szeker is a passionate advocate of sharing the darker stories that people shy away from. After seeing so many turn a blind eye in history to the horrendous injustices of asylum care, the unspeakable acts of childhood trauma, and the growing statistics of animal abuse—it is her mission to always use her platform and stories to spread awareness.

When she's not writing about soul-shattering love or reading about it, you can find her binge-watching TV shows with her mom: her first inspiration that started it all.

To learn more about Brandi, visit her at:
Author website & newsletter:
www.brandibookthought.com
Tiktok & Instagram:
@brandibookthought
Author Facebook Page:
https://www.facebook.com/brandieliseszeker/
Spoilers Facebook Group for TP&TP:
www.facebook.com/groups/thepawnandthepuppetspoilers/

www.ingramcontent.com/pod-product-compliance
Lightning Source LLC
Chambersburg PA
CBHW020248030826
48979CB00030B/2665/J

* 9 7 9 8 9 8 5 5 9 3 4 5 7 *